By the same author

Novels

The Husband
The Magician
Living Room
The Childkeeper
Other People
The Resort

Plays

Napoleon (The Illegitimist)
(NEW YORK AND CALIFORNIA, 1953)

A Shadow of My Enemy
(BROADWAY, 1957)

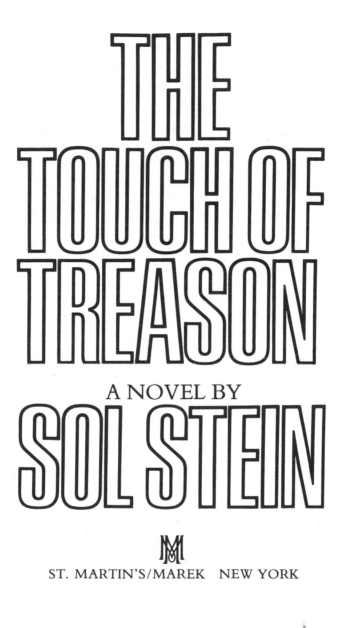

THE TOUCH OF TREASON

A NOVEL BY
SOL STEIN

ST. MARTIN'S/MAREK   NEW YORK

Design by Kingsley Parker

Library of Congress Cataloging in Publication Data

Stein, Sol.
    The touch of treason.
    "A St. Martin's/Marek book."
    I. Title.
PS3569.T375T6   1985   813'.54   84-23712
ISBN 0-312-80980-8

First Edition

10 9 8 7 6 5 4 3 2 1

For Toby
with love

□ A C K N O W L E D G M E N T S □

Four lawyers read the manuscript of this book and provided me with advice: my friend, Judge Charles L. Brieant, who has been instructing me in the law since the time of *The Magician*; his son, Charles L. Brieant III; his daughter-in-law, Joy Beane Brieant; and David Bernheim, whose knowledge of courtroom tactics was as useful as his understanding that when literary necessity and judicial convention clash, literature must govern.

Claire Smith's comments on an early draft encouraged me in a direction I am glad I took. Patricia Day and Toby Stein both provided me with literally hundreds of notes on several drafts of this book. Finally, it was Richard Marek's editorial reflections that as much or more than other factors influenced the publication of this book being in his good hands.

—SOL STEIN
Scarborough, New York

All men should have a touch of treason in their veins.

—Rebecca West

The Soviets are chess players. We play checkers.

—Archibald Widmer

□ CHAPTER ONE □

In the end you died. There could be a courtroom like this, Thomassy thought; all the good wood bleached white, the judge deaf to objections because He owned the place. The law was His, the advocacy system finished.

If that's what it was going to be like, George Thomassy wanted to live forever, because here on earth, God willing or not, you could fight back.

Thomassy took in the grained thick wood of the raised perch, the bench from which the Honorable Walter Drewson would look down and judge defendant, defense counsel, prosecutor, witnesses, jury. Drewson would swivel in that now empty high-backed leather throne to see that his actors behaved according to the canons, protected from the players by a moat of flooring that no mortal crossed until he received the judge's sign. The others, kept at bay by the promise of contempt, sought comfort in the knowledge that the judge's vision was subject to the clouding of his contact lenses, and that under his severe black robe was hidden the ordinariness of a glen plaid suit and a spine that consisted of bones on a string.

Some of the windowless courtrooms Thomassy had worked looked like half-deserted government offices, a prefab for the judge's bench, and a metal desk for the clerk. No criminal wanted his freedom decided on in a place that looked like the motor vehicle bureau. He wanted the accoutrements of authority in his theater. If he made it to a court like this, the walls paneled instead of painted, seven high windows letting in the morning light, he was prepared to be judged.

It had been some time since Thomassy had defended someone in a room this large, selected for this trial because it could accommodate more spectators and press than any other in the Westchester system. Thomassy, like everyone else who had paid attention in school, had learned that the Greeks used to kill the messengers who brought the news. But in this century, Thomassy thought, they're killing the men who send the messages: Jack and Bobby at the height of their power; Martin Luther King when things were turning his way; Hoffa, the truckers' hero, ready to make his comeback; and now, known only to specialists but perhaps, in the end, as influential as the others, Martin Fuller, the man who knew that you could more likely stop the Soviet spread over the earth not by the accretion of megatons but by understanding how a nation of chessplayers played its games. Martin Fuller had reluctantly agreed to put his system, his knowledge, the rules by which for several decades he had successfully predicted Soviet strategy, down on paper so that a few wise men might carry on his work to prevent Armageddon by insight rather than arsenals. Now Martin Fuller was dead, cut off from his work. In Washington the few who understood the import of Fuller's death were suddenly bereft. Thomassy wondered if there was jubilation in Moscow because the wrong man had been accused of murdering Fuller, and Thomassy, who was an innocent in foreign affairs, had been picked to defend him?

Well, this was going to be a whopper. Thomassy was a lawyer the way Robert de Niro was an actor. This courtroom was the set in which, during weeks to come, he would cross a line. Now only lawyers and judges recognized him in the street. After this, strangers would stare or stop him. You could get an unlisted phone. You could take your name off your mailbox. But you couldn't get back across that line once your face, seen on television, turned heads in the street. *The people* had you.

That's the skirt the government hid behind. *The people* versus whomever he was defending.

As on all mornings before a trial was to begin, Thomassy had arrived early to survey the field of battle. The defendant's table was always farther away from the jury than the prosecutor's table on the assumption that *the people* could be trusted. Thomassy preferred some distance from the defense table to the jury box so that he could saunter over, letting the line loose until he was right in front of them for the rhetorical question that would implant *reasonable doubt, reasonable doubt, reasonable doubt* like an echo that he could count on to reverberate when they were sequestered in the jury room out of his reach. If the courtroom was a tight fit, with perhaps only fifteen feet between his sitting self and the jury box, he'd have to spring to his feet for objection and in five strides be in front of them. Though he was addressing the judge, he'd be talking from the jury's position as if he were one of them, suggesting that the prosecutor was on the other side, a government worker. Thomassy helped the jurors understand that it was the government's heinous role in human affairs to assert itself in opposition to citizens against whom there were only unproved allegations to

2

which other citizens, chosen as jurors, could assert the technicality of innocence. Surrounded by people behaving like people, how could anyone stay innocent for long?

Kids somehow did. When he was invited to give one of the Mellon Lectures on Criminal Practice at New York University's law school, the students were surprised to see that their legend was only in his mid-forties, and didn't look like an Armenian but was as straight-nosed as someone from Amherst in the good old days. Thomassy's gray eyes surveyed his packed audience, surprised by the number of women now taking to the law and by how much younger all the students looked. Their naiveté reminded him of his at that age. *But Mr. Thomassy*, one of them had questioned, *aren't most criminal defendants guilty?* With a straight face he had answered: "It is the job of other departments in this university—psychology and religion—to train people to deal with guilt. Our job is to give those of us who are apprehended a defense so skillful that when prosecutors roll innuendo and circumstance at the jury we can say *No dice. You haven't proved it.* Some of you will become prosecutors. Well, I guess somebody has to work for the government." The students laughed of course, but one of them could be counted on to ask, as one did, *Isn't the end result supposed to be not just winning but justice?*

Thomassy knew you had to be patient with kids. He said, "Never talk to anyone of Armenian descent about justice." He waited for the laugh and added, "You don't tell your football team to go out there and get justice. You tell them to win." Then looking at one student in particular, the way he always at moments like this looked at one juror, he said, "When you go out with a young woman on Saturday night, are you worried about feeling guilty afterwards? Are you looking for justice or success?" And he turned his gaze to the dark-haired female law student in the first row, walked around the lectern and strode over to just a few feet in front of her and said, "Is there a woman alive in this world who wants justice more than she wants success?" Then his gaze lifted to them all. "If you want to lose cases, I suggest you switch to the medical school," and he sat down to a roar of laughter and the aphrodisiac of applause.

When he eased out of the lecture hall, nearly a dozen students clustered around him, most of them young women basking in his vitality who could not imagine, for all their quickening fantasies, that Thomassy lived alone.

Thomassy saw his life as a progression from innocence. As a boy he had thought himself cleverer than other boys because he pro-

3

vided favors before he might expect one in return. One evening, going to his house by a path that was shorter than going by road, he was accosted by four teenagers who were out to get the Armenian kid. Only one friend had ever accompanied him that way, a fat boy he had several times protected in the schoolyard from one or another of the four who were now blocking his way. In the distance, barely visible, he saw the fat boy, who had turned informer to curry favor with his enemies. Thomassy brought home a bloodied lip, a torn shirt, and the knowledge that boys do not bank favors.

When he began to practice law, on each occasion in which he had found himself surprised or vulnerable, he recorded a terse sentence or two in a notebook he kept in a locked desk drawer.

> *I believed Julio's story. Julio brought his mother in to confirm it. His mother didn't lie as well as he did. To get at the truth, question the accomplice.*

Some time later he added:

> *Question the accomplice first. It saves a lot of time.*

Once his secretary Alice referred to it as his devil book. Sometimes he was tempted to carry it with him for ready reference. Why do we forget what we learn? Life had snipers up in the trees. If God was as smart as He was cracked up to be, He'd have put eyes in back of your head, too. When he was a kid he'd foolishly thought WASPS like Judge Drewson were invulnerable. Drewson must be scared. He'd never had a case in County Court attended by reporters from abroad. He'll want to appear fair. He'll try not to allow more conniving by one side than the other. He'll be distracted by the television artists sketching him, and by his daughter, the bright beauty of his late middle age, home from law school for the recess and insistent on being slipped in as a spectator so she might judge him. This may be the fairest place on earth, Thomassy thought. Everybody's at risk.

"Good morning, Mr. Thomassy," said the white-haired woman who was clerk of the court, setting down her armload of folders. Of course he was glad to be recognized, and not at all surprised at the clerk's big smile because the grapevine always carried the news when Thomassy would appear for the defense and every clerk in the system knew that you could count on Thomassy to deliver the kind of show that made you eager to get up mornings.

If the clerk had been a young woman, he would merely have answered "Good morning" across the room. But he had watched his father being courtly to older women and had eventually understood the nature of this courtesy.

He walked briskly down the aisle to the lady, stretched out his hand, and when she took it, he lifted her from her daily anonymity by saying, "I'm afraid I don't know your name?"

"Marian O'Connor," she said, blushing, for attorneys do not usually shake hands or ask your name. She'd never seen a picture of him. He looked younger than she'd imagined him, tall, lean, relaxed-limbed, loose, clean-shaven, and his firm hand had been warm. His gray eyes looked at her as if to ask they once been lovers.

"I'm pleased to meet you," he said, his voice husky.

They both heard the double doors at the back of the courtroom squeak open.

"Excuse me," Marian O'Connor said quickly when she recognized the district attorney and hurried away through the door next to the judge's bench. Thomassy could see Roberts's handshake coming at him all the way down the aisle, above it that freckled face proclaiming *I can be friendly to everybody, I was born rich.*

Roberts's smile, Thomassy thought, is an implant. *I'm not a voter,* he wanted to say. *Save it.*

"I heard you get down to look things over on day one," Roberts said. "I thought we might chat a bit before we officially become adversaries."

"How's your wife?" Thomassy asked, pumping Roberts's unavoidable hand once, though he'd rather have let the embarrassing object drop unshaken.

Roberts was wearing his uniform, a vested gray suit, white shirt, striped school tie, Phi Beta key hanging from a watch chain across the vest. Thomassy didn't like any kind of uniforms—cops, soldiers, hospital attendants, businessmen. He had his dark blue suits made because he liked a touch of European flair in the jackets, nipped in at the waist, beltless pants, extra pockets for sunglasses and for the small cards on which he wrote the cues he wanted to remember. He couldn't imagine a woman going for a man's zipper if he had a watch chain across his vest.

"Janet's fine," Roberts said. "How's the girl who's eroded your bachelorhood? Same one nearly a year, isn't it?"

She's not a girl, Thomassy thought, she's a woman. "My bachelorhood's intact," he said.

"I heard—"

5

"I wouldn't pay attention to gossip, Roberts. What's on your mind?"

Roberts, shrewd as his Yankee forebears, preferred to plea-bargain away tough cases and bring the easy ones to trial. If he thought this one was going to be easy, Thomassy thought, he's lost his touch; or has the preelection fever got him in heat, ready to play Gary Cooper Lawman for his constituents? What pissed Thomassy was that Roberts built his cases on other people's backs—the investigators paid for by taxes, the paralegals paid for by taxes, the young assistant DAs paid for by taxes. He'd heard about how they brought their neatly organized garbage to Roberts's desk, with the menu on top, option A, option B, option C, so Roberts could check his choice of strategy and think he was a lawyer.

Thomassy pictured Roberts at the side of his swimming pool, swim trunks the length of Bermuda shorts, a beach jacket hiding the rest of his body from public view. Wonder if he lets other people do his swimming for him?

"What got you out of bed so early?" he asked the district attorney.

Here it comes, Thomassy thought. Roberts planned everything, like his career, like using this courtroom as a way station to a more suitable arena, the House of Representatives, the Senate. A man like Roberts fantasized about his inauguration day. If, like Thomassy, you were the only son of an Armenian immigrant horse trainer from Oswego, New York, you concentrated on the chinks in human nature, the space between a man's ribs. The fantasy guys, on the way to the White House, could trip on a cracked sidewalk. Roberts hadn't tripped yet because he was a peg smarter than the others. He collected paintings. The story was he didn't like paintings, he liked the way Nelson Rockefeller had got away with shit because he collected art.

Roberts said, "My people tell me you haven't been receptive to negotiating this case."

"I thought you might like to play this one out."

"I wouldn't be that glib about hard evidence or eyewitnesses," Roberts said, his smile sheathing his words.

"You've got someone who was hiding in the shower and saw it all? You're bluffing, Roberts."

"You're getting things mixed up. You bluff. I don't. If you've changed your mind a little about negotiating, we could have a little sit-down with the judge."

Mid-trial surprises make the headlines. That's what Roberts was

6

going after. "You don't want the judge reminding you," Thomassy said, "that we need advance warning of identification witnesses."

"Oh sure. When I know, you'll know. Unless we negotiate before—"

Thomassy cut in. "My client is not copping a plea under any conditions. Any."

"That his idea or your idea?"

Thomassy was silent.

"Koppelman thinks it was your idea," Roberts said.

"Who or what is Koppelman?"

Roberts smiled. "I thought you might remember him. A sandy-haired summa cum laude from Harvard Law who applied to you for a job last year. Brilliant kid. Said you agreed to see him because he said he was from Oswego."

"He wasn't from Oswego."

"Nobody's from Oswego," Roberts said. "He thought you'd be impressed by his tactic since you're reputed not to give interviews. He got in."

"For three minutes."

"You should have hired him," Roberts said. "He came to me next. He's putting in a lot of overtime on this case."

"I work alone."

"If you're intent on going to trial, you might need some help on this one."

Thomassy laughed. "You suggesting I hire Koppelman away from you?"

"Koppelman seems to have lost his admiration for you when you turned him down. I, of course, retain mine. It was Koppelman who suggested that you and I might have a little talk about keeping the witnesses down."

"Sure," Thomassy said. "We can keep it real short. When I move to have the case dismissed, don't fight it."

Roberts, the patrician, smiled at Thomassy's little joke. In a quiet voice, laced with what Thomassy thought of as North Shore divinity, Roberts said, "Five of us looked at the evidence, separately and together, before we decided to present the Fuller case to the Grand Jury. I hope you got your fee up front."

Thomassy moved his gaze from Roberts's confident eyes to Roberts's blond hair, then Roberts's chin, then Roberts's left ear, then Roberts's right ear. The four points of the cross. It made witnesses nervous. They couldn't figure out what you were doing. You weren't doing anything except making them nervous.

"I wanted to save time," Roberts said.

7

"You'd like to finish up before the campaign season starts."

"You're looking for trouble with me, Thomassy."

"I'm looking for enough time for the jury to get used to the idea that my client is a human being. I'm out to save years of his time, not days of yours. Every slip you make, I'll go for a mistrial until you're dizzy."

Roberts said, "You don't have to play Bogart with me. I'm not a juror. Fuller's life was taken."

"You'll have to prove it was taken."

"The Grand Jury was convinced."

"The Grand Jury eats lemon meringue out of the palm of your hand. The reason we have trials is to get you out of your closet and into a room like this where there are two sides. You've got the wrong defendant, Roberts."

"That's one mistake I've never made." Roberts paused, summoning disdain from the generations that had preceded him. "I've always tried to be fair with you fellows who didn't have the advantages."

"Don't patronize me, Roberts."

"I'm trying to tell you this trial is over your head. Look who you're defending."

Thomassy knew the clenching of his right fist was a street instinct he'd hoped to leave in Oswego along with the flowered tie his mother had given him, and the wing-tipped shoes. "I'm going to whip your ass in front of the judge, the jury, the spectators, the press, and your mother's DAR den if they'd like to come watch."

Roberts, fingering his striped tie, said, "I'd meant this to be a friendly conversation."

Thomassy stepped closer to Roberts and lowered his voice. "I mean, in the friendliest fashion, to show that the government has to prove that the death of Martin Fuller was not accidental, that if not accidental it was accomplished by the willful act of another person, and that that person is my client, that he had a motive to kill his teacher, and that you can prove your case, if there is a case, to a jury of my peers, not yours. This isn't going to be one of your one-two-three trials. I've got a footlocker full of reasonable doubt. You're going to get very tired. You're going to come out of this wishing you'd given it to one of your honchos."

Roberts had no choice but to turn to go. At the double doors he said, "The calendar says the people versus your client, not me against you or you against me."

"You don't represent the people, Roberts. You represent the government. I represent the people. We're all defendants."

It was funny the way Roberts tried to slam the swinging doors. You idiot, Thomassy thought, you can't slam swinging doors. They take their own good time.

CHAPTER TWO

On a particular morning half a year earlier Martin Fuller had caught himself thinking that before every murder, two minds are at work, the murderer's and the victim's. If each knew the mind of the other, if there were no miscommunication, would the murder take place?

The answer, Martin Fuller thought, was in most cases yes. Our thoughts are far worse than what we allow ourselves to say.

As he carefully put the manuscript he had just worked on inside the safe in his study, Fuller, then in his eighty-third year, thought of one particular murder. He imagined Trotsky with the small, pointed beard at his desk in his house of exile in Coyoacan, reading the manuscript of the young man who was standing behind him, looking over his shoulder. Trotsky knew the handsome fellow as Sylvia Ageloff's lover or husband—it didn't matter which—a Jacques Mornard who had come reportedly from a Belgian bourgeois family to succor Sylvia, and who was now beginning to seem a convert to Sylvia's conviction that Trotsky was the redeemer of the October Revolution. As Trotsky bent over Mornard's manuscript, the blow came, and in that millisecond Trotsky knew that Stalin's long-awaited messenger had arrived. For Mornard, Fuller and the whole world learned soon enough, had taken a *piolet*, an ice-axe, out of his raincoat pocket, and with the energy that comes to an ideological assassin at the moment he has been living toward, had struck Stalin's rival in the skull with the sharp point, releasing a scream that the assassin later acknowledged felt as if it were piercing his own brain.

Trotsky, Mornard reported, bit his hand as a dog might do, then stumbled out of the room, blood streaming down his face, yelling *See what* they *have done to me!*

They was the word that reverberated in Fuller's head.

Martin Fuller had known the antagonists, Trotsky and Stalin, and had quarreled with both. It was inevitable that Trotsky, in his

9

Mexican exile, would be writing a biography of the man he knew had sentenced him to death. Well, Fuller's writing was of a very different sort, a book that would never be published as a book. The stipend he received from the U.S. government, which supplemented his pension from the university, was for the creation of a manuscript intended only for the eyes of the National Security Adviser and his successors.

The man who had visited Fuller nearly a year ago to persuade him to accept the assignment was someone he had known casually for a long time, Jackson Perry. Fuller, who throughout his long life had forsworn neckties as a punishment visited upon men, thought Perry looked like a man whose necktie was as much a part of his presence as his close-cropped hair. When Fuller bade Perry sit, he noticed the tinge of pink embarrassment in Perry's face as he unstrapped his attaché case from his wrist before he could put it down.

Fuller could remember with amusement when the attaché case had been a sign of expense and rank. Soon afterward middle-management types started carrying attachés made of rougher leathers. Young men in suits began to carry metal and plastic attachés. It was said Puerto Rican runners on Wall Street carried their lunches in them. Once the Con Edison man showed up at the Fuller home carrying an attaché case; when opened, it revealed his work tools.

Perry's well-worn attaché looked like it might have been made of glove-soft leather darkened by wear and repeated restoration; but the leather strap, one end tied to the attaché and the other to Perry's wrist, Fuller had seen only once before, when a courier had caught up to him in the south of France. Fuller presumed that Perry was required to make a verbal presentation, and if Fuller did not reject the assignment out of hand, only then would Perry take out of his case a written summary of what he had just said.

Instead Perry reached into the case and from a blue folder removed two sheets of heavy bond paper with the great seal on top.

My dear Fuller, Three of my advisers in the field of intelligence agree—and they seldom agree on anything—that you more than any other living person have predicted correctly the likely conduct of the USSR based on the past behavior of specific leaders. Your knowledge of the system, they tell me, is profound.

They always began with flattery. Who was impervious, especially on this stationery? He wondered who had drafted the letter.

I am told that your advice to previous presidents has proved to be of even greater value than was anticipated. My concern is that while the principles of your system have been understood, no one else has yet demonstrated his ability to use those principles as effectively in the application to actual impending situations of great moment. Can you—with speed if possible—set down your method in such a manner that successors to my present National Security Adviser, of lesser or greater knowledge than the incumbent, will be able to see that your methods will be used even by future generations responsible for the safekeeping of the nation?

Lest you think this request discretionary rather than imperative, I need only to remind you that the Soviet leaders are presumably as concerned about the proliferation of our respective nuclear arsenals as we are, and also as concerned about the leader of some client state with covert nuclear capability seeking to trigger an irreversible cataclysm between the Soviets and ourselves. We must keep up with their thinking so that if fast action is called for, the chances for misunderstandings are curtailed. We need your guidance urgently in a form useable by others before it is late.

Fuller looked up at Perry. "He's worried about my dying."
Perry, motivated by politeness, started to object.
Fuller stopped him with a wave of his hand. "At my age, I think about it, too." His eyes returned to the letter.

I ask you to accept this burden in the full knowledge that it is an imposition you would abjure were you not as concerned as I am about the avoidance of misunderstandings that could lead to war.

Mr. Perry is empowered to discuss all terms and conditions. I trust your answer will be in the affirmative.

Fuller looked up at Perry's anxious face. "I'm sorry," he said, "I'm afraid the answer is no."
Perry's face crusted with dismay. He had been told not to fail. He tried to smile. "With all respect, Professor Fuller, I believe you'd rather leave this legacy than any other."
"Why me again?" Fuller said.
"Nicolaevsky is dead. Shub is dead."
I, too, soon, Fuller thought. They will have to get used to going to the younger generation. Those who had lived through it would

be gone. His prescience had never been based on subjective impressions but on transmittable guidelines, and he had taught those guidelines to others. It was not his fault that the government hadn't yet found a satisfactory interpreter of his method.

"What about some of the younger people?"

"It was discussed at length," Perry said.

"What about Tarasova? She's twenty years younger. I taught her everything."

Perry had looked down, as if embarrassed by what he knew. "She's an émigré."

"Forty years ago, Mr. Perry!"

"They wanted the perspective of someone born in this country."

"That's nonsense. A method has nothing to do with one's place of birth."

"He wants you, not one of your students."

For a moment Fuller had been tempted to say that he and Tarasova could work together on this, but he knew that was not possible. And so when Perry waited him out, Fuller finally said, "When I finish this one, will I be free to die?"

Perry, after so many years of surreptitious work, still had the laugh of a civilized man, textured with pain. "You'll outlive us all," he said. "We'll see to it."

Fuller protested the security arrangements that Perry told him would be installed. "Terrorists are multinational," he said. "They have institutionalized the gratuitous act, killing the wrong people as easily as victims selected with purpose. Is my life more in danger because I will be writing this manuscript for you?"

"If they know about it."

Finally they shook hands. It would all be arranged Perry's way, foredoomed. Perry slipped his papers back into the attaché, closed the case, then restrapped it to his wrist in the name of a security that Fuller knew no one in the world could feel any longer.

Now, after months of work on the manuscript, Fuller longed to be freed of his duties to history. He was more sensible than Trotsky, he would tell himself each day as he locked the safe in his study. For he allowed no one except Leona into the small room in which he worked. The door was deadbolt-locked when he was inside as well as outside. Trotsky was guarded by idealistic students and by Mexican police, neither a reliable category. Fuller's safety, on the one hand, was in Perry's charge, and Perry had given him Randall, a professional whose sole responsibility was to see that no harm came to Martin Fuller. Fuller referred to Randall behind his back as "my spook," but he appreciated that because of Randall his mail was safe to open, his phone line untapped, there were no bugs in his study or elsewhere in his home, and that, since he'd begun work on this project, an elaborate fire and burglary warning system had been installed in his home in Westchester at federal expense. Whenever Fuller opened the safe in the early morning, that act was registered by a green light on a board somewhere nearby. When Fuller, his work for the day finished, closed the safe some hours later, the light went out. If anyone not familiar with the combination tried to open the safe, or even jostled it—as Leona found out it was so sensitive you could not brush it accidentally with a broom—Randall or one of his lieutenants would be at the house within minutes. And he knew that if the phone lines from the house, though they were underground, were ever cut, the red light would go on instantly, even before the prospective intruder could enter.

Randall had pleaded with Fuller to make a carbon as he worked so that a safety copy could be lodged somewhere. Fuller said he couldn't be bothered with carbon paper. Randall suggested a copying machine be brought in and the manuscript reproduced under Fuller's watchful supervision. "That will give you two things to worry about," Fuller said. "My copy and the safety copy. And how can you make safe what I have not yet put down on paper?"

Fuller was aware that those who came to visit, whether from the U.S. or abroad, even the students who hung around to refresh themselves and him in what seemed to outsiders like abstruse debate, had had at least a cursory check without their knowledge. The problem was, of course, that so many people who were interested in Martin Fuller had what Randall referred to as "difficult backgrounds." The older ones may have once been Stalinists, Trotskyites, Lovestonites, or came from Asian and African countries that seemed to be unwilling or unable to provide background information on their own subjects. The younger ones were sometimes casual users of what Randall referred to as "controlled substances"; they sometimes lived out of wedlock and dressed intentionally in scruffy clothes; some of them had been to the Soviet Union in recent years as exchange students or tourists; others were former peaceniks making the usual migration of age from left to right. Fuller enjoyed the range of his guests and was purposefully delinquent in giving Randall the names of prospective visitors for advance checks.

Once, when Randall was insistent about the strangers coming to

13

a buffet dinner at the Fullers', Fuller said, "Why don't you tell me who's coming to visit you this weekend."

"Nobody interesting," Randall said.

"Then I'll lend you some of my guests," Fuller said. "If you're afraid to let them in your house, you can always frisk them first."

Randall, who'd gone to Georgetown University before becoming a Secret Service officer, was sometimes embarrassed by his role. "This isn't normal bodyguard duty," he'd been told. "It isn't something we can assign to just anybody. We need someone Fuller can respect, who understands the implications of what's being guarded." But Randall wondered whether he hadn't become the instrument of the government's paranoia. Fuller wasn't writing of military secrets. He was describing his method of analyzing the past conduct of each member of the Soviet leadership, whose protégé each was, how he'd climbed the ladder. He had studied those people the way good constitutional lawyers study the justices of the Supreme Court so they could try to predict their future actions on given subjects. "Don't let him die before he finishes," Perry had said. "Not with what's at stake." Randall knew the number of nukes didn't make the difference. Brains did. He was supposed to guard Fuller's brain. Perry, always joking, had said, "Your job is to see that Fuller dies from natural causes. After the work is finished." *I'm not God* Randall had wanted to shout at him. But he knew what Perry meant. Fuller himself had said *In previous centuries terrorists were crazy freelancers. Today they are psychopaths and ideologues trained by governments to traffic in premature death.* Randall remembered Perry saying, "The Soviets don't want Fuller dead. They want to know what he's telling us. Protect the manuscript first, then the man."

But Randall, being human, had his own priorities. Once he had showed up at the house with what he called an interim query from Washington while the Fullers were still at breakfast and he observed with alarm that on a paper napkin next to Fuller's bowl of cereal, there were eight pills and capsules, none of which he'd had a chance to have tested in the lab.

"Randall," Fuller had said, "I've been taking megavitamins for years."

Randall had to admit to himself that Fuller, at the age of eighty-two, had the lean, physical vigor of a much younger man.

"Does Doc know you're taking these?" Randall asked.

"Physicians," Fuller said, "know as little about nutrition as about Soviet affairs."

It was then that Leona Fuller said, "Those eight pills are his fountain of youth. See, I take them, too."

Randall knew that Mrs. Fuller, that remarkable woman, was not an imitator. She had to be independently convinced of everything. If she was taking all those vitamins, they had to be safe.

After he finished his present work, Fuller would presumably be free to loaf for the first time in his long life, to travel not out of necessity, as he'd done for the government from time to time, nor on the run, as he'd done long ago when he and Leona had been part of the movement, but to places of their choice where he and Leona could take the sun, or read the best books again, or talk to intelligent strangers who knew or cared nothing about Soviet affairs. He wanted as much time as the higher powers would give him. Ever since he had abjured authoritarianism in all its forms, he'd thought of gods in the plural, the way the Greeks did, male and female, each with a specialty in mortal affairs. Monotheism was too simple. If you examined life long enough, nothing was simple. Except the clock that ticked relentlessly over everyone, tolling each year that would not return.

Randall knew that the President had once remarked that Martin Fuller looked like he would live forever. The President thought of Martin Fuller's brain as a national asset of immeasurable worth to which no harm could be allowed to come. But the President's wish was Randall's responsibility. Few people knew that Randall had once had part of the responsibility for John Kennedy and then for Robert Kennedy. Randall was a realist; he lived in increasing fear that the successful conclusion of his assignment was ultimately impossible. Yet he found himself envying Fuller when he happened to see him emerge from his study after a fruitful morning's work, his eyes exuberant with discovery. Fuller's work gave Fuller life.

Randall had to put up with Fuller's teasing. The old man would tell him, "Go off and worry about the missile defenses with those fellows at MIT. Talk to them about laser satellites and defense screens."

"You are our first line of defense," Randall would say in an attempt at banter but feeling like a manservant.

And Fuller would answer, "I am older than the Maginot Line, and as much use."

Yet the time Fuller had received the Medal of Merit from the President in a private ceremony kept from the press, Fuller knew it was for that specific instance when his form of intelligence— insight based on intimate understanding of how Khrushchev

15

thought—was said to have provided the key that enabled a red alert to be wound down so the adversaries could return to the bargaining table.

The President had said, "You are a greater asset than our coal reserves."

And Fuller had replied, "Mr. President, your asset has arthritis."

The President had been briefed, of course, and knew that Fuller steadfastly refused to take anything stronger than aspirin so as not to numb his brain as long as the work remained unfinished.

Nor had Randall been able to change Fuller's lifelong habit of imbibing nourishment from interchanges with younger people, graduate students, former students, younger professors, specializing in Soviet historiography, intellectuals of the left and right who thought that debate with a mind such as Fuller's enriched them. Randall realized that Fuller needed their adulation to sustain the rigor of daily work at his desk seven days a week, every week of the year, but Randall, like some men of his generation, distrusted young people.

"I am not a monk," Fuller told him. "I will not isolate myself. I was not put on earth to teach only governments. I am, like all teachers, a snitch for the young, an informer."

It was therefore not unusual that on the evening in April, Leona Fuller, seven years younger than her husband, who had been beautiful when young, and had grown, not only in her husband's eyes, even more beautiful when old, presided with her husband over a dinner for four acolytes.

Leona Fuller served them *arroz con pollo*, which she had learned to make when they lived in Mexico. She had transfigured the recipe over the years till all of their friends renamed it Leona's chicken. She herself had the appetite of a small bird; her pleasure was in watching others enjoy her food.

Melissa Troob, as usual, had positioned herself on Martin Fuller's right. Long ago Leona Fuller had guessed correctly that Melissa's barely epicanthic eyelids suggested an Oriental grandparent. In fact, her Chinese grandfather had taught Asian history at Stanford, where Melissa had also taken two degrees. A specialist in Soviet history, she'd heard Martin Fuller lecture at Stanford during his happy half year in northern California and had fallen in love with Fuller's mind. If Fuller had been twenty years younger, Leona believed, the situation might have developed dangerously, for Melissa had not only a sharp mind, and an incredible memory, but was what she thought of as beautifully boned. Melissa's cheekbones were as visible as an Indian's, always touched with a blush of color. And whatever dress she wore, Melissa's hips revealed their bony understructure in a way that Leona Fuller knew Martin would find erotic. Other men viewed women as laymen viewed buildings. They saw the exterior. Martin, like an architect, saw structure in beautiful things.

Melissa, Leona suspected, had moved East for her doctorate less for the benefits of Columbia University than to continue to sit at Martin's feet, sucking in his wisdom as only a graduate student still in a fever of learning could do. Fortunately, the man sitting across from her, Scott Melling, had found Melissa attractive. And Scott, who was six-feet-two with a very black mustache carefully trimmed, was angularly handsome in a way that seemed to complement Melissa's beauty perfectly. Scott, now twenty-nine or thirty, Leona guessed, was lecturing at Columbia, his degrees behind him. He was said to be an instructor who each hour inspired rapture anew by a consciously thespian manner of teaching political science as if it were a dramatic combat between us and them. She liked him. Martin liked him. And Melissa, thank God, was probably in love with him, though Scott had a wife, and Leona Fuller, despite her long exposure to the young, still had difficulties with the looseness of that kind of tie. She and Martin, despite his long, now-dead affair with Tarasova, had remained an indivisible coupling, though they no longer spent the nights in each other's arms. Other people's bonds were children who grew away; theirs was the work, her thoughts enmeshed in his like threads in cloth. She was the coauthor of his life.

At Leona's right sat Ed Porter, who, though only twenty-four, had three degrees and was the brightest of the lot, a dimpled ferret who went after small facts that turned out to be the last pieces of the puzzle. Unlike the others, he seemed street-smart, something the Fullers themselves had never been. Ed was short, perhaps no more than five-seven or so, with tousled brown hair in the style one has come to accept among young people, not unattractive, not unkempt, what they call natural and some call wild. His hands as well as his face were quite freckled. He wore the standard uniform for his age, jeans and a sweater, though the tan sweater looked as if it might have been of camel's hair or cashmere, and Leona had long suspected what Ed had never acknowledged, that he came from a family that was very rich. Ed, unlike the others who had published only in learned journals, had written a book that had been well received. It was called *Lenin's Grandchildren*, and dealt with the lives of the Latin American and African revolutionaries of the last thirty years. But what mattered most to Leona was that when Sniffer, their Methuselah of a cocker spaniel, died, their friends conveyed their regrets with the special care one took with people who had no children, but it was Ed Porter who Leona had found sitting in the yard, rocking the dead dog in his arms.

Barry Heskowitz, who sat on Leona's left, was not one of the acolytes Leona cared for. A heavy-set young man with curly black hair, and eyes that were constantly busy, he had acquired the habit of compliments. He would admire Leona's dress, or a bouquet of flowers she had arranged; he would tell Martin, who rarely looked to see what tie he was putting on, that his tie was perfect for his suit. Leona had little patience with such sycophants. Martin liked to be congratulated on his perceptions, not his ties—but he'd made an exception for Barry because the young man, still working for his master's, understood the historic origins of Soviet intransigence better than any student he'd had in a long time.

Melissa was arguing that the most important member of the Politburo to track carefully was what she called the *Gletkin*, the pure Soviet man unsusceptible to the negotiating wiles of the West.

"If that's the case," Ed Porter interrupted, "we should have paid more attention to Suslov than to Khrushchev or Brezhnev, but Suslov died and your contention goes up in smoke."

Martin raised his right hand slightly from the table, a sign they all knew meant he was about to speak. "The gods, for those who believe, took care of Suslov by removing him. They have less time for studying these men than we have. Therefore, we always need to know who the backup man is. Sometimes the next-in-line for any ideological role is not only a standby, but an assassin."

After dinner, the talk continued in the living room, advancing in waves of contention, and then receding as the ocean does when it cannot push the shore. At one point Leona Fuller said, "We should know more about their women." Only Melissa did not smile.

Shortly after eleven Barry excused himself. "I live in the West Side combat zone. I don't want to tempt fate."

What he meant, of course, was that he had to be in class in the morning, as the others did not. He offered Ed Porter a ride. Ed said it was too early.

Less than an hour after Barry's departure, Leona closed the discussion. "It's midnight. Martin must get his sleep. You know how early he rises."

She knew that Melissa and Scott would use the lateness of the hour to take advantage of the standing offer of the upstairs bedrooms, in which, over the years, dozens of late-staying students had camped for the night. Ed Porter had missed the last train and he didn't have a car. So when Leona Fuller made her ritual offer of an upstairs bedroom, he, too, accepted with a show of reluctance, as if he had not in fact done so a dozen times within the last month. Ed cut the grass without being asked. He had combed Sniffer's coat. He split wood for winter.

Within fifteen minutes, the house was quiet. Leona, sliding into the huge bed in the large room at the rear of the house, remembered when Martin told her that lovemaking robbed him of some fraction of his intellectual vitality the morning after, that he would absent himself from the temptation by sleeping in a separate bedroom. That was thirty years ago and she had not believed his reason. When she saw him with Tarasova, both so aggressively pretending to be merely infatuated with each other's brains, she told herself that like a kidney stone, it too would pass. But the memory remained. Leona put her arms around her second pillow. You get used to anything in time.

In the morning, at first light, Martin Fuller opened his eyes. Immediately his thought was on the work at the point he had left off on the preceding day when he stowed his manuscript in the safe. Daily life was an impediment, showering, dressing, breakfasting. His body, he sometimes thought, was too elaborate a machine for housing his brain, required too much attention. He put his heavy robe around his cold frame and headed for his bathroom down the hall.

The bath off Leona's bedroom was far more elaborate and spacious than the one he called his own. But this way he could keep the kerosene heater in place since no one else used his bathroom and only he felt the chill before the steam from the shower warmed the room.

He turned the hot water on in the shower stall. It usually had to run a full minute before the tepid water in the pipes was pushed out of the showerhead to make room for the hot water from the basement tank.

He bent to turn the knob on the kerosene heater. As every morning, he took the packet of matches he kept in the bathroom cabinet, struck one on the back of the pack, and touched it to the proper place in the heater. Suddenly, the heater, which he always thought of as an accomplice against the morning cold, roared forth with a ball of flame that engulfed him. The floor-length robe was transformed instantly into a torch, and as Martin Fuller screamed

19

from within the incendiary mass, he had the presence of mind to unlock the door so help could reach him, thinking the one word: *they*.

Leona Fuller had heard Martin going down the hall, of course, but as usual picked up a book to read in bed so that Martin would continue to believe she was still asleep. Human contact before he got to work always interfered. He awoke thinking of the next paragraph he would write: the precise formation of his thought would take shape while he sipped at his orange juice and spooned the cereal into his mouth. It was his habit to take his coffee with him into his study, holding the cup carefully in his left hand as with his right he unlocked the door with the key that never left his possession.

She heard the loud *vroom* a moment before Martin's terrible cry. Her first thought was that something had made Martin fall. He'd broken his hip three years earlier when he'd slipped from the library ladder while trying to get a book from a high shelf, and she imagined him in bed for eight weeks again, demanding and restless to get back to work. She damned the fragility of old bones as she got quickly out of bed, slipped on her robe, and rushed down the hall, glad that some of the acolytes had stayed overnight because Martin was twice her size and she knew she wouldn't have the strength to pick him up off the floor. But then she heard him screaming again and again and realized that this was something more than a fall, that something was still happening, and then she saw the flames through the slit between the bathroom door and the jamb.

Leona pushed the door wide open and saw that Martin's bathrobe was ablaze and that Martin himself was burning like a fireball. He was trying to get the burning robe off himself, lunging at the walls as if to try to smother the flames. Leona pushed him toward the shower stall, not realizing she was burning her right hand, understanding that only Martin's eyes were screaming now and that the spray of water might not be enough. Then hands were seizing her from behind, and she was pulled out of the bathroom as Ed, wearing nothing—he must have been sleeping naked—pushed Martin into the shower. Half a minute later Scott came to help, and he and Ed together did whatever they had to do to beat the fire out.

When they pulled Martin out into the hall, his lips still twitched. When the rescue squad arrived minutes after Melissa's call, Martin

Fuller was still technically alive, but Leona knew that his life, her life, and his work were over.

CHAPTER THREE

Archibald Widmer was the kind of lawyer whose corporate clients would appreciate the fact that his desk had no encumbrances except a signature pen in a marble holder and an appointment book that he called a diary. When a client was about to enter the paneled sanctum of his office, Widmer's secretary, who had the demeanor of the headmistress of a school for wealthy young women, would put before him the client's folder. On top was a discretely small memo on which an associate had summarized everything Widmer needed to know about the meeting. The telephone was located on the credenza behind him in order not to mar the concentration that a bare desk brought to the matter at hand.

When he picked up the phone for the first time on that morning in April, his secretary asked, "Are you taking calls, Mr. Widmer?" for she knew that even when he was alone he did not always welcome interruptions.

In fact he had been gazing out of the window of his twenty-sixth floor corner office at the magnificent view of New York harbor and thinking of his daughter Francine, who was now twenty-eight years old and had been seeing George Thomassy for almost half a year. Widmer had introduced them because Francine had been raped by a neighbor and wanted revenge. Thomassy was the only lawyer Widmer knew who could bend a reluctant legal system to prosecute and win an uncomfortable case. In the process, Francine told him she'd found in Thomassy that combination of drive and tenderness she had not found in the young men of her generation. Whatever the ingredients, the chemistry was immediate and visible to others.

It was not exactly the match Widmer had in mind for his brilliant daughter, who contributed ideas, phrases, paragraphs to the speeches of the U.S. ambassador to the UN and might one day herself be that ambassador. Thomassy's family was Upstate Armenian Immigrant, and, sadly, dead. Widmer had always hoped that his daughter's choice would lead to what his own forebears had expected, an extension of family, not a mere acquisition of a solitary son-in-law. Perhaps it was luck that Thomassy's parents were no longer among the living; what in heaven's name would he and Priscilla talk about to a horse trainer and his wife whose world was bounded by inadequate English and an upstate farm?

Yet what he had wanted for his daughter was not a replica of himself. He couldn't have managed Priscilla if she'd been like Francine, a Roman candle you held as far away from yourself as possible without letting go as each colorful outburst went off with a bang. Widmer laughed to himself. A Roman candle was such a masculine image. Was that what was happening, liberated young women turning into part-men? In a drawer at home, Widmer kept a once-crumpled nude Polaroid photograph of Francine that he'd found in a bag of things she was throwing away. He assumed it'd been taken by an errant boy friend on a lark. Though she was recumbent in it, she looked as if she was ready to spring at the photographer, or was it to bolt away? When he'd seen it, it was a bite of the apple he could not spit back. It had stirred him, just for a second. His eyes told him she was a woman with a beautiful body that he had helped create and therefore—*therefore?*—could not touch. Only once was he tempted to get rid of the photograph, when it brushed his memory as he was making love to Priscilla. His only fear now was that if he was to die without warning, the photograph would be found among his effects.

"What is it, Miss Hargood?" Widmer asked.

"It's a man named Randall, sir."

"Please put him on."

The man spoke in a rush, without niceties. "Mr. Widmer, do you remember me? Jackson Perry introduced us."

"Yes, yes, of course."

"You were Martin Fuller's attorney?"

"Were?"

Widmer's other guilty secret, of course, was that he had several clients whom his partners thought of as eccentric to their corporate practice. Widmer's partners did not know that he had taken on these people at the behest of Jackson Perry, a very old friend who'd been a Skull and Bones brother at Yale and whose wealth had enabled him to indulge his proclivity for intelligence work, then thought of as a frivolous occupation during peacetime, except, perhaps, for Princeton men. "Ned," he'd said, "we need to know who their lawyers and accountants are. Take them on. You won't be sorry." Widmer remembered Perry's later call. "Ned, this

22

is the important one I spoke about. His name is Martin Fuller. Compared to the others, he's uranium."

The man Randall was saying, "Could I ask you to come to the Fuller house as quickly as possible?"

"Is he ill?"

He could hear Randall's breath but not a response.   .

"Out with it," Widmer demanded.

"I'm afraid Fuller is dead."

At moments like this one's immediate, uncensored thoughts are rawly selfish. Widmer thought *My education is over. I will die knowing only what I know now.*

Though Fuller was eighty-two, he could not imagine that storehouse of intellectual vitality stopped like a clock. His few meetings with Martin Fuller over routine matters such as a will and a real estate transaction, as soon as their business was done, provided Widmer with more intellectual stimulation than he'd had in thirty years. Widmer had said something about "balance of power" and Fuller had snapped back, "Nonsense. That concept misled three generations. The power of nations is constantly in flux. A surprise attack tilted it for the Israelis. Oil tilted it for the Arabs. An oil glut tilted it back. The power of nations rests not on balances, but on countervailing forces."

In that one perception Fuller had rocked Widmer's life-long view of himself as a man who understood how the world performed. And of course Fuller's conversation, brimming with insights, made Widmer realize the relative emptiness of his intelligent friends and successful clients who knew as little as schoolchildren about the transactions between nations. When he first listened to Fuller, he'd felt hollow. As the years went on, Widmer felt lucky. In Fuller's presence, his mind felt as alive as it had when he was an undergraduate discovering the world.

"Heart attack?" he managed to ask because that was the death he always imagined for himself.

"Fuller burned to death."

Widmer thought *I do not deal with people who burn to death.* "When was this accident, Mr. Randall?"

"This morning, early. Mr. Widmer, I must ask you to come now."

Widmer could not contain the sudden grief that seemed to fill his lungs. He wanted to cry his immediate anger to the world. As a child, his parents had made it clear: *Others are not to know.* His voice husky with embarrassment, he found himself saying, "I have several appointments."

23

"Please have your secretary cancel them. Don't tell her or anyone where you are going. Perry's flying in from Washington. There are some matters we must discuss with you before the police arrive."

"Police?"

"Mr. Widmer, we believe Mr. Fuller was murdered and his murderer may still be in the house."

□ CHAPTER FOUR □

Widmer drove. It was the only sensible way to get quickly from lower Manhattan to Chappaqua, more than an hour north. When he arrived, there were three black cars in the driveway where usually there were none. In front of them was a blue Datsun sports car. He parked in the street and walked up the bluestone path, conscious of each step's crunch. He remembered when Perry first brought him here to meet the Fullers. He'd said *Bluestone is better than blacktop. You can hear a car coming.* He'd thought, at the time, that people in intelligence work become overcautious.

The Fuller house, set well back from the road, seemed squashed by trees on all sides. You had the feeling of a house jammed into a stockade. The saplings were planted too close to the foundation. The branches grew toward the house as well as away from it, and if you cut the threatening branches back, they'd try again, while the roots went right at the foundation, searching for the water pipes. Widmer liked space. His own house was fifty feet from the nearest tree.

When he rang the bell, the door opened almost at once. The man in the dark blue suit put his hand out. "Randall," he said. "I'm glad you could come."

Inside the house, Widmer immediately noticed the lingering acrid aftersmell of a fire. There were several other men about the house. One of them was taking measurements in the hall. Another was taking photographs into the bathroom that Fuller used.

"Where is Mrs. Fuller?" Widmer asked.

"In her bedroom in the back. Try to be brief. Upstairs there are three former students of his who stayed the night. My people have been talking to them at length."

As Randall led Widmer past the men working in the hallway outside the bathroom, he said, "This is where it happened."

Widmer stole a look at the bathroom. Blackened wallpaper, bits of charred cloth. His eyes fixed on the kerosene heater.

"He used that every morning," Randall said.

"I thought those things were safe now."

"It seems to have exploded."

In the back bedroom, Leona Fuller sat sunk in an armchair that seemed much too large for her. A younger woman was holding both Mrs. Fuller's heavily bandaged right hand and good left hand in her own. Widmer had met the woman once. Leona Fuller had said, "Emily helps with the cleaning three times a week." Leona was the kind of person whose domestic could become a friend.

Widmer stooped to kiss Mrs. Fuller's cheek. Behind her, on the dresser, he could see a silver-framed sepia photograph of Leona Fuller as a young woman, taken, he had been told, by Alfred Stieglitz. She'd been a striking beauty, with eyes that could only be measuring the intelligence of the man looking at her. She was a woman devoid of gossip, who more than understood her husband's work, who actively contributed so much to its fine honing that Widmer suspected she merited not just the dedication of his masterwork but her name on the title page alongside his.

Widmer took her left hand just for a moment. It felt small and bony. "I'm sorry," he said. He was aware of the paintings on the wall—Orozco, Siqueiros, Diego Rivera—staring at him.

"Thank you for coming," Leona Fuller said.

"I am here to help," Widmer answered.

"He is beyond help."

"I meant you."

"I am beyond help, too." The maid took Mrs. Fuller's hands again.

"Will you excuse us?" Randall said to Mrs. Fuller.

Widmer's instinct was to back out of the room. He felt the need of alcohol, which, of course, he never drank except before dinner.

When Randall and Widmer were in the living room by themselves, Randall said, "The hospital gave out a statement with the time of death. I persuaded the public-relations director to say that Fuller apparently died from a household accident. Just to stall. At this moment, the *Times* is probably freshening up its file obit. It might be page one. If the cause of death gets out, it'll hit the tabloids.

Once the suspected perpetrator is charged, we'll have TV crews on our hands."

"I understand," Widmer said.

"It would help if you'd speak on behalf of the widow when the time comes. As family attorney and friend. If Perry or I do the talking, our presence will raise questions we don't want to get into."

"There's much that I don't know," Widmer said.

"Exactly. That's why you're the perfect spokesman."

When Perry arrived, there were quick handshakes. Perry and Randall whispered together. Then Widmer heard Randall say, "We pulled the fourth one, Barry Heskowitz, out of class. He admits he used Fuller's bathroom once before he left. He says he offered Ed Porter a ride back to the Columbia area, but Porter declined."

Perry, an energetic man who dressed in pinstripes and hand-crafted Napa leather shoes, saw himself as a diplomat of the new school. He would not spend a measurable portion of his career in meetings with foreigners, moving the alphabet of negotiation from A to B. Skiing, racquetball, indoor swimming skimmed his reservoir of energy but did not drain it. He was determined, despite a career in government, to get things done.

"The widow," Randall reminded him.

"Of course," Perry said. He hurried to the back bedroom to convey his condolences, returned in less than a minute.

"She knows it wasn't an accident," he said.

"Couldn't be helped."

"Damn."

"She'd know soon enough anyway," Randall said. "It's best she not feel we were deceiving her in any way."

"You're right. Did the hospital find the key to Fuller's study in the pockets of his bathrobe, what was left of it?"

"We looked through it before the rescue squad came. It wasn't there."

"You said he always carried it with him."

"Right."

"Into the bathroom?"

"Everywhere."

"Okay," Perry said. "I'm authorizing you to use the duplicate to get in there. Disconnect the alarm at central. Have McDougall with you at all times as a witness. Open the safe, check the manuscript in front of McDougall to make sure the pages are consecutive and none are missing, and have him fly it to Washington today in a

26

package marked 'Williams, Eyes Only.' Confirm all the steps you take in writing, handwritten will do. Have McDougall initial each paragraph. What do you think happened to Fuller's copy of the key?"

"I don't know yet," Randall said.

It was answers like that that subverted Perry's career.

How could he fly back to Washington? He wouldn't want to be at *that* meeting. *Fuller was the last of them. Now we've got to depend on the second-handers.* Somebody would say *Bring him back to life.* How could the United States be so dependent on what one man knew? *Why the hell didn't somebody get him on the project ten years ago? He would have been knocked off ten years earlier.* It was a meeting to miss.

"Let's go upstairs," Perry said. When faced with the insoluble, get busy with the diversions of detail. "Come along, Ned."

Widmer's feet were heavy on the stairs. The genie was out of the bottle. Fuller couldn't be brought back to life. How could you possibly deter the death of the next individual by finding out who caused this one? What was the use of the law when justice had no point except revenge?

Perry interviewed Melissa Troob first. "Mind if I ask you a few questions, Miss Troob?"

She sat on the edge of the bed, her spine straight, dabbing at the corners of her eyes with a scrunched-up handkerchief.

"I've already been asked a great many questions by that man," she said, pointing to Randall. Then she stared at Widmer. "Who's he?"

"I'm Mr. and Mrs. Fuller's lawyer," Widmer said. "And a friend."

"Thank God," Melissa Troob said, "you're not one of them."

"Miss Troob," Perry said, "Mr. Randall said you lived less than an hour away. Why did you stay the night?"

"When we'd have a late-night gab session, we'd often stay the night."

"Who's we?"

"His . . ." She hesitated. "How shall I characterize us? His permanent students?"

"Why did you particularly stay last night? You. Last night."

"I don't really want to answer that right now."

"You realize," Perry said, "that your lack of forthrightness can only cast suspicion on you?"

"Mr. Perry? You said that was your name, didn't you? I'm hesitating only because I don't wish to harm someone else needlessly."

"What about Professor Fuller?"

"I loved him," Melissa Troob said, a definitive pronouncement.

"As much as you love Mr. Melling?"

"You have no right to question my private life!"

Widmer saw the glance that passed between Perry and Randall. Randall must have briefed him on the phone. Widmer, in the dark, remembered Perry saying to him long ago, *You are making a contribution.* He despised being condescended to. They were using him like an actor who hadn't read the play.

In the hallway, the door closed on Melissa Troob, Widmer said, "Do you suspect her?"

Jackson Perry looked at his old friend as if to calculate how much information he owed him. "I was trying to ascertain if she would make a good witness if the case came to trial."

"And would she?"

"We'll see," Perry said, and strode into the next room, where Scott Melling faced the window, smoking his pipe. He turned to them, accepting the introductions, then said, "I apologize for all the smoke in the room. I'll open the window."

"Mr. Melling," Perry said, "how did you arrive here last night?"

"I told Mr. Randall. My wife dropped me off because she needed the car."

"How were you planning to get home?"

"I assumed it would be a late evening and that I'd stay the night. I have quite a few times, as you may already know."

"Mr. Melling," Perry said, "how long did you know Professor Fuller?"

"Six years. No, seven really."

"You teach at Columbia College?"

"The graduate faculties actually. Professor Fuller recommended me for the position."

"Did Professor Fuller recommend Miss Troob to you?"

"What do you mean?"

Widmer recognized the controlled anger. It was a way of gaining time to think.

Perry said, "You didn't sleep in your room last night, did you?"

"Is that a question or an answer? I don't think it's any of your damn business what consenting adults do."

Perry stepped closer to Scott Melling. "Did Professor Fuller consent to his death?"

"It was a terrible accident!"

"Was it?"

Melling's carefully groomed mustache quivered perceptibly. "What are you implying?"

Perry said, "Mr. Melling, you broke the law last night. You—"

"What law?"

"Adultery is illegal in this state."

"My wife knows about my relationship to Miss Troob."

"That doesn't make it legal."

"What the hell is going on? You've come all the way from Washington to bedroom-snoop?"

"Why do you think I'm here, Mr. Melling?"

"I thought to investigate the circumstances of Professor Fuller's death."

"You are one of those circumstances. A man who breaks one law with impunity can break several."

"If you're accusing me of anything, I want an attorney present."

"There is an attorney present!" Perry snapped.

Widmer said, "I'm sure Mr. Melling was referring to his own attorney."

Melling's face, despite his efforts, had reddened. "I'd like to make a phone call."

"To the Soviet legation?"

"What are you talking about?"

"You've phoned them at least four times in the last three months."

Widmer saw the delta of blood flushing into each of Melling's cheeks. Melling, like his English forebears, probably considered visible anger a form of self-betrayal. Widmer saw Melling take a deep breath through his nostrils, his lips together.

It drained Widmer's reservoir of pity to see a younger man not unlike himself confronted by rude incursions. What did Melling do to deserve this?

Widmer thought of the charred bathroom downstairs just as Melling finally spoke. To Perry he said, "Do you have a court order for tapping my calls?"

"I didn't say we were tapping anything. We routinely check out calls made by Professor Fuller's visitors."

"But I've never called from here."

"I didn't say you did."

"You mean you tap my line at home?"

"You seem more concerned about our attempts to protect Professor Fuller than you're concerned about his sudden death."

"That's not true. You're twisting things."

Widmer thought *He looks naked.*

Perry whisked Randall and him out of the room. As soon as they were in the hallway, Perry's harsh mask dropped. "I'm glad you're hearing some of this firsthand, Ned. Those two are opposites. She's soft on the surface, but controlled and credible when she speaks. He's got social armor that's full of cracks."

Widmer said, "I need to know more."

When they entered the third upstairs bedroom, Perry's personality seemed to change completely.

"Ah, Mr. Porter," he said, "I'm Jackson Perry. You've talked to my colleague, Mr. Randall? This is Archibald Widmer, a friend of the Fullers."

The last phrase had the desired effect. Ed Porter seemed to relax when he shook hands with Widmer.

"Mr. Randall tells me that you've been a welcome house guest at the Fullers' quite often," Perry said.

"We seemed to get on," Porter said. Widmer was taken by the young man's casualness. Such a contrast to Melling's stiff stand.

"Despite the age difference?" Perry asked.

"When you're Professor Fuller's age, it's kind of hard to have older friends."

Widmer, always appreciative of wit, restrained his temptation to laugh. The young man's eyes glistened. Fuller was dead.

"Excuse me," Porter said, and turning from them, blew his nose loudly into a handkerchief that he quickly buried in his pocket. When he turned to face them, the tears were gone.

"I hope you don't mind my asking you a few more questions," Perry said.

Porter sat down on the edge of the bed as if his legs had suddenly become untrustworthy.

"Are you all right?" Widmer asked.

"I'll be all right."

Perry said, "Mr. Randall says you were Professor Fuller's favorite acolyte."

"He used that word?"

"Student, friend, the term isn't important."

"We worked the vineyard together. That is, he led, and I helped wherever I could."

"Were you involved in the manuscript he was writing?"

"Oh no," Ed Porter said. "I told Mr. Randall nobody got near that. By the 'vineyard' I meant Professor Fuller's work in general."

"Can you be more specific?"

"Sure. Most people in polisci—political science—aren't very scientific. They just line up events to fit the pattern of their prejudices. Professor Fuller was a genius at studying track records and political moves for the purpose of trying to predict the likely course of future actions by the same people."

"Is that important?" Perry asked.

Widmer thought *It is impolite to pretend ignorance.* He corrected himself. Perry wasn't carrying on a conversation. He was digging.

"Fuller was worth an army," Porter said.

"You ran down naked?" Perry asked.

Widmer had to admire Perry's arrogance, relaxing the young man, fortifying his ego, and then the flash of an unexpected question.

"What do you mean?" was all Porter could bring himself to say.

"This morning," Perry said. "You ran down without any clothes on is what I mean."

"The screaming was awful. I didn't take time to throw something on."

"You wanted to see if you'd been successful?"

In the silence, Widmer heard an old clock in the corner registering the seconds until Porter, his voice uneven, his eyes brimming again, said, "What are you talking about, sir?"

"You know damn well what I mean. Didn't you try to open the door of his study while the rescue squad was taking him out to the ambulance?"

"You're crazy!"

"You're the crazy one, Porter. A signal went up on the board. It's a two-sided key that only works with the right side up. How did you expect to get the manuscript? The safe is locked."

"I don't know what you people are talking about," Ed Porter said. "I loved the old man. He was my teacher. I worshiped him."

Perry leaned over him. "What does that mean?"

"I was closer to him than . . ."

"Than who?" Perry pressed. The kid seemed suddenly frightened. "Than who?"

"My father."

"Who is your father?" Perry asked, as if he already knew the answer.

"I'd rather he were left out of this," Porter said, smearing the tears out of his eyes with the back of his right hand.

"You brought him up. What's his first name? Where does he live?"

"Connecticut. I haven't seen him in three years."

31

"His first name?"

"Malcolm."

"Malcolm Porter?"

Air escaped from the young man's lungs. "Malcolm Sturbridge."

"*The* Malcolm Sturbridge?"

Porter nodded.

"Are you his stepson?" Perry asked.

"What's he got to do with any of this?"

"You have a different name."

"I use my mother's name."

"What's your father's phone number?"

"I don't remember. It's unlisted." He hesitated only a second. "Of course that won't keep you people from getting it. Can I go now?"

"You stay put like the others. In this room."

"Can I talk to Mrs. Fuller?" Ed Porter asked.

"If you want to say anything, say it to us," Perry said, ushering the others out before him and closing the door.

One of Randall's men was standing at the head of the stairs. "The police are on the phone from the hospital. A detective named Cooper. He's ordered an autopsy."

"No autopsy. Tell him it was an accident."

"I did. He says an accident is an accident when it's proven to be an accident. He's coming over here. He's damn mad we didn't call in the locals four hours ago. He says we're obstructing justice."

"Jesus, one of those."

They were surprised to find Leona Fuller sitting alone in the living room. Randall went over to talk to her quietly. Widmer could see her shaking her head.

Leona Fuller addressed all of them. "I want to know what's going on?"

Randall deferred to Perry. Perry said, "We're investigating the causes of the accident. We believe—"

Mrs. Fuller cut him short. "I feel sorry for Randall. He went to so much trouble for so long to avoid something like this." She closed her eyes for a moment. "I just wish they hadn't used such a horrible means."

Widmer said, "Who is they?"

All three of them looked at him. Widmer felt a fool.

As soon as Leona Fuller had retired, to her bedroom in the back,

Widmer said to Perry, "I can't be her spokesman unless I have some better inkling of what's going on."

"Understandable," Perry said. They huddled around the end of the coffee table.

"What happens to the manuscript that Fuller was working on?" Widmer asked.

"It will be turned over to the national security adviser personally before the close of business today."

"As the attorney for the estate," Widmer said hesitantly, "I have to ask, will the manuscript be copyrighted in Fuller's name?"

"That manuscript will never be sent to the copyright office for registration."

"Mrs. Fuller has the right—"

For a second Perry seemed to lose his patience. "Fuller was an employee-for-hire under the terms of his contract. At the moment of his death he ceased to be an employee. The work belongs to the government."

Perry saw the shocked expression on Widmer's face. "I'm sorry, Ned," he continued. "That sounds raw. This thing is getting to me, too. I'm sure Fuller's widow will be taken care of discreetly, to supplement her insurance, of course."

"That's very kind."

"One of the better uses of taxpayers' money."

Widmer proferred the expected smile. Then he said, "All the complex security came to nothing."

"I wouldn't be that pessimistic, Ned. We'll have what he did so far. Someone else will continue the work."

"What if the manuscript had been copied somehow for the Soviets without your ever knowing it?"

Perry looked at Randall. They were getting beyond the need to know. But they did need the confidence of people who helped out, like Widmer, even in minor ways.

"Let us make an assumption. That's always safe. Let's assume— hypothetically, of course—that in the first section of Fuller's work there was one paragraph, just one, that was fitted in at our request. If that paragraph reached the Russians, they'd immediately cut off contact with a certain agent whom we've turned. We'd know in a minute that they'd got their hands on a copy."

"My God, that's beyond chess." Widmer wrung his hands.

Perry and Randall were looking at Leona Fuller, who had come back into the room and was waving away their help as she let herself down into a chair. "I can't rest."

33

"Please try," Widmer said solicitously.

"I'm the living half of all this. I need to know what's being planned."

Randall looked at Perry.

"Of course," Perry said.

Leona Fuller's good left hand adjusted her bandaged right on the chair's armrest. "Ned," she said, and when he heard his name he felt the windchill of fright that he was going to hear something private. He wished he were alone in the room with Leona.

"Long, long ago, Ned, when Martin and I were on the other side, we were so often on the run we didn't dare have a child. Once the movement got word to us in Mexico that the Federalistas were looking for a couple that fit our description. I went to stay with friends in Guadalajara and Martin lost himself in Mexico City. We were apart four months. I loved him so much. When we finally risked getting back together, it was as if we were struck by lightning while holding each other. We were flooded with insight. It was easier to avoid the authorities than our own former comrades. The authorities wanted to arrest us. Our former comrades wanted to kill us. To us, it wasn't as if we had switched sides. We'd been forced to confront the imperfect ability of the human race." Suddenly Leona was looking down at her lap. "I don't mean to lecture," she apologized. "When we finally met you, Ned, your innocence was a saving grace for Martin and for me. He needed to know that not everyone had worked in the jungle the way he and I did, and Mr. Perry and Mr. Randall still do."

Leona lifted her eyes and looked over at Perry and Randall. "I don't mean to derogate what you do. I hope you win your game. For Martin, and for me I must add, it was something different." She turned to Widmer. "Please don't misunderstand what I am about to say. Martin never put on blinders to the faults in our zoo. He was a specialist in their menagerie. He knew so much about how creatures in the totalitarian state leach, turn, twist, rise, fall, rise again. He understood Lenin's *Who Whom*. For Martin the twentieth century hit bottom the day the Hitler-Stalin Pact was announced because he knew it would happen." Leona turned to Perry and Randall so as not to exclude them from her final words. "But it wasn't the bottom. In the pit were Gulag and Auschwitz. Ned, everywhere Martin saw Christian cheeks like yours turning, finding hope somewhere. His books were written for you."

Leona struggled to complete her thought. "Martin saw himself as a soldier who studied the shapes of the enemy the way air-raid wardens studied the outlines of planes." She coughed into her

34

good hand. "Please go on with your talk, gentlemen. I won't interrupt again."

Widmer felt the silence as pain.

It was Perry who broke it, offering, "We have to deal with the three people up there. And the police. And the press. Are you sure you want to hear any of this, Mrs. Fuller?"

She sighed. "I'm eavesdropping for Martin. I'll be quite all right. You see, I don't need revenge. I suppose to appease society you must do something about this crime, but I'd rather the energy was devoted to protecting the living."

For a fleeting moment, Archibald Widmer wished that his Priscilla, thirty years younger than Leona Fuller, was more like that woman. Priscilla, alas, was like himself.

"Since I'm the declared innocent," Widmer said, directing his comment to Perry, "may I ask what's to keep any of the three up there from bolting?"

"Their knowledge that if they do they'll be communicating something they may not want to. Ned, Mrs. Fuller," Perry said, "I won't be able to talk as freely once the police are here. We're hoping that the whole thing goes down as an accident."

"I understand," Leona Fuller said.

"I don't," Widmer said.

"If it looks like Professor Fuller was killed," Perry said, "there'll be hell to pay. Our territory will be compromised. Everybody knows Irish terrorists operate with impunity in Britain. Arabs and Armenians and Turks work Paris all the time. In Italy they kill statesmen as easily as policemen. In Germany, there isn't a high-level businessman who isn't afraid. If you've read Claire Sterling's book . . ."

"I haven't," Widmer said.

"It shows how all the strings ultimately run to Moscow. Right now our turf seems safe. The FALN lets a bomb go once in a while. Quaddafi's had a hit or two here, but it quickly passes from memory. If Fuller's death is seen as an assassination—particularly if it's by an American and pulled off here—it'll make us look helpless to the rest of the world."

"I'm interrupting again," Leona Fuller said. "Mr. Perry, don't you think Americans are sick of cover-ups, which never work anyway?"

"Someone must be punished," said Widmer.

"Oh Ned," Leona Fuller said, "I'm glad you're not a Muslim."

Perry sighed. "I didn't say whoever did it would escape punishment. We don't want to see a public trial. If there has to be one—

35

the police are going to be all over the place soon, and all they want are arrests and convictions—that's where you come in, Ned. We'll need your help in finding a local litigator who's clever enough to get the case thrown out, or if it's tried, to be sure there's no conviction. We want to avoid appeals and all the attendant publicity. We want this buried." He turned to Mrs. Fuller. "I'm sorry."

Widmer was silent for a moment. Then he said, "What ever happened to our sense of law?"

"Nothing," Perry said. "It's always been an adversary system— them and us."

"I suppose you don't see this as cynical."

"I see this as practical."

"Who knows about these decisions? Is it at cabinet level?"

"I assure you we're not free-lancing."

"If I'm to have any further involvement, I insist you tell me who knows about this."

"The President."

In the stillness, Leona Fuller rose from her chair. Widmer rushed to help her. To Perry she said, "Please tell them Martin put most of the things that are important in the first third of the book."

Widmer, holding her arm, saw the relief on Perry's face. To Leona he said, "He knew this might happen?"

"Of course, my dear," she said.

□ CHAPTER FIVE □

Detective Cooper was glad April had come. People didn't realize how much outside work a detective had to do. Just writing down license numbers of cars was a pain in glove weather. He didn't need gloves to write down the numbers of the cars parked outside the Fuller house. Federal types ought to bodyguard the President or whatever else they did and stay off his turf.

He rang the doorbell twice, and engaged in his most common reflex, pushing his belly up with the back of both hands. Detective Cooper had been at least thirty pounds overweight for more than half of his forty-four years. The door was opened for him. He dropped his cigarette on the stone step outside and crushed it with his shoe before stepping into the house. He knew by heart what the surgeon general had said about cigarettes, but continued to smoke two packs a day. At night, in bed, he'd sometimes have conversations with the surgeon general. "If I stop," he said, "I'll be sixty pounds overweight."

Cooper showed his ID to Randall, then asked to see theirs.

Randall produced his.

Cooper said, "I thought you guys were all in Washington. Where's yours?" He was looking directly at Perry.

"He's my boss," Randall said.

"Where's yours?" Cooper asked Widmer.

"I'm the family lawyer," Widmer said.

"How come the lawyer gets called before the cops?" Cooper asked.

Cooper had blue eyes and black hair, a combination his wife, Meg, found attractive. She kept telling him he was really a very good-looking guy except for his overweight. Once she gave him a clipping from the paper about some new low carbohydrate-something-or-other diet and he'd said, "My mother was fat, my father was fat, it's genetic. My mother liked herself so she married a guy who looked like her. If she'd hated herself she'd have married a real skinny like you, Meg, so I'd have had a chance. I married, you, skinny, to give our kids a chance." His problem insoluble, he concentrated on solving other people's problems.

"Who's in the house?" Cooper asked.

"Mrs. Fuller," Randall said.

"Anybody besides Mrs. Fuller?"

Randall told him about the three overnight guests.

"The deceased work for you guys?" he asked.

"He worked for Columbia University," Randall said.

"You fellows always show up when a teacher dies?" Cooper asked.

Perry looked at Randall.

Randall shrugged. *It's not my fault this cop is a pain in the ass.*

Perry, his voice resonant with senior reason, said, "What we have here, Mr. Cooper, is a tragic accident in which perhaps the most accomplished man in his field, in the middle of important work, had his life cut short. It's a blow to his wife, of course, but also to the people counting on his finishing the work. However, what happened happened, nothing will reverse it, and the sooner we tidy this up, the better for all concerned."

"Nice speech," Cooper said. "What's this work Fuller was doing?"

"It's really not relevant to the fact of his accident, is it, Mr. Cooper?"

37

"We don't know that yet," Cooper said. "Or do you? I don't have to be a doctor to tell you he didn't die of smoke inhalation. I saw the body in the hospital. He wasn't singed. Parts of him looked like grilled steak. A guy don't stay to get third-degree burns unless he can't help it or unless it gets him all over at once, like in an explosion. I talked to the medical examiner. I ordered an autopsy."

Cooper went to the door. Beyond the parked cars in the driveway, two policemen in uniform waited. Cooper motioned them to come in, stepped aside so they could enter.

"Mrs. Fuller doesn't want an autopsy," Perry said.

Cooper ignored him. "Please show us where it happened," he said to Randall.

Cooper spent several minutes in the bathroom, then motioned Perry and Randall over to him. "If the fire was confined to that small space, and help came within a minute, and he was scorched like he was at Hiroshima, it doesn't sound like an ordinary fire to me. I've seen people who were torched. Anybody in this precinct dies of natural causes, that's not my bailiwick, but burning to death in a contained flash fire is not, in my book, a natural cause. I checked with Columbia from the hospital, Mr. Perry," Cooper said, his whisper gone. "Fuller was no teacher. He was eighty-two years old. He was on the retired list. You fellows aren't telling me everything you know. I'm here to do a job. What are you guys here for?"

Perry felt he had to say something. "I told you Professor Fuller was doing important work."

"That's a big help. What's in this room next to the bathroom?" He jerked a thumb at the closed door of Fuller's study.

"That's where he worked," Perry said.

Cooper used a handkerchief to try the knob. It wouldn't turn.

Over Cooper's hunched back, Randall mouthed to Perry, "I relocked it." Perry nodded his approval.

"Somebody better find the key," Cooper said.

Twenty minutes later Cooper asked to talk to the three people upstairs, one at a time. Jackson Perry suggested that Widmer be present. Widmer asked to speak to his old friend privately.

"I don't have experience in police matters," Widmer said. "Shouldn't we get someone in?"

"There isn't time right now. It's either you or me or Randall. Neither of us is a lawyer. If we object to anything this cop does, it won't carry the same weight."

And so Widmer listened to Cooper ask a list of questions, first of Melissa Troob, then Scott Melling, then Edward Porter. Miss Troob objected to a third round. Cooper showed his badge. "This one's official."

The first questions were routine: Spell your name. Where do you live? How often have you slept over here? How did you get here yesterday? What means will you use to get home? In each case the questions then took a different turn. What time last night did you get to this room? Did you fall asleep right away? Did you wake up at any time during the night?

"Miss Troob," Cooper said, "could I see the keys you have on you?"

"They're in my purse."

Cooper nodded, a patient man who expected all things to go his way in time.

She showed him the ring of three keys.

"What's this one for?" Cooper asked.

"My apartment."

"And this one?"

"That's for the Fox lock, also my apartment."

"New York's a tough place to live, eh Miss Troob?"

"I'd rather have two locks there than no locks in a lot of other places."

Smartass. He liked the old days when people said "sir" to a detective because they didn't want more trouble than they already had. "What's the third key?"

"What does it look like?"

"A car key," Cooper said.

"Very good," Melissa Troob said. "It's parked outside."

"Same key work the door and the ignition?"

She nodded.

"Any other keys?" Cooper asked.

"There's a duplicate of the car key in a magnetic holder under the bumper of the car."

"If we took you down to the police matron, any chance she'd find the key to Professor Fuller's study in one of your body orifices?"

That got to her, he could see that. It didn't mean a thing. All women reacted that way. *Keep out of my orifices.*

She said, "I've never seen the key to Professor Fuller's study. And there's no reason for you to be vulgar."

"Miss Troob, I'm paid to find out who kills people. If you can

39

figure out a real genteel way of doing that, write a book for young detectives."

In the hallway, after they'd questioned Melissa Troob and Scott Melling, Widmer touched Cooper on the sleeve. "I'm not quite following your line of questioning."

"No line," Cooper said. "I'm just trying to find out what each one is tempted to lie about."

"What makes you think any of them is lying?"

"Those two, the ones we just saw," Cooper said, "they're a couple. You heard him say his wife drove him up here?"

"Surely," Widmer said, "you're not investigating the extramarital habits of these people?"

"I'm investigating what you people call an accident. And what I call a death under very suspicious circumstances."

"May I ask what circumstances you find suspicious?"

Cooper looked at the chain across Widmer's vest. "You," he said. "You and Mr. Perry and Mr. Randall. I still don't understand what any of you are doing here, or the two we just saw."

Widmer followed Cooper toward Ed Porter's bedroom, wishing George Thomassy and not he were in attendance. Thomassy knew how to deal with policemen.

Widmer followed Cooper into the room.

"Shut the door behind you," Cooper ordered. Then as an afterthought, "Please."

Ed Porter was lying face down on the bed.

"Turn over," Cooper said.

Porter must not have heard him. Cooper poked the young man's back with his finger. Slowly, Ed turned around. His eyes were red, his freckled face a devastation of grief. He reached for the crumpled handkerchief on the night table and blew his nose several times.

"What's your name?" Cooper said, his notebook at the ready.

Ed started to speak but it was as if his lips were stuck together. He rubbed his mouth with the back of his hand. "Porter," he said, closing his eyes.

"That your first name or your last name?" Cooper asked.

"Ed Porter. I want to sleep."

The words echoed strangely for Widmer. When Priscilla intuited an overture from him, she sometimes said, "I want to sleep," as if that was the kindest way to fend off the possibility of unwanted lust.

Cooper said, "Didn't you sleep last night?"

Ed didn't answer him. He asked, "Who are you?"

"Cooper." The detective pocketed his notepad. He removed his wallet from his hip pocket and snapped it open, revealing a badge. "Where do you keep your gear?" he asked.

"What gear?" Ed started to sit up, then let himself fall back on the bed.

"Your overnight stuff. Your shaving kit. Your pajamas. Your fresh underwear. You wear clean underwear every day?"

"Do you?"

Widmer admired the young man's brashness in the face of authority.

"Don't get smartass with me, kid," Cooper said. "I've brained guys twice your size."

For the first time Porter seemed fully awake. "You heard his implied threat of violence, Mr. Widmer?"

Widmer believed his role to be that of a calming influence. "Gentlemen," he said, "wouldn't it be better if Mr. Cooper asked his questions and Mr. Porter got them over with?"

"I'm sorry," Ed said, his chest heaving. "I'm upset." He turned to Cooper. "My gear's in that blue duffle." He pointed to a small overnight carrier of ripstop nylon parked on the dresser.

"Empty it," Cooper said.

Ed looked at Widmer, who shrugged. He didn't know what the rules were.

Ed zipped open the duffle and turned it upside down on the bed. It contained some books, a notebook, a shaggy cable-knit sweater, undershorts, two white T-shirts, a toilet kit.

"Don't you put your stuff in drawers when you stay some place?" Cooper asked.

"I leave things behind. I prefer to live out of the bag if I'm staying a night or two."

"What's in the closet?" Cooper asked.

"I don't know," Ed said.

Cooper, angered, pulled open the closet door. There were wooden and wire hangers in it but no clothes. There appeared to be some things on the shelf. "Get them down," Cooper said.

"Mr. Widmer," Ed said, "can I see Mrs. Fuller now?"

Before Widmer could reply, Cooper snapped, "You're not seeing anyone now. Get those things down from the closet shelf."

Ed got off the bed and pulled the cane-webbed chair over to the open closet. "Be my guest," he said.

Cooper looked at the cane seat as if it might not hold his weight. Gingerly he got up on it, holding onto the top of the door for balance. From the shelf he threw off a blanket, then a pile of magazines that scattered over the floor. Widmer was surprised to see the kind of magazines they were. Cooper laughed. He reached around with his hand to the back of the shelf and brought out a half-pint curved flask. "This yours?"

Ed shook his head.

"Whose is it?"

"How should I know?"

Cooper unscrewed the top, which was attached to the body of the flask by a short metal chain. It was empty. He sniffed, then turned the flask every which way looking for identification of some kind. "Anybody in this place named Dunhill?"

Widmer stifled his laugh. Ed did not.

"What's so funny?" Cooper asked.

"It's the name of a store," Widmer said.

Cooper thumped down off the chair amid the debris of the magazines, strode over to the bed, and said to Ed, "Open that drawer," pointing to the bedside table.

Widmer thought he saw a stroke of fear in Ed's eyes.

"Open it!" he bellowed.

Ed slid the drawer open. Widmer saw a deck of cards, a nail file, and a small plastic bag. Cooper went for the plastic bag. "What is this?"

"I don't know," Ed said quietly.

"Whose is it?"

"I don't know," Ed repeated.

"What does it look like to you?"

"It looks like tobacco."

Cooper picked up the plastic envelope, opened it, lifted it to his nose. "This is a controlled substance," he said.

"So's spit," said Ed. "What the hell are you supposed to be doing here, searching people's drawers or investigating someone's death?"

"It doesn't belong to the Fullers, does it?" Cooper said.

"I doubt it," Ed said. "It could belong to any one of dozens of people who've stayed here."

Widmer, Perry, and Randall were conferring in the living room when Cooper came back in from giving the garage a going-over. He looked disheveled. His raincoat was dirty. His suit pants looked like he'd been on his hands and knees.

Perry was about to launch into Cooper about wasting time on a couple of ounces of marijuana when the detective preempted him.

"Gentlemen," he said, "one last time. Is there some official federal involvement here I don't know about?"

"In what sense?" Perry asked.

"Kidnapping, interstate traffic, anything like that?"

"Nothing like that."

"In that case, I want to remind you that unless the constitution's been thrown out the window in the last couple of hours, this is a police matter in our jurisdiction. We always cooperate with other law enforcement agencies if there's a reason, but we haven't been told that reason yet. Anybody want to volunteer any information?"

Widmer looked away. Randall again deferred to Perry.

"I'm sure you understand that some matters must be treated in confidence."

Cooper was a stone wall.

Perry said, "Professor Fuller was preparing a document for the President's national security adviser. His accident came at a most unfortunate time."

Cooper let out a profound sigh. "In this county most deaths aren't convenient. This wasn't an accident."

It was Widmer who said, "What do you mean?"

Cooper took two corked plastic vials out of his raincoat pocket, removed the cork from one, and walked over to Widmer, holding the plastic vial right under Widmer's nose. Widmer instinctively took half a step backward.

"What does that smell like to you?" Cooper asked.

"Gasoline," Widmer said.

Cooper recorked the vial and uncorked the second one. "And what does this smell like?"

"Different, I'd say."

"Kerosene," Cooper said. "No mistaking the difference. I took those samples from the two cans in the garage. The labels on them are two inches high, kerosene and gasoline. What I think is somebody mixed some of the gas in with the kerosene in Mr. Fuller's heater. Murder isn't a federal offense. It's a nice local crime. I want to see those three brains upstairs again." To Widmer, "You're not their lawyer, too, are you?"

"No," Widmer said.

Perry stepped forward. "Mr. Cooper, maybe I can get someone from Washington to talk to you on the phone before this goes any further."

"I don't care if you get J. Edgar Hoover's ghost on the telephone. This is my jurisdiction. Let's go upstairs and find out who put the gas in the kerosene."

□ CHAPTER SIX □

When his private line rang, Thomassy knew it was Francine.

"Where are you?" he said.

"Your place."

Before Francine Widmer he'd given no woman the key to his house. You let a woman feel at home in your house and the next thing she's running around the perimeter peeing, marking off her turf. He wasn't about to give anyone an exclusive on his life.

"I'll need a key in case you're late," she'd said, and he'd taken his duplicate off the peg and handed it to her. That was safer than telling her there was a duplicate under the edge of the third flagstone outside. The peg key he could always ask for back when it was over.

Was that what he was expecting, that this, like the smoke over an extinguished fire, would eventually drift away, as the others had? If she has your key, he told himself, your privacy is shot. You can't ask for that key back; it's a terminal message. You want her to keep coming. But when he'd asked her, on the spur of one glorious moment, if she'd like to move more of her things in, maybe give up her apartment, it was she who'd said *no thanks* to the only gift he'd kept for himself.

Her voice, those resonant chords within her gracefully long neck that caused, as now, an answering vibration he would prefer to control, said ever so casually, "I want you to do something for me."

The women before Francine were all askers. They'd never have said *There's something I'd like you to do for me*. The authority in her voice, something he'd always thought of as a masculine attribute, had attracted him. Judge Turnbell had said to him in chambers, "Thomassy, you're the only lawyer I've had out there whose voice doesn't have a whisper of subservience." Turnbell was black. He'd learned all about role playing long before he'd got his law degree. "Weak people," Turnbell had said, "reek with deference. Deference shows a deficiency of respect. They like to be surrounded by niggers and women. Who are you afraid of, Thomassy?"

44

"What would you like me to do for you?" Thomassy said to Francine.

"Remember that bar of glycerine soap you brought home from San Francisco?"

"Rain."

"Blue soap that smelled of rain. I found one in a pharmacy on Forty-eighth Street today. I'd like you to come home and lather my back when I shower."

"Your back?"

"My legs too if you like."

"You can reach your legs."

"Not as well as you reach them. Come home."

He drove a bit faster than usual. The streets were slick. A slight rain had brought oil out on the surface of the road. He liked his silver-gray Buick Electra, a heavy car that held the road, a solid defense against any errant made-in-Japan tinbox that crossed the double yellow line in his direction. Slow down, his head told him, you're not a kid anymore.

Before Francine he'd gone with women who'd say things like, "How about if we went to the movies tonight and had dinner at my place afterward?" That was okay, he preferred that to having them in his place, where they'd be tempted to get domestic and try to show him they belonged. In their places he could watch their ploys with a certain detachment. Joanne, who overdid the candlelight business; candles on the table, okay, but on the sideboard and windowsills, too? *Your place reminds me of church, Joanne.* Or Florence, who wore a bra with cut-outs that let her nipples show against her dress. *If you wear something like that again, I'll come in wearing a codpiece.*

Joanne and Florence were figurines. Nora was dangerous, a malpractice specialist, an independent who made more money from her one-third share of insurance settlements than Ned Widmer did down on Wall Street. He liked her crazy energy till he realized that it was all real for her, not a game; she wanted to bring every doctor who made a mistake—and who didn't?—to his knees because her father had been a great surgeon who, when she was a kid, never once held his daughter in his arms, or smoothed her hair, or made her feel like an incipient woman. Not even Thomassy, with all his skill, could unlock the steel box in which her sexuality rattled like

45

ball bearings. Maybe there was a safecracker for her somewhere, but it wasn't him.

Oh there were good ones, Elaine and Louise and others who had their own careers and lives and strengths. It was Elaine more than the others who made him realize that women seemed to see life in stages: this is what it's like now, this is what it'll be after we get married. Didn't they see that every time they gave him a glimpse of the future, they unnerved him because he liked them as they were? In New York City, on the occasions when he couldn't avoid the subway, Thomassy would watch the row of seated women opposite and pick out the long-married ones, the not-so-long-married ones, and the ones that were still single. How do you find a wild animal you can keep at home that won't domesticate? *Marry a Siamese cat.*

Francine was as direct as Nora had been, with a difference. Somewhere along the line Ned Widmer had given her the keys. Hell, she was as direct as a straight line. Lather my back in the shower. I want to eat. I want to be eaten. She didn't advertise her desires, she announced them when he was a little off guard, because she knew the value of surprise. And he had to admit that the most erogenous physical attribute he had ever encountered were the convolutions of Francine's brain, the light-and-sound show of Francine talking, flashes of insight that explained the world to a mere lawyer who hadn't learned how to get her high-watt stations on his dial. "George," she'd said to him, "you're smart, why don't you think?" and he'd wrestled her lovingly down to the bed, and she'd flicked the head of his ready member with her finger and said, "It's your other head that needs the exercise, George." Cracks like that turned him on, and she, the bastard, knew it. "I'll suck your brain dry," he'd answered, and she'd said, "That's not where my brain is, George, but keep looking." *You don't find a woman like Francine twice,* he warned himself. *Don't let her get away.*

Thomassy heard the siren, saw the motorcycle in his rearview mirror. The cop motioned him over. *Officer, there's a lady waiting for me in the shower with a bar of blue glycerine soap.*

Thomassy rolled the window down. "Was I speeding?"

"No, sir," the cop said. "Your license plate's about ready to come off."

Thomassy stepped out into the drizzle and followed the cop to the back of the car. The license plate hung at an angle by one loose bolt. Thomassy squatted, took a nail file from his wallet, tightened the remaining bolt enough to secure the plate until he could re-place the missing bolt.

"Thanks," he said to the cop.

"That's okay, Mr. Thomassy. Getting a replacement plate is a real pain in the ass." The cop mounted his cycle and roared off.

Some people liked being recognized. Last year, when he de-fended the Morgan woman, he was twice trapped by TV newsmen as he was leaving the courthouse by a rear door. Each time he said "No comment." And while his face was on the screen that night the reporter's voice said, "Defense counsel had no comment." Flo-rence and Joanne both called to say they'd seen him on TV. He'd liked his anonymity as much as his privacy. His house was hidden from the street. He was ready for someone who understood even before he'd met Francine.

Inside, not a sound. On the kitchen table was the bar of blue glycerine soap, its cellophane opened like a flower, the soap its centerpiece.

"Where are you?"

No answer.

Nobody in the bathroom.

In the darkened bedroom he could make out Francine wrapped in a bath sheet. Was her face as beautiful to the rest of the world as it seemed to him? He touched her hair.

She woke with a start. "George? Oh, I must have fallen asleep."

As he lay down beside her she rolled away to the other side of the bed, then pulled the bath sheet after her, and, standing up, wrapped it around her. "First things first."

After a moment, he got up and stood in the door of the bath-room. She had her back to him. He said, "There's something about a naked woman brushing her teeth." As she gargled she threw her head back. His gaze traveled the contours of her body. God's mira-cle was skin; in the Met the man-made miracles were of stone. He walked up behind her and with the ends of his fingers touched the indentation on each side of her waist. He looked up. In the mirror, he saw Francine's breasts, the areolae pinkish brown.

"Your suit is damp," she said.

"I can remedy that," he said, not wanting to take his hands away from her waist.

She turned almost the way a ballerina turns to let her partner know her escape is merely to the other side of the stage. She turned the overhead shower on, then stepped into the tub.

47

"The soap is on the kitchen table," she said.

"I know," he answered, hurrying to get it.

She dozed for only a few minutes afterward because she had cat-napped earlier. As he slept beside her, she remembered his saying a year ago, when it had started, *Falling asleep afterward is a compliment to the experience. Nobody falls asleep in a whorehouse.*

The skin of her inside thighs still felt his lips. To George love-making was courtesy: You opened the door for another; somehow you would pass through as well. Were the other men she'd known selfish or inexperienced? She opted for inexperience, then thought how many go through their lives without understanding what a woman wants. She wanted to spoon herself against his body but thought that that would wake him. Courtesy was mutual. She abstained, and suddenly felt a rush of profound loss.

In the early months of their involvement with each other, her days were buoyed by exquisite agony: Where was he this very moment, doing what? Her work, which used to be her primary source of excitement, suddenly became an office where time passed until she could hurry to his home and they would, in a great rush, kiss, undress, kiss, hug, glory in each other's bodies. She lived from evening to evening, from body clasp to body clasp, as if the waterfall of tumultuous orgasms was drowning everything she had been before. The thumping insanity of the first weeks, overcome by irrationality, suffocated her brain. Her father had so drummed into her: *Your mind makes you human, your power will be derived from the success of your brain.*

In time the carnival stopped. The sheer, crazy, minute-by-minute imagining and longing for the other had receded enough so that she could breathe, enjoy her work again, think of others, behave as if she were dressed and not running around the world naked. Her feeling for Thomassy now had resonance. They had a history together. Were they evolving into something longer range, or was that the trap of every woman's hope, the cave to which food was brought and where children were born? Francine still couldn't imagine herself in her mother's world, being someone's wife. Was that like being someone's automobile? What was it she wanted? she asked of her restored sanity.

Planning was hope-chest stuff. Let whatever would happen, happen.

The phone rang just as they were finishing dinner. Francine's instinct was to answer it, her movement toward the phone aborted

48

by the thought that this was still a bachelor's home. She stopped. Thomassy got it on the third ring.

"Yes," he said instead of hello to let the caller know this was not the time for a long telephone call.

Francine watched him. He had a way of cradling the phone between his shoulder and his neck so that both of his hands would stay free.

She stood in front of him and mouthed the words, *One of your old girl friends?*

"Excuse me," Thomassy said into the phone and covered the mouthpiece with his hand. To Francine he said, "It's your father. He says it isn't about you."

Widmer was saying, "A friend of mine from Washington and I would like to see you rather urgently this evening. Before you say no, it's truly quite pressing. What's the matter, George?"

The matter is that your daughter is running her fingers up and down my fly. "Nothing. Go ahead." To Francine he mouthed *Not you.*

"Let me give you the address."

"Hold on," Thomassy said. "I've got a full calendar, Ned. If this is going to take more than an hour or two, I don't see how I can get involved."

Widmer wanted to say *You are involved. You are a prisoner of your capabilities. You're the only lawyer around here who could defend a case like this and be sure to win.* What he said was, "A client of mine died this morning."

"You know I'm not into estates and trusts, Ned."

Widmer felt odd when Thomassy used his nickname. How few people in this country now awaited permission to use your Christian name. Francine had said, *What do you expect him to call you? Dad?*

"It isn't anything like that."

"You're not saying much." *I've got a restless relative of yours here.*

"This must be in confidence," Widmer told him.

"Come on, Ned."

"Do you know the name Martin Fuller?"

Only a moment elapsed before Thomassy said, "I thought he was dead."

"He is now."

"I meant long ago."

"He was still active at eighty-two."

"I didn't see anything in the paper."

"He burned to death this morning, George. Can you come over

49

to his house as soon as possible so that my friends can have a word with you?"

"I'm too busy. The answer is no."

Among Widmer's friends one said *I'm afraid I can't.*

"Please," Widmer said.

"I've got to prepare for trial tomorrow. Sorry."

Without a further word, Archibald Widmer's Armenian non-son-in-law hung up, and grabbed Francine before she could skitter away. "You know what I do to girls who play games while I'm on the phone?"

A half hour later, lying in bed, Francine asked him, "Who did you think was dead?"

"He is dead."

"Who?"

"Martin Fuller. Name mean anything to you?"

"Oh my God."

"You knew him?"

"Everyone in my field knows his work."

"His brain passed your test."

"Don't be facetious. He did what he did better than anyone else in the world."

"That's not like being the best lawyer in Westchester County."

"Oh, George," she turned to him. She hadn't meant to hurt him. "What Fuller did was change the balance of power."

"And I don't change the balance of anything, according to you."

She'd intended supplication, saw she'd hurt him worse. "You changed my life when you won my case."

"But my brain isn't as good as Fuller's, is that it?"

"It's not your brain. It's that you haven't used it for important things."

She couldn't heal him with platitudes the way the other women always had. This was one of the things he'd had to adjust to, like Radcliffe, which he'd thought of as a place other men's women went to. And her grasp of what went on behind the news. She read newspapers as if there were five lines for every one he saw. She predicted Beirut. He'd said she got it from her work at the UN. "I got it from my head. I put two and two together instead of reading the ambassador's instructions." "You are arrogant," he said. "I don't arrogate anything to myself except you," was her answer. *You can't conquer a country*, she'd said once, *you can only subdue it temporarily.* And he'd thought, you can't subdue even temporarily a woman who thinks like that. You have to learn to trust yourself

50

to a rare species named Francine who in some matters would always be smarter. In Oswego, women settled in to run things from behind the scenery. At the UN Francine put words into the ambassador's mouth and said she'd refuse the ambassador's job if offered because she wasn't going to be a Charlie McCarthy for anyone.

Francine's special relish was drafting a reply to an anti-U.S. diatribe by a Soviet client, "one of the monkey states," as she characterized them. When they'd first met, Thomassy'd told her all the UN gab was useless because it ignored human nature. She'd said, "When a monkey flashes its ass, it's a sign it doesn't want to fight. The monkeys at the UN flash their teeth the way other monkeys flash their asses."

Francine had seemed cerebral and smart aleck to him at first, until the morning she watched him sorting out the junk mail. When Thomassy got letters soliciting funds for blind people, blacks, veterans, orphans, et cetera, he'd throw them into the garbage pail unopened. Francine had accused him of being a heartless bastard. Thomassy said he didn't throw out the ASPCA envelopes, he sent a check. She said it was monstrous to care about animals and not people. Thomassy told her the other animals don't destroy members of their own species or torture each other for no direct gain. Criminal lawyers watch other people lie all the time by commission and omission but they can't lie, not to themselves, not to others. They've got too damn many enemies to let themselves get caught. Francine said Thomassy got his clients off because the jails are too full and don't rehabilitate anyone. Thomassy responded that he got clients off because that was his job. He'd told her he was an advocate for winning and she was a do-gooder who would like to believe in the perfectability of man. "The best proof that you're wrong," he'd said, "is that you've taken up with me."

Now, Francine, leaning her head on her hand, said, "Fuller was the only one of my father's clients I wish he'd taken me to meet. In his—I don't suppose you've read any of his books?"

He was damned if he'd go on the defensive.

"I'm sorry," Francine said. "No reason for you to have. His great talent is—was." She stopped a moment only, "Prognosticating Soviet moves with miraculous accuracy."

"Astrology?" There he went.

"You study judges. He studied Soviet leaders. He knew how each one's mind works. You do the same thing except . . . "

"I get punks off. He saved the world."

"What did my father want?"

"Me."

"To get some punk off or save the world?"

"I don't know."

"Take me with you."

"You're crazy. Besides, I turned him down."

Francine threw his robe around herself and went to the phone to call her father.

"He's not home," Thomassy yelled after her. "Please don't mix in my business."

"What goes on in the world," Francine shouted at him, "*is* my business, donkey."

□ CHAPTER SEVEN □

Leona Fuller called from the back bedroom, where Detective Cooper had insisted on interviewing her in private. "Ned Widmer, please come in here."

Leona said, "He wants to know how much insurance there was on Martin's life."

"Is that relevant?" Widmer asked Cooper.

"We're trying to establish a motive for someone mixing gas in with the kerosene. Who benefits?"

"We've been protected for a long time," Leona Fuller said, "but not now, and not from the police." She turned to Cooper. "I believe there is about four hundred thousand in two or three policies, does that sound correct, Ned?"

"Approximately."

"If you have no children," Cooper said, turning his back to Widmer, "why so much insurance?"

"If we had children, they'd be grown. My husband took the insurance out at least thirty-five years ago. That wouldn't be much per year if something had happened to him then and I lived till, say, now. After all those years of paying premiums, he refused to discontinue any of it. He wanted me to have a good time, he said. He also wanted there to be enough for me to get help in organizing his leftovers."

Widmer intervened. "She means his manuscripts, letters, and so forth. It could take several years to get them all in order for turning

52

over to the university. Did you find that any of the individuals you interviewed upstairs had anything resembling a motive?"

Cooper shook his head.

"Then perhaps we can all be left in peace now?"

"Just as soon as I put the cuffs on one of the ones upstairs and take him to the lock-up."

"Which one? Why?"

Cooper glanced at his notepad. "Edward Porter. Possession of two ounces of marijuana. We found it in his room."

"Oh," exclaimed Mrs. Fuller, "I told him to be careful about that tobacco of his."

"Maybe you better advise your client," Cooper said, "that if she knew about his use—that stuff ain't tobacco—in her house and didn't inform the police, she could be charged. I don't want to have to charge the bereaved."

After Cooper left the room, Widmer tried to calm Leona. He patted her good hand. She sat, shaking her head, as if, under this crude barrage, her loss was first coming home.

Cooper stuck his head in the door. "Oh, Mrs. Fuller, did the Porter kid cut the lawn for you?"

"He's not a kid. Yes, he kindly did the lawn from time to time since our gardener moved away. He's a sweet and helpful young man."

"He had access to the five-gallon can of gas in the garage?" Cooper asked.

Leona glanced at Widmer. "Anyone could have access. We didn't lock the garage door ever."

Widmer hurried upstairs in time to see Cooper formally charge Edward Porter with possession.

"You've got to be kidding," Ed said.

Cooper held the handcuffs out. "Turn around and put your hands behind your back or I'll put them there for you."

Ed looked at them as if they were some strange object never seen before. "No," he repeated.

"Yes," said the detective. He spun Ed around, and with two quick movements slipped the cuffs on and locked them with a click.

Widmer realized that for all of his years practicing the law he had never seen a man arrested before.

"I want a lawyer," Ed said, trying in the absence of hands to

53

shake his hair away from his eyes. "Somebody who knows how to handle these people."

Perry and Randall were standing in the open doorway. It was to them that Widmer said, "George Thomassy is expensive and unwilling. We'll have to think of someone else."

"I don't care about the expense, dammit," Ed said. "This charge is ridiculous. They didn't have a search warrant. I want someone who can get the charge thrown out at the arraignment."

Widmer thought *This young man knows how the law works.*

They heard the distant phone ringing, once, twice. Randall hurried to get it, returned, said to Widmer, "Ned, it's your daughter."

He couldn't imagine how she knew where he was.

"I made George tell me," she explained. "He's willing to listen now."

"How did you convince him?"

"I'll go into that some other time. Here he is."

He told Thomassy about the marijuana charge, then said, "What I'm really concerned about, George, is that this is just a pretext arrest to hold him until they can press another charge."

"What kind of charge?"

Widmer hesitated. His purpose was to enlist George. Therefore he said, "I think they're thinking this might possibly involve murder."

Marijuana didn't interest Thomassy. He got kids off all the time just to get it across to the cops to stop wasting time on victimless crime. Murder interested him if the dead man was someone whose brain interested Francine.

"Tell me where to go," Thomassy said.

"I'll have to find out," Widmer replied, putting the phone down. On the way upstairs, he passed the bathroom from which the acrid smell of burning still seeped.

The village justice was hearing a case in which the owner of a '79 Ford wagon was claiming under oath that this evening was the first time in his life that he had been within the precincts of the village, that he had never lent his car to a member of his family or anyone else, and he had no idea how an officer had put a ticket on his car if it had never been there.

Thomassy took Widmer into an empty room along the corridor outside the courtroom. "What's your interest in this defendant?"

Widmer coughed politely into his fist. "I . . . I—"

"Don't try to invent something, Ned. You don't do that well."

54

"The truth is I really can't answer you at the moment. When I can, I will."

"That's fine, Ned. I trust you. I'll be patient. Let's meet the kid. We haven't much time."

The first time Thomassy had met people like Archibald Widmer was in college, white-shoe boys who kept their left hands in their laps when they ate and didn't make jokes about it. His father used to remind him all the time that the Armenians were the first Christians. Well, these Ivy League silver spooners weren't Christians, they were Episcopalians. Oh how his father had fought against his going to a college like that. Thomassy remembered his father saying, "Why you no go college here, boy? Why you need goddamn fancy college where rich snots make fun of you?"

"I need that kind of college, Pop, to get into a good law school."

"Then what? You come back here or you stay down there?"

"Pop, here is nothing."

Haig Thomassian's eyes blazed from his leathered face. "Here is me, boy."

"I didn't mean that, Pop."

"Here is Mama's grave. What you want to be, a son who runs away from his mother's grave, eh?"

"I'm going to school, Pop, not running."

"Believe me, the Turks will find you down there."

"I'm going to law school, Pop, to learn how to fight Turks."

"You end up lawyer for gangsters."

"No, Pop, you don't understand."

"I understand more in my pinky than you ever learn. You going to be lawyer for pimps, crooks, murderers."

"I'm going to defend the innocent."

"Innocent people stay out of trouble, don't need damn lawyer. You going to work with junk people."

Thomassy couldn't bear the glimmer of tears in his father's face. Suddenly the old man's arms were around him, hugging hard. "You listen, George, the Turks kill the woman I loved before your mother. I didn't make my life. The Turks made my life. I ran. Like you running now."

"It's not the same, Pop. I want to make it in this country. Even the teachers say the best way is to be a lawyer. Why are you so worried, why are you crying?"

"I never cry. My heart cries when God gives me one son and he wants to be defender of Turks who kill other people."

Getting through to an old-world father held no hope, Thomassy thought. What you learn is everybody comes from a foreign country. Communicating heart to heart, mouth to soul, with anyone is like climbing Mount Ararat.

In three or four minutes Widmer returned to the room with Detective Cooper leading Ed Porter, his hands cuffed behind his back. The introductions were cursory, as if names didn't matter, except that Thomassy recognized Cooper and that meant a lot to Cooper.

Thomassy said, "I don't talk to clients with their hands behind their backs. Would you mind taking the cuffs off."

Cooper believed most lawyers that hung around the courthouse were preening pigeons who got in the way of quick results. But Thomassy wasn't just a mouth. He was the kind of lawyer you'd go to if you got into trouble yourself. Cooper took the cuff key from his pocket too quickly, and it dropped to the floor.

The key lay on the tile floor, the bright object of their attention. Well, Thomassy thought, if I bend and pick that key up, will Cooper think I did it because he's too fat to bend without looking clumsy in front of a prisoner? Thomassy picked up the key and handed it to Cooper, who mumbled his thanks.

Once the cuffs were off, Thomassy said to Widmer and Cooper, "Please excuse me."

When the door closed, Porter, rubbing his wrists, said, "Thank you. I like the way you handled that cop."

Thomassy looked at Ed Porter. The kid, fully grown, was short. Short people were one of Thomassy's prejudices. They made up for their shortness in too many ways that were trouble for other people. There were exceptions. The kid's eyes had a brain behind them. The brown hair was a bit too tousled for going before a village judge who could rule on appearance as much as on evidence.

"Got a comb?" he asked Porter.

Porter nodded.

"Use it. We can't change your clothes. We can at least go in with combed hair."

Porter said, "We don't want to disappoint the judge's bourgeois expectations."

"Don't use a word like bourgeois if the judge asks you any questions in there. I want you to understand two things. You may be an academic genius, I know how a courtroom works. What we're going into is a courtroom. Second, you haven't hired me yet. I agreed to handle this arraignment as a favor to a friend. If this goes

56

any further than tonight, we have to talk retainer. Where will you get it?"

"I'll get it. I've got a stipend from Columbia."

"That can't run to much."

"Four thousand a year."

"That won't get you through the first day of a trial with all the preparatory costs."

"I told you I can handle the retainer."

"Let's not take any more time over that now. You'll pay for whatever this arraignment costs. Then we'll talk."

"I just wanted to assure you," Porter said, "that I have adequate resources."

Not many of Thomassy's clients used expressions like "adequate resources." He remembered one of the first things that struck him about Francine Widmer when he took her case on was her vocabulary. Her face, her body, and her vocabulary.

Porter said, "They said you were very good at this sort of thing."

"What sort of thing?"

"Defending the innocent."

"They told me Cooper saw two ounces of grass lying around on your night table."

"Detective Cooper lied," Porter said.

"You didn't have any grass?"

"It was in the night-table drawer."

"Who opened the drawer, you or the cop?"

"I'm not crazy. The cop opened everything—the closets, the drawers—he even managed to get his fat ass down on the floor and look under the bed."

"He find anything under the bed?"

"Dust, presumably."

Thomassy felt the first small run of adrenalin. He hadn't anticipated liking anything about this unscheduled evening.

There was a sharp knock on the door. "Sorry, folks," the court sergeant said, "the judge is ready."

"We'll be out in a second," Thomassy said. When the door closed again, he said, "Porter, your job in there is to look respectable, serious, and responsible to somebody who doesn't associate that with the blue jeans you're wearing. At least let your face look like you're applying to get into Amherst."

"I taught at Amherst for a year."

"Terrific. But remember, in there it's only appearance. The rest is

57

street fighting. That's my job. Don't fuck it up just because you have a brain."

In arraignments like this Thomassy had two choices. He could do what other lawyers did, listen to the affidavit of complaint, plead for low bail for his client because he had strong roots in the community, watch him getting fingerprinted and mugged, and wait for a preliminary hearing to rip into Cooper's belly. Or he could try what he thought of as his short-order-cook routine. When he saw the Washington people in the courtroom, he remembered what Widmer had said. This isn't a two-ounce marijuana case. He decided on the fast route.

Just before things started Widmer got close enough to whisper to Thomassy, "When it comes to making bail, I'll be pleased to guarantee it if it's necessary."

Thomassy patted Widmer on the shoulder, a patient acknowledgment of ignorance. "A lawyer can't make bail in New York State, Ned, have you forgotten?"

Widmer's blush showed. "I thought, that is, I thought Priscilla might supply the funds."

"Sure," Thomassy said. He had to keep remembering that, one, Widmer was well-meaning, and, two, that he was Francine's father.

The judge looked down at Porter. "Do you have your lawyer here?"

Porter nodded and pointed at Thomassy.

"Use your vocal cords," the judge said. "The court reporter can't hear nods." The judge glanced at the papers before him. "You've been charged with possession of two ounces of marijuana." He said it as if possession of two ounces of a controlled substance was getting to be like groceries.

"Your Honor," Thomassy said, "is that Detective Cooper's affidavit?"

"It is."

"Since Detective Cooper is present I'd like to move for an immediate preliminary hearing to determine if there is probable cause."

That woke the judge up. It was a good way to get rid of cases, but most defense lawyers weren't prepared to do anything but try to keep their client's bail low and get it posted. "Are you prepared?" he asked Thomassy.

Like a boy scout with a condom in his pocket. "Yes, Your Honor," he said.

58

The judge turned to Cooper. "Will the arresting officer please take the stand and be sworn."

Cooper was surprised. He didn't expect to have to do anything.

Thomassy noticed that when Cooper placed his right hand on the court clerk's Bible, he closed his eyes while saying "I will." Maybe the closed-eye routine was Cooper's private absolution before the fact.

"Your Honor," Thomassy interrupted, "I wonder if the witness might be requested to repeat his affirmation of the oath with his eyes open."

The judge said, "If your concern, counselor, is for the dignity of the court—"

"That, too, Your Honor, but my greatest concern is that you and I both have to judge the reliability of the witness's responses by his demeanor on the stand, or his testimony may have no greater value than his affidavit. I need to see a man's eyes when he is answering questions or taking an oath."

The judge made the clerk and Detective Cooper do it all over again. Randall and Perry, sitting way back in the small room, were amused.

Cooper was not. It showed in his voice as he answered the police sergeant's questions and described the events that led to the charge. When he was through, the judge nodded to Thomassy. "Does counsel wish to cross-examine?"

"Counsel wishes," Thomassy said, unraveling his body from the chair. "Your Honor, this issue here is not just probable cause. Two ounces of marijuana found in my home or your home, I mean anybody's home of course, raises the question as to whom did the proscribed substance belong, and how did it get there. Did it belong to you or me or to a guest of ours or a previous guest who'd left it are all questions of fact. And whether the marijuana got there by means of the host, or the guest, or a previous guest or were introduced, as is unfortunately sometimes true, by a police officer, these are all—"

"Counselor," the judge interrupted, "the police officer is waiting for your cross-examination."

"Of course." Thomassy walked toward the stand until his face was less than two feet from Cooper's. Cooper was trying to control the fire Thomassy had lit in his chest.

"Mr. Cooper," Thomassy said, "did you have a search warrant when you entered the residence of Professor and Mrs. Fuller?"

"I didn't come to the Fuller place to—"

59

"Your Honor, Mr. Cooper is an experienced witness. Perhaps he could be reminded that his role here is to answer questions yes or no. He can elaborate on his answer, but we have to have the answer before the elaboration."

The judge nodded.

"Will the court reporter please repeat the question."

Cooper said, "No, I didn't have a warrant."

Thomassy said, "Do you know whether the defendant lived in the Fuller house?"

"I was told he stayed overnight."

"Mr. Cooper," Thomassy said, "that's hearsay, which may be admissable in federal court but has no place here. I asked you whether you knew whether the defendant lived in the Fuller house. Is the answer no?"

"Yes."

"Your yes means that your answer is no, is that correct?"

There was a titter in the room.

"Mr. Cooper, as an experienced police officer, do you know whether the defendant, whether he was a guest in the house or a resident in the house, had a reasonable expectation of privacy when he decided to stay the night?"

"Yes."

"Did you in fact deny him his reasonable expectation of privacy by going into his room twice without invitation by him in order to interrogate him about various matters?"

"Yes. I believe—"

"Mr. Cooper, the court is interested in your answers, not in your beliefs. Your Honor, I'd like to save time by stipulating that Mr. Cooper as a detective investigating a serious matter had a right to interrogate possible witnesses. Now Mr. Cooper, may I ask if your interrogation of the defendant involved asking him numerous questions?"

"It did."

"Did it also involve opening closet doors, dresser drawers, and a night-table drawer in which you found a user's quantity of marijuana?"

"I saw it."

"You are not answering my question again, Mr. Cooper. Are you familiar with the plain-sight doctrine?"

"Yes, sir."

"And was the marijuana in plain sight before you opened the drawer?"

Cooper was silent.

"Mr. Cooper," Thomassy said, "I could interpret your silence in one of three ways. Two of them would not be a credit to your profession or responsive to the oath you took. Was the marijuana in plain sight?"

"It was in the drawer."

"Did you order Mr. Porter to open the drawer?"

"I did and he refused."

"Did you then open the drawer?"

"Of course I didn't. I insisted he open it."

"Your Honor," Thomassy said, "It doesn't matter who opened the drawer. I would like to suggest that when a police officer asks a citizen to do something, that the citizen takes that as an order, not knowing the law, and that in the absence of a search warrant, and in reliance on a guest of a reasonable expectation of privacy, and the plain-sight doctrine, that the investigating officer, investigating an entirely unrelated matter, was clearly in violation of the defendant's constitutional rights as much as if he had searched his pockets without reason, and unless every single person in this room—" Thomassy turned to take in the spectators as well as the police sergeant and the judge—"is ready to turn his pockets inside out at this moment or at any moment on demand by a police officer without the right to do so, then we have a clear instance of one choice and one choice only. Your Honor, we either throw out statutory and constitutional protections afforded all citizens or we find no probable cause and throw out this unmeritorious case and discharge the accused."

Ed Porter was fulsome in his gratitude. "I don't want your gratitude," Thomassy said. "I want your address so I can send you a bill for my time."

It was almost midnight when Thomassy got home. He found Francine scrunched up on the window seat in the living room reading.

"Wouldn't you find a chair more comfortable?"

"I'd go to sleep in a chair. I wanted to finish this. That's not true. I was waiting up for you."

He kissed her lightly, lips on lips, a touch of sweetness, someone else's warmth. *Domesticity* was the word that hovered in Thomassy's head.

"It went well," he said.

"I know. Dad called."

"I thought you don't like to answer the phone in my place."

"I thought it might be you. It doesn't matter, does it?"

61

"Not anymore."

"He said, among other things, that what one needed in life besides a passion for one's work, was a good doctor, a good lawyer, and a good man. In my case he said he thought that perhaps all I still needed was a good doctor."

"He's condoning us."

"Slightly."

They slid, eventually, into their respective sides of the large bed in the hope of sleep. Francine was about to turn off her bedside lamp when Thomassy said, "Do you own a copy of Fuller's book? The famous one, whatever it's called?"

"Sure."

"I'd like to borrow it."

"To prop up something?"

He pinched her nose closed till she gasped for air, her mouth wide open.

"Aren't you," she said, "a bit advanced in years to beg a political education?"

He ignored her crack. "I'd like to know everything you know about his work."

"Did you ever defend a cocaine dealer?"

"Sure."

"Did you study up on the pharmacology of cocaine?"

"This is different. I have a feeling that everything that happens to us—taxes, wars in the Middle East or Latin America, line-ups for gas, nuke fear, all of it—oozes out of the basic confrontation. Them and us. I know something about us. Fuller knew about them."

"Right."

"The government wanted Fuller's manuscript the way my broker would like to have Big Board numbers for December thirty-first." He glanced at her face. Why did she look so happy? "Get me some stuff to read," he said brusquely.

She hadn't expected the wave of satisfaction from thinking about the photocopies she could make from journals and other people's books. Once upon a time people had farms, divided up the chores, helped each other.

Thomassy's voice interrupted her thought. "How long has your father been connected to the government?"

"I didn't know he was connected. He's been a partner in that law firm for thirty years, and he was an associate there straight out of law school."

"I didn't mean he was on the government payroll or anything. Just a connection."

"Some of his school friends ended up in government."

"Intelligence?"

"I don't know," she said.

"Maybe," he said, turning out his bedside lamp, "we've both got an education coming."

□ CHAPTER EIGHT □

Before visiting the Fullers at home for the first time, Ed had wondered about what kind of woman Leona Fuller would turn out to be. She had to be smart—Fuller was so quickly bored by anyone of either sex whose mind didn't bubble like a percolator. What Ed hadn't expected was her directness. She said, "Martin has told me about your talent. Why don't *you* tell me about your anger?"

How could he deal with a question like that? His anger got worse whenever he went home for a visit so he stopped going home. It wasn't like a suitcase. He couldn't leave it in a locker or get another. It went around with him like a boil ready to burst.

"You don't have to answer me," Leona Fuller said. "Perhaps some other time."

Ed could see that her question was meant solicitously, but he knew that if she had had a son of her own she wouldn't ask recent acquaintances questions like that.

Ed had to say something. "Inequities," he said. "Inequities make me angry."

"Well," she said, "be prepared for a lifetime of anger. Inequities abound because God is smarter than we are. He demands variety of His creations. And from variety, inequity."

Ed was accustomed to women being like his mother, shutting up even if they were smart. Leona Fuller was a new experience.

"What I just said," she went on, "aroused a touch of anger in you."

He hated that it showed. He valued control.

"Don't deny it," she said. "Think about it. Our brains are for understanding ourselves first and societies second."

63

When Ed was very young he heard some adult say that his father was a very impressive man. He didn't know if they meant large or imposing mannered or rich, all of which he was. The first time he heard Martin Fuller speak, lured back for one of his perennial guest lectures, the word came back to him with a bounce: *impressive*. In his father's circle there were other men as successful as he was, but Martin Fuller did what he did better than any other man on earth. That was impressive. Ed couldn't believe his luck when Fuller took time to talk to him after class. Ed made him laugh, something he said about the bowel imperative being more imperative than the categorical imperative. Ed didn't want to overdo it, or seem to be sucking up to Fuller, but he stopped by after his lecture the following week and sneaked in a word about the book he was finishing, *Lenin's Grandchildren*.

"Bring me ten pages," Fuller said.

"I could bring you all I've done," Ed volunteered.

"Ten pages," he said.

Ed photocopied ten pages and dropped them off when Fuller wasn't around. He didn't want to be there when Fuller read them. He felt like a kid physicist working on a formula and showing it to Einstein.

Ed sweated the time away. After the next lecture he hung behind, waiting till the others got their little after-lecture ass kissing out of the way, then stood in front of Fuller, waiting.

He just looked at Ed. He didn't say a thing.

"Is it that bad?" Ed asked.

Fuller laughed with his whole chest. "I want to read the rest."

He could see Ed was still nervous. He said, "You have a good mind."

He could have said Ed had two legs for all it meant.

Ed brought Fuller the rest of the manuscript. Several weeks went by. Was he reading it? Finally, Ed asked.

"I've read it," Fuller said. "Why don't you come for dinner next week. We live in Westchester. It isn't far."

Ed felt as if he'd suddenly been asked to sing at the Met.

He didn't know how he was supposed to dress and he was embarrassed to ask, but he did. "Wear clothes," Fuller said, and that time Ed laughed.

Ed thought there would be other students there for dinner, but that night there was only him. Was that their way of getting acquainted with a new person? Or did Fuller want to talk about Ed's manuscript in private?

At one point in the evening the conversation got around to the progressive income tax. Ed said, "How can you call something like an income tax progressive?" That made them both laugh. Ed desperately wanted them to like him enough to invite him back. He felt comfortable there. He'd be even more comfortable the second time.

Fuller could turn any topic into something worth looking at again as if ideas were sculpture to be turned and seen in a different light.

"Of course, Ed," Fuller said, then, "Is it all right if I call you Ed?" He didn't wait for an answer. "Please call me Martin." *I couldn't do that*, Ed thought.

Fuller was saying, "It's the people in the middle who pay most of the tax. The rich—all you young people know that first—devote their energies to tax-avoidance schemes. The poor are trapped by sales taxes on necessities. But the Soviets," he said, "are cleverer than the rich here. They are not about to impose a graduated income tax or eliminate their tax-free perks. Their chief tax—few people know this—is on vodka, the big contributor to the government's coffers, the drug of choice and imposition. Since the unhappy man in the gutter and the unhappy men in the Kremlin have an approximately equal capacity for vodka before their livers give out, most of the taxes fall on the lower- and middle-income classes since the vodka served at the top probably comes out of public funds. That's socialism?"

He believes what he wants to believe, Ed thought. You can't argue fact with him. Ed opted for letting loose. "Why doesn't the CIA package a thousand bales of first-class marijuana in heavy plastic, tie them to floats, and let them loose off shore around the entire periphery of the Soviet Union during the summertime when there's no ice. The bales'll drift to shore. The whole country will get turned on tax free. Vodka consumption will plummet, the Soviet exchequer will shrink, the Kremlin'll have to cut the arms budget drastically, and the KGB'll be running around the country trying to stop pot smoking. The peasants are clever. In a wink they'll have private plots growing their own weed. End to the cold war!"

Oh did the Fullers laugh, both of them. Watching them appreciating something he'd said gave Ed a high. All those years he had longed to have somebody he admired appreciate him.

"As for your manuscript," Fuller said, "it's a good beginning."

Was that a put-down? Fuller had seemed to like the first ten pages. Was the rest a disappointment? What the hell had Fuller written when he was Ed's age?

Mrs. Fuller was watching them both as if she could sense the web of tension between experience and enthusiasm.

"Hope is an intellectual aphrodisiac," Fuller said. "Your book sings with hope. As you go on in life, your work will fill with observation and insight."

"Instead of hope?"

"Insight gives us hope," Fuller said. "Hope does not give us insight." Fuller smiled at him. "You must come again soon. And bring a friend."

He was being dismissed. Ed didn't want the evening to end, but they were standing and so he had to go. He mustn't take it personally, he told himself. People Fuller's age conked out early.

It took Ed four days to reread his own manuscript through Fuller's eyes. Was it naive? Of course it was a first book. Fuller would always know more than he did. Was there no catching up? Suck his knowledge like marrow from a bone. Get whatever he has to teach, then drop him. Fuller was wrong about hope, about youth, about socialism.

The next morning Ed woke with a giant's feelings in his bones. *It was a good beginning.* Fuller had said next time to bring a friend. He was sure they meant a girl. He thought of Sonya.

Sonya had dark hair, black eyes, and a tiny body in the right proportions. He had met her with some people at International House and when they shook hands he had wanted to drop to his knees—that was his fantasy—and stretch his lifeline out in front of her like a necklace and put it in her hands.

The first time he came to pick her up for a meal and movie, she yelled for him to come in. She had seen him from the window and taken the Fox lock down and opened the deadbolt. Ed opened the door and saw nobody, then heard her yell, "Won't be a minute!" and saw her down the hall bare-ass naked, beautiful, actually waving hello to him and then disappearing for a second and coming out slipping into T-shirt and panties and jeans and sandals, a kind of reverse striptease that was so natural he stood there like an idiot spectator. Finally he shook hands with her and felt love drowning him from the inside.

All through the movie he was torn, thinking if he came on too strong it might end right there, so he kept his hands on the armrests during the movie and afterward at her house when they shared a joint. He didn't know what she expected. He was afraid he'd come before she was ready, or like he once did, before he even got inside. So he just kissed her hand. He licked the palm and Sonya said, "That's sweet," and patted his hair and he didn't know how to interpret that. He went home and stayed up half the night writing her a poem, full of his agony for her. What he got back in the mail three days later was a note saying, "Listen, I'm not turned on by pseudointellectual poetry, I want a man with balls."

How could he risk having Sonya put him down in front of the Fullers? He kept remembering Leona Fuller's question, *Why are you angry?* and what Sonya had said to him and how it had brought back everything, his father saying *You read too much junk. You'll end up wearing fishbowl glasses like your mother. You need to work out in the gym with me. You need to practice on rabbits and squirrels so you can go hunting with me for decent-sized game. You need balls.*

Ed remembered looking in the bathroom mirror. If anything, his balls seemed bigger than other boys' because he was smaller. It's a metaphor, you idiot, he told himself. What did his father want, that he should lie about his age and enlist for some suicidal war in South America?

The morning after Fuller's death Ed stayed in bed longer than usual. Just because Fuller isn't there, he thought, doesn't mean the sanctuary is closed. He could still visit Leona. It wouldn't be the same kind of homecoming.

As Ed lit a joint, his mind filled with the recurrent memory of Samuel McAllister and the tennis racket.

Ancient Sam McAllister, a widower, had come to work for Ed's father as a gardener long before Ed was born. His accent was that of a man born in Scotland. Before Ed was officially awake, McAllister would arrive each morning in a car that he acknowledged with pride had been built in 1934. In good weather, when Ed was very young, he'd go out on the grounds to find wherever it was that Sam was working on his hands and knees, preparing a flower bed, or bending over, pruning, always. Without turning around, McAllister would boom his accented "Good morning to you, Eddie," as if he could sense Ed's presence even before he saw him. When it rained or in the dark months of winter, Ed would find Sam—he had to be in his seventies, Ed thought of him as being nearly a hundred years old—in the greenhouse, preparing seedlings for spring. Sam would motion to one of the high stools so that Ed could clamber up and watch him, a leather-faced god intent on turning seeds that were the size of nothing into plants that grew and grew.

One day when Ed was ten, he witnessed a scene between his father and Sam McAllister. Sam was gathering his things—a lunch box and thermos, a sharpening stone he frequently brought from home to give a fine edge to the tools in the greenhouse—when Ed's father, who always looked so formidable in his dark blue business suit and tie, said, "One moment, Sam. Did you see a Dunlop tennis racket around the back of the house?"

"Oh yes, sir," Sam had said.

"Do you know where it is?" Ed's father demanded.

"In the trunk of my car. I saw it lying on top of the garbage can and assumed you were throwing it away. Some of the strings were broken."

"I was planning to have it restrung."

"I'm so sorry, sir," Sam said, scurrying to the trunk of his car, getting the racket, and offering it back to Ed's father with both hands. "I know you have several new rackets, and I never thought—"

Ed's father cut him off. "You should have asked. Taking without asking is stealing." His father had glanced at Ed, as if this was an object lesson for him, too.

Sam's leathery face reddened. "Sir," he said, "As God is my witness, I have never stolen anything in my life."

"What could you ever possibly want with a tennis racket?" Ed's father said, his voice raised like a scythe.

"To tell you the truth, sir," Sam said, "I played tennis quite a bit until the arthritis, and I thought to cross this one with mine on the wall of my living room as a kind of decoration, a memento."

"You planned to sell it," Ed's father said.

"Oh no, sir. Never."

"Theft is inexcusable. Your employment here is terminated, Sam. Please remove your work clothes from the greenhouse—and nothing else—while I make out your final check."

Ed saw a terrible shadow cross Sam McAllister's face. "I've worked here more than thirty years!" he said. "You know how difficult it is to find a job at my age!"

But Ed's father's back was already turned as he strode off.

"Will you give me a letter of reference, at least," Sam called after him.

Ed's father stopped only long enough to say, "As a thief. Are you sure you want it?"

Sam McAllister had driven nearly halfway home in a trance when he thought he heard sobbing in the back seat. He saw Ed's tear-streaked face in the rearview mirror, and pulled quickly over to the side of the road.

"What are you doing here?" Sam asked.

"I don't want you to leave."

"Thank you, Eddie. I don't want to leave. But your father has the say. Until socialism comes. Maybe things will change then."

For the next fifteen minutes, sitting in the ancient auto at the side of the road, Ed heard for the first time about capitalism and socialism and the views that Sam had kept to himself all these years.

Finally, Sam said, "I'd better drive you home. Your father will say I kidnapped you."

"Can I come and visit you?" Ed asked.

"Only if your mother gives permission ahead of time."

"Will you come and get me?"

"You'll have to find a way of getting to my place. I will drop you off at the gate today. I will never enter those grounds again."

"Even if I make my father say he's sorry?"

Sam McAllister laughed, and it was the memory of that sound that brought him to mind, now as many times before, even long after Sam McAllister, as Ed's mother had said, died of loneliness.

For a while Ed spent time in the greenhouse trying to continue at least some of Sam McAllister's propagation work, but the new gardener, a Filipino who smiled a great deal but never laughed aloud the way Sam had laughed, told him, "Go play."

Play for Ed now became the realization of a secret ambition, to try to read all the worthwhile books in the world, starting with those that Sam had mentioned. Some were difficult, but he read books about those books, which he bought with money his mother slipped to him for other things. Once he made the mistake of leaving one of the books face down and open on the hallway table where his father glanced through the mail when he came home at night.

"Jenny," he shouted to his wife, "have you seen this garbage Edward is reading?"

Jenny Sturbridge had come in from the living room and said, "He's trying to find his way. All kids read a lot that doesn't stick. He gets good grades, that's what counts."

"If he keeps reading junk like this," his father said, "he'll turn into a goddamn commie."

When she answered him she sometimes ducked her head a little deferentially. But this time her eyes and body were unswerving. "I think he's trying to become a decent human being," she said, then turned to where Ed was standing until Malcolm Sturbridge turned his head and saw his son.

Ed didn't know if it was his father's embarrassment at having been overheard or the fact that his pacemaker had to be replaced and he was in bed for a few days contemplating the possibility of his own death again that resulted in their having a frank talk.

Malcolm Sturbridge looked lonely propped up on pillows in the big bed, no longer imposing, pale, probably frightened. Ed had come in because his mother had said he ought to at least say hello to his father, but when he saw what his father looked like he sat down on the edge of the bed. Ed expected to be ordered off, told to pull up a chair, but instead his father just nodded as if to declare a truce before saying something he had been saving up.

"I'm glad you stopped in, Edward," he said.

Ed wanted to say to him *Will you ever call me Eddie or Ed before you die?*

Malcolm Sturbridge said, "It's been a very long time since we had a peaceable talk." He paused for a moment to gather strength, or was it courage? "You're a very bright young man. I think you inherited your mother's sharp mind without her passivity about using it. Can you focus on a question I've been thinking about?"

Ed said nothing, waiting.

"What do you think, Edward, is the chief difference between yourself and me? I'm not talking about physical things. I mean character."

"That sounds kind of heavy, Dad," Ed said.

"The doctor put no limitations on my thoughts, just on my physical activity. What difference do you see?"

Once Ed had feared that if he gave his father an answer he didn't want he'd reach out and slap him. That time had passed.

"In the world of business," Ed said, "the end is profit, the impulse greed. If you spend your life in it, I suppose you become part of it."

Sturbridge sighed. "I suppose that is intended to characterize me. What about you?"

"I'm concerned about the people, trying to puzzle out answers we don't yet know. My feelings," Ed said, "are with the perpetually powerless."

Sturbridge took a sip from his bedside water beaker through the bent glass straw.

"Businessmen are said to look at the world with a cold eye," he said, touching a tissue to his lips. "I know your heart bursts with demands for justice. Ask yourself, where do the poor remain poor despite the most radical changes in government, here or there? Your mother says you're aiming to become a specialist in Soviet affairs. Will you be able to look at the causes of poverty there as well as the alleged causes of poverty here? If you do, you will gain some remarkable political insights."

Ed had always wanted to learn to argue with his father successfully but instead felt his face flushing with anger. "I'm on the side of peace," he blurted out. "What side are you on?"

Perhaps because he was sick, Sturbridge didn't snap back at Ed. He said quietly, "The greatest cause of war is naiveté. Even a superficial view of history has to acknowledge that the appeasers gave Hitler his chance. Churchill saw that, and yet the moment we ostensibly won the war, Churchill got thrown out and the appeasers came flooding back into power. Doesn't it strike you as ironic that when the Churchills were no longer in charge that we began getting into the game of escalating arsenals on both sides of the Atlantic? All appeasement gets you is a bigger fight when you're less prepared for it."

Ed's mother came into the room. Ed didn't know whether it was because she heard his slightly raised voice or thought it unusual for him to be in there for more than a minute. "What are you two up to?" she said.

Malcolm Sturbridge said, "We have decided that we are both on the side of peace."

Ed thought his father was trying to disarm him. He was trying to win him over. And so he said, "Why did you fire Mr. McAllister? He wasn't a thief."

Jenny Sturbridge watched her husband's dehydrated lips. Would he look away? His gaze lifted to meet Ed's. He said, "Because he stole you from me."

You couldn't erase the memory bank even after all these years.

Ed stared at the ceiling.

If only Sam McAllister were alive somewhere.

If only Fuller were still alive.

Thoughts like that came from lying in bed too long. It was time to get up. His gaze wandered over the bookcase closest to the bed. He reached over and pulled out Fuller's book. Oh how they'd joked about it in grad school, the seminal work on the revolutionary ovum. Ed never joked about it after Fuller inscribed his copy:

> *Dear Ed, as a scholar be loyal to your senses, to your memory, and to objectively verifiable fact. As a passionate human being, be loyal to friends and to the innocents who depend on your knowledge. With affection, Martin Fuller.*

Ed hoisted himself to his feet. His reluctant body felt ten times its normal size, moving against the tremendous force of gravity. He sat back on the bed. How much had he smoked? Had he popped any pills? People died sleeping in the snow. Up from the bed he struggled once more, made it to the bathroom, raised the toilet seat with his toe and let his stream splatter into the water of the bowl, poisoning it with yellow.

In the mirror his face told him he had not shaved for two mornings. The stubble seemed like decay. To shave is to start clean. He stung preshave on his cheeks, got his Phillips rechargeable, pushed the "on" button. Nothing happened. Had he allowed the battery to go dead? He got the AC adaptor and plugged it into the outlet at the mirror. Nothing. What a time for it to fail!

He was looking in the cabinet for the throwaway razor he'd kept when he heard the knock on the door. As he went to the door he looked around. God the room was a mess.

"Who is it?" he shouted through the door, but he knew.

When he opened the door, Cooper said, "This time I have a search warrant." He waved the piece of paper in front of Ed.

"Isn't this out of your jurisdiction?"

"This is a New York City search warrant. And that's a New York City cop behind me."

"Why are you picking on me?" He looked at Cooper's protruding belly. He had no respect for people who couldn't control their appetites.

"That was your button I found in the garage, wasn't it?" Cooper said. "You had a button missing from your jacket, didn't you?"

"You're going to arrest me because of a button? You know you'll be held responsible for false arrest."

"Listen, big brain," Cooper said, pointing a finger at Ed's face, "you used the downstairs bathroom during the night, didn't you?"

Ed said nothing.

Cooper said, "There's a bathroom up there on the second floor. Why'd you use the downstairs bathroom?"

"Out of courtesy. That's something you wouldn't know about. The upstairs bathroom is between Troob's and Melling's rooms."

"There's a door from the hallway."

"That door was locked," Ed said.

"Not when I checked it."

"I'm talking about the middle of the night. Melissa or Scott must have opened it in the morning."

"We found traces of an inflammable fluid on the floor near your bed."

"I spilled it filling my lighter. You're wasting your time."

"Mister, I don't waste time. Where's your lighter?"

"I don't know. Somewhere around."

"Look for it."

"I'll look for it when you get out of my hair."

"Don't get fresh with me, kid. I don't like your attitude."

"When you start behaving like a public servant, I'll change my attitude," Ed said.

Cooper, his face reddening, tried to control his voice. "You smoke?"

"Sure."

"Where are your cigarettes?"

"Somewhere around."

"Where somewhere? Show me. I don't see a lighter, I don't see cigarettes. What was that hip flask doing in your closet?"

"I don't drink."

"You saying that flask wasn't yours?"

"I said I don't drink."

"That hip flask, mister, was empty, but my nose said it had been filled with an inflammable fluid. Do you fill your lighter from a hip flask? Don't answer."

Cooper would be damned before he'd pull out a plastic card and read the Miranda. "You've got a right to remain silent," he told Ed. "Anything you say can be used against you." Then he said, "Can we come in now?"

"I want to read that warrant."

Cooper put it in front of Ed's face without letting go. Ed read it through word for word. He needed time to think.

"I want to call my lawyer," he said.

"It's your dime," Cooper said.

Ed looked in his wallet for Thomassy's number.

The phone in Thomassy's office was answered by a secretary, who said Thomassy was in court, could she help?

"Can you get word to him? This is Ed Porter. Tell him Detective Cooper is here with a warrant. Yes, the same address I gave him for billing me."

After Ed hung up, he asked Cooper, "What if he doesn't call me back?"

"He'll find you in the station house."

"You're arresting me? I thought the charge was dropped the other night."

"This isn't grass. It's murder."

Ed put his hands on his belly. "I think I've got diarrhea," he said.

Cooper pointed in the direction of the bathroom. "Don't lock the door."

In the bathroom, Ed tried to organize his thoughts, shake off whatever was cluttering his brain.

"Hurry up," Cooper yelled from the other room.

Ed looked in the mirror. Thomassy would hate the fact that he hadn't shaved.

Ed had to sit in the chair in the corner and watch the two of them, Cooper and the man in uniform, going through everything. The grass was in the refrigerator in a plastic container, under leftovers Ed would never eat. They didn't look in the refrigerator.

Cooper spotted Fuller's book on the bed, opened it, found the inscription to Ed that ended *With affection, Martin Fuller.* Cooper looked at him as if he always suspected that eggheads had a hole in their brain and this was proof.

The shrill phone rang.

Cooper jabbed a finger at Ed and then at the phone.

Ed picked the phone off the cradle.

"What's up?" Thomassy asked. "I'm in a phone booth. Make it fast."

Ed tried to tell him, Cooper, the warrant, the New York City cop with him. Thomassy sounded exasperated, as if Ed was taking too much time. "Give me Cooper," he snapped.

Ed held the phone out to Cooper.

All Ed could hear was Thomassy yelling at Cooper just like he'd yelled at him. Cooper said, "Sure it's a search warrant. But I've got probable cause for an arrest."

Cooper listened, his face reddening. "Look, Mr. Thomassy, the form is he goes to the station house to get booked. You want to talk to him, you talk in the station house."

Cooper glanced over to make sure the other cop was at the door. "I know how you feel about station house interviews," he said to Thomassy, "but I can't bring him to your office. You want the captain down my throat? He'll think I'm on the take. No, no, no, I don't want you talking to the captain. I'm running this. You deal with me. Don't give me that false arrest shit, Mr. Thomassy, I'm too old for that. You what? You can't do that."

Cooper turned away. He didn't want Ed to see how angry he was. "Sure I know you're an officer of the court. You're making a lot of trouble for me. Suppose—"

Ed still couldn't hear anything Thomassy was saying, but his voice was less strident, as if he had stopped yelling and was giving instructions.

"Okay," Cooper finally said, "Okay." When he hung up, he said, "Shit." Then to Ed, "Come on."

"Where are we going?"

"Thomassy's office."

Ed couldn't help saying, "Is that usual?"

"I don't want any extra grief from that son-of-a-bitch," Cooper said, grabbing Ed's arm.

"Then," Ed said, "let my arm go. If you're angry at him, grab his arm."

"Get going."

Ed looked around the room for his jacket. The apartment was sure a mess. He slipped the jacket on and Cooper held the hand-cuffs out.

"Do we need to do that?"

"Just shut up," Cooper said. He hated the idea of a lawyer who made the law come to him.

□ CHAPTER NINE □

Thomassy got to his office a bit out of breath, wanting to be there before Cooper arrived with Ed Porter. Alice held up a warning hand.

Alice, though "comfortably married" for six years now, still occasionally had the fantasy about her boss lifting the sheet and sliding in beside her, touching her waist with the tips of his fingers. His hand would never move up to her breast, or down to her thighs, just stay safely in the isthmus between erogenous zones, her soul longing for his fingers to move down or up. About six months after her marriage, she'd gone to a counselor because of that recurrent fantasy, and he'd said, "Why don't you find employment somewhere else now that you're married?" She'd wanted the fantasy explained, given some harmless excuse, not eliminated. Working elsewhere wouldn't have stopped her thinking, would it? She hadn't gone back to the counselor. She was Thomassy's proximate woman, more than any other woman, even when there was a closed door between them. And if her mind set was right, she could feel his emanations through the door. Thomassy might fire her, though he had no reason to, but she'd never quit.

Alice's warning hand having stopped Thomassy in his tracks, she said, trying to keep her voice neutral, "She's in there."

"She who?"

"She who is right," Alice said, her voice losing its grip on neutral.

"I forgot to tell you Miss Widmer was dropping by," Thomassy said.

"I'll bet."

The truth was that he had forgotten.

Francine was sitting behind his desk, in his chair. Thomassy closed the door. He didn't want to lose a good secretary.

"Sorry I'm late," he said.

She waved away his apology. "Why do you keep my picture face down?"

On the credenza next to the desk was her swan-neck photograph, as if she was turning away from the camera and got caught at the precise angle that made her seem what she was, fleet yet catchable.

"I'm glad you could drop in, Francine. Got a couple of semi-stupid questions for you."

"You haven't answered me. Why face down?"

Thomassy sighed. "In this office I try to find out as much as I can about my clients. I don't want them finding out much about me."

"You mean you want to be thought by female clients to be available."

"Don't be silly."

"I was a female client. You just lied to me, George. Alice turns my picture face down."

Thomassy's smile flickered for a moment. She'd guessed a half truth. Alice had turned the picture down the first time. She claimed she'd been dusting around and forgot to raise it again. Men, he thought, fought about women with their antlers. Women scratched.

"Before you ask me anything, counselor, I have three questions to ask you."

Oh well, he thought, making himself comfortable in the chair he reserved for visitors, if Cooper comes, Cooper will wait.

Francine stretched her legs, her body seeming to elongate itself in his chair. "You're staring," she said.

"I am a student of your body."

"Don't distract me," she said.

76

"I could say the same."

"Enough. George, would you take on the case of an ordinary seaman who'd—"

"Is this a hypothetical case?"

"I'm not saying. Yet."

"Go ahead."

"This seaman," she said, "jumped a ship from one of the Warsaw Pact countries and asked for asylum under the following conditions. He told the immigration authorities he was bored with socialism, and they found that insufficient reason to accept him as a political refugee and risk a rumble."

"Nothing else?"

"Nothing I'm going to tell you before you answer. Obviously he doesn't have any money so all you'd get was a promise to pay something out of his future wages if he stayed. Would you take his case?"

"Why did he give a frivolous reason?"

"Boredom frivolous? George! Boredom is one of the great instigators of migration, domestic and international." She sat up straight in his chair. "Come on risk it, gamble."

"How?"

"By answering truthfully."

"I'd take him on."

"Based on?"

"Anybody who votes with his feet has got guts. Anybody with guts ought to be defended. Are you fronting for a prospective client or testing me?"

Francine touched her long fingers together, forming an arch. He remembered her father doing that.

"Question two," she said. "Presumably you'd defend an adolescent who killed a parent."

"As a matter of fact I have. What are you getting at?"

"Would you defend a mother who killed her baby?"

He was silent.

"Is this hypothetical?"

Francine said nothing.

"I'd need to know a lot about the mother," Thomassy said. "Her life. The circumstances."

"How do you distinguish between the two cases, then?"

"Well, if you've read the books . . ."

"I've read the books."

"I don't mean law books. I mean Aeschylus, Freud. Killing a parent is like all killing, wrong, but it's a not-unknown response to the relationship, held in check by most people. Killing a baby is not natural. Insanity cop-outs are not my dish."

"If the baby had an incurable disease?"

"You're loading it on, Francine."

"If the baby weren't born yet?"

"Look, this is turning into the kind of discussion I like to have after hours."

"I'm trying to see if your brain is functioning and you're copping out."

"I'm asking for a postponement, Your Honoress."

"You try calling a female judge that and you'll get your brass balls tarnished."

"I've got a client coming soon. You're getting your questions in and I haven't asked one yet."

"I have one more before you get your turn."

He held up a finger. "One," he said.

"Don't panic. My lease is up in less than two months. Do you think I should give up my apartment?"

"Have you found a place you like better?"

"Yes," she said.

"Where?"

"On Allerton, a house set back from the street, occupied by a bachelor with lots of room to spare."

Thomassy examined the fingernails of his left hand.

"Need a manicure?" Francine said.

"I'm thinking."

"Once, on the spur of the moment, you invited me to move in. This isn't spur of the moment, George. We've come a long way. Are you worried about what your cleaning lady will say if I move in? She'll say she finds the house a lot neater."

"You're not pregnant?"

"No. And what the hell's that got to do with it? Your cleaning lady do D&C's on the side? You don't like contracts, I'm not asking for one. I was just being practical. I'm there half the time I'm not at work. It'd save nearly five hundred a month. Just think of the vacations six thousand a year could buy. Please don't just stand there, say something. Say you don't want a roommate under any conditions."

"That's not it."

"Then what the hell is it? You waiting for a woman who's two inches taller than I am and three points higher on the Richter scale? Look, forget it. This is your meeting. I didn't mean to preempt it. What did you have in mind?"

78

Thomassy closed his eyes. He could handle the worst surprises in cross-examination, why was he tongue-tied now? And as he asked himself that question, he remembered his father pointing to a new brown-and-white filly he'd acquired that looked like she'd grow into a stallion instead of a mare. *What you see, Georgie,* his father had said, *is a horse you ride where she wants to go. Other horse, you give apple, piece sugar. Not this horse. This filly eats respect. Can't buy respect in feed store. You think you handle horse like that, Georgie?*

He had left Oswego thinking he could handle anything or anyone in or out of a witness chair, but nothing had prepared him for partnership with a woman who could sometimes churn him like a judge instead of allowing herself to be manipulated like a jury. *You can appeal from decisions easily, Thomassy, but not from this one.*

"You were going to ask me some semistupid questions," she prompted.

Was it the fact that she knew so damn many things he didn't know?

"George, you're drifting."

That brought him back, unsteady, unready, but it was his turn. He could hear his stomach rumbling. Nerves. She was one case he wanted to win more than any other. She wasn't a case. Was he incapable of risking sounding less bright than she was? If not with her, whom?

"I thought you were pressed for time," she said.

"Question," he said, a word to get started. "I need some litmus for this case I'm on. You've spent time with all those Third-World creeps at work. How do you tell the difference between the fuzzy-brained ones and the ones who squat when the bear tells them to?"

Francine was relieved. All that pressure building in him. "Try self-determination. Not straight out, just ease around to it and ask do they mean people who go elsewhere when they can't vote at home. If they say only malcontents emigrate, you know you're probably listening to a Russian ventriloquist. Or mention self-determination for the Puerto Ricans. That always gets the puppets because the damn Puerto Ricans vote to stay with us imperialists. That's a giveaway word. Ask how Portuguese imperialism in Angola differs from Cuban imperialism in Angola. If they say the Cubans are just trying to help little old Angola's economy, you know where you are. If they start on antinuke talk, ask them if they are opposed to war. If they insist they are opposed to nuclear weapons, ask about biochemical weapons. Gas. Lasers. You get to see the difference between a jerk and a party liner pretty fast. Why

79

this lesson now? I thought you didn't get into Kunstler's kind of law?"

"I'm not. I'm defending a kid who's supposed to be a whizz bang in Soviet studies. I just want to find out if I'm defending a kid or a cause. I don't like causes."

Alice buzzed on the intercom. "Detective Cooper is here," she said. "And two others."

"One in handcuffs?" he asked.

"Yes," she said.

To Francine he said, "Thanks for the prepping. I wish I wasn't so dumb about the things you know."

"Would it make you feel better if I asked you how you can tell if a witness is lying?"

"I've got to see these people now."

"When we talked you looked pale. Now you've got high color in your face. We have to talk some time about what makes your juices flow. Right now you have the look of a walking adrenalin pump."

"What's eating you?" he asked.

"I wish I could turn you on as quickly as clients do."

She was gone.

In the anteroom, Francine stopped short when she saw Cooper, Ed Porter, and the uniformed cop. The one she was staring at was Ed Porter.

Thomassy came out of his office, saw Francine still there, wanted to say something to her, but the other three were seeing his agitation. So was Alice from behind her desk. He watched Francine close the outside door without a glance back at him. He heard her heels clatter on the stairs going down. He felt as helpless as a fifteen-year-old kid. Everything he had learned to outsmart opponents was useless up against Francine's maddening advantages, the curves of her skin, the ultimate cove, and worst of all that female brain that despite his long bachelorhood was enticing him toward capture.

□ CHAPTER TEN □

"Very attractive client you've got there," Cooper said, jiggling his head toward the exit door.

Thomassy still wanted to run after her. The remedy was work. "Who's your friend?" he asked Cooper.

"This is Detective Hoffman," Cooper said. "I brought him along to help keep an eye on your client and to have a witness that you're not bribing me for bringing your client here instead of you coming to the station house."

"Much obliged," Thomassy said, nodding at Hoffman.

Cooper handed Thomassy a piece of paper. "This is the name and badge number of the New York City patrolman who witnessed the arrest."

Thomassy said, "Thanks. These walls are thin. I want to talk to the defendant in private. Why don't you gentlemen have some coffee. Downstairs, three doors right, there's a coffee shop. And would you mind removing Porter's cuffs."

Cooper said, "I'll leave Detective Hoffman at the outside door."

"Thanks," Thomassy said. "That'll make me feel real safe."

Outside, Cooper said to Hoffman, "Come on, Hank, coffee time."

The detective, addicted to coffee as are many policemen who spend so much of their lives waiting, said, "I thought I was supposed to guard the door."

"I was only pulling that prick lawyer's leg. Come on."

Perched on a stool inside the coffee shop, Cooper spotted Francine in the public phone booth. "Hey," he said, poking Hoffman, "isn't that the babe that just huffed out of his office?" He slid off the stool and placed himself to the side of the booth where she couldn't see him. He leaned his ear against the wooden booth. Oldest trick in the world. He could hear as clearly as if she were talking into his ear. "Dad," she was saying, "Dad, remember you asked me to urge George to take on a young client. I think I just saw him brought into George's office. Short, wildish brown hair, lots of freckles. Is that the one?"

Cooper strained to hear.

81

"No," Francine said. "I didn't catch his name, but I swear that he's the same one I saw—"

Detective Hoffman, sipping hot coffee, was looking straight at her, the same man she just saw in Thomassy's office. "Hold the line, Dad." She opened the accordion door. Cooper pulled his head away, but she recognized him, too. Back in the booth, she picked up the dangling receiver. "Sorry. Someone's been listening in. I'll call later from another phone."

Cooper watched her leave the coffee shop. Some ass, he thought. Wonder if that lawyer's banging her? He jotted a few words into his notebook. The DA might want to have a talk with the lady. He wouldn't mind having a little talk with her himself. But he had learned early not to make a play for a woman that was out of reach.

Hoffman said, "I guess I shouldn't have stared at her."

"Never mind," Cooper said, stuffing his notebook in the side pocket of his jacket. "I got what I wanted."

Inside his office, Thomassy gestured at the straight-backed chair he wanted Porter to sit in. Then, as a reflex, he sat on his desk, overlooking Porter, his knees on a level with Porter's head. Until he got to know a criminal client, he always wanted to be in a position to kick a head quickly if he had to.

This isn't your usual client, he told himself. *This is a well-educated pothead.*

"All right," Thomassy said. "Why did you kill Martin Fuller?"

Blood rushed to Ed Porter's face. He put a hand quickly through his hair, as if to quiet his reaction.

"Why don't you ask me questions," Porter said, "instead of assuming things. I didn't kill anybody."

Thomassy looked at Ed Porter's eyes. The kid's gaze did not waver.

The clock on the shelf ticked.

"I have never physically hurt anybody," Porter said.

This kid can testify on his own behalf, Thomassy thought. He looked away so that the kid could look away.

Instead Porter asked him, "Who have you defended?"

"You. I got you off at the arraignment, didn't I?"

"This seems to be a more serious matter," Porter said.

This kid had nerve. "You want references?"

Porter nodded.

Thomassy took a piece of scrap paper from his desk and wrote a name and phone number on it. "You can call him," he said. "Be my guest." He pointed to the phone.

"Who is this?" Porter asked.

"The DA. He probably remembers who they were better than I do. I forget about cases when they're over. He remembers."

"How often do you lose?" Porter said.

"I don't lose. Clients lose," Thomassy laughed. "Don't worry, kid. I don't lose cases that go to trial. If I don't think I'll win, I plea-bargain."

"I won't bargain. I didn't do anything wrong."

"You smoke grass, don't you?"

Porter shrugged his shoulders. "Well?"

"You just lied. You said you didn't do anything wrong."

"I didn't say I didn't do anything illegal."

Good boy, Thomassy thought. Roberts will have a hard time sandbagging him if I put him on the stand.

"You going to call the DA for references?"

Porter stuck the piece of paper into his jeans pocket.

"Do you know why your ass is in a sling? Why they picked you to charge?"

Porter looked at Thomassy for more than a few seconds. "Don't they have to charge somebody," he finally said, "before the public gets antsy?"

"Not this soon. And why you?"

He was waiting for Porter to squirm. The kid looked reflective.

"I don't think this Cooper fellow likes people who work with their brains."

"He works with his brains."

"I mean intellectuals," Porter said.

"That would include pretty much everybody who visited the Fullers. Why you?"

"I use grass. In some people's minds that's three steps from murder, isn't it?"

"Don't be facetious. What is his evidence?"

"He found an empty flask on the back shelf of the closet in my room."

"Empty of what?"

"Of whatever'd been in it. How'm I supposed to know, it isn't mine."

"Whose is it?"

"Do you know how many people use that room? He found skin magazines in the closet, too. I like skin, not magazines. I don't know why he's sniffing in my direction. You tell me."

"I don't know yet. Are you foreign born?"

"What kind of stupid question is that?"

83

"Answers can be stupid, not questions."

"I was born in Connecticut, is that foreign?"

"What kind of ID do you have?"

Porter took out his wallet. Thomassy could see cash, checks, the usual debris. Porter put a driver's license in front of Thomassy.

"I want to see all of it. Including dirty photos."

"I don't carry dirty photos."

"All of it, on the table."

Thomassy looked at the driver's license closely. Connecticut all right. "What are you doing with two driver's licenses?" Thomassy asked, picking up the second one. "Who is Richard W. Bates?"

"I don't know. I bought the card years ago when I was below drinking age."

"You expect me to believe that?"

"Sure. Lots of kids do that."

"You've been drinking age for four or five years. Why didn't you tear up this second ID. Or sell it?"

Porter sulked in silence.

"Mr. Porter," Thomassy said, "you go around thinking you're smarter than most people you meet?"

"I am."

"Maybe you are," Thomassy said, putting the ID right under Porter's nose to see if he'd grab it. "But some people have a lot more experience. Why didn't you get rid of this?"

"I thought you were supposed to defend me?"

"I haven't agreed to do anything. I want to know what I'm supposed to be defending. Why the other ID?"

"My father had people looking for me. We didn't get on for a while. Hey, don't tear that card up!"

Thomassy hadn't intended to tear the card. He just wanted to see Porter's reaction. "I'll keep it. Anything else in your wallet we might not want them to see when they book you?"

"No."

Thomassy handed Porter an eight-and-a-half-by-eleven pad, and a pencil. "Draw a human being," he said.

"Draw a what?"

"I said a human being."

"You a psychologist?"

"I'm a lawyer."

"What's this, some kind of thematic aperception test?"

"No, and you're flunking it by asking a lot of questions. Draw the picture."

Thomassy looked at the result of his infallible test carefully. Aggressive, yes, crazy, no. He wrote the name Edward Porter in the corner, and the date. "If I'm to undertake your defense, I'll need a retainer of twenty-five thousand dollars."

All his childhood Ed Porter had lived in a world without money. There was always someone with him, a governess at first, a companion, a tutor, whatever she was called, who paid for anything he wanted and marked it down on a three-by-five card for reimbursement. In high school he secretly saved most of his allowance. His high energy enabled him to be a good student and still put in work for pay—in the library, waiting on table—that his parents didn't know about. When he finally cut loose, the bonds that were to provide his tuition had been irrevocably committed by his father for the required ten years and a day to a Clifford Trust. When he stood next to his packed suitcase in the living room to tell them he was off, his books and stereo had already been shipped off to a friend via UPS. He felt immensely free that day because there was nothing his father could do to stop him.

"That twenty-five thousand," Thomassy said, "includes the six hundred you owe me for the arraignment."

"That's a lot of money," Porter said.

"If we have to appeal, it'll be double. You're lucky. I usually don't have to appeal. If you can't afford it, I'm sure they can arrange for someone cheaper. Or legal aid."

"I can get the money from my father. I think."

"Use that phone," Thomassy said, pointing to the second phone on the side table in the rear of his office, away from his desk.

Thomassy shut the door of his office behind him. He held up two fingers to Alice, her signal to use another line to get time and charges and number called so they wouldn't have to wait till the bill came in to know the number Ed Porter was calling.

On the table next to the phone he'd let Porter use were several old telephone message slips held down by a silver dollar, head side up. Sometimes he'd find the silver dollar tail side up, evidence that the client had fingered the coin, perhaps been tempted to pocket it. Four teenage clients had actually taken it, enabling Thomassy to ask for the coin casually. They'd always given it to him and Thomassy had thus communicated his message: *I know you're a crook and can't be trusted.* It helped control a young punk more than any other trick he used.

After a few minutes, Porter came out of the office, saying, "My father wants to talk to you. I didn't tell him the trouble I was in just yet."

Thomassy went in and picked up the phone. The silver dollar was gone.

"George Thomassy, Mr. Porter," he said into the phone.

A voice laced with dust that might have come from an Egyptian tomb, said, "Mr. Thomassy, my name is Sturbridge. My son tells me that he needs a check for twenty-five thousand dollars immediately for some business scheme that you and he are engaged in. Is that correct?"

Sturbridge? I could have asked for a hundred thousand, Thomassy thought. Why didn't Widmer tell me? Did he know? Did he not tell me because he knew?

"What else did your son tell you, Mr. Sturbridge?"

"That the check was to be made payable to you. It sounds like some kind of swindle to me, Mr. Thomassy. I think I'd best have Franklin Harlow, general counsel for my firm, be in touch with you. I don't want Edward involved in any hanky-panky."

"Mr. Sturbirdge, why does your son use the name Ed Porter?"

"I imagine he likes his mother's name better than mine. Perhaps he doesn't want to be identified with Sturbridge Pharmaceuticals. As to this deal of yours—"

Thomassy cut him off. "Mr. Sturbridge, this isn't a deal. Did your son tell you I was an attorney?"

"No."

"Did he tell you the hanky-panky he's involved in is a charge of murder in the second degree and that the twenty-five thousand dollars was my retainer for defending him?"

Sturbridge's dusty voice started to say something that proved unintelligible. There was a moment's silence at the other end and then a woman was on the phone saying, "This is Mrs. Sturbridge. My husband wears a pacemaker. He is not supposed to be exposed unduly to upset. I don't know what you just said to him but I'm afraid he can't go on with this phone conversation."

Ed Porter stood in the doorway. Behind him, Thomassy could see Alice, always alert for trouble.

Thomassy said into the phone, "Mrs. Sturbridge, I had no idea of your husband's condition. Is he all right?"

"Yes. I just don't think he should continue the conversation."

"Mrs. Sturbridge, please don't hang up. This is a matter of some urgency. Is your maiden name Porter?"

"Yes, of course."

"Why does your son use your name instead of his father's?"

"He's not supposed to. He shouldn't. I don't know why he does. What is the matter?"

"Your son has been charged with second-degree murder here in Westchester County. He has asked me to represent him. He will be booked today and arraigned as soon as possible. I'd asked him for a twenty-five-thousand-dollar retainer and apparently he gave your husband some unconvincing reason for needing that money. Perhaps it would be best if you'd reach your husband's general counsel and have him call me right away." He gave the woman his number. He asked her to repeat it to be sure she got it right. Her voice had undergone a marked change, from protector of her husband to despair.

"Who is dead?" she asked.

The newspapers were out. He had to tell her.

"Martin Fuller."

The voice said, "Oh my heavens, oh my dear God." Then, "Ed worshiped him. Ed's a scholar, not a killer. It must be some mistake."

"I hope so. My name is George Thomassy. Please have your husband's lawyer call me back at once."

"Where is Ed."

"Here with me."

"May I speak to him?" Her voice was coming under control.

Thomassy looked up at the kid in the doorway. "Your mother wants to talk to you."

Ed Porter shook his head.

"Talk to her," Thomassy said, his hand over the mouthpiece.

Porter took the phone.

"Hello, Mom."

Thomassy did not give the kid privacy. His eavesdropping presence kept the pressure up.

"Professor Fuller died in an accident," Ed said, his voice cracking. "His bathrobe caught fire from a kerosene heater. Some crazies are trying to hang it on me. You know I wouldn't do anything like that, Mom. Please do as Mr. Thomassy says."

Thomassy closed the door of his office on himself and Ed, assuring Alice with a nod that everything was all right.

"You don't use your father's name," Thomassy said.

"There's no law against that, is there?"

"It raises questions."

"My occupation is focused on raising questions. I don't see why people should know my father's rich as Croesus. You think I want some kidnapper sending him my ear for verification? If you knew who he was, you'd probably have asked for a higher retainer, right?"

"Why did you tell your father that cock-and-bull story?"

"Because I know about his heart condition."

"Well, if you scared him enough, maybe he'd pop off and you'd inherit his money instead of having to crawl to him for it."

"Are you trying to provoke me?"

Thomassy waited him out in silence.

Then, Porter, his voice calm again, said, "My father says he cut me out of his will."

"Did he? Or did he just say so?"

"How the hell am I supposed to know! Why are we getting off the subject?"

"We're dead *on* the subject, which is you. I want to know what I've got to defend."

Alice was at the door. "It's a Mr. Franklin Harlow, calling at Mrs. Sturbridge's suggestion."

That was quick. Thomassy went around to his desk. Harlow said, "I just had a brief talk with one of my former law partners who practices in Westchester now, Mr. Thomassy. He says you've got quite a reputation for making the DA's office work overtime."

"Thank you."

"Mr. Thomassy, the Sturbridge family is profoundly shocked by what they just heard. Is there any truth to the charge?"

"I don't know. Yet. Ed was one of three overnight guests at the Fuller home. It could have been any one of them, or a fourth who didn't stay overnight. Or it could have been an accident. The police claim they have a button of Ed's that they say was found in the garage. Some circumstantial evidence perhaps. I don't know enough yet. I can't tell why they've focused on the Sturbridge boy."

In a stern whisper, Porter said, "Don't call me that."

"I hope this can be quashed at the earliest possible moment, Mr. Thomassy," Harlow continued.

"This isn't just a local police matter," Thomassy said. "There were federal agents there before the police. At least one of them quite high ranking. Fuller was apparently engaged in some very important national security project."

"I see," Harlow said, which is what people of his class and station said when they did not see. "I'll have a check sent by Purolator. Will you be good enough to keep the family posted through me if possible?"

□   □   □

88

When he got off the phone, Thomassy asked Porter, "Where's my silver dollar?"

Edward Porter Sturbridge laughed.

Thomassy repeated, "Where is my silver dollar?"

"On that bookshelf," Ed said, pointing.

Thomassy looked. Sure enough, it was there. He put it back on the phone table, on the message slips. "Why did you move it?"

"I figured it was an entrapment ploy," Ed said. "I moved it to see how tough you were."

□ CHAPTER ELEVEN □

The Sturbridge family home was just across the state line in Fairfield, Connecticut, an attractive haven to which the wealthy had once been drawn when it was income-tax free. Malcolm Sturbridge's rationale for the move, made just before his only child, Edward, was born, was that instead of the state distributing a portion of his earnings to others inefficiently, he would retain his right to donate it as he saw fit. As a rule he gave to organizations that saw to the welfare of the kind of people he never associated with socially: the chronically unemployed, blacks, abused children and beaten wives, unwed pregnant women, and in more recent years, Haitian refugees, whom he referred to as the new Mayflower people because they crossed rough seas in makeshift boats with exemplary courage.

Courage was like an irregular beacon to Malcolm Sturbridge throughout his life. When caught in its light he was seen to be a mountain climber in Yosemite at sixteen, a lieutenant of infantry at eighteen, an ocean-racing yachtsman at twenty-six; an American who made his way to the heights of the business community, proving himself acceptable by the definition of others. He had once set himself the goal of collecting the modern equivalent of the great library of Alexandria, not to read but to *have*; of course he kept this activity a secret from his business associates, who thought an interest even in collecting books an occupation for women.

To Sturbridge's puzzlement, his son Edward from an early age took advantage of his extensive library, actually read the books, and seemed to enjoy devouring the knowledge in them. But to

89

Sturbridge's dismay, the boy had no interest in displaying courage. Once, when Ed was thirteen and had four or five friends from Exeter staying over a holiday weekend at "Chateau Sturbridge" as the boys called it, a commotion in the wing occupied by them drew Sturbridge to witness his son on the bed, each limb tied to a bedpost, being beaten by the other boys. When Ed was released, he asked his father that the boys not be sent home. Later, alone with his father, he was asked, "Why didn't you fight back?" Ed answered, "Fight whom?" That day, Malcolm Sturbridge had the impression that "whom" meant him.

Sturbridge worried about a son who would accept comradeship at the price of brutality. Had he created a child that nobody wanted except to use him? He decided he must discuss the matter with Jenny.

He never got around to it.

The Sturbridges were given to parties of some magnificence, held in the grandeur of their living room for the benefit of selected charities. The room could accommodate a hundred people dancing at one time to a small orchestra. On other occasions, with the equally worthy objective of entertaining their numerous intellectual friends, the Sturbridges would have a hundred and fifty people conversing comfortably in small groups until the evening's recital began—a well-known poet who would have been paid a suitable honorarium to read his latest work, and a quartet that could handle the later works of Beethoven. They maintained their large circle of friends because the friends liked each other's company and the fact that they could be entertained royally with the proceeds of capitalism in the hands of a cultivated liberal with good taste.

On those occasions, of course, the two crystal chandeliers splayed bright light throughout the room. But now, as every evening after dinner without guests, it was the recent habit of Malcolm and Jenny Sturbridge to turn the wall rheostat all the way down so that the room was illuminated only by the individual brass lights over the Rouault, the Modigliani, and the Cezanne— each given a wall to itself so that it seemed framed twice, the second time by the expanse of burnished mahogany that focused the eye on each wall's centerpiece. In the large hearth—Sturbridge used to say you could roast an ox in a fireplace that size—the flamelets jumped at random from the logs providing focus to the fourth wall in front of which two matching armchairs and ottomans gave the Sturbridges a place from which they could talk in peace, safely looking at the mesmerizing flickers rather than each other.

Of all the suitable women available to Sturbridge when he was young, he had chosen Jenny because while the others deferred to him, as was the practice of the time, Jenny never hid her sense of leading a separate life. He liked resilience in a woman as he did in negotiation. He hadn't expected her to prove to be more perceptive than he was, perhaps even more intelligent. Even Edward at times struck him as having intellectual abilities that outraced his. Certainly Edward's curiosity was greater.

Whenever one of Malcolm Sturbridge's significant stockholdings went down, he prudently bought an equal quantity at the lower price to average his cost basis. With two inches of port still virgin in his glass, he said, "We could have had a second child, Jenny."

Jenny Sturbridge sipped from her glass. She'd always thought port too sweet for her taste, but she considered it one of the easier accommodations. She said, "I thought by giving Ed no rivals, we could help him perfect himself."

"You spoiled him, Jenny."

"Perhaps you were too severe with him."

"I tried to establish boundaries of the permissible. I thought that's what children wanted, to know what the rules were."

"He found out, didn't he?" Jenny Sturbridge said.

Her husband glanced over at her to see if the edge of sarcasm he heard in her voice was corroborated by her expression.

"He crossed every line I drew," Malcolm Sturbridge said. "I wanted him independent, he became a rebel. I wanted him to taste the joys of mastering a scholarly field and he becomes a specialist in Soviet affairs. I thought only today, Jenny, of that first lover you took as a sophomore. You wanted to demonstrate the unshakeability of your liberalism so you became intimate with a Negro."

"I've told you a thousand times, I liked him, and we were together only for a single weekend."

Mr. Sturbridge's laugh was that of a sick man clearing his chest. "You picked him for the effect it would have on others. You dehumanized him and yourself. I can't help but think that what Edward has done all along is emulate you as a challenge to me."

Jenny Sturbridge, who had once loved her husband but who had now settled down to being his companion until he died, said, "Perhaps you can understand this. When Ed was a baby and a toddler I loved him unreservedly, unabashedly, fully. But as he became a person, I felt he became in stages someone I loved who was not really part of me, like an adopted child. There's a limit to how we can fashion our children."

Sturbridge cut in, his voice harsh. "If I weren't rich, he couldn't have played with cocaine."

"Wrong. He would have had to steal perhaps, but he would have done what he wanted to do. Do you remember when he brought the Fullers here for a visit, the awkwardness we felt, the awkwardness the Fullers must also have felt with the rich parents of their protégé? Do you remember Fuller saying the revolution eats its children? I think our children eat at our tables until they are strong enough to push their chairs back and then they begin the natural process of eating us."

"Unless we have the strength to live without whatever we derive from having them."

"Not strength," Jenny Sturbridge said. "Will. You had a great will once."

He laughed. "Sapped by age."

"Oh no. By accomplishment. You got what you wanted. You left the field clear for Ed to want something else."

Malcolm Sturbridge touched the button on the sidetable. A minute later, a manservant appeared. "Justin," he said, "we will leave a half hour earlier in the morning. I want to stop at the police station before going on in to the office."

"Yes, sir."

When Justin vanished through the sliding doors, Jenny Sturbridge said, "So you bought the gun. I thought you had agreed not to. What will you tell the police when you register it?"

"After the Macready house being robbed, I'm sure they're not going to ask a lot of stupid questions."

"You're putting me in danger, Malcolm."

"What nonsense is that? I'm concerned about criminals breaking into the house."

"Six out of seven handguns, the papers say, are eventually used against loved ones."

"That means you're safe, dear."

District Attorney Roberts had asked to see Jackson Perry "outside of channels. Just an office visit. I have a few questions."

When Perry showed up in Roberts's office, he had Randall with him.

Shaking hands, Roberts said, "You fellows always travel in twos? Have a seat, gentlemen."

After the secretary brought the requisite coffee and shut the door behind her, Roberts said, "We're on the same side of the fence.

That flag in the corner isn't a county flag or a state flag, it's an American flag."

Perry had long ago learned when a nod was preferable to speech.

"This Fuller thing," Roberts went on, "isn't a smoking-gun case. It would be very helpful to the prosecution if we knew more about how the security system in the Fuller house worked."

He had listeners who were saying nothing. He continued, "I'm particularly interested in whether, to your knowledge, anyone other than Fuller tried to get into his study before or after the killing." Roberts's eyebrows posed a question.

Perry said, "Someone did try. Very soon after."

"That's very helpful. Who?"

"Our system doesn't tell us who, just that someone is trying to get in who doesn't know how the key works."

"I'd like to get a layout of the wiring," Roberts said, "and someone, either of you or someone else, could take the stand to explain to the jury the methods by which Fuller and his work were kept secure."

Randall could have guessed what Perry then said. "Mr. Roberts, obviously we'd like to cooperate with your office in every possible way. What isn't possible is to reveal the workings of a system that is in use elsewhere to protect other persons."

Roberts coughed into his left hand. He was always careful to do that because people didn't like to shake hands with a hand that had been coughed into. "I would hope subpoenas wouldn't be necessary."

Perry said, "You wouldn't get anywhere. The county executive would get a call from the governor who would have had a call from the White House on behalf of the National Security Agency. Why go through the hassle? As citizens we'd like to help out any way we can in a murder case, but national security comes first."

Roberts felt the cellophane over his composure wilting. His forehead glistened. "The people must get a conviction in this case."

"I'm certain that if your evidence is strong enough, you will."

Roberts reached over and touched twice one of the buttons on his intercom. He wanted to say something casual to pass the seconds but he could see that Perry was not in the mood for small talk. The door opened and a young man strode in, tall with ambition. His shoulders seemed to roll with his walk. His thick tortoise-shell eyeglasses looked as if they had been chosen to look severe.

"This is Mr. Perry and Mr. Randall. Mr. Koppelman is a recent

93

addition to the trial staff. Koppelman, we've been talking about the Fuller case. If you had to bet your career on the evidence in your hands right now, would you go for a conviction?"

"Yes, sir."

"Koppelman, twelve jurors need to be convinced. George Thomassy is a very crafty defender, and these gentlemen from Washington are not inclined to cooperate on the few matters we discussed."

Most people's faces improve when they smile. Koppelman's did not. He said, "That may not be as significant as we thought, sir. I think I've found Thomassy's heel."

"Heel?"

"His Achilles' tendon, sir."

Perry rose. "Then you won't be needing advice from us."

Roberts was not letting them off that easily in front of his new recruit. "I have a feeling you folks in Washington use national security as a big blanket."

Randall was about to say something, but Perry touched his arm. Then Perry said, "It covers two hundred twenty million people, Mr. Roberts. If you ever run for national office—and make it— you'll understand."

They left Roberts standing behind his desk, his uncoughed-on hand unshaken, not turning to Koppelman for comfort, trying to remember who in law school had said that all the homicide corpses the entire class would have to deal with during the rest of their professional lives, laid end to end, wouldn't cover one side of the perimeter of the cemetery in Normandy he encouraged them to visit at least once to keep local murders in perspective.

□ CHAPTER TWELVE □

The first morning of a trial sometimes, as today, brought back memories to Thomassy of the first day of a new school year. As a boy he had viewed each upcoming semester as a body of books and lectures to be dominated so that he could go on to the following year's dares. An affable English teacher, a man who seemed always relaxed, once said to him, "George, can't you think of each new subject as a sport to be played, enjoyed?" "Oh I enjoy it, sir," fourteen-year-old Thomassy had answered. "I get a kick out of

94

tackling something new." The teacher said, "There you go, tackling." And Thomassy had said, "I can't help it, sir. My father said that if an Armenian doesn't figure out how to win, he'll learn to lose."

Lawyers like Francine's father, judges like Drewson, could afford the WASP stance: *Beneath our orderly surfaces, we sit first in judgment of others and only then of ourselves.* Thomassy felt the need to prospect a landscape, to investigate circumstance. You never knew behind what boulder a Turk lay in waiting. You never wanted to become a prisoner of anyone because you knew what the French as well as the Algerians did to their prisoners. Civilization was not a saving grace. He understood the terrors of a tribal world.

"George," his father had gone at him again in the year before he died, "you lawyer for who? Crooks, cheats, bad kids? You a toilet for everybody?"

In that last year Thomassy had learned to respond to Haig Thomassian's railings without anger. "Pop," Thomassy had said, "in the old country, the lawyer for the guy who's accused is more interested in what the government wants to happen than in getting his guy off."

"The people you work for, they stink!"

Not always. I would defend you, Pop.

"All rise!" the sergeant-at-arms suddenly shouted, and Thomassy had the sense of the whole crowded courtroom struggling to its feet. The sketch artists in the front row of the press section were the last to get up, putting down their lap boards and crayons for the ritual rise of respect to the man in the black robe who would be one of their models. Drawing judges was easier than drawing witnesses; they sat still more of the time, witnesses twitched and turned. Harry Layne, who sketched for CBS-TV, was there; his drawing of a judge wearing a cellophane robe through which all was visible was probably the most famous unused sketch of this new craft that bypassed most judges' exclusion of television cameras.

Thomassy caught a glimpse of the expression on the face of Judge Drewson's daughter as she stood for the arrival on the bench of her father. Thomassy wouldn't have recognized her if Marion O'Connor, the court clerk, hadn't pointed her out. The young women were getting younger. He was glad Francine had not come. Was it possible that at some point he would stop thinking about the whole female half of the human race as eligible for more than his admiration?

Standing next to him, the defendant, Edward Porter Sturbridge,

95

looked like a boy scout. Perhaps he had been. It wasn't the worth of the defendant's soul, much less his innocence or guilt, that would determine the outcome. It was how well Roberts played. How well Thomassy counterplayed. And how the twelve-part audience reacted. The jury was standing too as Judge Drewson accidentally bumped the stand holding the American flag. As it teetered, the members of the jury seemed transfixed as if much depended on whether the flagstand would topple.

The flagstand, heavily weighted at the bottom, did not fall. The judge motioned everyone to sit. Thomassy noted how the jury sat first, as if the connection between them and the judge was that of soldiers and officer. Then the spectators, like a massive disorganized flutter of unconnected beings, found their seats where they had left them, underneath and behind. The press, which was reluctant to stand for anyone, was the last to sit as if that tardiness also declared its independence from the ritual.

Thomassy's eye caught the face of one of the jurors, the one he had had second thoughts about. The man's jacket seemed to weigh him down like a blanket. Beneath it, he was poised to bitch. Thomassy was usually wary of jurors who might try to dominate the others by whining. More people gave in to that than to reason. He hadn't thrown a peremptory challenge at the man because Roberts had let him get by and it was late and he was only an alternate. He should have knocked the guy out. It was sloppy to have an alternate who would make you hope none of the regulars got sick.

He liked the foreman, a woman who taught anthropology at Hunter College. He'd latched on to her because when he asked her about her attitude toward young people—a question he'd put to everyone—she'd said, "I teach because I like young people. They remind me of my own time at school, when life seemed endless." That woman had a brain one didn't often want in jurors. But with the defendant a twenty-four-year-old perpetual student with tousled hair, she wouldn't see Ed as someone who ought to be put away. She was a natural leader; and the others, at some prolonged long-ago period of their lives, had been students when teachers were still respected and listened to.

Thomassy leaned over toward Ed and whispered in his ear, "I hope you peed before this began."

Ed nodded.

The judge's eyes met Thomassy's. He shouldn't have spoken to Ed amidst all that silence. But the judge was merely acknowledging Thomassy's presence. Then he turned to Roberts and intoned the usual. The play could begin.

Roberts touched the watch chain across his vest, the Phi Beta key to be noted. *If you have enough brains for the job*, Thomassy thought, *you don't need to advertise.*

"Ladies and gentlemen," Roberts said, his eyes on the jurors from a distance of at least twenty feet so that it wouldn't seem unnatural for his voice to be raised—he wanted to be sure the press caught every word—"there are two kinds of crimes. Those that may attract our momentary sympathy—like crimes of passion—and those that produce a profound sense of revulsion, as in this case when a great man with a unique capability is killed by one of his own closest students, who pretended to love and admire him."

Thomassy had to give Roberts credit. In one breath of openers, he had used the word *revulsion*, designed to create a crime not on the statute books, a crime worse than murder, a crime that didn't come down from the Grand Jury but had just been invented. And in the same first breath, Roberts had pulled a rug from under Gordon's case, *pretended* to love and admire him, Roberts had said. Maybe he'd been too complacent about Roberts. It wasn't Thomassy Roberts had to convince, it was—as always—the jury of nonpeers who now had *revulsion* and *pretended* implanted in their heads. At least the anthropology professor wouldn't go for that. Or would she, too? *Hey Roberts*, he wanted to yell, *tell us what you're going to prove.*

Roberts made the mistake of glancing in Thomassy's direction, and as if he could imagine Thomassy's thoughts, converted to a businesslike tone. "The people will prove Professor Martin Fuller died not of natural causes or an accident, but as the result of the willful intent of another person, that person being the defendant, Edward Sturbridge, also known under the alias Edward Porter."

Alias was a tar-brush word. Thomassy saw Ed squirm.

"The people will prove," Roberts continued, "that the defendant had the means to cause the death of the deceased, that in the early-morning hours of April fifth Professor Fuller died a horrendous death as a direct result of certain actions taken by the defendant. The people will present proof in the form of evidence and then ask you to decide if the defendant is guilty as charged . . ." Roberts's voice became nearly inaudible as he added, ". . . or innocent."

97

Thomassy got to his feet. "Your Honor, I request a conference at the bench."

Judge Drewson nodded.

Thomassy could see the reporters' restlessness. A conference always shut the door in their faces. Thomassy wondered if any of the papers were smart enough to hire a lip reader.

"Your Honor," Thomassy said *sotto voce*, with Roberts next to him, "the people, in their presentation, did not specify that they would provide evidence showing conclusively that nobody else could have committed the alleged crime. I'm prepared to move for dismissal on the grounds that the people did not make a *prima facie* case for the guilt of this particular defendant."

Roberts's face flushed red. Who, besides Thomassy, would fuck around like this? The man was trying to get him angry.

Judge Drewson admired Thomassy's ability to keep a straight face.

He leaned toward both men. "Mr. Roberts," he said, "your opening certainly elided the issue of other possible suspects. However, Mr. Thomassy, if you move for a dismissal, I will rule against. The court has it in its discretion to permit Mr. Roberts to continue his opening to correct his omission, or we can get on with this case. What do you say, gentlemen?"

Roberts looked relieved.

When Thomassy returned to the defense table, Ed asked him, "What was that about?"

"About forty seconds."

"I have a right to know."

"You're supposed to sit still, smile, and look confident, not ask questions."

"Mr. Thomassy," Ed said, "you are working for me, and I expect an answer."

The kid was right. "I was about to move for dismissal on a technical ground, but the judge turned us down."

"Us?" Ed asked.

"You."

The judge, his face a fixture of fairness, said, "I can understand the defendant wanting to consult with counsel, but I would appreciate if such consultations could be kept to a necessary minimum. Mr. Thomassy, your opening statement, please."

Judge Drewson had never presided over a trial worked by Thomassy. He watched with curiosity as Thomassy stood in front of the jury box. *He is letting them get a good long first look at him so*

98

that when he starts to talk, they will listen instead of dividing their attention between taking him in and hearing what he says.

To the jurors, George Thomassy, long armed and lanky, appeared taller than his six feet. They, nervous in public, noted how remarkably loose Thomassy seemed, his gray eyes looking in turn at each of them as if he were about to begin a very private conversation.

"Ladies," Thomassy was saying as he looked at each of the three women in turn, "and gentlemen of the jury," he continued, taking in the rest, "the deceased, Martin Fuller, was acknowledged to be this country's senior expert in the ways of the Soviet Union. If he were standing in my place he might say that over there, if you see a man being arrested, you assume him to be innocent. Over here, if you see a man being arrested you assume him to be guilty."

Some of the reporters in the front rows laughed.

"It is an unfortunate trait of the human animal," Thomas said, "to think in categories. It *is* convenient. But it is quite possible that a policeman arresting someone on the street in Moscow is taking him in not for alleged crimes against the state but for consuming too much 100-proof vodka in an area where he might be seen by foreign tourists. And it is quite possible that in this country, a police officer might pull a car over because it had been driven erratically, or a taillight was out, or because the driver was an attractive blonde."

Suddenly Thomassy's affability vanished. "In this courtroom," he said, "we cannot think in categories. We are concerned only with the allegation against a particular individual. In this case, the individual . . ." Thomassy turned his back on the jury and did not speak till he was standing alongside Ed, ". . . is a twenty-four-year-old student who graduated from Columbia College summa cum laude and then received an M.A. from Columbia in just eight months, and went on to study for his doctorate at Columbia's Russian Institute. He has taught at Amherst, one of this country's finer private colleges. Recently, this young man has been continuing his education in his field by working with the deceased, who'd become his mentor, his teacher, his friend. He spent many hours a week with Professor Fuller and his wife, he was their guest at mealtime dozens and dozens of times, he was their overnight guest on many occasions when he and Professor Fuller and others would converse long into the night on their subject, which should matter as much to us as to them, because our future may to some degree depend on what they know and learn."

Thomassy strode to the jury box again. "Does it make sense for a

99

hungry man to cut off his supply of food? Does it make sense for a man hungry for knowledge about a particular subject to cut off his principal source of that knowledge? I say this because the government must prove—I said prove—that the accused had the intent to commit a crime, and unless it provides facts to prove to your satisfaction that he had such intent, then they have no case. Before you deliberate, His Honor, Judge Drewson, will, of course, instruct you in the law, but before the government starts, I want you to keep in your minds as if branded in there: Without proof of intent to kill there can be no guilt."

Thomassy was standing directly in front of the foreman. Quietly, Thomassy repeated, "There can be no guilt."

Thomassy turned from the jurors toward Roberts, letting his last words hang in the air. Then, his voice back to normal, he said, "The government—sometimes mistakenly called 'the people'—"

He got the laugh of support, and walked toward Roberts, knowing the man would have liked to strangle him for that one. He stopped a few feet in front of Roberts. "The government," Thomassy said, "is represented here by the district attorney, Mr. Roberts. Every juror should know that Mr. Roberts, by the standards of the American Bar Association, is here not merely as an advocate for the government. It is the duty of the prosecutor to seek justice, and it is your role as responsible jurors . . ."

Thomassy had already turned from Roberts and was striding back to the jury box. ". . . to judge whether he is fulfilling his duties, whether he is seeking justice. Mr. Roberts was recently in a different forum, in the Grand Jury room, where the government had itself a field day because the attorney for the accused was not present. There was no one to counter what Mr. Roberts alleged or to test his so-called evidence. People who work in the law know that prosecutors tend to have their way in the Grand Jury room because they are unopposed in that one-sided forum. Well, things are different in this courtroom because if Mr. Roberts and his legion of assistants haven't done their homework properly, I'll know it, and you'll know it.

"The government has got a lot of work cut out for itself. First, it must prove that Martin Fuller's death was not caused by accident. Well, I'm going to save a lot of your time and taxpayers' money, ladies and gentlemen, by agreeing that Martin Fuller's bathrobe caught fire from the heater in his bathroom and that despite efforts by his wife and the accused and others to save him, he died. You won't have to listen to the coroner's morbid details. Prosecutors like to put coroners on the stand because they want to permeate

100

the atmosphere with death, but the horrible death of Martin Fuller is something we will stipulate to not only to spare you the gruesome details but because the issue in this courtroom is determining whether the accused and no other person or persons were responsible for causing Martin Fuller's death. I remember," he said, suddenly relaxing, "the time I went with a friend to see a movie, and we left before it was over. As we went out into the parking lot, my friend, who is not a lawyer, said, 'Boy, that was murder.' Well, it wasn't murder, it was a bad movie. And what we may be dealing with here is a bad accident, and if it wasn't, the government has to prove to your satisfaction that it wasn't, that Martin Fuller died because someone or ones had the will and the means to do it. We will prove with witnesses that when Martin Fuller started to scream because his bathrobe was on fire, the first person to reach him was his wife and the second was the accused, seconds later and stark naked, because that's the way he sleeps, without pajamas, and he dashed down from upstairs without thinking to put anything on because his mentor was screaming for help. Does that sound like someone who had the will to kill? Or was it to help?

"The government has not said it will present irrefutable, objectively verifiable evidence because its so-called case is based on circumstantial evidence that will be refuted by other circumstantial evidence. The government's case does not exclude other hypotheses based on the same so-called circumstantial evidence, and I am here to tell you in advance that our system does not operate on hypotheses. If a policeman walked into this courtroom this minute and came over to this jury box and put his hand on the shoulder of one of you and said, 'You're under arrest,' that doesn't mean you're guilty, and this young man—" he strode over to Ed—"is, according to our system, according to our law, and according to the main tool every juror has—common sense—innocent."

As soon as the judge adjourned the trial for the day, Ed asked to talk to Thomassy somewhere privately. But the clerk came over to say the judge wanted to see Thomassy and Roberts in the robing room.

"I'll be back," Thomassy said to Ed. "Stay put." He looked at the deputy sheriff standing behind Ed as if *stay put* were an instruction from a higher authority than had granted Ed bail.

In the robing room, Judge Drewson said, "Those were interesting presentations, gentlemen. Since rhetoric comes easy to both of you, now that we're past the opening remarks I'd like to see the

101

jury confabulated less so that they have an opportunity to examine the facts, which is what they're here for."

"Alleged facts," Thomassy said, his smile fleeting.

Judge Drewson laughed. His laugh gone, he said, "I suppose you both know there are federal officers in the courtroom?"

They nodded.

"Is it your belief," the judge asked, "that they are here in preparation to arrest the defendant on federal charges?"

"I'm confident that's not the case, Your Honor," Thomassy said.

"Then what the hell are they doing in my courtroom?"

"I suspect they are observers. Their job was to protect the deceased at least until his work was finished. They failed in their job."

"Do you believe they are here to pick up anyone other than the defendant?"

"That might be a precautionary purpose of theirs, Your Honor," Thomassy said. "I don't know. I think they want to see justice done."

"We all do, don't we?"

"Yes," Roberts said.

Thomassy thought *Not necessarily.*

"By the way, I'm sure you also know there's a contingent of TV cameramen out front. I'd be careful what I said to them. I'll be watching the news tonight."

"Suppose I go out by the back door," Thomassy said cheerfully.

"Then tomorrow they'll have crews at the back door as well as the front door. Good luck."

Thomassy and Ed went through a long corridor to reach the room where Thomassy and his client could confer in private. Ed spoke the moment the door shut on them.

"I don't get your strategy. Why'd you bring in all that analogy?"

"What analogy?"

"Someone arrested in Russia presumed by others to be innocent. And then all the Russian Institute stuff about me? What are you trying to do?"

"Defuse," Thomassy said, "in advance. I can guarantee you that Roberts is going to make something ominous out of your special field, and the best way to deal with that kind of crap is to bring it up first in your context instead of their context."

"You could have waited to see," Ed said.

"And get caught on the defensive? That's a loser's game."

"I just don't like playing on the jurors' anticommunist sympathies. I want to win because I'm innocent."

Thomassy moved his face very close to Ed's and his voice was almost a whisper. "Listen, innocent," he said, "who is Ludmilla Tarasova?"

Thomassy came down the steps. There must have been thirty reporters down there with cameras and notebooks. He was used to juries who could be warned that the fifth amendment was not to be construed as a sign of guilt. If he said *no comment*, they'd put it in a context that'd make it look like he was ducking.

"Mr. Thomassy, hold it right there, on that step," yelled one of the TV people.

A newsman with a pad asked the first question. "What is your reaction, Mr. Thomassy, after the first day of this case?"

"What case?" Thomassy said. "The government has no case."

He recognized the Channel 4 reporter, who asked, "Mr. Thomassy, what do you make of the fact that there are reporters here from Reuters, Agence France Presse, et cetera. Are there international implications in the charges?"

"The charges," Thomassy said, "are absurd. Excuse me, gentlemen." He moved forward and away.

"Where are you going?" one of them yelled after him as his cameraman swiveled around to catch the departing lawyer.

"I'm going for an acquittal and a Scotch and soda," Thomassy said, and hurried his pace because he needed to know a lot more about Ludmilla Tarasova before tomorrow.

□ CHAPTER THIRTEEN □

Thomassy noticed that Francine had parked her bright red Fiat in the driveway headed out instead of in so that he would see the page of notebook paper under the windshield wiper. "If you're bringing company home," it said in her rectangular handwriting, "ring three times and wait a full minute before opening the door."

In the years before Francine he'd known women who were skilled in the craft of arousal, who'd developed nuances in their

103

voices to match the seductiveness of dresses and blouses and skirts chosen with care. But Francine was the first to administer what he thought of as prearousal arousal, an appetizer before the appetizer. Well, why not? Wasn't it the kind of thing he sometimes did in the courtroom, getting the jury anticipating something and then stirring them up just before he was ready to deliver? Proverbs eleven, Thomassy's book: *You tingle their balls. You give them a hard-on. Then you let them have it.* Well, here's life full of reciprocity again. He'd come home with a mission, to *talk* to Francine, to use her role at the American delegation to get at information he couldn't get directly without Roberts getting his antennae up. And all of a sudden he was moving on another track because that lady left a note under the windshield wiper of her car that was causing his loins to hum even before he'd set foot inside the door.

Thomassy turned the key in the lock and opened the door halfway. Francine was parked legs up on the ottoman watching the TV news and wearing what he had seen only once before and termed the ultimate flimsy, a diaphanous cover-up that covered up nothing, a translucent shimmer of thinly woven silk that called more attention to her breasts and pubic triangle than if she were naked.

"Come in, Bob!" Thomassy shouted over his shoulder, causing Francine to bolt out of the chair and scurry across the room to the bedroom.

Thomassy closed the door behind him.

Francine poked her head around the corner to see into the living room. "You bastard," she said.

"I could have you arrested," Thomassy said, "under two forty-five point eleven of the penal code."

"Which is what?" she said, offering him a full kiss that stifled the possibility of response. Thomassy dropped his keys to the floor so that his right hand would be free to caress the very top of her behind.

"The public display of nudity is a Class A misdemeanor," he said.

"I'm glad it's Class A in your opinion."

"Two forty-five point ten defines nudity as the showing of the human male or female genitals, pubic area, or buttocks with less than a fully opaque covering of any portion thereof below the top of the nipple, or the depiction of covered male genitals in a descernibly turgid state. I think I got it right.".

She glanced downward. "You'd have to have us both arrested. Here." She handed him the telephone. "Call the police."

Thomassy took the phone from her. He took his jacket off, removed his tie. Francine turned the deadbolt on the front door. "That's just in case Bob shows up," she said, laughing.

The fact that the TV kept going had been an additional aphrodisiac, a splatter of words and changing pictures that caused their lovemaking on the living room couch and then the thickly carpeted floor to be as if in the presence of witnesses they were not paying attention to, the anchor man, the anchor woman, faces flashing on the screen. Happily exhausted, they finally lay quietly in each other's arms.

Thomassy laughed and said, "We wouldn't do this if we were married, would we?"

"Why not?"

"Because that's what going to contract does. It increases your goddamn sense of responsibility and diminishes your sense of play. Proverbs fourteen, Thomassy's book. I know what marriage would hurt. What would it help?"

Francine, unprepared for the question, got up out of the witness box, and grabbing her diaphanous gown in anger as she passed the chair on which it had been flung, disappeared from his view.

They decided to have dinner out. They settled for the Greek restaurant because it was within walking distance and they both felt the need to walk, as if the exercise itself would restore some balance to their equation. Once they'd had their stuffed grape leaves in lemon sauce and a bottle of retsina, which tasted like no other wine in the world, and the Turkish coffee had been served, Thomassy broached the subject that had been on his mind when he spied the note under the windshield wiper.

"You've met Mike Costa," he said.

"Once. It was enough."

"I don't give a damn about the clothes he wears. He's a first-rate investigator. I don't like surprises at a trial."

"Unless you spring them."

"Exactly. Mike came up with the name of one potential witness Roberts was thinking of using. He had two meetings with a Ludmilla Tarasova. He must have decided not to use her. Maybe that means that we should. Her name mean anything to you?"

Francine nodded.

"I need to know everything you know about her. I asked Ed Porter, but I can't tell if he's giving me a distorted version."

"I don't know that much," Francine said. "She does some work for Washington on occasion."

"What kind of work?"

"In her field. Analyses of first- and second-level characters on the Soviet scene. Backgrounders on shifts in the Politburo, that kind of thing. My boss knows her. I haven't met her. I hear she's a tough and attractive lady."

"Could fit you."

"Tarasova's sixty."

"What's her background?"

"The usual. Russian born, escaped West during the war, probably been a U.S. citizen for some time. Have to be to do what she's been doing. She teaches political science at Columbia. I haven't read her books, but I've seen them quoted, sometimes alongside stuff from Fuller."

"Any other connection between the two of them?"

"Why don't I arrange for the three of us to have lunch, you, me, my boss. He can fill you in. He's known Tarasova for a long time."

"Look," Thomassy said, acknowledging the delivery of the check with a nod at the waiter, "I'm up to my ears with this trial in Westchester. If I run down to the city for lunch, with travel time it's half a day lost. And when am I supposed to do it, on Saturday? Does your boss work on Saturday? You're in town every day anyway. Just lunch with him, find out what he knows about Tarasova."

"What reason could I use?"

"I'm sure a lady as clever as you proved to be this evening can figure out something that won't get him unduly suspicious. Will you help?"

"What do you pay Mike Costa for snooping?" Francine asked.

"I make love to him regularly."

"You are an arrogant man, Thomassy."

"If I were really arrogant, I'd have political ambitions, like Roberts. I just like to win my cases."

"A modest lawyer. Let's go home and watch you on the late night news."

Despite the Turkish coffee, Thomassy found himself dozing off for seconds at a time in front of the TV. He glanced over at Francine to see if she had noticed. If she had, she was being polite, her eyes straight ahead. She must have had just as tough a day at her diplomatic zoo as he'd had onstage in the courtroom, but she was twenty-eight and he was forty-five and hating it because the energy that had once seemed limitless was failing him. He'd been saying ridiculous things to himself for years, that he had half his life still to go. He wasn't going to make ninety. Hardly anyone made ninety. What does over the hill mean, when you're finished or when you've passed the peak and are coming down the slope on the other side? Maybe it was the television? If he were playing tennis, he'd be feeling exhausted and young, not like a washrag resting on the edge of the kitchen sink.

Francine's elbow alerted him just as the anchorman was saying, "The international press was well represented today as the prosecution presented its case in the murder trial of Edward Porter Sturbridge, scion of the Sturbridge pharmaceutical family. The ex-Columbia University graduate student is accused of murdering his former professor, Soviet expert Martin Fuller, in a case that is being prosecuted by the Westchester district attorney personally." And there were the reporters crowding around Roberts on the courthouse steps. "When asked how the first day had gone," the anchorman's voice said, "District Attorney Roberts said . . ."

Roberts flashed onto the screen, first full length and then in tight close-up. "The people today presented their case against the defendant, who stands accused of having committed the most hideous of crimes. Mr. Thomassy, counsel for the defendant, tried to turn things around to make it seem the people are on trial. Mr. Thomassy has the reputation of being quite a magician in the courtroom, but I think his bag of tricks won't work in this case. We're lucky to have a good jury and an experienced judge and despite Mr. Thomassy's obfuscations, justice will be done." The image went blank. A Ford commercial usurped the screen.

"Where the hell were you?" Francine asked.

"On those same steps."

"Maybe your brilliance overexposed the film."

"Some son-of-a-bitch in the cutting room left my segment on the floor."

"Don't get paranoid. Maybe your remarks were dull compared to Roberts's."

Thomassy grabbed at her as she got up.

"Missed," Francine said.

"That prick Roberts."

"Why don't you send him around sometime?" Francine said.

"You're supposed to be providing aid and comfort to me, not the enemy."

She left him sitting in the living room. He'd have to learn how to handle the damn press. Roberts made it seem like it was an open-and-shut case. It's a good thing the jurors aren't allowed to watch television. But, he thought, most people he knew watched the late

107

news. As far as they were concerned, wherever in the world Telstar beamed its message, he had lost the first round.

When Francine came out of the bedroom, she was dressed for the street and carrying the Lark bag with the multicolored stripe in which she had first brought what she called her "live-in essentials."

"George," she said, "you're going to be able to concentrate on your case better. I won't be here evenings. I'm not pulling a Lysistrata. I just want to be by myself for a while."

He couldn't bring himself to plead with her. She wasn't asking anything. She said quite a lot. He didn't interrupt her. When he found his voice he said, "I'll carry your case out to the car."

"I carried it in, George. I'll carry it out."

Ten minutes after he heard her Fiat disappear down the driveway, he went over to the bottle of Scotch and emptied it down the sink because he suddenly didn't trust himself not to wreck his brain for tomorrow's day in court.

□ CHAPTER FOURTEEN □

Toward morning Thomassy woke to the drumming of rain on the roof, reached out toward the other side of the bed, pulled back his disappointed arms.

It wasn't as if Francine had moved out. She had never moved in. But for a year his expectation was that after work she would come to his home as if she lived there.

Thomassy listened to the rain. She'd said he didn't respect the idea of a permanent relationship. She'd said she had no obligation to nest in any particular place.

His leather-faced father, Haig Thomassian, breeder of horses in Oswego, had said *I swear by your mother's memory, to catch a woman you walk away.*

Thomassian's son, the courtroom manipulator, felt the center of pain in the hollow of his chest. He never longed like this for the women who used to come and go. His mind could not shut off images of Francine, the line of her neck, her hair, her eyes, the way she crossed her legs, whatever she was doing elsewhere. His father was wrong. Walking away was too big a risk. Besides, he hadn't walked. She had. If he pulled away, that would double the distance.

If he didn't get his minimum sleep he'd be like an angry kid in the courtroom. Thomassy reached into the drawer of his bedside table. His fingers found the earplugs he used to shut out sound. Counting sheep always seemed loco to him. He counted Francine's hips walking across the screen of his mind. He needed not to think of her. He thought of his mother singing an old-country lullaby, her voice a whisper of itself, something about a sailor coming home from the sea.

When the alarm shattered him awake, he sat up with a start, expecting to see his mother still sitting at his bedside. How could it still be dark outside? The rain was now a continuous, angry fall of water blocking the sun and his sense of life.

He put his feet into slippers. From the window, he could see water cascading down his driveway, too much for the ground to absorb.

He remembered bad-weather mornings when he was a school kid reluctant to get out from under the blankets, his father standing in the doorway saying *Hey George, terrific outside. God teach men God is God. Get your ass out of bed, George.* Ghosts move us, Thomassy thought, heading for the bathroom. He turned the shower on, hot only, to let the enclosure steam up before he stepped in. Francine's peach bath sheet was still on the towel rack, waiting to be used again. For a second he thought of using it instead of his own. He balled it up and threw it into the hamper, slamming the lid down. A small brass nail fell out of the hinge, spun on the tile floor, went under the radiator.

He stepped into the shower stall, turned his face into the rapidly heating water, mixed some cold in, used the long-handled brush's coarse bristles to punish his shoulders. She had stepped in to soap his back, saying you won't need that brush anymore. Like hell.

Twenty minutes later he was behind the wheel of his Buick, turning the ignition unsuccessfully for the third time. Maybe he'd flooded the carburetor. He grabbed the umbrella from behind his seat and went out into the maddening downpour again. His trousers, already wet between the bottom of his raincoat and his shoes, got wetter still.

On the line, the local taxi service was telling him no chance, not for an hour. He slammed the receiver down. He'd once thought of having a second car just for situations like this, but it'd seemed crazy for a single driver to have two cars. If Francine had stayed over, she could have given him a lift. Or at least gotten him to somewhere where he could get a damn taxi. This rain is going to make everyone in the courtroom act as if they're on downers today, the jurors, the judge.

He went out to the car once more, opened the driver's door, sat down sideways, then tried to close the umbrella from inside the car, and succeeded only in splashing himself as he closed it. The battery, already weak from his having left the parking lights on one night last week, was further weakened by the nonstarts. He tried again, and suddenly the engine caught. He pumped the gas pedal carefully. Thank you, God. Probably Haig Thomassian from the Oswego corner of heaven, rewarding him for thinking of the dead.

Traffic inched. In places, the water was deep enough to hydroplane. When the run-off pipes in the area were installed half a century ago, some brilliant engineer had twenty-four inchers emptying downhill into eighteen inchers and then into twelve inchers. Whenever it came down like this the sewers backed up quickly, flooding the low places. He longed for revenge against the long-dead engineers.

He glanced at the dashboard clock. Thomassy proverb number seventeen was *always* arrive in court early. He'd seen too many lawyers get the judge going by arriving minutes late. It was hard enough representing people in a system that called the accused *defendants.* We're all guilty, Your Honor; today the prosecutor is just picking on this particular defendant. He swung out of the traffic and took a shortcut to the Sprain Brook Parkway, which didn't flood the way the Taconic and Saw Mill River did because its engineer had a functioning brain.

Thomassy arrived at the courthouse parking lot twelve minutes late. He ran, his left arm hugging his briefcase, his right trying to keep the umbrella vertical despite the wind that whipped rain into his face. Inside, he stopped in the john to paper-towel his face and hair. Then he tried to comb it, remembering the days when it was short enough not to need a hair blower. Nothing he could do about his soaking pants bottoms. Or his spirits.

The second he was behind the counsel table, the court officer shouted "All rise!" as if in reproof for Thomassy's late arrival, and Judge Drewson swept in. Ed wanted to ask Thomassy something.

"Not now," Thomassy said. He hoped everybody had wet pants bottoms.

Roberts called Leona Fuller to the stand. Thomassy knew what

110

was coming this rain-drenched day; the widow routine. Focus on the loss instead of who did or didn't do it. The ancient strategy worked on the jury if the widow played her part.

In the confines of the witness box, Leona Fuller looked like a diminutive of her stoic self. Few old women sat ramrod straight as she did. She affirmed the oath as if she were granting a decree. He wondered if Francine would have that kind of majesty at Leona Fuller's age. It didn't matter. He wouldn't live to see it.

Thomassy knew that Roberts might try to make her cry. He sat on the edge of his chair, ready to rise and shout "Objection" to make the jury see that this had nothing to do with a life that was already lost; it was a game in which one player had to cast the widow's chip.

Roberts's voice had the expected gentleness. "Please tell the court your name and your relationship to the deceased."

"Leona Albright Fuller. I am Professor Fuller's widow." Flat words caught by every ear in the suddenly silent courtroom.

"I will try to keep my questions to a minimum, Mrs. Fuller," Roberts said. "Please tell us in your own words what happened the morning your husband was killed."

Thomassy was on his feet instantly. "Objection, Your Honor. The defense has stipulated that the deceased died from burns. The prosecution has yet to prove that the fire was not accidental. The use of the word killed is improper."

He had turned away from the judge to see Leona Fuller's reaction to the word "improper." Not a flinch.

"Sustained," Judge Drewson said.

Roberts collected himself, tried again. "Mrs. Fuller," he said, "tell us what you heard and saw the morning your husband was burned."

Thomassy was on his feet again. "I'm sorry Your Honor. The same objection. 'Was burned' implies the commission of an act by another person. The 'was' is improper."

The judge shook his head. "Mr. Thomassy, this isn't a course in linguistics."

"I understand, Your Honor, and I have no intention of making petty objections with regard to Mr. Roberts's misuse of words except where they clearly could incorrectly prejudice the jury with regard to the circumstances of Professor Fuller's death."

The cost of rattling Roberts was rattling the judge. But now Thomassy could see a slight crack in Mrs. Fuller's composure. She had readied herself to get her testimony over with as quickly as possible.

"Strike the question," Judge Drewson said, a touch of annoyance in his voice. "Please rephrase it one more time, Mr. Roberts."

Articulating each word, Roberts said, "Mrs. Fuller, tell us what you saw and heard the morning your husband burned."

He should have said died, Thomassy thought. Repeating burned wasn't helping her maintain her composure.

Her hands clenched, Leona Fuller told her story without further interruption. Thomassy jotted down just one word on the pad in front of him. *Love.*

"Mrs. Fuller," Roberts said, "in describing the events surrounding your husband's death, you mentioned the name of Edward Porter several times. Is he in this courtroom?"

She sighed as if to lament the barter of words that contributed nothing to anyone's understanding. "Yes," she said.

"Will you point him out to the court, please."

How could one point without it being the widow's accusing finger? She did as she was asked.

"What was the defendant's relationship to your husband?"

She thought for a moment. "At first a student, then a friend in the GPW. That's what they called the Great Political War."

"Was the defendant a friend of yours as well?"

"In a different way. He and my husband had a mentor-disciple relationship that worked well for both of them. There was a warmth between them."

"Like father and son perhaps?"

There go the harp strings, Thomassy thought.

"More like brothers distant in age."

"Would you say that they were close?"

She nodded.

Judge Drewson said, "Please speak up a little, Mrs. Fuller, for the court reporter."

"I'm sorry. Yes, they were close."

"But not like father and son?"

"Increasingly like colleagues."

"Like Brutus and Caesar perhaps?"

Thomassy was on his feet shouting "Objection!" and Mrs. Fuller glanced over at the judge as if to plead for his intercession.

"You will not lead the witness, Mr. Roberts," Judge Drewson said. "Nor will you offer your own opinions in the guise of questions. Questions are not evidence. The jury will disregard Mr. Roberts's comments about Brutus and Caesar."

Thomassy thought old Brutus Roberts got *his* knife in. The

112

judge's instructions to disregard were as useless as Francine telling him *Don't think of me.*

"Mrs. Fuller," Roberts was saying, "did there come a time when Edward Porter Sturbridge stayed over frequently?"

"Yes."

"For what purpose?"

"To sleep."

There was a guffaw from where the reporters sat, snuffed out immediately by the judge's glare in their direction.

"To your knowledge, did the defendant have a place of his own?"

"Yes, of course." Her impatience showed. "We'd all talk long after dinner, and whoever stayed the course, usually slept over."

"Would you say that the defendant stayed over more often than other students and friends did?"

"In recent months, perhaps."

"Mrs. Fuller, would you say that the defendant had the run of the house?"

"Yes."

"And of the garage?"

"Yes, of course."

"For what purpose?"

"He frequently cut the lawn for us. He put snow tires on our car in the fall and took them off in the spring."

"Did he ever put kerosene in your husband's bathroom heater?"

"My husband usually did that himself. Ed would have if Martin asked him to. I don't know."

"Do you know how the kerosene would be transported to the house?"

"The kerosene was kept in a five-gallon can. My husband couldn't carry anything that heavy so he kept a one-quart plastic lamp-oil container in the garage and would bring in fuel for his heater that way." She paused for a moment before saying, "He hated keeping kerosene supplies in the house."

Roberts coughed into his left hand. "Mrs. Fuller, in your description of what happened on the morning of April fifth, you said that when your husband screamed, of the three overnight guests the defendant appeared first. Is that correct?"

"He helped me push Martin into the shower."

"What was the state of his dress?"

"His bathrobe was burning."

"I mean the defendant's dress."

113

"He was naked."

"Stark naked?"

"Yes."

"How did the defendant seem to you, excited?"

The judge anticipated Thomassy's objection. "Mr. Roberts," he said, "please try not to lead the witness."

"What did the defendant's state of mind at the time seem to you, Mrs. Fuller?"

Thomassy objected. "The witness cannot testify to someone else's state of mind, Your Honor."

"Oh Your Honor," Leona Fuller said, "I know what he means. Of course Ed was agitated. He rushed down naked because it was an emergency. I respected his not stopping to put something on."

The judge looked at Roberts and Thomassy in turn. "If neither of you objects, I'll let that answer stand. Proceed."

"That's all for this witness, Your Honor," Roberts said.

He didn't get a tear out of her, Thomassy thought. He didn't get anything out of her. Roberts had promised brevity and produced a long drawn-out nothing.

Thomassy walked up to the witness box and placed his hands on the edge. Leona Fuller looked as if she expected him to shake hands with her. *Such civil greetings are not permitted in this court. All I want to get across to you is that you are not on the other side.*

"Mrs. Fuller," Thomassy began, "I know how difficult this procedure must be for you. It's my duty to represent the defendant and I am required to ask just a few questions to help the jury decide the facts. You do understand that?"

"Yes," she said.

"Thank you. Mrs. Fuller, do you yourself know for a fact that a kerosene heater in close quarters can be dangerous?"

"Oh yes, I'd warned Martin about that when we first bought it."

The rule was you never asked a question of a witness you didn't know the answer to. Sometimes you had to gamble.

"Mrs. Fuller, did you ever discuss with your husband his wearing of a long and possibly flammable bathrobe in the close quarters of his bathroom with the kerosene heater on?"

"Many times. He thought I was a crank on the subject."

"You testified earlier that your husband hated keeping kerosene in the house. Why was that?"

"Because he knew it could lead to a dangerous accident."

"Was kerosene used for any other purpose in your house than for the bathroom heater?"

"Oh yes," she said. "We have a couple of hurricane lamps on the dining room table."

"Are those lit daily?"

"For dinner."

"When you have guests?"

"Even when we eat alone. Martin . . . Professor Fuller and I enjoyed that kind of light almost as much as candlelight. We used to use candles, but the wax dripped on the table and was a chore to remove sometimes."

"When the small container you say was kept in the pantry had to be refilled, was the five-gallon container brought into the house or was the small one taken out to the garage?"

"The latter, of course. Martin never allowed the five-gallon one into the house. And it doesn't make sense to carry the heavy one in when you can carry the empty out."

"Quite right, Mrs. Fuller. And who did the refilling?"

"Usually Martin. I did once or twice when he had the flu, though I found it difficult to lift the large can for pouring when it was rather full. Lately we've been asking younger people when they're around to refill the container."

"Any younger people?"

"Usually the ones we know best. The ones who come frequently or sleep over."

"Could you name those young people who to your knowledge ever refilled the kerosene container?"

Thomassy glanced over at Roberts. So far he hadn't given the district attorney an opening.

Mrs. Fuller said, "Now let me see. Of course, the three who slept over the night of the accident. Melissa Troob was always very helpful that way. And so was Ed Porter. And Scott Melling, I remember him doing it at least once or twice."

"In other words, all three guests who stayed in your house the night preceding your husband's death had not only had access to the kerosene, but had actually used it, taken some of it into the house?"

"Yes."

"Do you recall any other guest who might have had access to the kerosene and/or gasoline?"

"Well, Barry Heskowitz, he was with us the evening before but didn't stay over. Barry did the lawn for us at least once. I don't remember if he filled the kerosene up, or just used the gasoline for the lawn mower."

"Anyone else?"

"Well, there was a young man named Yuri something or other who was studying at the Russian Institute and for a period of weeks was around the house a lot, but I think he and Martin had ideological differences and the young man stopped coming."

"How long ago was that?"

"Oh, months."

At last Roberts was on his feet objecting. "Your Honor," he said, "I object. Unless counsel can demonstrate that the student who has no last name yet was in the house more recently, I don't see how this line of questioning is relevant to what happened on the night in question. I move to strike the last two questions."

"Your Honor," Thomassy said, "I am exploring other hypotheses not excluded by the alleged proof, and it is certainly relevant that people other than the defendant, perhaps many other people, had ordinary access to the kerosene and gasoline that were kept in the Fuller garage, quite apart from the fact that the gas needn't have come from the Fuller garage. It could have been siphoned from a car. It could have been brought in from anywhere by anybody."

Judge Drewson leaned forward. "Mr. Thomassy, I think relevance ends at a certain point in time, and that the people are correct in objecting that anything that happened weeks before the incident is not proximate enough to the date of the occurrence to be relevant. It has been testified to here that Professor Fuller used the heater every morning, and since there has been no testimony that the heater exploded on previous mornings, your questions, Mr. Thomassy, are relevant only to the persons who were present on the premises during the previous day and evening, namely Miss Troob, Messrs. Melling and Heskowitz, and the defendant, all of whom were admittedly guests the evening before the event. The jury will disregard the last two questions and answers and the reporter will strike them from the record."

Thomassy smiled. The judge had done his job for him. It had been twice implanted in the jury's minds that four people could have put gasoline in the kerosene. *Let's just add a few more.*

Thomassy's voice was very quiet when he asked the next question of Mrs. Fuller. He wanted Roberts straining to hear. If he wasn't sure he got it all, he'd be less likely to object.

"Mrs. Fuller," Thomassy said, "did you and your husband keep the garage door locked at all times?"

"I don't think we ever locked it except when we went away on vacation and left the car. It's not that kind of neighborhood, Mr. Thomassy."

"Does that mean that anyone from the outside could slip into the garage for a minute or two?"

"I suppose so. When Mr. Randall first was put in charge of security—"

"Objection!" Roberts said. "The witness has answered the question. There was no question about Mr. Randall or security."

Judge Drewson touched his fingers together, a gesture he used to remind himself that he wanted to come across as a man of infinite patience. "Why don't we let the witness complete her thought, Mr. Roberts. If it's hearsay I'll consider striking it." To Mrs. Fuller he said, "Please continue."

"Well, when my husband began work on this project, Mr. Randall or one of his associates would always check the underside of our car in the morning. He was worried about car bombs."

Roberts stood. "That's hearsay, Your Honor."

"I'll phrase a question," Thomassy volunteered. "Mrs. Fuller, did there come a time when Mr. Randall or one of his associates said anything in your hearing about car bombs?"

"Yes. He said it was important to check the underside each time before we used the car. Professor Fuller and I really considered it a nuisance."

"Did they ever do their inspections in the garage where the kerosene and gasoline were kept?"

"If that's where the car was, of course."

"Your Honor," Roberts said, approaching the bench, "is counsel trying to leave the impression that officers of our government are also on his suspicion list in connection with the crime being tried under the current indictments?"

Thank you, Thomassy thought. "It is my duty, Your Honor," Thomassy said, "to have available for the jury all other possible hypotheses as to the perpetrator. If the district attorney wishes to prolong this trial by calling the federal people as witnesses, Your Honor, I certainly won't object, but my purpose here was simply to put on the record the witness's clear testimony that more than four persons had access to the garage, and anyone, including persons whose identities we do not and cannot know, may have entered the garage where the kerosene was kept. Your Honor, I have an ancillary question or two to ask the witness."

"Proceed."

"Mrs. Fuller," Thomassy said, "to your knowledge, did Mr. Randall or any of his associates ever purchase kerosene for you?"

"As I recall Mr. Randall may have once or twice when the can was empty. Usually, my husband would put the empty can in the

117

trunk of the car and have them fill it up with kerosene when he went for gas."

"To your knowledge, Mrs. Fuller, did he do the same when the can containing gas for the lawn mower needed filling up?"

"I think so."

"You're not sure."

"He probably did."

"Mrs. Fuller, you and your husband were both students of the imperfections of mankind. Did your husband ever speak to you about his concern that someone at the gas station might inadvertently put kerosene into the gas can or gas in the kerosene can?"

"My God!"

"Would you answer the question, please."

"No, he never spoke to me about it. It's just the thought!"

Thomassy let the thought hang out there where it could be absorbed by the jury. Then he turned to the judge.

"Your Honor," Thomassy said, "I am aware of the fact that in a criminal prosecution the defendant may introduce reputation evidence, but rather than put Mrs. Fuller to the pain and inconvenience of a second appearance I would like to ask her one question relating to the defendant's character on cross."

"Objection!" Roberts said, not knowing where Thomassy was headed.

"Overruled," the judge said. "Let's see where this takes us."

"Exception," Roberts called out, confused and angry.

Thomassy put both his hands on the witness box. "Mrs. Fuller, do you know of anything negative about Ed Porter's character that would have caused you to keep him out of your home as a potential danger to any member of your family?"

"No."

"Thank you," Thomassy said, turning to the judge.

Archibald Widmer, sitting halfway back among the spectators, thought Leona looked worse than she did when he first saw her after Martin's death. Had he made a mistake in recommending Thomassy? He looked up, because Roberts was starting his redirect examination.

"Mrs. Fuller," Roberts said gently, "I made a note that during the cross-examination, you referred to, and I quote, the three who slept over the night of the accident endquote. Did you mean to use the word *accident?*"

Thomassy was again on his feet. "Your Honor, I object. What the witness said on the record is on the record—"

The judge held up his hand to cut Thomassy off in mid-sentence. "Let the witness answer."

Roberts said, "Did you mean to use the word accident?"

Leona Fuller looked not at Roberts but at Thomassy. "I should have used the word murder," she said.

Thomassy moved for a mistrial. Judge Drewson dismissed the jury, then told both lawyers he wanted to see them in chambers.

Seated opposite the judge, Thomassy and Roberts listened to him say, "Gentlemen, I want you both to know I have every intention of seeing this trial through to a finish. Mr. Thomassy, I am well aware that you will be dropping little tidbits along the way in the hope that they will give you a basis for an appeal should you think that necessary at a later date. But since neither of you has tried a case before me, I think you should know that I will not tolerate digressions, nonsensical objections, forays into fantasy, or any of the other tricks of the trade unless they speak to the point at issue: the facts on the basis of which the jurors must determine whether the defendant is guilty or not."

Thomassy was about to speak, but the judge raised his voice just a bit to cut him off. "I am well aware of your aim to demonstrate that others in addition to the defendant had access to the combustibles, which I have and will continue to allow. We operate under strict rules. I'm not interested in filling newspapers full of gossip. We're trying a case of homicide."

Again Thomassy tried to speak, and again was kept silent.

"Just a moment, Mr. Thomassy. Unlike some defense counsel, I don't think the Grand Jury sits up there handing down indictments just because the district attorney presents a case. They must have reviewed sufficient evidence of the defendant's potential culpability to warrant the expenditure of thousands of dollars of taxpayers' monies on this trial. Mr. Thomassy, would you mind telling us what you're up to?"

"I moved for mistrial, Your Honor."

"Denied. I'll put it on the record when court resumes. Now answer my question."

Thomassy coughed into his fist. "Your Honor, Mrs. Fuller was, I believe, a very convincing witness. When she uttered the word 'murder,' she may have irreversibly and irremediably implanted in the jurors' minds that the event of April fifth was not an accident. I think it is fair to say that she doesn't have any direct evidence to contribute to the supposition of murder, but her outcry may well be based on her knowledge of the danger her husband was in since he began that project. That is certainly supported by the watch that the federal government put on the Fullers' home and Professor

119

Fuller's person. Therefore, Your Honor, I must introduce an expert witness who can speak to the point of who—and there might be many such persons—might have had a motive for putting a stop to Professor Fuller's life if it was not an accident. I intend to subpoena as a witness for the defense a woman by the name of Ludmilla Tarasova, who, for more than two decades, I'm afraid, had a continuing intimate relationship with the deceased. I don't intend to refer to that relationship unless I am forced to."

He was looking straight at Roberts. Warning received?

Drewson tapped his fingers on the table. "To what specific end are you planning to introduce this testimony?"

"Your Honor, with all respect, I don't think it is fair to the defendant for the trial to be conducted in chambers. My obligation is to advise the prosecution, as I have now done, that I intend to call a certain witness. What the witness will say under oath and in front of the jury may well not only jar the prosecution's flimsy case against my client but may disturb a lot of other people who have not appeared in your courtroom."

"Such as?"

"Such as the CIA, the FBI, the incumbent on Pennsylvania Avenue, and whoever is running things in the Kremlin these days.

Thomassy stood up.

"Where are you going?" Judge Drewson asked.

"I thought the conference was over, Your Honor."

"Mr. Thomassy, I'm running this trial."

"Of course, Your Honor," Thomassy said, and left Roberts and the judge alone together.

Judge Drewson had from time to time reflected on the difference between the reporters and himself. They were voyeurs. He was an observer. He knew exactly what Thomassy was doing, throwing the proof back into Roberts's lap while forecasting trouble to come. Out of the broth of confusion came reasonable doubt.

"Mr. Roberts," he said, "between us, if you were ever in serious personal trouble with the law, would you engage George Thomassy to defend you?"

Roberts, standing, looked at the still-seated judge.

"You don't have to answer that," the judge said, rising amid the swirl of his death-black robes.

CHAPTER FIFTEEN

Ed, getting a cramp sitting in the chair waiting for Thomassy to phone, thought *I should take that clock off the wall.* He felt as if he'd been doing time ever since Pope Sturbridge put up the bail. A hundred fifty thousand was crazy, except they knew he could afford it. *Suppose I did take off?* Ed thought. If it cost him a hundred and fifty million it wouldn't make up for what he cost me.

Ed wanted to lie down on the bed, smoke some grass, drift. He wished he had resisted Thomassy's order to get rid of his stash. Nobody was going to come looking here anymore. Thomassy said being out on bail would give Ed a chance to clean up his life. His life didn't need cleaning. It needed Martin Fuller to say, "Never mind Sturbridge, genes are a retrogressive reactionary explanation that pleases the American fascist mentality. You are not like your father. You are shaped by your environment, namely me." If Martin Fuller gives great head, the head is the source of talk, brain sparks, firestorms. But he never once put his arm around Ed.

That's not true. Why had he thought that? Fuller put his arm around Ed the day they went to the Turkish bath.

Ed was amazed at how that skinny old man looked naked. His skin was tight against the muscles underneath. He had the spots of age, but his body, despite all the pills Ed knew he took, looked like it could live on for another eighty years. He saw Ed noticing the three inked numbers separated by dashes on the inside of his left forearm. *My katzet numbers,* he said, laughing, but Ed knew that Fuller had never been in a concentration camp. Katzet numbers had more numerals. These had to be the new first-of-the-month combination changes that Randall brought to him and that Fuller must have kept on his forearm till he was certain his faltering memory for recently learned numbers would not be betrayed.

Ed got up out of the chair, feeling the exhilaration he'd felt that day in the Turkish bath. Martin Fuller had let him see his body, and with it, the numbers on his arm. And then after the steam and the shiver-cold shower, they'd gone to eat in the small cafeteria downstairs, and on the last stair he had put his arm around Ed's shoulders and turning him till Ed was facing him, his eyes unavoidable, said, "You are hungrier for affection than any human being I have ever met."

"What's wrong with that?" Ed was caught by surprise. Fuller so rarely was personal.

"You are better with the dog—both Leona and I have observed it—than anyone who has visited with us. You understand his needs. A human should not be so continuously needy, lest he become as vulnerable as a dog."

Ed wanted him to understand he didn't need the approval of faceless mobs like a dictator or an actor. He wanted Fuller to say that he was someone special in his life, the best of his students, not another body to be replaced in a year or two.

"Ed," Fuller said, "you don't appreciate enough what you have already accomplished. How many at your age have written a book that will live?"

Ed wanted to say that the most important part of the book was its dedication page. *To Martin Fuller, mentor and friend.*

"You should leave the nest," Fuller went on. "You don't need me anymore. We will remain friends. We will see each other from time to time. Scott and Melissa have flown into each other's arms under my roof, and they stay not because they need to anymore but because of the convenience. You are not bound. You need to fly."

I will break my wings to stay, Ed thought.

"I envy you your youth," Fuller continued, "take advantage of it. I envy the time you have left to do your work. Remember the affection you give your work is always reciprocated by the work itself." He held Ed physically by the arms, as if they might threaten him if he let go. "I know, I know, one needs the affection of a woman. Some day you will meet one who will be to you as Leona has been to me, coworker, battler, a friend."

Ed wanted to shout back at him, *What about Tarasova?* Everybody in the field knew about him and Tarasova. *Man is a treasonous animal! You betrayed Leona.* Where was trust between human beings? Fuller himself had said the revolution is a history of betrayal not just during but even more after, like the marriage he had betrayed. He would say Tarasova was part of his work, there is a need in the heart to be part of something with another to avoid the terrible anomie of working alone. Did at some point Leona desert *him?* Did she leave him alone in the midst of his battlefield?

Out loud Ed said, "Do people join people just as they join movements, to turn longing into belonging?"

"You and your aphorisms!" Fuller replied.

"And what's wrong with aphorisms?" Ed demanded.

"They bend truth to appear clever."

"Therefore I am a good student," Ed said. "Having learned all of your aphorisms, I now invent some of my own."

Fuller roared with laughter. He slapped Ed on the back. They went into the restaurant and sat down at a small table for two near the window. "I shouldn't laugh so," he said, laughing again. "Better stop before I have food in my mouth or you'll be the death of me."

Ed remembered staring at him when he said that as if he could read his mind. *Thomassy, where are you, you said you would call. I'm counting on you now.*

□ CHAPTER SIXTEEN □

Thomassy got to his office long before Alice was due to arrive. He thought of the early-morning hours as his time of peace, when he could work undisturbed by the rest of humanity, having only himself to deal with, only the work he wanted to do before him. He knew there were people who felt alive in crowds, in theaters, casinos, at dances, in Times Square on New Year's Eve. Thomassy avoided crowds; they sapped his privacy. They used to say three's a crowd. His answer was two's a crowd when you're looking for the still center, where communion begins. Was that why he'd been a bachelor so long, afraid to be cut back by another? The war was between you and crowds, you and the state, you and the first other person. Eve with the apple, and peace fled.

He put the newspaper under his arm so he could turn the key in the lock. It was the first issue of *The New York Times* in which the Fuller trial coverage appeared on page one. The *George* part of his name appeared on page one, followed by *continued on Page 14* where *Thomassy* was the first word of the continuation. If his father were still alive, he'd have to phone him. *Hey, Pop, guess what?* And his father, who would never have known about the *Times* story in Oswego, would have said, *That your name in the paper, George, not mine. My name Thomassian. You think I want show neighbors you change my name?* The old man was dead. The dialogue continued.

The red light on Alice's answering machine blinked, meaning

messages. I saw Mr. Thomassy on television, can he defend my wife. She's not a crook, she's a kleptomaniac, she's sick, she needs help not jail. Beep. I read about Mr. Thomassy in the Times. *I want him on retainer in case I get into trouble again with the Liquor Commission. Beep. My son is in Attica with hardened criminals. He's only nineteen. He swears he didn't mean to shoot the gas station attendant. The gun wasn't his. Will Mr. Thomassy try to get him out?*

Fuck the messages. Publicity was supposed to be good for business, but he had all the cases he could handle without taking on associates and starting a school for baby lawyers.

Wrong, George, he told himself. Publicity gets you the chance to drop all the nickel-and-dime cases that can be handled by some jerkoff just out of Pisswater Law School or a well-meaning clunk from legal aid. Wrong again. Those are the guys who screw up the little cases. George, big-rep lawyers pick their cases. Big-rep lawyers make a lot of money.

What would I do with a lot more money, buy four more neckties?

This is my hour of peace, he told the blinking red light. It commanded: pick up.

He'd always been able to resist the command.

He picked up. It was Francine's voice. If he looked up at the ceiling God would be sitting there, pulling the strings.

Alice, this is Francine Widmer. Please have Mr. Thomassy call me, at my home if it's before eight-thirty, at the UN after nine-thirty. The earlier the better. If he calls from the courthouse, please have him try to get in touch with me during a break. It's important.

At her home? Her home was his place until she deserted.

It'd been so long since he'd dialed her at her apartment he had to look the number up. Dialing it brought back the early days, when he'd be nervous about her state of mind.

Her sleepy voice said, "Hello." That's all it took to make his steeled heart turn back into a pump beating faster.

"You called?"

"George, where are you?"

"Office."

"This early?"

As if nothing had happened.

"I can't forget my other clients just because I've got a trial on. I need to get some paperwork moving. What's up?"

"You sound angry."

"I'm just wanting to get some work done."

"My mother and father have invited us to dinner this evening."

124

If you're a trial lawyer, you lose the ability to take ordinary conversation at face value. The unexpected elicits suspicion.

"Do they know that we have semi-busted up?" He heard humming on the line. "This is a bad connection. Let me call you back."

"No, you won't call back. I don't mind the humming. We have not semi-busted up. I needed air, space, to think about . . ."

"About?"

"About where we're going. Or not going."

"You've got a mighty circumspect way of referring to the unmentionable."

"It's the iffiness of what we have now, George. I feel like a transient."

"Well, what's going to happen at dinner? Am I supposed to act like you and I are strangers?"

"George, you're hurting."

The day he was twenty-one he had told his mirror while shaving that detachment was the key to adult life. Mama and Papa, the original governors, had not been in charge for years. The point was not to let anyone else take their place. There were three ways of standing: on someone else's feet, letting others stand on your feet, or standing alone.

He had vowed never to be dependent on anyone. Wasn't that what the women were demanding for themselves? Of course he was hurting.

"George?"

"I'm here."

"It's just dinner."

"No ulterior motives?"

When she said "None," he thought that's not the answer she would have given under sodium pentathol. Francine was a great manipulator but a lousy liar.

"What time?"

"Eight okay?"

"It's a lot more convenient to come straight from court. Or is that early too working class?"

"Eight. Please, George?"

You please George. You used to please George. George is not acquiescent by nature. With your voice on the line, where is his famous strength?

"I'll be there," he said, and hung up, no good-bye, no chance for further chitchat. His fucking heart was going like a kid's. He worked as if he were possessed.

□   □   □

When Alice came in that morning, he'd gone, but the number of tapes he'd left for her, including revisions of a lengthy memorandum of law, made her think he'd been there all night instead of just a few hours. She'd once had a fantasy about them working all night on some pressing matters, then toward morning, tired, coming together in each other's arms.

She'd said to him, "I can get more money elsewhere."

"Alice," he'd said, "you're not going anywhere. If you want a raise, why don't you just ask for it straight out."

And he'd given her one. But that wasn't what Alice wanted.

When Roberts came up to him in the hallway just outside the courtroom, Thomassy had a feeling the meeting wasn't coincidence. He saw Koppelman the Insidious drop behind.

"Just one question, George," Roberts said.

That was the first time he'd called him George.

"I hear you're planning to put the defendant on the stand."

"I'm still thinking it through," Thomassy said.

"Let me know when you've decided."

"I'll let the court know."

"Mind if I ask a personal question?" Before Thomassy could respond, Roberts continued, "You're first-generation American-born, aren't you?"

"It was crowded on the Mayflower," Thomassy said.

"How do you feel about defending a traitor?"

Thomassy felt his right hand tighten. "This isn't a treason trial."

"Maybe not for the defendant," Roberts said and walked away, his leather heels echoing Thomassy's rage all the way down the corridor.

□ CHAPTER SEVENTEEN □

Driving to the Widmer house, Thomassy couldn't stop the debate with Roberts in his head. *I let him get to me.*

He saw the red light late, jammed the power brakes. His tires screeched. Pedestrians looked at him, *crazy driver.*

Roberts was doing to him what he always did to others. Get them angry so they can't think straight.

The honking behind him made him see the light had turned green. *Go.* Starts like that use half a gallon of gas.

Maybe it was all Fuller's fault. He was eighty-two, wasn't he? Maybe he poured some of the wrong fluid in, a mistake. It could have been one of the others upstairs. God knows what the truth is, my job is to defend. Did a surgeon check to see who was under the anesthesiologist's mask in the middle of an operation? He'd told the kids at NYU *You are not the law, you are a tool of the law. Every last son-of-a-bitch in the world is entitled to the best defense you can give him.* And that black-haired girl in the front row had raised her hand and asked *What about Eichmann?*

He'd been cool with the kids. *It isn't the dimension of the crime that matters. Mothers who bash their babies' heads against the wall have a right to a lawyer.* The black-haired girl had persisted. *What if you're sure the defendant is guilty?* He had answered *How can you be sure until you've heard every last word the jury hears, and even then?*

Thomassy, who knew when a witness sounded unconvincing, was unconvincing to himself. He pulled off the road, onto the shoulder, hearing the gravel thrown up against muffler and tail-pipe, stopping, taking out his handkerchief to mop his brow, and to let the hammer of his heart slow down.

When he turned into the splendid, curving driveway of the Wid-mer house, it was a quarter to eight. He didn't want to kill time for fifteen minutes, but when he rang the bell, there was a delay as if his early arrival presented a problem inside.

Finally, it was Priscilla Widmer who came to the door, gave him a pleasant smile touched with frost, led him into the living room, where Ned rose and Thomassy saw the two others, Perry and Randall, the men from Washington. What the hell kind of family dinner was this? Where was Francine?

Thomassy the Pigeon shook hands all around. Was Francine in the kitchen, ashamed to have maneuvered him here under a pretext?

Mrs. Widmer disappeared as if on cue, and the lead man from Washington came right out with it. "Please don't hold this meeting against any of the Widmers, Mr. Thomassy," Perry said. "We thought it might be awkward to meet with you in your office or anywhere around the courthouse. If we're ever asked about this meeting, it was a social occasion, unexpected by you, unexpected by us. It was very kind of the Widmers to provide the circumstances."

Thomassy sat in the armchair pointed out to him, an unre-

127

hearsed witness brought into the courtroom where everyone knew his role except him.

Ned Widmer offered drinks. Thomassy noticed that Perry and Randall were having refills. They must have been here for some time discussing strategy. That's why Francine hadn't wanted an early dinner.

"Mr. Thomassy," Perry said. "How much do you know about your client, Edward Porter Sturbridge?"

Thomassy looked over at Ned Widmer. "Where's Francine?"

"Oh George," Widmer said, "I'm afraid she's not here this evening."

Thomassy stood up. "Perhaps I'd better leave." He turned to Perry. "I don't discuss my cases or clients with strangers."

Perry and Randall looked to Widmer to speak.

"George," Widmer said. "These gentlemen, whom you've met earlier, are not strangers in any sense, especially not to this case. You'll recall it was I who asked you to represent young Sturbridge in the first instance. It was Mr. Perry who asked me to recommend someone like you."

"What does 'like you' mean?"

It was Perry who interjected. "An able defense counsel. As near perfect a track record as possible defending the guilty."

"Mr. Perry," Thomassy heard himself saying, "the prosecutor is a long way from proving guilt in this case." That was robot talk. Inside, his lungs were ballooning against his ribs. "They are going to have one helluva impossible time," he heard his voice go on, "sticking anything to my client only. There were others staying right there in the house."

"Do sit down," Widmer said.

Thomassy eased himself back down into the armchair. "There're at least half a hundred other lawyers you could have picked."

"With your record for acquittals?" Widmer said.

"Why's the government so itchy for Sturbridge to get off? His father a heavy campaign contributor?"

"No," Perry said. "Definitely not. May I show you something, Mr. Thomassy?"

Perry removed a five-by seven photograph from a manila clasp envelope. He didn't pass it over. He stood up and held the photo in front of Thomassy.

Though an enlargement, it seemed blurry. Thomassy thought it might be his vision misting. Then it seemed to clear. There were twenty or thirty people walking in both directions in what looked like the large lobby of an office building.

Randall passed a circular magnifying lense to Perry who handed it to Thomassy. "Look at the people who aren't walking."

Thomassy could feel the dampness of his shirt under his armpits. *Is this what witnesses feel like on the stand when I put a photo in front of them for identification?*

At the left edge of the photo he could now make out two men, annoyance—or surprise—on their faces, stopped by a short man with his back to the camera.

"The one on the left," Perry said, "is Semyonov. He's with the Soviet Mission to the UN."

"Where is this?" Thomassy asked.

"Public lobby of the UN. The man with him is Trushenko. Do you recognize the man who's stopped them in the corridor?"

"Can I hold the picture?" Thomassy asked.

"Sure," said Perry, handing it over. Thomassy peered through the magnifier. "It could be anybody from the back," he said, "anybody short."

"Maybe this will help," Perry said, and slipped a second five-by-seven out of the clasp envelope.

It was taken from a different angle. The short man could be seen from a side view.

"When was this taken?" Thomassy asked.

"Two days after Fuller died. Recognize the man?"

"Why was it taken?"

"All right," Perry said, sitting back down. "In order to answer that we have to take you into our confidence."

"Maybe you'd better not. I won't make any promises that might jeopardize my client's case."

"I'll take that risk," Perry said. "The government is preparing a group of candidates for expulsion from the United States for espionage in retaliation for an expected expulsion of several U.S. diplomats from Moscow. The FBI has been photographing Semyonov surreptitiously whenever he makes contact with anyone else, Russian or otherwise. There's a smart young assistant DA named Koppelman who's trying to get his hands on some of these from the FBI. We have a problem in the government. When it comes to espionage, the FBI has what you'd call narrow-angle vision. They're classy cops caught up in spy catching, not foreign policy. Our national security people have to have wide-angle vision. If these were our photos, a county DA would never get his hands on them, but that Koppelman fellow might be able to persuade some simplistic patriot in the FBI that he needed them to make the government's case against an American working for the other side. Here, take a look at this one."

He slipped another photo from the envelope.

"It's blurred," Thomassy said.

"Yes. But you can make out that Semyonov has turned away from the young man and is heading in the opposite direction. Look at this last one."

It showed the Trushenko person, his back to the camera, hurrying away through the crowd, followed by the young man, holding his arm out as if to try and stop Trushenko.

"Now," Perry said, "if you don't mind, look at the left side of that last picture very carefully."

Thomassy felt his heart's drum pound.

"What's Francine got to do with this?"

"It was fortuitous," Widmer said quickly.

Nothing seemed accidental anymore. Thomassy was being hoisted up the scaffolding of a building that didn't exist. He didn't want to play games with Russian finks or Washington finks or anyone else. *Georgie*, his father had said, *never show fear to a horse or worry to a man. They'll both stomp you.*

He handed the photo back, hoping the tremor in his left hand was visible only to himself.

"Does Francine know about this picture?"

"She hasn't the slightest idea that it was taken, Mr. Thomassy," Perry said.

"Can I see the second photo again."

"Sure." Perry handed it over.

The slightly blurred figure on the right had to be Francine.

"The first one again?" Thomassy asked.

Perry handed it over.

There she was. Thomassy looked up. "She saw the whole thing?"

It was Widmer who spoke. "Apparently. She would recognize Semyonov, of course, and possibly Trushenko, and must have slowed down because something in the interchange with the third person caught her eye."

Perry leaned forward. Thomassy thought he was going to take the photo back, but he didn't. Instead he said, "Semyonov has been her boss's leading adversary at times. I suspect she noticed him, then Trushenko and the young man trying to stop them. Look closely at that picture, Mr. Thomassy. Look at the young man's right hand."

It was clear now. He was trying to hand a piece of folded paper

130

to Semyonov, who was rejecting it, scowling, as if the young man was unknown to him, a crank.

"You'll want to look at the second photo again," Perry said.

It looked like the young man had tried to shove the same piece of paper at an unwilling Trushenko as Semyonov was turning away to head in the opposite direction, possibly to get away from him.

Thomassy looked up at them. His rib cage hurt. He shifted his weight in the chair. In a calm voice he said, "It would have to be proved beyond a shadow of a doubt that the third person is my client. Even so, there could be many grounds for his wanting to communicate with these people. If that's Porter, please remember he's a Soviet affairs specialist. He may have needed information for his work, anything. Surely an open contact in the lobby of the UN building . . ."

Perry's upheld hand stopped Thomassy's voice.

"There's no need to speculate. Your client knows why he tried to pass a message to these people. I'm certain that in the context of lawyer-client confidentiality, he'd fill you in. You don't expect clients to keep essentials from you?"

"Of course not. But I don't see—"

"Mr. Thomassy, you don't know what we know. The prosecutor doesn't know what we know and we're not about to tell him. We're on your side in this one, please understand that. We'd rather know his version of what he was doing in private than from testimony in open court. It's in his interest to tell you."

"Are you implying that if I relayed to you anything he told me, that piece of information wouldn't get to the district attorney?" Thomassy turned to Widmer. "Ned, you know the sanctity of the client-attorney relationship."

"As I understand it, George, it's to protect the client's interests. It seems to me that what Mr. Perry is suggesting would protect your client because the information wouldn't be used in the trial, don't you agree?"

"How can I trust any of you?"

They all looked at him. Perry was the one who spoke. "You know who we're working for, Mr. Thomassy. You are working for your client. The question is who is your client working for?"

"That's a very serious allegation without an iota of proof!" Thomassy said, wishing he hadn't raised his voice. "You couldn't get a man a traffic ticket on evidence like that. Are you pushing me to throw the game?"

He knew where that came from. Joe Siston. Thomassy turned his anger on Widmer. "You got me into this to defend the kid, didn't you?"

"Of course."

"Please," Perry interrupted. "We certainly don't want you doing anything unethical or that would jeopardize your client's case. We think if you found out what happened, it might help your client's case."

Thomassy remembered Joe Siston, the star of Oswego's basket-ball team, invincible in 1954, suddenly playing like a broken-legged giraffe in the last quarter of the final game, missing shots he'd never missed, and when the booing started, pretending to limp, calling time, fast-talking the coach, wanting out, the coach ordering him back into the game to play like the winner he'd been all season long. Afterward Doc had said there was nothing wrong with Siston's leg, only the inside of his head, and the coach had called the bank every day for five days until Siston deposited the bookie's cash. They threw Siston out of school but that hadn't helped; every last kid in Oswego High felt betrayed, and it was Armenian George who confronted him in front of the ice cream parlor and said *If you needed the fucking money so bad, we'd have chipped in five bucks a piece for you to win!* He'd wring Ed's neck if what he was doing was throwing the game!

Game was the word Francine had thrown at him. Treason isn't a game. He'd thrown back her State Department types, weren't they playing? And he had said wasn't that what the spy novels all missed, that the Russian players knew that if they fucked up they could be caught by *either* side.

They were all looking at him, the man they'd shown the photographs to.

Perry sensed Thomassy's unease as accurately as if he'd had two fingers on his pulse. He said, "If your client was in fact involved with the Russians—that's just hypothesis right now—I can assure you that there are other possible suspects in the Fuller case."

"Like who?"

"Isn't it true, Mr. Thomassy, that the more suspects, the fewer chances that the jury would find Porter solely responsible beyond a reasonable doubt?"

"I said like who?"

"The others who stayed over." Perry leaned forward. "And others who came to visit frequently, who knew their way around the Fuller house. Maybe one or two who had it in for Ed Porter?"

"Who are these people?"

132

It was Randall who spoke. "We've been tracking all Fuller's visitors for years."

This is crazy, Thomassy found himself thinking. *They're playing with me. They're making this up.* "Are you talking about hard evidence? Admissible evidence?"

Randall looked at Perry.

Perry said, "Possibly."

"Would that information be made available to me?"

"If it became necessary."

"And what you want in exchange is whatever I find out from Gordon about what transpired in the UN building?"

"We would be interested in one aspect particularly."

"You think he's broken with the Russians and you want to turn him," Thomassy said.

"It's too late for that if they distrust him, Mr. Thomassy."

"Then why the hell are you jeopardizing my lawyer-client relationship?"

Perry sighed. "Mr. Thomassy," he said, "if what you learned was communicated to us and we determined that we had to make immediate use of it, you could always resign the case retroactively, as it were, making your resignation effective sometime before you communicated the information to us. Porter would be in no position to tell anyone. In the measure of things, you'd be helping your country. That isn't exactly unethical, is it?"

"Ned," Thomassy said, "you'd better tell these fellows you picked the wrong pigeon. You know I wouldn't do anything like that." To Perry standing above him he said, his face flushed, "Who do you think I am?"

"An astonishingly good advocate," Perry said, "whose knowledge of foreign affairs . . ." Perry took the photographs and sat back down. "If we ranked knowledge of Soviet Affairs on a scale of zero to ten, I think everyone would rank the late Professor Fuller as number ten, and anyone who knew Ed Porter's work—we've talked to a number of people—would rate him eight or better. Where would you rate yourself, Mr. Thomassy?"

Perry was no cop, detective, prosecutor, the kind of people Thomassy put down with practiced regularity. What Perry was doing was as clever as some of the things Thomassy did in the courtroom. Perry was working a field Francine knew. "I'm a beginner," Thomassy said.

Perry smiled. "That's not a sin. Most people, most lawyers, judges, and politicians know very little about how this game

133

between us and the other side really works, where to find the opportunities, where the dangers are." He leaned forward. "Mr. Thomassy, there are a few people in State and the National Security Council who know almost as much as Fuller did. I don't. But I know that the people who know are very concerned at this moment that any Soviet move to revive détente, even as a mood, is seized by Western sensibilities, making us vulnerable unless there are people like Fuller around to demonstrate that playing the Soviet game with our sensibilities always works to the Soviet advantage and never to ours. Moreover, we've got a domestic handicap that's become a national leukemia. When we play tough it means ballooning the deficit. Do you follow me?"

"What's that got to do with my client?" Thomassy asked.

"Another drink, George?" Widmer asked.

"No."

"Our hope," Perry said, "is to avoid the extremes. Just as détente lulls people, getting the electorate hot under the collar about Soviet actions adds to the pressure for the administration to do something. That's why we hoped the Fuller affair would blow over as quickly as possible. He was a great loss, but my motto is, if you've got a body, bury it. This trial could swell up into an international scandal, and if it does, the media are not likely to let it go because it's good long-haul copy, not just a one-shot. Roberts tells us you're planning to put Tarasova on the stand. That will fuel the fire."

"My job," Thomassy said, his voice tremulous, "is to get my client off. If an expert in the field of Soviet affairs as high rated as Ludmilla Tarasova has something to contribute, I want her testimony."

"Don't you think you can get an acquittal without her testimony?"

"Only a fool would attempt to predict how a jury will react to a string of circumstantial evidence. With Tarasova's testimony, I could build the possibility that half of the KGB was out to assassinate Martin Fuller."

Perry glanced at Widmer. Widmer looked jumpy. Then Perry said, "We mustn't lose perspective. A murder charge is one thing. If you put into the jury's head the idea that this murder might have been committed at the behest of a foreign government, you'll have opened a can of worms. He'll never stand a chance with a jury of quite ordinary people who see treason clearly, not in the complex way, say, that intellectuals like Porter do. If he's convicted—"

"Now wait one minute!" Thomassy interrupted. "Nobody's getting convicted. I'm using Tarasova to show that any one of a zillion guys in the KGB could have been on an assignment to take out Fuller while my client was peaceably pursuing his research."

Perry's rude finger pointed straight at Thomassy. "I said *if* he's convicted, and if you'll let me finish, I'll add that when and if that happens we'll be obligated to use him. Youngsters like Porter don't do very well in maximum-security institutions. Once he's had a taste of prison he might listen to the kind of postsentence bargaining we very rarely get into. In other words, if you don't get him off, Mr. Thomassy, we could get him out of prison subsequently with a sealed court order. However, the pictures you saw would indicate that Porter and the Soviets are not in tune, probably because what they wanted is what we would have wanted under similar circumstances. I can see us wanting to know what a Soviet expert on America might be thinking, but we wouldn't want to stop his mind from working. That's amateursville. If Porter's convicted, the Soviets will be on edge. They know we'd visit him in prison and that every day would create pressure for him to talk to us. I assure you it's only in the movies that men resist the chance to get out. The Russians would be afraid Porter might reveal who recruited him—we don't know that yet—and who his control is or was. If you get Porter off without Tarasova's testimony the publicity stops, and we can all return to the détente mirage for our own reasons."

"What happens to Porter?"

"Who knows?" Perry shrugged. "Does it matter?"

Thomassy looked at Perry. What had he been like at Porter's age?

Perry said, "I'm afraid that what Ned and we have got you involved in has repercussions outside the criminal justice system that outweigh the case itself. May I make a few suggestions?"

Thomassy grunted. "You can make all the suggestions you like. I'm going to be guided by my principles, not yours."

"A declaration of a closed mind is hard to talk to."

"I didn't say my mind was closed to anything, Mr. Perry. I've been sitting here listening to stuff that makes a man's skin crawl. I said principles. And one of them is my responsibility to my client to use every possible avenue to suggest that others might have committed the crime."

"Whether he's guilty or innocent?"

"How many times do you think criminal lawyers get hired by innocent people? I'll do what I have to do for my client."

"For your principles?"

"Now you've got it," Thomassy said.

"They come ahead of your clients?"

Thomassy felt suddenly peaceful because he was beginning to understand. "I suppose your client, if we wanted to put it that way, is the United States."

"Of course."

"Not a particular agency, or party, or person?"

Perry didn't like where the conversation was going. "The interests of the United States come first. Always."

"As a matter of principle?"

"Certainly."

"Because your principles and the principles of the United States are the same?"

"They are congruent."

"Then do you think it was in accord with the principles of the United States, as you understand them, for you people to have helped smuggle known mass murderers from Nazi Germany into Paraguay, Uruguay, Bolivia, Argentina, and into the United States so they could escape justice in the countries in which they committed their crimes, and to do so on the alleged grounds that they might be useful?"

"We used the mafia in Sicily to facilitate the Allied landings there."

Thomassy wanted to stand. *This is not a courtroom,* he told himself. *Every place is a courtroom,* he answered himself.

"That was the Sicilian mafia in Sicily to save American lives during a war. What's that got to do with rescuing Nazi criminals after the war? Do you think the American people would have ever voted for anybody who proposed such a move? Do you people think that you aren't responsible to anyone? I've got one lousy client in court at a time, and I try to get him a fair shake before the law, but I don't try to spirit him out of the country. My clients stand trial. Your fucking clients are living it up all over South America and you dare talk to me about my principles against your principles?"

Thomassy stared straight at Ned Widmer, who looked like a man whose candle was barely flickering. "Ned, what's your role in this? You're not working for the government the way these people are, are you?"

"No," Widmer said, sighing. "Not in any sense except in which all citizens give something of their lives to it from time to time. Perhaps in error. I think we ought to go in to dinner now, George."

"Where's Francine?" Thomassy asked.

"I believe she's at your house, as a matter of fact."

"Mind if I skip dinner, Ned," Thomassy said. "Please convey my regrets to Priscilla."

"She's gone visiting to some friends for the evening. I'm doing the serving," Widmer said.

"I'm sure you and your friends from Washington will have some things to discuss," Thomassy said, heading for the door.

"Well," Widmer said, "I guess he's going to call Tarasova. I'm sorry you couldn't persuade him not to."

"On the contrary," Perry said. "The best way to reinforce an obstinate man's decision, is to try to talk him out of it."

"You *wanted* him to call Tarasova?"

Perry didn't answer. He turned to Randall. "Tell the boys we've got a green light."

Thomassy drove home keeping his speedometer at exactly seven miles over the speed limit. If you spoke friendly to a cop, not arrogantly, not scared, he'd never known one to give a ticket for seven miles over. Ten maybe, not seven. That's what his grade-B head was full of, junk facts. Francine, trying to puff up his ego, had said, *George, the UN is a big stage, with nothing going on. You're on a small stage, with a lot going on.* He'd believed her for the wrong reasons. He'd accepted the justice system as a game he could play as well as anyone. All those years since Oswego he had let himself believe that crap about law. He had always worked his way around the law on behalf of his clients. He had worked his way around something that didn't exist. The courts were as much a pretense as diplomacy. There was no law. And if that was true, what the hell was he practicing?

He'd always worked crime. Now he was in Madison Square Garden working something else. He had been yanked out of orbit. He wasn't up against Roberts. He was up against two governments, neither of which was on trial. *They both ought to be.*

He couldn't pull his car into its usual place in his driveway because Francine's car was already there, blocking the way.

CHAPTER EIGHTEEN

Thomassy remembered coming home with his parents from his first sleep-over trip away from Oswego, a Thanksgiving weekend visit with his aunt and uncle Thomassian in Binghamton. He'd slept in his mother's arms most of the way home in the Model-A his father called "the rattletrap," but as they neared home, he stirred and woke as if he knew it was almost time and then he saw their house, isolated from all other houses, outlined in the moonlight, and he'd asked his mother in alarm, "Why aren't there any lights on in the house?" And his mother had patted him on the head, and in her Armenian accent he could still hear, said, "Because we not there."

For the fourteen years that he'd been practicing law in Westchester, Thomassy had arrived home to a darkened house. Known to all of his women as a bachelor by choice who did not want to share his life the way he saw other people sharing theirs, he had sometimes thought that if he'd had a family, at least there'd be a light on in the house when he came home. Once he'd mentioned that to Alice and she'd said, "You could leave one lamp on. It wouldn't cost that much." He'd told her, "I don't want to advertise an empty house. One steady light says nobody's home. A darkened house might have a security system on. I've defended burglars. I know how they think."

In the last year he'd usually gotten home before Francine since she commuted all the way from the city. But five or six times she'd been there first. And the inside lights had been on, as now.

Thomassy turned his key in the familiar lock as if it were to a vault he was opening for the first time, unsure of what he would see when he swung the door open.

He saw Francine in front of a fire she did not need except as a focus for attention outside herself as she sat, legs up on a hassock.

"Hello, George," she said.

He wished she didn't look so painfully attractive. "You set me up at your father's."

Francine swung her legs off the hassock. "Before we start that

138

argument, I have something to say. Let's talk first and fight afterward."

Thomassy, his anger thwarted, loosened his tie, slipped his jacket off his shoulders and onto the back of a chair. Over on the counter an uncorked bottle of Cabernet Sauvignon and two empty glasses caught his attention. He poured some wine slowly into each, brought one to his antagonist, slipped into the other chair in front of the fire. His shoes felt weighted. Would it seem too domestic if he took them off? Hell, her feet were bare.

"You are pouting," she said.

"I am not pouting. I'm angry. You shared this place for most of nearly twelve goddamn months and you left on two seconds' notice."

"They weren't goddamn. I didn't leave. I went away to think."

"You could have done your thinking here."

"Maybe some people can meditate in the middle of Times Square. I can't be around you when I'm thinking about us."

"And what conclusions have you come to, Your Honor?"

She smiled. The trouble with most of the men she'd met is that they behaved like boys when ostensibly courting, a game with goals, a kiss, a feel, a grope, a lay. And when they talked, it wasn't for the fun of it but for points in the game. They played tough but had no sinew. They spent their ambition climbing a ladder that ended in the sky, nowhere, instead of living rung by rung. There was some of that in Thomassy, too, maybe in all men, hunters who went out to feed a family and got trapped in the skills of the hunt. Thomassy wasn't interested in feeding anybody, including himself. He wasn't out to get richer lawyering like daddy's friends. He wasn't a spectator. The play he was interested in was the one he was playing, in the courtroom, or with her in bed, or out walking on Sunday. Thomassy was the first to give her hope of a partnership. Their game would be them against the others, whoever the others turned out to be. She soared on thoughts like that, and then he'd say things like *Your Honor* to her and he was suddenly a boy like the rest. Maybe she wanted too much too fast.

"George," she said, "you've been conditioned by years of trying crazy cases that people either win or lose. Even trial marriage is not like a trial. Either both win or both lose."

"Yes, Spinoza."

"Don't play high school with me. I am not lecturing. This is the beginning of what I hope you will allow to become a conversation."

139

At last the muscles in his cheeks relaxed, boyish belligerence fled.

"I've never seen a trial except in the movies," she said, "but the impression I get is that each side makes points for the benefit of the judge or the jurors, correct?"

"Go on."

"There are no third parties in a marriage. Making points is only useful if you're keeping score. There's no score in marriage. It has ups and downs, but if in general it's going right, there's no judge, no jury, and no witness to anything that's important in it. The minute partners start assembling witnesses, the fracture's there."

"Who's talking marriage?"

"It applies to living together, married or not," she said. Was she trying to box him in, do what men did to women in the game?

Thomassy stared at her profile, lit by the fire.

Was this his way of deflecting himself from what she was saying? "I thought we were headed *somewhere*. Are you listening, George?"

He nodded. Throughout his childhood, having seen his father's horses die, he had thought that one of his ongoing duties was to prepare himself for the death, first, of beloved horses, then people, including his father, and then himself. He had taken his mother, Marya, for granted, just as his father had, and she had died first, even before the horses, and he had realized how out of control life was in its ending and that what even a kid had to seize on was *this day*. For many years now the joys of this day were winning: motions, battles, courtroom cases, women; settling for the joy or work well done or a woman who would be glad to come back again. The Future—he always envisioned it with a capital letter—was in whatever breach of luck God flung down. A career was too long range. A permanent woman was equally long range. Before Francine he hadn't prepared himself to meet a woman whose mind was crisp in places his was sodden, who could percolate an idea freshly that he'd long ago segregated in a drawer like his socks and handkerchiefs. Whenever he thought of her, present or absent, he felt her sense of life. If Marya had known her, she would have had to live longer.

Francine touched his hand. "You aren't listening!"

"Sorry," he said. "I was listening to myself."

"That's an improvement over some of the people you listen to," she laughed. Even her laugh was a death-dispeller. He'd come in wanting to vent his anger.

"George," she was saying, "when a couple starts producing evi-

140

dence of the malfunctions of one side or the other, they've put themselves on trial, but we've done something better. We've put ourselves into a kind of trial first. We're exchanging information, experience, getting to know, filtering in stuff from the past. I've got all that primordial WASP junk, you've got all the neanderthal Armenian ready-to-be-massacred-unless-you-fight-back-first junk. We're exchanging junk now so that if we end up living together more than a year, we won't get sandbagged the way my friends did who got married five or six years ago, innocent about everything except sex and money. You know what I'm afraid of, George?"

"Not sex."

"Not money either. I'm scared of palpitations because I can't control them. Love sure fuzzes up a clear picture, which is why, I suppose, the palpitations vanish after a time so you can get used to seeing the other person without the damned glow."

"Finished?"

"Those are my views, and I'm not ready to be cross-examined on them. Before you respond, maybe you should spend three days thinking about it the way I have."

"Why did you set me up tonight?"

Francine got up slowly. "You'd rather fight than fuck, wouldn't you?" she said, striding across the room.

Thomassy wanted to shout *Sit down!* loud enough to shatter glass, letting the irrational roar like a rocket taking off. He wanted to yell *The most important thing you want from a friend is not to betray you.*

He cut the switch. The WASPS thrived everywhere on *control.*

She'd gone into the bathroom, slamming the door. *You see,* he wanted to tell the invisible jury, *they go bananas just like Armenians and Italians and Jews.*

The fire glared back at him. Was the courtroom the place he hid from his own life?

Did she think she could set him up with impunity because he loved her? Did Porter pretend to admire Martin Fuller in order to betray him? Or did he really love Fuller and betray him anyway? Thomassy, he told himself, you're thinking sick. The only thing you're supposed to be thinking about is that they can't prove their case. Photographs don't make a case. You've had photos submitted in other cases and made fuzzy pretzels out of them for the jury. And Roberts doesn't have the photos, the Feds do, and they're ready to deal.

He sipped the wine. He put a pinewood log on the fire because he wanted to hear the sizzle. When the wine in his glass was gone, he finished Francine's.

Why did you set me up tonight? was a lawyer's question, an accusation. If he learned to be civil to her, would it hurt his courtroom style? That is sick thinking, Thomassy. Like screaming at somebody. Had the Widmers learned that it was inappropriate or merely useless?

He stretched his left foot toward the fire, the foot that worked the clutch when he'd had a gearshift car. You needed to be able to disengage the clutch that left you vulnerable to your own emotion. You can't drive around life with automatic transmission.

He got up and in his stockinged feet went to the bathroom door and knocked on it.

"Please come out," he said, thinking that in all the courtroom trials of twenty years he had never heard the word please.

When she came out Francine looked like she'd washed her face after crying. He took her hand and tried to lead her into the bedroom, but she said, "Sex doesn't cure everything."

And so he led her back into the living room. He stretched out in front of the fire. She insisted on sitting in a chair.

"Tell me your version of how I ended up at your father's with the National Security Council instead of you."

"Where's my wine?"

"I drank it. I'll get you another glass," he said, starting to get up.

"Never mind. I'll get it."

When she came back, she sat down beside him on the floor. Be grateful for small improvements, he told himself.

"When I was twelve," she said, "I once asked my mother if Daddy worked at two jobs. When she asked me to explain I said that he always seemed to be doing a little something for the government. I didn't know exactly what it was. Neither did she. But we both knew that whatever it was—a few phone calls, an occasional trip to Washington on some pretext—gave him the same kind of kick other fathers got from golf. It was his thing. He didn't parachute behind enemy lines, but on his scale of adventure, it was obviously rewarding. However busy he was, he always had time when Perry asked him to do a little something that mother and I weren't supposed to know beans about. I remember how upset he was when Christopher Boyce escaped from jail. He doesn't show upset easily."

"Who is Christopher Boyce?"

"The kid from California who stole our satellite secrets from TRW and passed them, through a friend, to the Soviets in Mexico. Don't you read the papers?"

He remembered the case vaguely. Then less vaguely as Francine filled him in.

Suddenly he said, "I don't want to hear any more about it."

"Because it reminds you of what kind of person you might be defending now?"

"Nobody has proved anything."

"I love your absolute loyalty to your client. Who is your client loyal to?"

"You lied to me about tonight," he shouted.

"I thought you were trying to learn not to shout."

"You betrayed me. You set me up!"

"George, George, this was the first time my father included us in. He didn't tell me what it was about, just that it would be of immense help in something important if I could get you to come to the house. I told him we were on hold, that it was a bad time, but he said it couldn't wait, so mother cooperated by letting the cook off, fixing dinner herself, and going off to eat hers with a friend and I cooperated by inviting you to a party I wasn't part of. Was it bad?"

Funny, he thought, how he felt the need for a lined yellow pad. In the courtroom he'd trained himself to jot down pointers for countermoves while listening.

"Why'd you come back?" he asked.

"I was coming here before this dinner thing. I said I wanted three days. I took three days."

"Did you know," he said, "that they showed me photographs of a scene in a UN lobby that included guess who?"

"Who?"

"You."

Francine blanched involuntarily like any witness he'd ever surprised.

"Who photographed me?"

"They weren't photographing you. They've been taking pictures of a man called Semyonov—that mean anything to you?"

"Of course."

"And there was another one, Trushenko. That mean anything?"

Francine nodded. A flicker of memory.

"Why did you stop?" Thomassy asked.

"What do you mean?"

"Everyone in that lobby was walking in one direction or other

143

except Semyonov stopped and Trushenko stopped and then you stopped."

"I saw someone come up to them and they reacted weirdly. Semyonov turned around and walked back fast in the direction he'd come from, Trushenko kept going. The young man who'd come up to them went after Trushenko, which is odd."

"Why?"

"Because Semyonov's the senior man. He left for Moscow the next day. My boss was surprised. He'd expected to have a sidebar with Semyonov later that week."

"Did you recognize the young man who stopped them?"

"He didn't stop them. Semyonov just turned and went back the way he'd come. The fellow went chasing after Trushenko."

"You're avoiding my question. Did you recognize him? Stop looking at your hands, look at me. Francine, please don't lie to me. You've seen his picture in the papers. You've seen him standing next to me on television. You saw him in my office. If the DA subpoenas you to testify to where you saw Porter and the circumstances, what do I do, cross-examine to destroy your testimony or take myself off the case? You remember how I got this case, don't you? You nudged me because your father nudged you because Perry didn't want to see the Porter case explode because he was defended by some schmuck!"

He was letting the anger mount again. Sit on it, he told himself, hang it on the wall so you can look at it instead of just feeling it.

She said, "I can see why you would be upset."

She stretched out on the carpet, face up, her hands behind her head. Would he ever leave himself so vulnerable to another person?

"I don't want to get those photos as an exhibit in the record," Thomassy said. *I don't want you on exhibit. I don't want you on the stand.* He took her hands. "Once you testify, or those photos get printed somewhere, some newsman will dig out the link between you and me. How we met." *Your rape case.* "We avoided the papers when it happened. Now every goddamn camera in the world is focused on us."

"Why did they show you those pictures?"

"It's the line on which they can reel me in. They want me to dig some stuff out of Porter and pass it on to them."

"Will you?"

"In violation of my lawyer-client confidentiality? Like hell I will. What I want to know is when you'll finish filling me in—completely, everything—on Ludmilla Tarasova?"

Francine sipped at her wine. She said, "If I smoked, this is the time for me to light a cigarette."

"What's rattling you?"

"You, Dirty George. You want to get out of their dirty hands by making mine dirty. I'd feel like a thief ransacking government files for you to use against the government."

"I wouldn't be in this if it weren't for you!"

"I didn't push."

"You don't have to when it comes to me."

"And now you're telling me that to keep their dirt from rubbing off on me, all you want is for me to rub some dirt on myself. What the hell are you up to, George?"

"I'm planning to get my client acquitted."

"How?"

"If I don't tell you, you won't be able to tell your father."

"My father may never speak to me again if you blow this thing up."

"Has he ever?"

"Ever what?"

"Spoken to you the way you do to me?"

"No."

"I'm glad to hear that you have a different relationship to me than you do to him."

"George, I can see your brain whirring. You're going to do something that will get the government very upset."

Thomassy smiled. "I consider that a prime objective. My flag says *Don't tread on me*."

He was standing over her, and she said, "Don't tread on me, George," and they laughed together for the first time that evening.

"I'll bet you haven't eaten dinner," she said.

"Have you?"

"No. I don't need to. I like to skip eating once in a while. It's a way of proving to food who's boss, it or me."

"Can I offer you an after-dinner drink?" he asked. "I have," he said, inspecting his bottles, "Grand Marnier, a little Kahlua left, and some Armagnac, if you can take the strong stuff."

"I can take," she said.

"I can give."

With deft hands, he undressed her, setting her clothes aside carefully so as not to wrinkle them. Only when he removed her skimpy panties did he roll them into a ball and as if he were playing basketball made believe that he was aiming at the backboard behind a hoop and threw them against the wall.

145

"You should have played for the Celtics," Francine said.

"I'm much too young."

She caught his stare, crossed her legs, and supported her head on an elbow, a nude odalisque.

"I want to touch you," he said.

"You waiting for permission?" she asked.

He said nothing.

"Permission granted."

He bent over her. He watched her breast move with her breathing. Then, with the tip of his index finger, he touched her right toe.

"You're a model of restraint," she said, feeling the cavernous longing.

"I'll get the Armagnac," he said, rising.

She looked at him across the room looking at her.

"You are overdressed for this climate," she said.

"That can be remedied."

She watched him take his clothes off, not the way most men did, hurriedly, but one careful movement at a time, like in a ballet. Who said only women undressing could be erotic in their effect?

When he slipped his shorts off, she said, "Hello."

"At your service," he said, pulled the cork out of the Armagnac bottle with his teeth, then with great deliberation came over to her and tipped the bottle, letting the viscous liquid flow over her breasts and past her naval, down. He set the bottle down on the coffee table, then let the cork fall from his lips so they would be free as, like a huge tomcat flicking his tongue, he fell to his knees and then bent his head to her.

□ CHAPTER NINETEEN □

Jenny Sturbridge had given the servants an unexpected evening off because, like all servants, they lived part of their lives vicariously, and she did not choose to have them overhear what might transpire when Franklin Harlow visited. Even if they didn't hear a thing, just the presence of the family lawyer was enough to feed their appetites for gossip. It was bad enough they had to read about the case in the newspapers.

She answered the door herself. "He's in that study of his," she said. "I'll lead the way."

Between the large kitchen and the pantry a door led down steps to the cellar. "We must be careful not to startle Malcolm," she said.

Past the door to the boiler room Harlow could see the long cool corridor in which hundreds of bottles of wine were racked in bins against the walls. Seldom-worn jewels, he thought, collecting in a jewel box.

Jenny Sturbridge was a few steps ahead of him. "He's aging me faster than the wine," she said.

Harlow's wife Elizabeth had been a magnificent eccentric in his view, a lady who cared for injured birds till they no longer need fear cats, a lady who told idling policemen how to direct traffic better. But one day he had watched Elizabeth folding towels, putting them in the linen cupboard, then removing them and refolding them in a slightly different manner. Was that the first time he had realized her eccentricity had slid over the line? She was in an institution now and that presented him with a congeries of problems, including the shape of Jenny Sturbridge's body as she walked in front of him, a man deprived.

A long time ago Malcolm Sturbridge had had a wall built across the far end of his wine cellar and behind it had created a small room with paneled walls, a desk, a chair, a locked filing cabinet. He called it his second study. Unlike his upstairs study, there was no phone. Jenny suspected that the papers in that filing cabinet were ones she would not want to go through if Malcolm died. He didn't like to be interrupted in this room, and so Jenny knew the risk when she rapped her knuckles against the walnut door.

"What is it?" came the annoyed voice from within.

"Franklin is here," she said.

After a moment, Sturbridge opened the door. He glanced at his intruding wife, and then smiled, extending his hand to Harlow. "Franklin," he said, "how unusual of you to pay an unexpected visit. Have you been cozying my wife while I've been working away in the depths?"

"Hello, Malcolm."

"What brings you here?" Sturbridge said, shutting the door of the room behind him.

"I asked him," Jenny said quickly.

"I volunteered to come," Harlow said quickly, "when Jenny told me you were troubled about the possibility of being accosted by reporters at the trial."

Sturbridge said, "It's cold down here. Why don't we all make ourselves comfortable upstairs."

Franklin Harlow said the only thing he could say. "Of course," and gained the advantage of walking back through the wine cellar behind the graceful body of Jenny Sturbridge, thinking what a waste of love that a client's wife was beyond the pale.

In front of the fireplace, a third armchair pulled close for Harlow, Sturbridge said, "It's a pity you haven't been attending the trial."

"You know what my schedule's like, Malcolm. Do you want me to abandon supervision of the SEC case?"

"Of course you can't. But your lawyer's eye could tell me more than mine do. I sit there, trying to listen as a juror might. Jenny thinks things are going against Edward despite that talented lawyer."

"Jenny," Harlow said, "is a pessimist."

"I wish Malcolm would listen to the doctor," Jenny said.

"Rachlin thinks all those flare-ups in the courtroom are going to outpace my little mechanical implant. My only concern, Harlow, is the newsmen."

"Have they detected you yet?"

"Jenny and I sit all the way in the back. It's just that Edward cranes around once in a while until he's certain where we're sitting. I'm not sure he finds our presence a comfort. Jenny has to steel herself to keep from going up to Edward during the breaks. If the newsmen identify me, what do I say? What will they ask me?"

"Malcolm," Harlow said, "I guarantee the first question would be 'How does it feel to have your only son being tried for murder?'"

"I could say 'no comment,' couldn't I?"

"That's the trap. Industrialist says no comment when asked how it feels to be the father of an accused murderer. Newspapers hang you for not answering as well as for answering. Avoid them. Just walk away if they come after you."

Jenny said, "You're both being very self-centered. What about Eddie? Look at the agony he's being put through day after day. He's not that kind of boy."

"What kind?" Malcolm said, staring at Jenny as if she had just trespassed on his moral code.

Harlow said, "I don't like it when you get that flush in your face, Malcolm. Rachlin wouldn't either."

Malcolm Sturbridge smiled, pharoah in his tomb looking at the

living. "Are you giving me medical, moral, or legal advice this evening?"

Harlow glanced at Jenny. "I thought I might put out a statement
from my office to the effect that you have a profound faith in your
son's innocence."

"Jenny put you up to that."

"Not really."

"Don't start shading the truth with me now. We've known each
other too long. I am not going to usurp the function of the jury."

Jenny Sturbridge said, "*You* were his jury for the longest time."

Malcolm ignored her. "Franklin," he said, "you've been infi-
nitely valuable to me over the years. I've listened to your advice
not only as the company's advocate but as mine. The decisions,
however, you will recall, are finally my prerogative. No statement
to the press. That's final. Sherry, or something stronger?"

Harlow asked for whiskey with a splash.

"Jenny?" Sturbridge asked.

"Not for me."

"Well, the doctor says a bit is good for the ticker," Sturbridge
said, as he poured some whiskey into a second glass. He handed
the first glass to Harlow, then clinked his own against it.

"To our friendship," Sturbridge said. "May it never end."

□ CHAPTER TWENTY □

Thomassy was just coming into the courtroom when he saw the
couple taking their seats in the back again. On the first day he had
suspected who they were because Ed had inherited enough of the
features of each for the kinship to show. Ed had confirmed his
guess. And now that they were just a few feet away, Thomassy
thought he'd go over and shake the hand of the man who was,
after all, paying the bill.

As he came near, the man he thought was Malcolm Sturbridge
turned his head away. It was the woman who faced him. She motioned him close enough so she could whisper, "He's not being
rude. He doesn't want the reporters to identify him. It's better they
leave him alone. Because of his heart condition."

149

"I understand," Thomassy said.

She couldn't help touching his sleeve. "Good luck," she said.

Thomassy continued down the aisle. He hated the idea of luck. Fools counted on it.

The guard standing near the court reporter saw Thomassy and nodded. Guards, Thomassy had learned, didn't bet on the outcome of trials. As far as they were concerned, a defendant got this far, he was guilty. The question was would his lawyer get him off?

"Hello," said Ed with a smile.

Without responding, Thomassy sat down next to Ed at the defense table. He suddenly felt as if he and not Ed were the defendant. What was this trial becoming?

Ed stared straight ahead as if he felt that eye contact would ignite whatever seemed to be boiling in Thomassy's brain.

"It's your job," Thomassy had told the students, "to use every legal means to give your client the best defense you can." "What about tricks?" someone had asked. "You mean tactics," Thomassy had said, getting a laugh.

You are becoming unfit to practice criminal law, he said to himself as he got up and walked back out of the courtroom to the surprise of the guard and Ed and anybody else who might have been watching.

The court attendant found him in the washroom, putting cold water to his face with cupped hands.

"Okay," Thomassy said, "I'll be right there."

Thomassy was finding it hard to pay attention as Roberts continued his examination of Detective Cooper. He hadn't interrupted for five minutes.

"Detective Cooper," Roberts was saying, "on the day of Professor Fuller's death, did you examine the contents of the Fuller garage?"

"I did."

"Did you do that personally, or did one of your men do it?"

"Personally."

"Tell us what you found in the garage."

"In addition to the automobiles, there were a number of floats and other pool items stored in the rafters, and on one side, some mechanical equipment."

"What kind of mechanical equipment?"

"A lawnmower, a leaf-blower, a five-gallon can containing gasoline and a similar-sized can containing kerosene."

"Were the cans labeled?"

"Yes, sir, they were."

"Did you determine whether the contents of each of those cans was what the label specified?"

"Well, sir, I removed the screw caps and smelled. Gas smells pretty different from kerosene. I took a sample of each."

"Are you satisfied that the cans were correctly labeled?"

"Yes, sir."

"To the point where you would not have hesitated to use the gas in the lawn mower?"

"Yes."

"And would you have used the contents of the kerosene can to, say, fill a kerosene lamp that you would light or a kerosene heater that you would use?"

Thomassy could swear the judge was glancing at him for the second time, waiting for him to intercede. *I'm not a robot, Your Honor, I'm having trouble with this case.* A surgeon could be sued for malpractice for sleepwalking through an operation.

Thomassy rose to his feet. Was that relief he saw on the judge's face?

"Your Honor," he said, "I've been very patient about the witness responding to what he saw or smelled, but I think we're into the area of opinion here, and if the government wants some qualified expert opinion, they ought to call an expert and not ask this police officer about opinions he is no more qualified to answer than anyone else who uses a lawnmower."

"Sustained," Judge Drewson responded with a sigh.

Thomassy sat down. Maybe if he could avoid looking at Ed for a while, he'd be all right. *Think of it as a case.*

"Detective Cooper," Roberts continued, "did you find anything in the garage that was unusual?"

Thomassy was on his feet again, but before he could say anything Judge Drewson said, "Mr. Roberts, would the people confine the questions to those that will bring forth factual responses rather than opinions about what might or might not be usual." The judge said, "Strike the question."

Thank you, said Thomassy to himself.

Roberts pulled down on his vest again. "Detective Cooper," he said, "what did you find in the garage besides the items you have enumerated?"

"A button, a jacket button."

"What did you do with the button?"

151

"I put it into an envelope, sealed the envelope, and marked it for identification."

"I show you an envelope with markings. Is this the envelope into which you put the button?"

Cooper glanced at the envelope. "That's the one."

Roberts ripped open the end of the envelope and shook it over the palm of his left hand. A button fell out. "Is this the button you found?"

Cooper nodded. "Yes, sir."

"Okay," Roberts said, "I'd like to have the button marked as People's Exhibit E."

Thomassy rose. "Your Honor, a button is a very common object and may mislead the jury into thinking it has some relevance unless the witness can distinguish this button from the thousands of similar buttons in existence."

"Detective Cooper," Roberts said, "what makes you certain that this is the button that you found on the floor of the garage?"

"Well, sir, it has four holes for thread like other buttons but the area between two of the holes is broken."

"Thank you. And did you in the course of your investigations find any garment that was missing such a button but had similar buttons still sewed on the garment?"

"Your Honor," Thomassy said, "that's two questions, not one question."

And so Roberts, his exasperation beginning to show, divided his inquiry into two questions.

That was stupid, Thomassy told himself. He had focused too much attention on the button.

"Did there come a time," Roberts asked, "when you found an article of clothing with similar buttons that had one button missing?"

"There was a jacket in the defendant's room, that is the bedroom he had slept in in the Fuller house, and I asked the defendant whether the jacket was his and he said yes."

Roberts glanced over at Thomassy.

Don't count your chickens yet, Thomassy thought.

"Detective Cooper," Roberts asked, "did you have occasion on that same day to inspect the floor near the defendant's bed?"

"I did."

"And what did your inspection reveal?"

"Someone had spilled some inflammable fluid on the floor."

"And did you confront the defendant with that information?"

"I did."

"And what did the defendant say in response?"

"He said he was trying to fill his lighter."

"And did you ask the defendant to produce the lighter he was allegedly filling?"

"He couldn't find it. He couldn't find his cigarettes either."

"And what conclusion did you come to?"

"That the defendant didn't smoke and was lying about—"

Thomassy was on his feet. "Objection!"

"Sustained," Judge Drewson said. "The jury will disregard both the question and the response."

The son-of-a-bitch has got me in a box, Thomassy thought. *If I bring up the marijuana on cross, it'll just contaminate Ed's reputation with the jurors.*

"Detective Cooper," Roberts said, "did you make an examination of the bathroom where the fire took place?"

"Yes, sir, I did."

"To your knowledge, were you the first person to examine that bathroom?"

"No, sir. I believe that one or more federal people charged with Mr. Fuller's safety examined that room before I arrived."

"Not police officers?"

"No, sir."

"Did you uncover anything in your examination of that bathroom that seemed out of the ordinary?"

"Well, sir, there was extensive flame and smoke damage from the fire. The rug, or I should say the wall-to-wall floor covering, was burned in places. The toilet seat was raised. The covering of the toilet was of the same cottonlike material that covered the floor. When I started to lower the toilet seat and cover, I found jammed between the cover and the tank a man's wristwatch with a well-worn leather strap."

Roberts went over to the prosecution table and one of his assistants handed him a plastic envelope containing a wristwatch.

"Would you examine this watch and tell the court if it is the watch you found in Professor Fuller's bathroom?"

Cooper looked down at it just for a split second. "Yes, sir, it is."

"Did you subsequently ask Mrs. Fuller if it was her husband's watch?"

"No, sir."

"And why did you not?"

"Because there was an inscription on the back of the watch that said, 'On your graduation, with love Mom and Dad.' It was a quartz-type watch that came available in the seventies. I figured Professor Fuller must have graduated before that."

The laughter came mainly from the press section.

"Was there anything else significant about the watch in your opinion?"

"Yes, sir. It had a date."

"And what was that date."

"Six thirteen seventy-five."

"And what conclusion did you draw from that date?"

"Objection!" Thomassy stood.

"Overruled," said Judge Drewson impatiently.

Cooper couldn't wait to speak. "That it belonged to someone who graduated from something on the thirteenth of June, 1975."

"Did you then make inquiries to determine who might have graduated on that date?"

"Not personally, sir. But one of my men checked on the high school and college graduation dates of Miss Troob, Mr. Melling, Mr. Heskowitz, and Mr. Sturbridge, and the only one that graduated on or about that date was the defendant."

"Your Honor," Roberts said, "The people would like to have this watch marked as an exhibit."

"Have it so marked."

"Detective Cooper," Roberts said, "did you have occasion to search the room in which the defendant slept during the night of April fourth to fifth?"

"Your Honor," Thomassy interrupted, "may we approach the bench?"

Judge Drewson motioned Thomassy and Roberts to come up.

"Your Honor," said Thomassy, careful to keep his voice low, "during Detective Cooper's search of the bedroom in which the defendant stayed, he found a two-ounce packet of marijuana in a bedside drawer that the defendant opened at Detective Cooper's request at a time when Detective Cooper did not have a search warrant. That issue was dismissed. Because of the prejudice many people, including some possible jurors, might feel toward anyone who used marijuana, I think it most important Your Honor not to have that incident referred to in front of the jury."

"I would agree with your thinking on that, Mr. Thomassy," the judge said.

"I will be extremely careful not to raise that issue, Your Honor," Roberts said.

Back at the witness box, Roberts said, "Detective Cooper, did you have occasion to search the room the defendant slept in?"

"Yes, sir."

"During that search did you find anything that could relate to the charges in this case?"

Cooper said, "In my search I went through the closet carefully. Stowed on the upper of two shelves, way in the back, were what looked like some old curtains folded, and in back of the curtains was a stack of skin magazines, and in back of those was a leather-covered metal half-pint hip flask."

"Was there anything in the flask?"

"Well, sir, I expected I might find liquor of some sort, but it was empty except for a few drops that didn't seem like liquor to me but water. What aroused my suspicion was it had a smell to it. Not water and not liquor."

"Did you have occasion to ask the defendant whether the flask belonged to him?"

"When I arrested him in his apartment in New York City in the company of a police officer from that jurisdiction, the defendant said he didn't drink liquor."

"Did he deny ownership of the flask?"

"Not in so many words."

"Objection!"

"Sustained. Mr. Cooper, would you answer the question yes or no. Would the reporter repeat the question."

The reporter read from his tape. "Did he deny ownership of the flask?"

"No," Cooper said.

"Did you have the contents of the flask analyzed?"

"Yes, sir."

Roberts removed the top page of the papers in his hand and showed it to the witness. "Is this the report you received from the chemical lab of the Police Department?"

"Yes, sir."

Thomassy was on his feet again, exasperated. "Objection, Your Honor, that report is not admissible."

The judge called both attorneys up to the bench for a sidebar out of the jury's hearing. "Mr. Roberts, is the chemist who wrote that report alive and well and available to you?"

"I spoke to him this morning," Roberts said.

"Then he should be called as a witness. The jury has a right to hear his testimony and Mr. Thomassy has a right to cross-examine him."

Thomassy felt himself caught in the fulcrum of a scissor. The jury always perceived chemists as scientists, and he'd never seen a chemist who didn't try to snow the jury with his jargon. It would put too damn much emphasis on the contents of the flask.

"We haven't all day," the judge told him.

"Sorry, Your Honor," Thomassy said. "I will stipulate that the report be received." The jury knew that cops could shave the truth. Better a cop than a chemist.

The chemist's report was marked and entered. Then Roberts handed it to Detective Cooper. "Have you read this report?"

"Yes, sir."

"Would you please refresh your recollection of page three, last paragraph."

Cooper turned the pages, quickly read the paragraph.

"What conclusion did you draw from that paragraph?"

"That only a few drops of liquid were available from the subject flask. Under examination, these appeared to be largely water with a trace of a petroleum product."

"And what did you conclude from reading the report as a whole?" Roberts asked.

"I concluded that the flask may have contained a combustible fluid and had been washed out with water after use."

"Your Honor," Thomassy said, feeling the sweat on his forehead for the first time during this trial, "I have to object to a chain of conjecture unsupported by the evidence."

The judge asked for the report to be handed up. "Sustained," he finally said, handing the papers over to the court reporter.

To Thomassy, it didn't matter that he had been sustained. He could see the effect of Cooper's testimony on some of the jurors' faces. *Damn*, he thought. He didn't hear Roberts say "Your witness," until he said it a second time.

Thomassy asked for a moment's respite to consult with his client. "Ed," he whispered, "I don't like surprises. Is there any way that flask can be definitively linked to you? Initials, anything like that?"

Ed was taking time to think, which to Thomassy meant the flask was Ed's, not somebody else's.

"No," Ed finally said.

"It's your flask," Thomassy said.

Ed opened his dry lips. "What are you going to do?"

Ten years or so after Joe Siston, star player of Oswego's basketball team, had gotten kicked out of school for throwing a game, he came downstate to see Thomassy. Siston said a trucker who owned two upstate counties was trying to squeeze Joe out of his one-truck beer business.

"What are you coming to me for?" Thomassy had said.

Joe Siston hadn't shaved in a week. His eyes were rimmed red. "My regular lawyer is scared," he said. "They're setting up a frame that includes him. He's chicken, George. He might throw the game. You won't."

One of Thomassy's first entries in his devil book had been *If you want angels for clients, practice in heaven.* He could live with the guilt of a client, he'd had to many times. But if the flask *was* Ed's, what was his crime, murder or something else?

Ed pulled at his sleeve.

"Don't do that!" Thomassy snapped. "The jury's watching."

"What are you going to do?"

Thomassy stood up. Looking around the courtroom he felt the sudden vertigo of being atop a ferris wheel that had stopped, the electricity he had counted on snapped off. Had he ever been in greater danger of blowing a case?

He touched the counsel table with steadying hands.

"Is counsel ready to resume?" the judge asked.

Is counsel permitted to have an anxiety attack in front of a hundred and fifty people? Can Your Honor please ring the curtain down? Roberts was looking at him, ready to spring.

Thomassy nodded. He took a sip from the water glass and started toward the witness box, walking mechanically, a wound-up toy pointed at Cooper.

Close up, he looked at the detective. Cooper couldn't avoid Thomassy's gaze. Thomassy nodded as if to thank the detective for his cooperation.

"Mr. Cooper," Thomassy said, "did you happen to notice the make of the jacket Ed Sturbridge said was his?"

Cooper smiled. "It was a MacGregor."

"Mr. Cooper, do you know how many MacGregor jackets with those buttons were manufactured each year for the last five years?"

"No, sir."

"Then how do you know with such certitude that the button you say you found in the garage came off the jacket you say was in the room occupied by Ed Sturbridge?"

"The jacket had some long thread hanging in the place where the button used to be."

"*The* button or *a* button."

Cooper looked at the judge as if wanting the judge to help him out. Finally, he turned back to Thomassy and said, "The button I found was busted between two holes. The jacket had thread hanging."

"Mr. Cooper," Thomassy said, "did you wear a jacket that day?"

"No, sir, I wore a raincoat."

"Does your raincoat have buttons?"

"Yes."

"Are any missing?"

"Not to my knowledge."

"Is the raincoat you wore that day, Mr. Cooper, anywhere in this courthouse?"

After a moment, the judge asked one of the court officers to retrieve Detective Cooper's raincoat from an anteroom. While they were waiting, Thomassy asked, "Mr. Cooper, do you know the color of the buttons on your raincoat?"

His voice rose as if with a question. "I assume they are brown?"

"Well, we don't have to deal with assumptions. The court officer is just bringing the raincoat over. Is that the raincoat you wore on the day in question, Mr. Cooper?"

Cooper nodded.

"Please speak up," Thomassy said.

"Yes!"

"Would you say that the buttons on your raincoat and the buttons on Ed Sturbridge's jacket are approximately the same color?"

"It was—"

"Your Honor," Thomassy said, "may I respectfully ask that the witness be instructed to answer the question."

The judge nodded.

Cooper, his color showing, said, "Yes, they're about the same."

"Would you then look at each of the buttons on your raincoat that the court officer brought over, Mr. Cooper, and see if any of the buttons are missing?"

The judge had to gavel the audience back to silence, as Cooper examined his raincoat.

"What are you finding, Mr. Cooper?"

Cooper fidgeted. He looked over at Roberts, then at the judge. "There's a button missing on the sleeve. There are three buttons on the left sleeve, and two on the right, so I assume there's one button missing on the right sleeve."

"Is it possible," Thomassy asked, "that the button you found was the button now missing from your own raincoat?"

158

"That button was probably missing for the last five years!" Cooper shouted.

"I move that the response be stricken, Your Honor," Thomassy said.

Judge Drewson leaned forward. "You asked a hypothetical question, Mr. Thomassy, which is your prerogative, of course. But I agree that the response was inappropriately speculative. Strike the question."

"Now then, the question stricken," Thomassy said for the benefit of the jury as the court reporter hastily reached into the well behind his machine and noted the place, "I will rephrase. Mr. Cooper, I'm going to ask you to look closely at one of the buttons on your raincoat and the button that the prosecution has moved to put into evidence as an exhibit and answer the following question: Are the buttons similar?"

Cooper studied the buttons. "Well, maybe yes," he said.

"Are they similar. Are they the same?"

"I don't think they're the same."

"Are they, or aren't they!"

"They look very similar."

"Mr. Cooper, do you know for a fact whether you or your wife or anyone else sewed any replacement buttons on your raincoat during the five years that you say you have owned that garment?"

"She could have."

"And would she or the tailor who did the job for her have found an exact duplicate, or would they have used a button that looked pretty close to the one that was missing?"

Cooper did not reply.

Thomassy went on, "How many replacement buttons may have been sewn on your raincoat in the last five years?"

Roberts was objecting. The judge said, "Mr. Thomassy, I don't think any witness is likely to be able to answer a question like that with any certitude."

"I'm sorry, Your Honor," Thomassy said, his voice low. He glanced at his notes. Mike was a good investigator. It had been his idea to check on Cooper.

"Detective Cooper," Thomassy said, "do you know for a fact that *you* didn't lose a button while you were examining the Fuller garage?"

"I didn't hear anything fall to the floor."

"Mr. Cooper, isn't it true that you have a forty percent hearing loss that might interfere with some aspects of your work?"

Cooper was livid.

"Answer yes or no," Thomassy said.

"Yes," Cooper said.

"Did the police department records ever show that you had such a significant hearing loss?"

"Of course."

"Is it true those records do not now show any reference to that impairment?" *Bless you Mike Costa*, Thomassy thought.

"I don't know."

"You don't know or you're not sure?"

"I'm not sure."

"Did your hearing improve or were the records altered?"

Roberts was on his feet, objecting.

"Overruled."

"Thank you," Thomassy said. "Your Honor, if the button introduced by the prosecution is going to be admitted as People's Exhibit E, then I ask that Detective Cooper's raincoat be admitted as Defendant's Exhibit A so that both may be examined by the jury in the jury room."

"Hey," Cooper said, "I need to wear that raincoat."

"I'm sorry for the inconvenience," Judge Drewson said. "Please mark the exhibit."

"Now Detective Cooper," Thomassy said, "with regard to the watch you said you found in Professor Fuller's bathroom. The federal security officers who examined that room earlier, they didn't find a watch, did they?"

"They did not."

"Are you implying that those federal security officers were incompetent in the performance of their duties?"

Thomassy watched Cooper shove his rear end back against the witness chair. A lot of witnesses did that, changed position to give them a moment to think, to count to ten. Cooper said, "I only said that they didn't find it and I did."

"Detective Cooper," Thomassy said, strolling over in the direction of the jury and leaning back against the box, "are you familiar with the slang expression used by police officers who plant a gun next to the body of someone they've shot so that they can claim they shot the person in self-defense?"

"Objection!" Roberts's voice was striated with anger.

"Your Honor," Thomassy said, still at the witness box so his voice was raised to ring across the courtroom, "the prosecution has introduced in direct examination a watch that they imply is an important piece of evidence. On direct examination of a witness for

160

the defense, I have every intention of proving that that so-called piece of evidence bears no relation to the alleged charges. But as an officer of the court I am very concerned about the fact that more than one experienced federal security person thoroughly examined the locus of the fire and didn't find something as large as a wristwatch that a local police officer then found simply by lowering the raised toilet seat. I have no desire to prolong this trial by calling as rebuttal witnesses each and every one of the federal security people who examined that bathroom before Detective Cooper appeared on the scene and to put their extensive experience and credentials on the record. I simply feel the responsibility for pointing out that it is not unknown in police practice for putative evidence to be placed by police officers at the scene of an alleged crime as a cover-up for their own conduct. Detective Cooper admitted under oath to a thorough search of the bedroom in which the defendant slept and I wish to ask him now, so that the jury can hear his answers from his own lips and judge the truthfulness of his answers by seeing his expression, did he pick up the watch he alluded to during his search of the defendant's room and later pretend to find it in a room that had been thoroughly searched previously by federal security officials?"

"That's a goddamn lie!" Cooper shouted, red-faced, standing.

Judge Drewson said, "Will the witness please sit back down and try to confine his comments to answers to questions asked by counsel. Mr. Thomassy, would you state your questions one at a time."

"Of course, Your Honor," Thomassy said, leaving the jury box and coming over to the witness stand, bringing himself as close as he could to Detective Cooper, "Did you find the watch marked as People's Exhibit D during your search of the bedroom in which the defendant slept?"

"I did not," Cooper shouted at Thomassy's face.

Quietly, Thomassy continued, "You did not search the bedroom carefully?"

"I didn't say that!"

"You did not find the watch in the bedroom?"

"I did not."

"Yet your search was so thorough, according to your testimony, as to find on the upper shelf of a closet, some stowed curtains, magazines, and a hip flask that had been washed out with water, is that correct?"

"Yes."

"Did you attempt to determine whether the stowed curtains belonged to the defendant or someone else?"

"I assumed they were part of the household belongings."

"Is it your assumption that good detective work requires the detective to ascertain facts or to make assumptions without further investigation?"

"I've got a record as a detective, Mr. Thomassy."

"Oh?" Mike had gotten a copy of Cooper's record. "And would you care to have that record introduced in evidence in this trial?"

Cooper seemed flustered.

Judge Drewson said, "Mr. Thomassy, do I take it that your line of questioning is intended to impeach the veracity of the witness?"

"Your Honor, since veracity might involve the question of perjury, I would prefer to direct my queries to the professional competence of the witness."

"Proceed."

Cooper didn't want that record introduced. It was enough to have let him know that Thomassy had it.

Thomassy said, "Detective Cooper, did you attempt to ascertain whether the stack of magazines you found in the closet belonged to the defendant, or to some previous transient occupant of that bedroom?"

"No, sir, I did not."

"Did you attach any special significance to the flask that you did not attach to the curtains or the magazines or anything else you may have found in that closet?"

"Yes, sir."

"Did the flask have initials or any other identifying markings on it that would link it to the defendant?"

"No."

"Have you ever owned a flask, Detective Cooper?"

Cooper's face flushed again. "I used to take one to football games."

"Did you ever wash the flask out afterward with water?"

"Yes."

"Did your wife accompany you to football games at which you employed the flask?"

"No, sir, I went with some male friends."

"Did you wash out the flask after the game as a rule?"

"Yes."

"With water?"

"Yes."

"Until it no longer smelled of alcohol or anything else?"

"I suppose."

"Getting back to the flask you say you found in the defendant's room, did you personally hand it to the chemist who made the analysis of its sparse contents?"

"No, sir. I turned it in to Sergeant Petkov, and he sent it down."

"In other words, several people handled the flask before its contents were subjected to analysis?"

"Yes."

"Did you in your investigation attempt to find out if this flask belonged to any previous occupant of a room frequently slept in by people visiting the Fullers?"

"No, sir."

"Did that flask by any chance belong to you?"

"No, it did not."

"There's no reason to be angry, Detective Cooper."

"I'm not angry," said Cooper, angrily.

"No more questions," Thomassy said. As he went back to his table, he stole a glance at the jury. Several of them seemed amused by the exchange they had just witnessed.

At the table, Ed whispered into Thomassy's ear. "I think you're terrific," he said.

"Quiet," Thomassy whispered back.

□ CHAPTER TWENTY-ONE □

Less than ten minutes before Thomassy's critical meeting with Ed, he received a phone call from a calm-voiced Malcolm Sturbridge.

"What are my son's chances?" Sturbridge asked.

He'd heard that question dozens of times, from a parent of a kid busted on a drug charge, or one with a kid who took someone else's car for a joy ride, or the mother of a kid who got a pocketknife from dad for Christmas and who, during a high school locker-room scrap over who put a wet towel down on the bench, stabbed another fifteen-year-old to death. Some parents ought to be charged with environmental pollution for spreading kids onto the world. *Son's chances?* What did they think he was, a bookmaker?

163

"Mr. Sturbridge," Thomassy said, "what do you think your son's chances were when he was eighteen years old?"

"Chances for what?"

"For being a law-abiding citizen."

"Mr. Thomassy, I have paid you a considerable retainer to defend my son. Surely, you have some idea as to how it is going?"

"I don't want to mislead you."

"I'm not pushing for an answer you can't give. Just an interim appraisal. Please?"

"Mr. Sturbridge, I'm intent on preserving my reputation with regard to the defense of people charged with murder. But your son has also been charged with reckless endangerment in the first degree, which is a class D felony."

"What does that mean in layman's language?"

"It means, Mr. Sturbridge, that under circumstances evincing a depraved indifference to human life—those are the law's words, not mine—he is accused of recklessly engaging in conduct that created a grave risk of death to another person. If the state convinces the jury that Ed mixed gas into the kerosene, they could nail him on that charge. There's also assault in the first degree. That's a class C felony."

"Surely Edward didn't assault anybody, that's not at issue."

Be patient, Thomassy told himself. *He's a worried parent with a pacemaker.* "Under the law, assault in the first degree means that the individual intended to cause serious physical injury to another person by means of a deadly weapon or dangerous instrument. I think there was a rolling-pin case, and one about the heel of a high-heeled lady's shoe. But I don't think there's been one with a kerosene heater as the alleged dangerous instrument. Kerosene heaters have killed a lot of people by accident. It gives me some room to work in."

"I see."

"My main concern's the murder charge. Mr. Sturbridge, do you think you know your son well?"

"As well as any father knows his son."

"Do you think he intended to murder Martin Fuller?"

There was a moment's silence.

Thomassy said, "Don't worry, Mr. Sturbridge, it won't influence me. I just want to know if you think Ed intended to murder Professor Fuller."

Malcolm Sturbridge said, "I think the only person he ever thought of killing was me."

□   □   □

Thomassy watched Ed scrunched into the armchair opposite as if he were having a touch of postadolescence, not knowing what to do with his gangling arms and legs, trying to look everywhere in the room except at Thomassy. Not a word passed between them for minutes. Finally, Ed said, "Okay, counselor. What's on the agenda?"

That's all right, Thomassy thought. *I'll need him cool in the courtroom. Let him practice on me.* He said, "I'm thinking of having only two witnesses."

"I thought you'd round up a dozen character witnesses from Columbia."

"Juries don't fall for that anymore. A former concentration camp guard can get half a hundred people in Queens to swear he's a teddy bear. On television, the neighbors always say nice things about crazies in their midst. Juries know people are blind. I'm having two witnesses period."

"Which two?" Ed asked.

"First, Ludmilla Tarasova."

He saw Ed's lip twitch. "What do you want her for?"

"I'll probably have to subpoena her. She may not want to get involved in your defense voluntarily."

"What would you want to drag out of her? I know she—"

"Shut up a minute," Thomassy said. "I don't want you to know what she's going to say until she says it because when she gets off the stand, you get on."

"What the hell do you want to put me on for?"

Thomassy watched the panic flicker. Then the control. Paul Newman as Cool Hand Luke. How much of how we live comes from what we see in the movies?

Thomassy said, "Most jurors don't understand the fifth amendment. Ever. They just think that if someone, anyone, refuses to take the stand, even if it's his right not to, that he's hiding something. And if that someone is the defendant, they want to hear from him. They want the man accused to deny the charge in front of them, to explain what happened. It's a very rough chance, Ed. You could help get yourself acquitted. You could hang yourself in one sentence. Or in the way you act. And remember, it won't be me asking you the hard questions. It'll be that prick Roberts who wants to see you convicted so he can add your head to his watch chain for the coming election. Don't answer me now. Think about it. Make sure. If you decide to testify, you'll need to be rehearsed so well that every answer seems spontaneous and true."

"What's the worst kind of question anyone can ask me?"

"They can ask you to identify the people in a set of three pictures taken in the UN lobby. If the prosecution gets their hands on those pictures. What were you doing there?"

"Pictures?"

"I saw them."

"You sure it was me?"

"I'm not sure of anything."

"Is the person who's supposed to be me clearly identifiable?"

"Not clearly."

"It wasn't me."

"Suppose, just suppose, they can produce a witness who says it was you?"

"People make mistakes. Besides, what's wrong with being in the UN lobby? They have thousands of visitors, don't they?"

"Not all the people in the lobby are visitors. Some of them work there. You know the name Semyonov?"

Ed stared into space.

Give him time, Thomassy thought. Then he said, "Did I pronounce it correctly?"

"I've heard of a Russian playwright named Semyonov. He's had a book or two published over here."

"You know a man named Trushenko?"

Ed looked at Thomassy as if wondering if a question would lead too far. "What's the relevance?"

"He's in the picture, too. He and the other guy. And someone who looks like you trying to talk to them."

"What's this got to do with the charges against me?"

"All they need to do is link you with the Russians in some way and the jury will pounce on it."

"I've seen you object," Ed said. "You're terrific at it."

Thomassy felt strangely relieved. Ed was very careful not to appear to lie. He'd make a good witness on the stand if they didn't sandbag him.

"If I knew you were going to deliberately lie on the stand," Thomassy said, "I couldn't let you testify."

"I don't intend to," Ed said. "I don't have to."

Thomassy thought *We're both lying by omission. I haven't told him Francine was in the photos, too.*

"You know," Ed said, "I sure don't like the way the law works."

"In the end, nobody does. We just use the system because it's what we've got. What they've got is worse."

"Who's they?" Ed said.

□ □ □

166

Haig Thomassian had used the word *they* often in front of his son. *They* were the Turks who massacred Armenians. *They* were the cops you never saw except at Christmas with their hand out. *They* were nuns who married God instead of farmers. *They* were Jew counterfeiters who manufactured money inside their brains. Haig Thomassian hated to go to the movies to eat popcorn while the good guys won because when you went outside you realized that nothing had changed. Thomassy thought *Our theys are different now, Pop.*

He'd tried to discuss that with Francine, his father's *theys*. "He was wrong about nuns, Jews, and bureaucrats," Thomassy said. "He was right about the Turks."

Francine had said, "We have our Turks, too."

He'd meant to talk about his father and she was going to come back at him about him. He smelled it.

Finally she said, "George, you don't like the Russians much because they wear baggy pants."

"I know they're unreasonable," he shot back.

"You're absolutely wrong," her eyes were shouting at him, "they're perfectly reasonable. They know what they want, they wanted the same thing all along and they're getting it. Someone like you'd have to take to the hills in Afghanistan."

"I'm not going to Afghanistan," he shrugged, wanting her to stop.

"They couldn't let you walk the streets in Moscow."

"I'm not going to fucking Moscow."

"You've never been anywhere. You wouldn't give a damn if the Russians took over everything except Oswego and Westchester."

"Stop talking to me as if I'm a political idiot."   .

"You're defending a spy."

There it was. A cat he loved had left a mangled bird at his front door.

"Nobody's proven anything yet!" he yelled.

"Don't shout. You sound like every innocent of the last fifty years."

"I don't want you talking down to me. I'm not dumb!"

"Einstein wasn't dumb. But in my field he was as innocent as you are. Maybe worse. He let fellow travelers use him like a borrowed pen. But you, they'd see you couldn't be pushed around. If the Russians ever got their hands on you, George, they wouldn't put you on trial. They wouldn't try to force a confession out of you. They'd lock you up in a lunatic asylum."

"I'm not crazy!"

"That's just the point. You're an innocent. To them that puts you on the other side. To them you are *they*. And because you won't stop fighting, eventually they'd have to kill you."

He'd sat frozen, convicted, not wanting her hand to touch his fists. But she surprised him. She reached out and touched his face.

"Innocence is like a hymen," she said gently. "You can't put it back."

She had fallen in love with his strength. Now that she saw him split open, she loved him not less but more. Very quietly she said, "Your father would have fought in the hills with the Afghans, and so would you. That's one of the many reasons I love you. I don't want anybody using you except me."

□ CHAPTER TWENTY-TWO □

Somehow he knew it was a dream while he was dreaming it. He and Francine were twins, male and female, looking the same, running down a boardwalk together hand in hand, laughing in one synchronized sound.

He woke from the dream with a start, needing to tell Francine about it. She wasn't in the bed. He checked the bathroom. Not there. Grabbing a bathrobe, he ran down to the kitchen. He looked out the window. Her car was gone.

Each stair up seemed too high. He dropped back on the bed, weighed down by the pain of utter loss. She had had her three days away. After their talk hadn't it been understood that they would be together from now on? Even sons-of-bitches like Roberts kept their end of a deal. He and Francine hadn't talked about her moving back. He had assumed it. And what was that crazy dream all about? Did he make them similar because if there were two dissimilars on God's earth it was the two of them and he feared their differences would drive them apart? The ultimate test of a dream was like the test of any truth, was it fact or fancy, could you put it to someone on the witness stand: "What did you dream last night?" Objection! Sustained! Dreams were for couches, not for forums where you got sentenced on the basis of fact. That wasn't true either. In summation, he was the interpreter of the jury's imaginings.

Suddenly the face of the clock on the nighttable screamed: *You'll be late to court!* Quietly he got himself showered and dressed and, breakfastless, raced to the courthouse, unprepared for the day, wanting only to get there in time to have two minutes inside a pay phone before entering the courtroom.

She was at her desk in her office. To her simple "Hello, George," he said, "You took off without saying good-bye. We need to talk."

"Talk."

"Not on the phone. Phones are for teenagers. I want to see you."

"You'll see me soon enough."

"You going to drop in on court?"

"I can't."

"You could if you wanted to."

"I've got to go now, George."

As she hung up—safe for the moment—she realized how close she had come to telling him why she was forbidden to appear as a spectator. They'd warned her that a potential witness cannot observe the other witnesses testifying. George works with suspicion all the time, she thought, but he doesn't suspect me. When he finds out, it'll destroy us.

Scott Melling, so tall in the witness chair, seemed a purposeful contrast to both the gruff detective and the diminutive woman who had preceded Cooper. Melling's carefully trimmed black mustache-framed lips ready to answer whatever was asked of him with the precision of a British colonel out of some technicolor movie he had seen long ago. Among the other young professors at Columbia who strove to look casual, Melling, who had come from Omaha, was accepted as a colonial Englishman. For him it had been an excellent disguise for the ache he felt for having marrried half a dozen years ago the wrong beautiful woman, who had poisoned his brain with the smallest of small talk over breakfast and dinner and every before and after in bed till there was no more after. That military exterior was of a man on the hunt for a new bride so he could discard the old one. When he'd found Melissa Troob it had been across the Fullers' table, which to him had become a holy place, and when he'd first made love to Melissa it was in an up-stairs bedroom at the Fuller house. Fuller's death doomed the environment in which he'd come alive again. He would need the courage to face his wife and say why it was over, in truth because plain-brained as she was, she had never accepted any of the fic-titious reasons he had invented for wanting a divorce and she kept

169

insisting that she would not permit him to make an irremediable mistake.

Roberts took Melling's background and credentials quickly and as quickly got to the events of the night of April fourth. Dinner, conversation, the lateness of the hour, and the convenience of his host's having bedrooms upstairs in which guests were welcome. Had he heard anything during the night? Nothing special, nothing worth remembering. Only the scream in the morning. When he got downstairs, Mrs. Fuller and Ed had already pushed the professor into the shower but nothing they tried worked. He was still alive when the rescue squad took him away, but no, there was no doubt in his mind that Professor Fuller would die.

"Have you ever mowed the lawn for the Fullers?" Roberts asked.

"No, sir."

"Did you ever volunteer to do so?"

"Regrettably I did not, sir. Frankly it never occurred to me. Ed seemed to have that well in hand."

"Have you ever been in the Fuller garage?"

"No, sir."

"Your witness," Roberts said turning to Thomassy.

Thomassy understood Melling's type of man. "Mr. Melling," he said quietly, "a few moments ago you testified that you had never been in the Fuller garage. When Mrs. Fuller testified, she said quite clearly that you'd refilled the kerosene container, according to her memory, once or twice. In the light of that contradiction, do you want to change your testimony?"

"Objection!" Roberts said at the top of his voice.

"Overruled," Judge Drewson snapped. "The witness will answer."

Melling, who'd been sitting straight-backed, bent forward, both hands on the wooden rail before him. "I may have forgotten."

"Is your memory normally good, Mr. Melling?"

"Yes, it is. For important matters."

"Mr. Melling, in the context of this case the refilling of a kerosene container once or twice is a most important matter. Did you or did you not do so?"

"I may have. If Mrs. Fuller remembers that I did, I probably did."

"Does Mrs. Fuller also remember your lecture notes?"

The judge's gavel came down once. "Mr. Thomassy, will you please confine your questions to ones that are proper to this proceeding. Strike the question."

Thomassy sensed the jury turning against Melling. He was not about to let go. "Mr. Melling," he said, "did you at any time during the evening before the tragedy, or during that night, cause gasoline to be mixed with the kerosene in Professor Fuller's heater?"

"No, sir."

"Is that response as reliable as your response to my first question, or are you now telling the truth?"

"I'm telling the truth, damn you!" Melling said, half-standing.

Roberts moved toward the bench. "Your Honor, counsel is badgering the witness."

Judge Drewson said, "Mr. Thomassy, I think you've made your point. As for you, Mr. Melling, your outburst is entirely uncalled for. You are to answer all questions here and not to indulge yourself in expletives or I will be forced to hold you in contempt." Judge Drewson, who had liked Melling before his memory slipped from grace, might have responded in the same way to Thomassy's attack had he been on the stand. He had to credit Thomassy, though. He was performing for the jury, not the judge. He gestured to Thomassy to continue.

"Mr. Melling," Thomassy said, "you testified that you heard nothing during the night."

"That is correct."

"Your Honor," Thomassy said, "I'd like to have this schematic diagram of the upstairs hallway and bedrooms in the Fuller home marked for identification." He passed the diagram up to the judge.

Roberts was quick to say, "May I see that?"

"Of course," Thomassy said. "Your Honor, this sketch will lay the foundation for testimony as to the movements of various persons in the Fuller household during the hours preceeding the accident. May we have this marked as Defendant's B?"

"Have it so marked."

For a moment Thomassy wasn't sure whether Roberts would object. How could he? Roberts handed the sketch back to Thomassy, who handed it to Melling. "Mr. Melling, does this diagram seem to you to be an accurate rendering of the approximate location of the rooms on that floor?"

"It does."

"Would you say, then, that the bedroom closest to the stairs leading down was the room occupied by Miss Troob?"

"Yes, sir."

"And next to it is a bathroom?"

"Yes."

"Does that bathroom have three doors, one leading to the hallway, and one to each of the adjoining bedrooms?"

Melling tried very hard to preserve a neutral authority in his voice. "Yes," he said.

"And is the bedroom on the other side of the bathroom the one you occupied on the night of April fourth?"

"It is."

"I apologize for asking this, but did you by any chance use the bathroom during the night?"

"I may have," Melling said. "In fact I think I did."

"Did you enter it by exiting from your room into the hall and then using the hall entrance to the bathroom?"

"No, sir, I would have used the door leading directly from my room into the bathroom."

"Might not Miss Troob have locked that door?"

"I assume she might have while the bathroom was in use by her."

"I see. Mr. Melling, did you turn the light switch on when you used the bathroom?"

"Of course."

"Is that one of those ordinary switches that one hears or a mercury switch?"

"I remember it as being an ordinary switch."

"Is your hearing normal, Mr. Melling?"

"I've never known it to be otherwise."

"Then surely you would have heard the light switch when you flipped it on?"

"I assume so."

"But you said you didn't hear anything—anything at all—during the night. Is it not true that now that you have refreshed your recollection that you heard the light switch go on, perhaps the tinkle in between, perhaps the flush if it is your habit to flush, and the light switch turning off again?"

Melling's face was red with the strain of trying not to show his anger. Thomassy had accomplished his objective, and Roberts was on his feet objecting. "Your Honor," Thomassy said, "some people take an oath to tell as little or as much of the truth as they choose to tell at any given moment, but my client is here because charges were filed against him and not against the other two guests who stayed over that night."

The judge interrupted. "Mr. Thomassy, it may not have been clear to the witness that you meant your question literally. He may have thought you meant did he hear anything significant."

"Your Honor, I appreciate your attempt to clarify this matter, but I am not dealing with a semi-articulate witness who doesn't know the precise meaning of commonplace English words." Thomassy looked up at Judge Drewson. Again his choice was getting the judge annoyed or scoring his point with the jury. Thomassy opted for the jury. "Your Honor," he said, "I would like to pursue my line of questioning with this witness on the assumption he understands the meanings of common words unless the witness tells me to the contrary." Without waiting for the judge's reaction, Thomassy turned to Melling. "I will repeat the original question as it was asked of you by Mr. Roberts. Did you hear anything during the night?"

Everyone in the courtroom was waiting for the inevitable "Yes." Melling said it almost in a whisper.

"Well then," continued Thomassy, "besides the light switch and miscellaneous bathroom sounds, was there anything else you heard during that night."

Melling remained silent. He was no longer the unmoving guard at the sentry box.

"I repeat," Thomassy said, "did you hear anything else?"

So this was the way he was finally going to be able to get the message to his wife. Melling was about to speak when Thomassy said, "Let me help you. Specifically, did you hear anything from the room occupied by Ed Porter?"

With great relief, Melling said, "Well, yes sir. I heard him out in the hallway during the night."

"Was that after or before you used the bathroom?"

"After."

"When you used the bathroom, did you lock the outside door leading to the hallway?"

"Yes."

"Did you, afterward, open the door leading to the hallway?"

Melling blushed. "I may have forgotten to do that, sir."

"Then if Porter had to use the bathroom during the night, he would not have been able to get into it, is that right?"

"I suppose so."

"That wasn't very considerate, Mr. Melling, unless it was your intention to leave that door locked to prevent outside access to the bathroom between your room and Miss Troob's room. Is that a correct interpretation or is it not?"

Melling wasn't aware of having taken out his carefully folded handkerchief. He wiped the beading sweat from just below his

173

black mustache. "I suppose it wasn't very considerate. To Mr. Porter, I mean."

"Who, if he needed to go to the bathroom, would then have no choice but to go downstairs and use Professor Fuller's bathroom, not a very convenient thing to have to do during the night. Is it possible, Mr. Melling, that you *wanted* Mr. Gordon to use the downstairs bathroom in order to try to implicate him in a plot hatched by yourself and Miss Troob?"

"I resent that, sir."

"You resent the conspiracy?"

"I resent the implication that there was one."

"But Mr. Melling, if you had in fact visited the downstairs bathroom yourself for inserting gasoline into a kerosene heater or any other purpose earlier, it would have worked out just dandy to keep the upstairs bathroom unavailable to Mr. Porter so that he would be forced to go downstairs!"

"Objection!" from Roberts. "Your Honor, the defendant's counsel is asking Mr. Melling a hypothetical question, and such questions can only be addressed to an expert witness."

"Sustained. Strike Mr. Thomassy's last question."

"Mr. Melling, now that we know your hearing is normal and that in fact you have testified to entering the bathroom, turning on the light, using the bathroom, and hearing Mr. Porter later going downstairs because he could not use the locked-door upstairs bathroom, will you please tell us truthfully what other sounds you may have heard?"

Melling, poised on the edge of his cliff, jumped. "During the course of that night I entered the bedroom on the other side of the bathroom—"

"The one occupied by Miss Troob?"

"Yes."

"Did you go there to borrow a cup of sugar?"

"You know damn well why I was there, Mr. Thomassy."

"I am not a mind reader, Mr. Melling. The court stenographer is not a mind reader. His Honor is not a mind reader and none of the jurors can read your mind. This is a court of law in which you stated on direct examination that you had heard nothing during the night and it is clearly the right of the defense to know what you were covering up during the crucial few hours before Professor Fuller's life was forfeit."

"I had nothing to do with that!"

"You needn't shout, Mr. Melling. If a combustible mixture was put in the kerosene heater before everyone went to bed, perhaps it was the assumption of whoever did that that the person who might turn on the heater was the person denied access to the bathroom on the same floor as his bedroom and that the prospective victim was none other than Ed Porter!"

"That's crazy!" Melling said, out of control.

"What's crazy, Mr. Melling, your locking the hall door so that Ed Porter was forced to use the downstairs bathroom?"

"I didn't intend to inconvenience anybody."

"This isn't a trial about inconveniences, Mr. Melling. Very serious accusations have been made and it is imperative that in your further testimony you do not elide the truth. You know what 'elide' means?"

"Yes."

"Did you tell the truth when you said you heard nothing?"

"Not the whole literal truth, of course."

"Well, would you mind telling this court the whole literal truth of what you heard and did when you entered Miss Troob's room."

Melling was glad Melissa was not permitted to hear this testimony. But would she then perjure herself to protect his marriage?

"We are waiting, Mr. Melling."

Melling spoke slowly. "I went into Miss Troob's bedroom and made love to her. I love her more than I love my life."

"Did you say wife?"

"I said life."

Melling dabbed his once-neat handkerchief at the corners of his eyes. Thomassy felt sorry for the man. Roberts should have coached him better if he was going to use him on the stand. Thomassy had had to throw Melling in the jury's path so that they could watch him stumble over his deception. Maybe the ideal defense was to prove that everybody was covering something up. Everybody had something to lie about. Why pick one man to hang when the woods were full of fallible human beings?

If Melling had been a woman, Thomassy would have held out a hand for the lady's hand and helped her off the witness stand.

Roberts waited till Melling wandered disconsolately from the room, allowing enough time before calling Melissa Troob for them to meet in the outside hall so that by word or gesture Melling might convey to her that their cat had run free in the courtroom. Thomassy could have kicked himself. He should have asked that the next witness be brought in by a different door.

There was no denying that God had vested a strange beauty in Melissa Troob's face.

175

Roberts got her name and relationship to the Fullers into the record and then asked her only one question. "Did Scott Melling leave your room at any time during the night before you or he heard the screaming from downstairs?"

"No," she said.

"Your witness," Roberts said.

The bastard, Thomassy thought. He's put my red herring back in the barrel. "No questions," he said, letting the surprised Melissa Troob out to join her lover in the hallway, where they threw their arms around each other, oblivious, until the flashbulbs startled them, that photographers were taking pictures of them for everyone to see.

Thomassy's attention was drawn back to the courtroom by the sense that someone was staring at him. It was Roberts, tugging at his stupid vest, a restrained smile on his lips. Thomassy had told the law students *If you think your adversary is dumb, beware. If he's on a different wavelength, he could surprise the hell out of you.*

What was Roberts up to?

Suddenly Thomassy had a premonition, the way horses do before an earthquake. Roberts, his voice stentorian, was saying, "Your Honor, I call Francine Widmer to the stand."

□ CHAPTER TWENTY-THREE □

For a moment Thomassy thought Francine was coming down the aisle to where they would both turn to the judge, who, with a few ceremonial words, would pronounce them man and wife. The way things went now they could still be forced to testify against each other.

She looked determined, and determination made her radiant. Her radiance struck him like paralyzing rays. She was coming down the courtroom aisle to testify against his client, twist the case out of joint, offer the one link that could, by turning only one juror, turn the verdict.

He could stop her, of course. He could tell the judge they had a Wade-Simmons problem, non-notification of the defense before trial of a possible identification witness. Was Ned Widmer double-timing him? Was Francine betraying him?

As she passed the defense table he thought she would ignore him, but as inconspicuously as possible, like an amateur ventriloquist trying anxiously not to move her lips, she said, "Hello, George."

Thomassy glanced up at the bench. Judge Drewson had seen that. Then he felt the yank at his elbow and heard Ed Porter whispering, "What the fuck is going on?"

The worst thing that can happen between two people not indissolubly bound. Thrust on opposite sides, she is suddenly his adversary's pigeon. If she harms his case, he will have to pluck her feathers out in front of everybody.

Ed didn't repeat his question. He'd learned to leave Thomassy alone when he got that dark Armenian glare.

After Francine had taken the oath, Roberts began. "Please state your name."

"Francine Widmer."

When Roberts asked her, "Where do you reside?" Thomassy looked around the courtroom, expecting to see every man who thought her as beautiful as he did writing down her address.

"How are you employed, Miss Widmer?"

"I work for the American delegation to the United Nations."

"In what capacity?"

"As a political analyst."

"Describe your duties, please."

"I do research for the speeches delivered at the UN and elsewhere by the ambassador. I sometimes contribute some of the actual writing, a few paragraphs here and there."

"Would you say then," Roberts went on, "that you are employed for both your research abilities and your perception?"

Thomassy stood impatiently. "Your Honor, I don't see this line of questioning leading to something pertinent in this case."

Roberts came on strong. "Your Honor, this is one of the peoples' most important witnesses and her powers of perception are directly relevant to what will emerge in her answers to the next few questions."

Judge Drewson said, "I guess we'll both have to be a little patient, Mr. Thomassy."

Haig Thomassian's son folded himself down into his chair. Francine looked so damned self-assured. She and Roberts were sud-

177

denly of one class, the comfortably born, the comfortably educated, allies in control of the realm.

"Miss Widmer," Roberts continued, "did there come a time on the morning of September twenty-first of this year that you witnessed anything unusual on your way to work through the UN lobby and if so, would you describe it."

Francine glanced at Thomassy. He turned away.

"The lobby is usually crowded at that hour. There were quite a few people headed in both directions. Two people walking in the opposite direction from me caught my eye because a young man was attempting to catch their attention. The two men stopped just for a second. I think the young man was trying to thrust something at one of them, perhaps a piece of folded paper, I'm not sure. But that man turned on his heel and started walking rapidly in the direction from which he'd come. The second man then started walking rapidly in my direction, followed by the young man still holding the piece of paper, trying to catch up to him."

"Did he?" Roberts asked.

"I think so."

"Can you be more specific?"

"It seemed to me that the second man, in exasperation, stopped as if he'd decided to take the piece of paper just to get rid of the young man."

"Did you observe all this while continuing to walk?"

"No, I'd stopped."

"Why did you stop?"

"Because I recognized the two men coming toward me as members of the Soviet delegation, Igor Semyonov and Julian Trushenko. Semyonov is assumed by the members of our delegation to be KGB."

"To the best of your knowledge, is that unusual for a member of the Soviet delegation?"

"Not at all. It's just that Semyonov is assumed to be quite senior."

"What about the other man?"

"He's supposed to be an agricultural specialist."

"You mean he works the farmers' lobby?"

Roberts's crack drew some chuckles from the press section.

"Miss Widmer," Roberts continued, "during this interchange you observed did there come a time that you recognized the young man who attempted to stop or pass a note to the Russians?"

"I believe it was the same young man I saw briefly in the outer office of the defense counsel."

"Miss Widmer, can you tell us if you see that individual in this courtroom?"

She pointed at Ed, slouching in his chair.

"You're not pointing to the defense counsel, are you?"

"No, sir, the younger man sitting next to him, with the curly brown hair."

"No more questions, Your Honor."

Thomassy rose. Slowly he walked to the witness box. In the Mellon Lectures, he'd told the kids *One of the high arts of defense is the destruction of a credible witness.* He hadn't told them that the witness might be the person they most wanted to protect. He looked at Francine in the box, lovely, perhaps a touch afraid. *If you learn to fly the high wire,* he'd told his students, *you no longer have the option of missing.* Anything you say in court is not retractable; it's in the record for keeps.

"Miss Widmer," he said, "do you consider yourself to be a law-abiding citizen?"

"Objection!" Roberts shouted.

"Your Honor," Thomassy said, "that question is directly relevant to the impeachment of the character of this alleged eyewitness."

"You may proceed. Will the stenographer please repeat the question."

The court reporter, in a voice perfectly suited to his task, droned as if he was reading from the telephone book. "Miss Widmer do you consider yourself to be a law-abiding citizen question mark."

"Yes," Francine said, her voice sinking.

"Did you believe that what you allegedly saw transpire in the crowded lobby of the UN building was unusual or unlawful?"

"Unusual."

"Did you report what you saw to the police?" Thomassy asked.

"No, I did not."

"Did you report what you saw to any other law enforcement agency, the FBI for instance?"

"No."

"Then can you tell this court how you came to be a witness in this trial."

"I was subpoenaed by the district attorney."

"Are you trying to tell this court that the district attorney is a mind reader or did you in fact tell someone of what you saw in the lobby of the UN building?"

"I told my father."

The judge had to use his gavel to stop the buzz.

179

"What prompted you to tell your father of this alleged incident?"

"I recognized the defendant in the anteroom of your office, Mr. Thomassy."

"And what were you doing in my office?"

"I came to see you because you are my friend."

Again the judge had to gavel down the noise in the courtroom.

"You gave this court your address," Thomassy said, repeating it. "But isn't it also true that you have in fact been living in my house for the better part of a year, Miss Widmer?"

"Better or worse, yes."

She was angry at last. Let the jurors think this was some off-shoot of a lovers' quarrel.

"Miss Widmer," he said, "I asked you what prompted you to tell your father of this alleged incident. Would you please answer the question asked."

Francine hesitated for a second. "Because my father asked you to represent the defendant in this case."

The press section came alive like a swarm and had to be gaveled to silence by the judge.

"And what precipitated your father's involvement in this matter?"

Roberts was on his feet objecting even as Francine in a louder voice than Thomassy'd ever heard her use shouted, "I don't know!"

"May I remind you you are under oath," Thomassy said, and then snapped, "No more questions!" and sat down, leaving her desolate in the witness box.

Roberts was yanking at the bottom of his vest, trying to think of how he might restore the importance of Francine's testimony from the shambles Thomassy's tactics had left it in. Koppelman handed him a folded piece of yellow paper. Roberts glanced at it.

He tried his best. "Miss Widmer," he said, coming up to the stand, "are you certain the defendant is the person you saw in the UN lobby?"

"I object," Thomassy said, "Your Honor, I move that this witness's entire testimony be stricken as irrelevant and immaterial. The facts that the jury are considering have to do with an incident concerning a kerosene heater inside the Fuller residence. I don't see any connection between this testimony and that incident."

"With respect, Your Honor," Roberts said, "this testimony is relevant with regard to the defendant's possible motive in perpetrating his crime."

Thomassy felt the blood surging to his face. "I beg the court to remind the jury—perhaps the distinguished prosecutor as well—that the defendant is under our system innocent until proved guilty beyond a reasonable doubt and cannot be referred to as a perpetrator of anything until and unless a jury finds him guilty. May I request a conference at the bench?"

The judge summoned both lawyers to him. "Yes, Mr. Thomassy?"

"Your Honor, while I realize we are out of earshot of the jury, I am concerned that the matter I am about to raise will become part of the trial transcript and later seen by the jury."

"Mr. Thomassy," Judge Drewson said, "I believe I know how to conduct a trial without reminders from counsel. You always have the prerogative of appeal if I err. Say what you have to say."

Thomassy knew that however low he spoke, if the court reporter were to hear, Francine would hear. He could ask for her to be excused. He couldn't do it. She would hear.

"Your Honor," he said, "this is not a treason trial." He heard his own subdued words echoing in his mind. Thomassy cleared his throat. "None of the charges against the defendant allege that he was working for one government and passing on classified information to another government. Yet we must all be aware that a jury does not draw distinctions the way Your Honor and honorable counsel do, and if Miss Widmer's testimony is allowed to stand, there is the undeniable risk that even one juror will interpret some connection between Soviet officials and this defendant and react emotionally to the implied charge of treason rather than to a judgment of the facts at issue in the specifics of the indictment."

Judge Drewson, watched by everyone, could not let his own disquiet show. He didn't like what had happened to the justice system, people being tried under the grab-bag of the conspiracy statutes instead of for what they did do because the government couldn't prove it. He didn't like people being tried for perjury in lieu of what he thought of as their original crime that they later lied about. He didn't like mobsters having to be sent away for income tax evasion. He was doomed to judge an imperfect world under an imperfect system he had sworn to uphold.

"Mr. Roberts," he said more sternly than he might have under other circumstances, "none of the charges in this case concern the espionage statutes, which would in any event be a matter for the federal bench and not for this jurisdiction. I don't want the jury left with any implication that a possible sighting of the defendant trying to communicate with Soviet nationals at the UN is related to the crimes he is here charged with unless you are going to be able to produce witnesses who will clearly, concretely, and without ambiguity associate this defendant with a foreign government and address the issue of intent."

Roberst glanced over in the direction of Koppelman. Koppelman shook his head.

"Your Honor," Roberts said, "it is possible that the people may have access to photographs supporting Miss Widmer's testimony."

"Do you have such photographs?"

"Not yet, Your Honor."

"Are you certain you will have access to them?"

"No, Your Honor."

"And no witnesses such as I just described?"

"I have no such further witnesses, Your Honor," Roberts said.

"Your Honor," Thomassy said, "I have moved to strike Miss Widmer's testimony. I now move for a mistrial."

"Denied," the judge said. "Mr. Thomassy, I'm going to leave the testimony stand but when I instruct the jury I will make it clear that even if the other evidence offered provides them with sufficient proof that the defendant was the only possible perpetrator, they may consider Miss Widmer's testimony solely as substantiation of motive or intent. If they are not impressed by the other evidence beyond a reasonable doubt, I will tell them that they cannot consider Miss Widmer's testimony in any respect and are to treat it as if it were not given by her or heard by them."

Roberts objected to the judge's news in vain.

Thomassy said nothing. The breath of treason had brushed by. If it was by the skill of his argument, was he then the traitor?

As they went back to their respective places, the judge dismissed Francine.

You son-of-a-bitch, Thomassy told himself, *you love to win, but at what cost?* Francine was just being ushered out by one of the guards. She should have told him. He'd have told her to get lost so they wouldn't find her. And she'd have said he was obstructing justice. She's been contaminated by that damn UN mentality, moral farting into the wind, when the only thing that counted here or in the spats among nations was winning. Then why did he feel as if he had suddenly lost something irretrievable?

During the recess, Ed said he wanted to make a phone call in private.

When he returned, he seemed to have regained his self-confidence.

"Who were you talking to?" Thomassy asked him.

182

"Franklin Harlow."

"You thinking of changing counsel?"

"Of course not. I was merely asking Mr. Harlow if an attorney heard conflicting information from his client and from a so-called personal friend, did that make representation of the client difficult?"

"And what did Mr. Harlow say?"

"He said that given the blanket of confidentiality that exists between you and me that does not necessarily exist between you and a friend, you are to assume for purposes of this trial that what I say is what you act on. To do otherwise, Mr. Harlow said, would be against the code of ethics. You are *my* lawyer and you are bound to help *me*."

"I will talk to you later," Thomassy said. "If I talked to you now I'd tell you what I thought of you."

□ C H A P T E R T W E N T Y - F O U R □

Alice finally connected with Ludmilla Tarasova in her Central Park West apartment. She put Thomassy on.

"Miss Tarasova," he said, "do you know who I am?"

"I read the papers," she said, her accent guttural spice.

"I would like to call you as a witness in the Porter Sturbridge case."

"I don't think I have much to contribute," she said quickly.

"You know a great deal that I want the jury to hear and that I believe to be extremely relevant. If you would give me the courtesy of an hour of your time—I'd be glad to go wherever it would be convenient for you—I think I could persuade you that you would prefer to appear voluntarily rather than under a subpoena."

"I must speak to my lawyer."

"You can have him present if you like."

"I will call you back."

She was ready to hang up so he said, "You'll need my phone number," and gave it to her.

As he suspected, she didn't phone back. And so the following day he called Ludmilla Tarasova again.

"You are very persistent," she said.

"Have you spoken to your attorney?"

"He will be at my apartment at eight this evening."

"Would you like me to come an hour later?"

"You can come at eight, too, Mr. Thomassy. My lawyer and I have already spoken."

Thomassy reached Francine at her office. "I called you last night."

"I was out."

"I wanted to apologize," he said.

She left him hanging in her silence. Then, a flutter in her voice like a bird suddenly bereft of its air current, she said, "I'm sorry I had to testify. I knew how angry you'd be."

"I guess I was a bit rough with you on the stand. I'm sorry. It's the way the game is played."

"They say pretty rough things at the UN sometimes," she said, not meaning the touch of frost in her voice, "but it's not *personal*."

"Mine wasn't personal, Francine, believe me. We both got caught in somebody else's trap. I was hoping to see you this evening, but I have to go somewhere in connection with the case."

"I'm going out, too," she said. "No connection to the case."

"Oh," he said.

She, skilled mind reader, laughed. "Matilda Brewster's flying in for a quick visit to New York. We roomed at school. We're doing the night on the town. I can't let her stay at a hotel. And I can't ask her to stay at your place, so she's staying at mine."

"You're being decorous. There'd be no problem with her sleeping in the living room. Does she think you're still a virgin?"

Francine laughed. "Let's say that Matilda, like all married people, thinks unmarried types like us fuck all the time, and I don't want her staying up all night trying not to listen."

"Have a good time."

"If the show's good, we will. I know she'll enjoy dinner. I'm taking her to an Armenian restaurant."

"Very funny."

"George, I want to say something to you."

"Shoot."

"Are you listening carefully?"

"Sure."

"Sure you're sure?"

"Come on!"

"Despite yesterday," she said, "I love you."

He hated the way people parrotted each other, so he didn't say *I love you, too*. But after he hung up, he stared at the phone wonder-

184

ing whether, after law school, he had stopped learning about himself.

Thomassy drove down toward New York City, got off the West Side Highway at the Seventy-ninth Street exit, made his way crosstown through light traffic, saw someone pulling out of a parking space just east of Columbus Avenue and did what New Yorkers do—he backed up to claim the precious space. If you parked in a garage these days, you were taking a chance on the cassette deck vanishing or an unexplained dent that they'd claim was there when you drove in. If you left your car in the street, you could still lose the cassette deck, but at least no parking lot jockey would use his car to practice U-turns in reverse.

Ludmilla Tarasova lived in one of those grand old buildings he'd liked when he first came down from Oswego. Now, in addition to the doorman, they had a security guard and a TV monitor. The doorman looked him up and down to see if this unfamiliar male was a potential problem. The security guard called the Tarasova apartment, mispronouncing his name. The guard gestured him in.

He stood in front of her apartment door. He'd expected her to be standing there, the door open. After a moment, he rang the bell. He heard steps. Then he realized there was a peephole magnifier at the door that was at the height of his Adam's apple. He bent a bit so she could see his face. He heard the chain come off. Then the door opened.

He was surprised at how female a sixty-year-old woman could be. Her hair was shoulder length, and he could imagine her brushing it vigorously. Her eyes, dark in a bright face, looked at him as if with a glance she could fathom his thoughts. Her figure was spare, though fuller in the breast. She shook his hand with stark strength. "Come in, Mr. Thomassy."

He wished he was wearing a hat so that he could take it off. The apartment had a slightly musty smell, which was immediately explained by the thousands of visible books, lining the hall, and then the living room.

"I believe you know my lawyer," she said.

From his armchair, Archibald Widmer rose to shake Thomassy's hand.

□ CHAPTER TWENTY-FIVE □

As Francine made the right-hand turn from the service road into LaGuardia, she thought *Departures are from stages.* For her, airports, railroad stations, intercity bus terminals provided expectations of drama. According to the dashboard clock, in one minute Tilly Brewster was due to arrive from Detroit. Did that mean touchdown, arrival at the gate? Maybe the plane was ahead of schedule. Fat chance. And the baggage wait, at best, was twenty minutes. Though Tilly was coming for two days, she was always loaded with presents as if it were Christmas. Even in school Tilly had felt she had to buy her space on earth.

The parking lot was jammed. Francine spied a child-loaded station wagon backing out of a slot, and positioned her bright red Fiat. *Fight for the space if you have to.* No opponents, a potential fracas aborted, she slipped into the spot, got out, locked the door, and ran through the lot to the walkway, pushed the button on the pole. The light seemed to take forever to say "walk." When there was a momentary gap between taxis, she ran across to honking and made it, breathless, into the terminal. She checked the *Arrivals* side of the TV monitor: the plane was *in*. Down the stairs—don't run!—Francine scanned the grouped crowds waiting for baggage. "Tilly," she shouted, just as Tilly was reaching for her large red suitcase. Tilly glanced up, and the bag went by ungrabbed. They had a good laugh, hugging each other, till the winding carousel brought the red suitcase around again.

The bag retrieved, Tilly stared at Francine the way old friends permit each other. Finally Tilly said, "How do you stay the same?"

"I'm not," Francine said.

"You look the same."

"I feel different," Francine said.

"Ooooh."

"What's that supposed to mean, Tilly?"

"What's his name?"

"He's a crazy lawyer named George."

"Not the Princeton George who jilted Arabella?"

"This is an Armenian George. I told you about him months ago."

"I guess it didn't register. You know I never knew anyone who actually knew an Armenian," Tilly said.

"Maybe you did, and didn't know he was Armenian."

They both guffawed as if the word Armenian triggered the memory of how they once laughed together at school.

"Is he very handsome?"

"I don't know how to answer that."

"You're in love, Fran. It'll pass in three weeks. Don't give it a thought."

"It's been nearly a year, Tilly."

"Oh my God, what are Mummy and Daddy saying?"

"They're not in the prompting box anymore. Besides, my father dotes on criminal lawyers like George who—"

"He's not the man . . ."

Francine nodded. Tilly paid a moment's respect to the rape. They'd spent many hours on the phone around that time.

"How're the kids?" Francine asked.

"Would you believe Harriet is six and Frieda is nearly five? Harriet's in school, Frieda's in kindergarten."

"Ready for another?"

"Only by immaculate conception."

"The other way's more fun."

As Tilly fluttered words, changing the subject, Francine remembered that in school it had been Tilly's humor that had made her every girl's best companion. Each of them had swings and spirals, preexam, premenstrual, pre-big-date, but Tilly was the constant, that rarest of all human animals, an unremittingly happy person it was a pleasure to be with.

"I know, I know," Tilly said, under observation patting the sides of her hair. "Premature graylings before thirty are a sin against nature. A sin against my nature," she said, and her attempt to slough it off suddenly, like a squirrel jumping from limb to limb and missing, fell precipitously to earth. "Never mind about me," Tilly said, "where's your car?"

Francine took Tilly's bag. "Just out in the lot."

They walked side by side, the hurry, by understood mutual agreement, over. "Still the red Fiat?" Tilly asked.

"Twelve thousand miles older," Francine said.

"Sounds like me."

On instinct, Francine said, "How's Burt?"

"I hope dead."

Francine put the bag down. "What's the matter, baby?"

"It doesn't matter. Let's go on."

"Of course it matters. Tell me."

"What's to tell? The kids are with Mother. I can't stay in Detroit. Burt's squiring his new woman all over the places we used to go to together. He sees our friends. He sees my friends. He invites them to her apartment."

"Oh Tilly, I never guessed."

"*You* didn't? *I* didn't! I was the last goddamn woman in Detroit to know!"

"Are you separated? Officially?"

"We're not anything. I went to talk to Jim Magruder and he said that if it came to a divorce, he'd have to be Burt's lawyer, would you believe that?"

Francine opened the passenger side of the Fiat first so that Tilly could take her tear-stained face out of sight of passersby, then put Tilly's bag and the armload of presents in the trunk. As Francine turned the key in the ignition, Tilly said, "Since your friend's a hotshot lawyer, maybe he knows somebody who kills for hire and is willing to travel to Detroit."

Traffic sped away from the airport, racing the descending darkness. Francine tried to concentrate on the road ahead, watching for the Whitestone Bridge sign she had once missed and vowed never to again. In college, they had all expected happiness at the end of the line, an amorphous reward for getting through the tortured years, a vent into what they used to call real life, meaning a job or marriage, a settling without a settling down. Of all the boys they had dated then, Tilly's Burt had been the highest flyer, learning commodities trading from his father at the time that he learned to drive a car. He had scored with money made by himself while the rest of them were still on the family dole. Francine hadn't cared for Burt's talkathon—speak first, think second—but she had accepted him as she would have accepted anything that was good for Tilly.

"Watch out!" Tilly said.

"Watch what?"

"Didn't you see that car?"

"What car?"

Tilly pointed right to an ancient tail-finned white Cadillac. "He nearly sideswiped us. He came that close."

Francine pulled the Fiat ahead. When they were parallel with the

Cadillac, she glanced right. There seemed to be three Hispanic-looking men jammed into the front seat, all grinning at her.

"They're drunk," Tilly said.

"How can you know?"

"Burt drinks now. I know what drunk looks like. Let them get ahead."

Francine eased off on the gas pedal, checked her rearview mirror, and then clicked on her right-hand turn signal and moved over behind the offending Cadillac. Suddenly the Cadillac braked sharply, and Francine had to brake fast. She could hear the tires of the car behind her squealing, too.

"He's playing games," Tilly said. "He didn't have to do that."

Francine was glad they were now on the bridge. Carefully she pulled left one lane, then another, and then speeded up. "I'll tell the toll booth attendant," Francine said.

Suddenly the Cadillac was in front of them again, braking.

"He's crazy," Tilly said. "I thought they're supposed to be cracking down on DWIs?"

Behind them somebody was honking because they had slowed down in the fast lane.

Francine wondered what George would do. Would he go to the toll booth? He'd ram that damn car!

She'd moved right and right again to get away from the Cadillac till she had a clear path to the toll booths ahead. She had the quarters for the automatic toll machines, but she had to queue up for the manned booth. As she waited while car after car in front of her paid the Whitestone toll, she caught sight of the Cadillac going through the automatic collector somewhere to her right. When she reached the booth she handed her money over and told the young man, "That Cadillac that just passed through there, on the right, the driver is drunk. They've been driving recklessly."

"What do you want me to do, lady?"

"Can't you radio a police car? Something?"

"I can't do that. Look at the lineup behind you. Did you get the license number?"

"No. It's one of those ancient Cadillacs with tail fins. And white. There can't be more than one of them on the road up ahead."

"Come on, lady, move on."

Francine tried to spot something, an ID tag on the attendant, a booth number, anything. She'd tell George, he'd know what to do. He'd say the world was falling apart. She zoomed onto the Hutchinson River Parkway.

Tilly, whose mind was probably somewhere in Detroit, said,

"Look, Fran, I didn't know what your living arrangements were. I didn't—"

"You're staying at my place. We're staying at my place. He's got a house."

"Sure it's okay?"

"It's okay."

Francine had never liked the Hutchinson River Parkway, two narrow twisting lanes in each direction, one of those roads you couldn't wait to get off of. Suddenly, up ahead, there was something. Francine pumped her brakes, switched her brights on. In the right-hand lane, stopped, was the white Cadillac.

"I hope he's run out of gas," Tilly said.

"I hope his engine block cracked," Francine said, and they both laughed, and Francine pulled the Fiat over to the left and realized they'd both been wrong. The Cadillac was starting up again, it'd just been waiting for some more sport, preferably with the two young ladies they'd already given a few scares. There was no exit on the right, the double guard rail on the left, and cars behind wanting to speed up. Well, she had the space, Francine thought, the Cadillac was just starting, and she put her foot down on the accelerator, never dreaming that the Cadillac would dare pull into the left lane ahead of her.

"Watch out!" Tilly screamed, and Francine put her full weight forward on the brakes, screeching, stopping, and suddenly whatever it was behind them slammed into them, pushing them violently into the angled side of the Cadillac in front of them with an explosion of smashed metal and glass and sudden, terrible pain.

□ CHAPTER TWENTY-SIX □

Amid the chitchat of arrival, Thomassy decided that Ludmilla Tarasova's apartment was the kind of place he could imagine himself holing up in for weeks, eating small special meals of exotic foods, listening to music with his feet up, sampling her voluminous library. If Tarasova had been twenty years younger, he could have seen her as someone whose sharp mind and self-comfort made her a suitable companion for an arrogant bachelor like himself.

190

It was a good thing Ned Widmer couldn't read his mind. *Warn your daughter, Prospero. Every bright and interesting woman interests me.*

"Good to see you, George," Widmer said.

"I assume," Thomassy said, "your presence here is not a coincidence?"

Tarasova took charge. "Mr. Widmer and I have known each other many years. I haven't had the need of a lawyer until now."

Thomassy's was an old trick. *Don't answer the speaker. Talk to the weaker party on the other side.*

"Ned old boy, it looks like you're part of the federal witness protection program."

Widmer said cheerfully, "This case is in state court, George."

"Sure. And Perry and Randall are spectators. With all the international press, I'm surprised we don't get moved from Westchester to the Hague. What the hell is going on, Ned? I don't like mysteries I don't create for tactical purposes."

"No mystery. Miss Tarasova is the heir apparent now that Fuller's dead."

Tarasova, whose back while standing or sitting was as straight as a soldier's, bent as she calmly poured tea. She straightened up, handed Thomassy his cup. He thought she looked like a beautiful tree overseeing the lawn of life.

"I was asked to consult with Miss Tarasova more than a dozen years ago," Widmer said.

"On some pretext," Thomassy offered.

"Of course it was a pretext," Tarasova said. "In a society that allows you one phone call when you are arrested, I had to be given someone trustworthy to call, yes?"

"George," Widmer said, "you don't doubt that I'm worthy of trust?"

Thomassy sipped at the strong tea.

"I know how you feel, George," Widmer went on. "Nobody likes surprises. The fact is that I share your annoyance about the government's intrusiveness. In normal times. Most people—" He looked at Thomassy as if to be certain that Thomassy did not exclude himself. "—are not aware that we are at war."

Francine, Thomassy thought, *help me.*

"I don't mean the obvious fronts," Widmer continued, "Afghanistan, Poland, Cambodia, Nicaragua, all that. I mean the positioning. Photographic satellites, laser-armed satellites, silent submarines. People *notice* wars like they notice stock market crashes, too late. Some of us get involved at earlier stages because of coincidences. I met Perry at Yale. Miss Tarasova was born in the Soviet Union. We were introduced because this country needs her and she might one day need me. As now." Widmer leaned forward. "George, you've always sneered at lawyerlings who play by the rule and lose. We both should be grateful that we have some people in Washington who are not unlike you in a different arena. They are determined that the best way to win is to avoid the uncontrollable. The naive think counter-intelligence involves the keeping of secrets. Only in part, George. The clever part is letting the other side know the strength of some of our hands. The naive also think that intelligence consists of ingathering the other fellow's secrets. The real function of intelligence is using experience to evaluate what we know. Martin Fuller learned his trade the hard way. Miss Tarasova had the advantage of cultural as well as geographic osmosis. She may catch up very fast if you don't blow everything by putting her on the witness stand."

In his head Thomassy opened a door to admit a Ned Widmer he had not previously known.

"George," Widmer said, "the Soviets are chess players. We play checkers. Tarasova is one of our very few chess players. If you're calling her to the stand to acknowledge that twenty years ago she had a long-lasting affair with Martin Fuller, I don't see how that contributes to your case."

Widmer waited for a response. Instead Thomassy turned to Tarasova.

"It was my thought," Thomassy said, "that the jury should be aware of the many people other than my client who might have had a good motive to remove Professor Fuller from the scene."

Tarasova's face flushed. "Surely, Mr. Thomassy, you don't think—"

"I do think, Miss Tarasova, before I make my moves. No, I'm not suggesting you were in any way responsible for Professor Fuller's death. I'm sure you have an excellent, objectively verifiable alibi, witnesses you were with, et cetera."

"Of course."

"What I want from you is a roll call of all the political assassinations on behalf of the Soviet Union you know about from, say, 1931 through today."

Tarasova leaned forward. "Do you know who Trotsky was?"

He hated to say *vaguely*. "What's the relevance?"

"He was killed by a student he trusted."

"Where?"

"In Mexico. Coyoacan."

192

"I'm talking about right here in the United States," Thomassy said, anxious to get back to familiar turf. "Can you provide me with the précis of the assassination attempts here?"

Widmer interrupted, "That would be hearsay."

"I'm sure the judge would permit it as expert testimony since, I gather, Miss Tarasova includes KGB foreign operations in her lectures to students and, in fact, has an extensive section on that subject in her next-to-last book."

"Congratulations on your homework, George."

"Congratulate Francine when you see her next. The UN library's been very helpful."

"In other words, you're preparing to drag every red herring you can across the screen, as it were."

Thomassy clasped his hands together and pointed his two forefingers at Widmer. "Ned, I was hired through you to win this case. Why are you interfering? I'm beginning to find this whole thing ugly."

"You've dealt with the unpalatable before, surely."

"I've never defended a traitor."

Thomassy noticed the quickening of Tarasova's expression. He continued, "You want me to drop the ball?"

"Of course not!"

"Then pay attention. Have those photographs your friends from Washington showed me the other night gotten into the hands of the DA?"

"I don't know."

"Ned, let's not play games. Roberts knows about those photos or he's seen them. He didn't find out about them by getting overnight service under the Freedom of Information Act. He heard about them or saw them through your friends or by someone acting on their behalf."

"I swear I had nothing to do with it."

"You do now because if those photos hadn't attempted to connect Ed Porter with some Russians, the DA wouldn't have dared put Francine on the stand and I wouldn't have had to fight like a madman to destroy the value of her testimony." Thomassy lowered his voice. "And risk our relationship."

"Yours and mine, George?"

"Hers and mine! Her testimony is still hanging there as the only plausible intent they've been able to throw against my client. If one juror believes that Ed Porter was in cahoots with the Soviets, I won't succeed in what you fellows wanted me to do."

Widmer was avoiding eye contact.

"Or," Thomassy continued, "was I set up for some propaganda stunt? We got him a real hotshot defense lawyer, but the Soviet connection hung him anyway, was that the plant?"

"George, I swear I knew of no ulterior motives."

"You just let them use you. And then me. Well me is not used to losing ball games. Now that the jury's heard Francine's testimony—I don't give a damn about it being stricken from the record—I'm going to have to demonstrate that if this was not an accident but murder with intent, and if that intent is linked to a foreign government, that a lot of others might have acted for that government, that it wasn't a one-on-one between Ed Porter and his mentor."

"George, some of your phrases escape me. What does one-on-one mean?"

"Somebody killing somebody else for a reason that's between them. I've come to think that Professor Fuller died because a foreign government wanted him dead—I hope to hell it was a foreign government and not our own."

Tarasova leaned forward. Her voice was not unkind. "Mr. Thomassy, you are much less naive than most Americans, but when it comes to understanding how the Soviet government accomplishes its purposes, I think you have a lot to learn."

The phone rang. Tarasova went to answer it. Thomassy'd been called a prick by district attorneys whose cases he had flattened. But naive? He'd fled Oswego to escape naiveté.

"It's for you," Tarasova said to Widmer. "Your wife."

Widmer looked at Thomassy for a moment. Thomassy hoped he wasn't going to make a small joke about how his wife always knew where he was. Widmer said nothing, went to the phone.

Tarasova touched the side of the brass samovar. "Some more tea? It's still quite hot."

"Thank you."

As she was pouring, Thomassy took in the striking shape of the woman's face. She must have been a very great beauty. He could understand why Fuller was unable to restrict his relationship with her. Her brain invited friendship. Her face invited more.

Thomassy looked up to see Widmer in the doorway of the living room. For the first time since Thomassy had known him, composure had fled from Widmer's expression, his blanched skin stretched across the skullbones of his face.

"There's been a terrible accident," he was able to say hoarsely.

"Who?" said Thomassy, rising.

"Francine was picking up a friend at the airport. They were both in intensive care at the hospital in New Rochelle. One of them died."

Thomassy's heart, dressed against surprises all his life, was caught naked. "Which one?"

"They couldn't say. The contents of their purses were all over the place. We need to get down there. Priscilla will be there before we will."

Tarasova already had Widmer's coat.

"Thank you," he whispered.

She kissed his white cheek, a blessing for the distraught.

"Look, George," Widmer said, "I'm not certain I can drive right now. Could we go in your car?"

Thomassy, needing the camouflage of motion, said, "Come on, then!" and headed for the door.

□ CHAPTER TWENTY-SEVEN □

Some time ago Archibald Widmer had determined that the inadequately brought-up human animal was at the mercy of his adrenalin, as if predators were still at large. The virtue of a proper upbringing was the ability, in the presence of stress, to curb one's inner dance with a presumably inherited biofeedback mechanism. In Thomassy's car, more than halfway to their destination, he said, "I keep remembering a comfort attributed to Niebuhr. It's like a nursery rhyme in my head. *God grant me the serenity to accept the things I cannot change, the courage to change the things I can, and the wisdom to know the difference.* His lungs accepted air. "You must have heard that before?"

"I think so," Thomassy said.

"I don't suppose you care for that kind of thing?"

"No."

"I imagine you think it's a slaves' litany."

"Something like that." *Tarasova had called him naive.*

"Will the Armenians find serenity when the last Turk is dead, George?"

"Somebody will hatch a new Turk."

Without plan, they were having a conversation each of them might have postponed forever. What the hell, Thomassy thought, he might as well know why the daughters of men like him flee to men like me. "Ned," he said, "in my end of the law, you know what serenity is good for? For making your antagonist nervous."

"Did Francine know how manipulative you were?"

He's talking of her in the past tense. Oh pioneers, the Indians are winning.

"You knew how I was," Thomassy said. "You brought her to me because she wanted Koslak in jail for what he did to her. Would you have picked me if you wanted a kid-glove lawyer? You picked me because you knew I knew what human nature looks like with the ski mask off and can deal with it."

"That you did. And very well. I guess we're used to a different way of negotiating with our adversaries," Widmer said.

"I can't let you off with that, Ned. When one of your daughters gets into trouble, you don't hire some Chamberlain to negotiate by walking around with a white feather seeing if Hitler wants his ass tickled."

Widmer sighed. "Yes, I brought her to you. For better or worse."

"If that's a question, you'll have to ask her." Yes, the present tense. He was her life-support system now, the kind you don't find in hospitals.

He remembered the biggest faux pas in his life. His law school friend Jeremy had a younger sister who died of meningitis the week before graduation. The night before the ceremony, he and Jeremy had gone out for beers. When they'd sat down, Thomassy had said to Jeremy, "How's your sister?" as if she were still alive.

He was betting on life, though the odds were exactly even. He glanced over at Ned Widmer, a man who was brought up to believe in fair play, got caught in Perry's web, and was now trapped in the same vehicle with his daughter's lover, who'd just come down off the trees in Oswego, New York, and operated as if the twentieth century were a jungle.

They entered the hospital, Widmer walking slightly ahead. Thomassy thought of hospitals as holding pens where the soon-to-be-back-among-the-living were sorted out from the soon-to-be-among-the-dead. The sorters were doctors. Not too many would put up a strong defense if they thought the odds were high. Too much work. Too little hope of winning. Corporation lawyers in white coats. He was too rough on Widmer. Practicing hanky-panky for the spooks took more guts than playing racquetball in Chappaqua.

Widmer was up ahead at the desk making inquiries. *A father has precedence*, Thomassy thought. If he and Francine were married, he'd have precedence. Was there something more to marriage than a contract?

Widmer, leading the way, motioned for Thomassy to follow. Widmer was walking fast. Then Thomassy saw Priscilla Widmer coming toward them in a rush. She took her husband's hands. He couldn't hear what she was saying.

Thomassy, the outsider, wanted to bellow *I love her, too. Tell me.*

"She's out of shock. She's stable," Priscilla Widmer said.

"Who?" Widmer asked.

"Francine. Of course, Francine. Oh Ned," and her arms were around him.

Thomassy, a waxworks dummy, suddenly felt his blood coursing, his face hot, the madly happy machine of his heart pumping. Priscilla Widmer was noticing him, and he took her extended hand. "George," she said, "I'm glad you're here. I think she was asking for you. She's sedated. Her words aren't clear."

Widmer said, "Tilly's dead?"

Death was not final until it was acknowledged. Priscilla Widmer nodded as if her neck were in great pain.

"What happened?"

In self-defense, Priscilla Widmer waved the question away. If it had been his mother, Thomassy thought, she'd be screaming at God.

The Widmers stood at the left side of the bed, Thomassy at the foot. Most immediately noticeable was the tube in Francine's nose, the death drain. And a nurse whose stare said *All of you are interrupting.*

"'lo," Francine said to her mother and father. "'lo," she said to Thomassy at the foot of the bed, lifting several fingers of her right hand in a kind of wave. Her left arm, in a splint, was suspended from above.

The complex instrumentation behind the bed monitored what? Her life? The hospital bill? NO SMOKING. OXYGEN IN USE. I am not smoking. We're all using oxygen all the time. By not looking at the three Widmers he was allowing a family moment in which he could not be included. When he finally couldn't keep from looking at Francine, her eyes caught his and he knew she wanted him to step closer. Mother and father parted to let him step between. For a moment he thought he would drop to his knees as he had as a boy in church.

She was trying to say something. He took her proferred hand. He made the soundless words *I love you* with his lips.

Suddenly the nurse seemed to want all three of them to go, but Francine shook her head, trying to speak.

Thomassy leaned down.

"Nunfair," he heard her say, struggling to articulate despite the nose tube. "I buzz driving."

"It's okay," he said.

Francine shook her head. "She ad hids."

Priscilla Widmer touched Thomassy's elbow. "What's she saying?"

"She had kids."

"Has anyone called Tilly's husband?" Priscilla Widmer said.

Francine closed her eyes.

The nurse was being insistent. Thomassy ignored her. Francine was opening her eyes, wanting to say one more thing. "Wadn't an accident."

And then they were hustled out into the corridor. Widmer's eyes looked awful. "Was she saying it wasn't an accident, George?"

"Get ahold of yourself," Thomassy told the older man. "Let's get the facts."

The policeman who had been sitting on the bench outside stood up. "Mr. and Mrs. Widmer?" he asked.

Thomassy, his precedence lost, listened to the officer asking, "Will your daughter be all right?"

"I hope so," Mrs. Widmer said.

"The best we can make out," the policeman said, "is that your daughter's car was in the middle of a three-car pile-up on the Hutchinson River Parkway. The station wagon in back of her ploughed into her when she stopped short. She left a lot of rubber on the road. That old white Cadillac she hit was angled in front of her, no blown tires, must have turned into her lane sudden like."

Archibald Widmer, schooled in reticence, almost touched the policeman in trying to get his attention. "Did the driver of the white car try to cut her off on purpose?"

The cop took his eyes off his notebook. "Sir," he said patiently, "I wasn't there. The Cadillac had three drunk spics all in the front seat. One's in the hospital here. He's been charged with DWI and reckless endangerment."

"My daughter says it wasn't an accident," Widmer said.

"What about vehicular manslaughter?" Thomassy cut in.

"That's up to the DA," the officer said.

Widmer said, "Does anyone know why they did it?"

The cop shrugged. "Personally, I think they were just girl chasing. The one in the hospital, he's been arrested twice before, once for nearly going into a toll booth instead of next to it. The other time it was on complaint of a woman who got his license number and pressed charges."

Thomassy said, "Ned, I know what you're guessing. Believe me, the Russians wouldn't hire three drunks, one with a record, to stage a fake accident. Give them credit. They're as smart as we are. This has nothing to do with the trial. Just animal life. Those drunks were playing games on the road."

"They ought to be shot," Widmer said.

The cop looked miffed because only the mother was paying attention to him. "We'll do everything in our power to pin it on the perpetrator," he said, trying to say *perpetrator* with brio, the way they always did on television.

Widmer put his arm around his wife.

"It seems so gratuitous," she said. "So unnecessary." She seemed to be trying to keep herself from tears.

Thomassy suddenly felt himself outside the family circle again. Widmer was hugging his wife. What was Thomassy supposed to do, hug the cop?

□ CHAPTER TWENTY-EIGHT □

The rooms they provided for lawyers to confer with clients were small courthouse cubicles, windowless monks' cells with nongreen, nongray, dirty walls warning the client: you screwed up; now if your lawyer screws up, you'll spend years in a room this size.

Ed Porter, sitting opposite Thomassy, chewed on a cuticle.

"Take your hand away from your mouth," Thomassy said.

"Look, Mr. Thomassy, would you mind not speaking to me that way?"

"What way?" Thomassy wanted to be at the hospital.

"I had enough of that do-this, do-that shit when I was a kid."

"People assume nail biters are guilty. I don't want you nibbling at your nails in front of the jury. Let's finish this. I don't have much time.

When he phoned the hospital, they said they were moving her to a private room. That had to be good news. He'd always thought of the intensive part of intensive care: we pay a lot of attention to you here because you're nearly dead. The hospital said the nose tube had been removed. Whatever blood or fluids had collected in her stomach were out. She could talk intelligibly. *Oh could that woman talk intelligibly!*

She'd spoiled him for all the other women whose talk was so predictable he had to resist the temptation to finish their sentences. What if she said *George, I really don't think we should keep seeing each other. We're not going anywhere.* She wanted some kind of pact. We are engaged to be engaged. That's as useless as a letter of intent. A contract was a contract when both parties signed it. What was he afraid of? Permanence? His father had said to him, *If your brain talk like your enemy, go for swim in river.* I would have drowned if she'd gone under. Is that what the link was, a life raft that'd stay afloat even if only one of them could manage for a time?

"I'm waiting," Ed said.

Everybody wants your exclusive attention, but the brain goes its own way. *He's paying for your time, Thomassy. His father forked over a big retainer so let's pay attention to getting his boy defended. Forget Francine for a few minutes. You're a minister in the middle of a sermon.*

"I was just thinking," Thomassy said.

"Sure." Ed nodded. *He doesn't give a damn what happens to me.*

"Tarasova is testifying without a subpoena. I've promised to limit her to certain areas. She's going to be our only witness besides you. Your ass may depend on how that goes. And to handle her, I need some straight answers."

"From her?"

"From you. I want you to think about your answers. People who think while they're talking instead of ahead of time are a danger to themselves and everybody else. Ready?"

"You're the one who's in a hurry."

"Put your hands on the table."

"What for?"

"I'll tell you later."

Porter put his hands on the table.

"Did you kill Martin Fuller on your own or under instructions from someone else?"

"Are you crazy?" Porter stood abruptly, knocking over his chair.

"Pick up the chair and sit down," Thomassy said. "If you react that way to questions from Roberts on the stand, Clarence Darrow couldn't get you an acquittal. Cool it. Think. Did you kill Martin Fuller by—"

"I heard the question."

"Keep your hands on the table."

"I didn't kill Martin Fuller period. What's the next question?"

"There isn't any," said Thomassy, rising. He'd watched Ed's hands.

"Where are you going?"

"You just flunked my lie-detector test."

Ed's face was the color of panic. "You're supposed to be defending me, not attacking me."

"I think you ought to think about getting a new lawyer, some schmuck who'll make sure you get hung."

"What's wrong? What's changed things? You trying to hold my father up for a higher fee?"

"You're cutting your throat, kid, you're losing your case," Thomassy said, heading for the door.

Ed yelled after him, "It's not your case, it's my case. Tell me what the fuck you're doing!" but the door had already closed.

□ C H A P T E R   T W E N T Y - N I N E □

The sidewalks seemed filled with people determined to get in his rushing way. Ned Widmer was the logical one to call. He'd put Thomassy on to the case, he needed to be told first that he wanted out. Ned would say *You don't quit in the middle of a game.* That wasn't Ned, that was coach's talk. *It's important in ways you don't understand. Please don't quit.* He understood as much as Ned understood, they were both put-up jobs, puppets for someone else's intentions. Was that what Ed Porter was, were they three of a kind?

In Thomassy's head, murder cases he'd handled flipped over like cue cards. Some of his clients had disgusted him from the word go; some he'd despised only when he'd seen through their pity-me papier-mâché masks to the stinking glob of sick brain inside. *You don't quit while the patient's on the operating table.* That's not Ned, either.

□   □   □

201

The empty phone booth smelled of recent piss. He looked down and stepped away from the stain, put his dime in, got Ned's secretary, asked that his meeting be interrupted. He imagined Ned took the call because he suspected it was something about Francine. Thomassy said, "It's not about Francine. I need to talk to you, Ned. I'm thinking of talking to the judge, seeing if he'll let me off the case."

"What's happened?"

That was when he had to tell himself that nothing in itself significant had happened, just a congealing of suspicions and smells. "I don't know what Ed Porter is guilty of," he said.

Widmer said, "It would be wrong under the ethics code to quit now. I've got people just coming in. I can't talk. We'll meet after Tarasova's testimony. Okay?"

He didn't say goodbye. He just hung up. *I thought people like Ned Widmer didn't do things like that.*

The thought grew in his head like a balloon. Everybody did the unexpected sometime. Ned Widmer. Francine Widmer. George Thomassy. Ed Porter Sturbridge.

If anybody was up there watching us handing out sentences to each other, He'd have a good laugh, wouldn't He?

The clerk administering the oath to Tarasova spoke in a drone that drained meaning from the words. Tarasova seemed amused as she said "I do" and lowered her hand. She was promising to tell what no self-respecting intellectual could promise: the whole truth, never known, its bits and pieces sewn together by memory, embroidered at the interstices. When she was sixteen, an idealist wanting to right the wrongs of the world, she would have refused with derision the offer of an untrue oath. What is it one learned? One learned to live.

Thomassy, from twenty feet away, observed her curious combination of dress. A skirt and jacket of bristly wool were set off by her white ruffled shirtwaist blouse, femininity accentuating authority. She turned to face him, as if to give him his cue. *A gazelle,* Thomassy thought, *with a steel trap at her feet in case anyone ventures too close.* There were women you could win by charm. Tarasova's demands were more severe: brains, wit, strength.

Thomassy began, "Would the witness please tell the court her name, place of birth, and occupation."

The TV artists were already sketching her in case her testimony should prove short.

"My name is Ludmilla Tarasova, I was born in Odessa. I am

sixty-two years of age, and I am a professor at the School of Soviet Studies at Columbia University."

He hadn't asked her age. Was she getting her seniority on the record?

"Professor Tarasova, would you tell the court where Odessa is?"

She looked at him as if he had asked where Chicago was.

In the Mellon Lectures, he had told the class the essence of examining a clever witness was to establish control. Sassy answers would be stopped by the judge. But facial expressions disdaining the ignorance of the questioner would be seen by the jury.

She said, "When I was born, Odessa was in Russia. The country is now called the Soviet Union." *Naive young man.* She might as well have said it. Her expression conveyed it.

It was time for his gamble. He wanted the jurors to believe her. She was his witness. If he attacked her, their instincts would rally to her corner. If he destroyed her credibility in the process, he'd lose his gamble. He had to enhance her credibility by pinning down one lie that would make him seem the enemy.

He looked at Tarasova and hoped she would forgive him. Then he said, "Professor Tarasova, are you now a citizen of the United States?"

"Yes. I was naturalized in 1945."

"When you filled out your naturalization application, did you answer all the questions truthfully?"

She turned to the judge, as if for help. Or was it the district attorney she should look to? She was Thomassy's witness. What was he trying to do, impeach the testimony she had not yet given?

"I can't remember," she said. "It was a very long time ago."

"Professor Tarasova, a moment ago you took an oath to tell the truth, the whole truth, and nothing but the truth. Was it your habit to tell the truth in 1945?"

"My dear Mr. Thomassy," she began. No one had ever addressed him in court that way. "What one imagines to be the truth when one is young is often altered by experience. I will tell you the truth as best I can today and not look back to when you and I had less experience of the world. May we go on?"

In the courtroom, Thomassy did what most men try to do: to subdue. But when alone with a woman, she was at the center of his attention, his eyes, his words, his mouth, his tongue, his strength, his care. He decided to make love to her.

"Madame Tarasova," he said, almost in a whisper, then turning his back to her and walking toward the jury, he continued, "you have been asked to appear here because of what you know. If we could turn to someone more expert for the answers we are seeking, I assure you I would have done so." Leaning back against the jury box, he faced her. "Because it is to your expertise we have come, my questions are directed toward establishing your qualifications and your authority, please understand that." He moved across the space between them. Truce. She could be herself.

Tarasova's nod was that of an empress giving permission to her minister to visit her quarters privately. The rules were agreed.

"Well then," Thomassy said, "can you please tell the court when you left the Soviet Union."

"After the Moscow trials and before the Nazi-Soviet Pact."

Women normally dated things from the births of their children. "Would you please be more specific?"

"The year was 1937. I cannot be precise about the month. It was a long walk, not in a straight line. I am not sure when I crossed the border."

The remark drew a small laugh from some of the reporters.

"And where and how did you enter the United States?"

"Hmmmmm. A bit complicated. Let us say that the legal time was from Canada. I have been a legal resident for more than two-thirds of my life."

"Where were you educated?"

"In Odessa, through *gymnasium*, high school, and here Barnard, and Columbia."

"Professor Tarasova, you said you teach at the School of Soviet Studies at Columbia University. Do you have a specialty within that broad scope, a specialty perhaps characterized by the subjects of your books?"

Roberts stood, objecting. "Counsel is leading the witness, Your Honor."

"I withdraw the second part of the question, Your Honor," Thomassy said. It didn't matter. He'd got his message across.

"I have perhaps two specialties," she said. "The KGB, which, now that the former leader of the USSR has had the same specialty, makes it less of a specialty."

The judge didn't do anything about the laughter in the courtroom because he couldn't help laughing himself.

"My second specialty," she continued, "may be said to be the evaluation of data in order to attempt to predict future conduct."

"Without going into great detail, Professor Tarasova, can you tell us what kind of data?"

"Certainly. We know more about Joan of Arc than we know about most of our contemporaries because everyone who ever

204

knew her, from infancy on, was interrogated at great length during two trials. By comparison we know very little about the leaders of a closed society. However, there are bits and pieces gleaned from the press, defectors, other sources."

"Do you mean intelligence sources?" Thomassy glanced at the third row, where Perry and Widmer were sitting as strangers, separated by others.

"All sources are intelligence sources," Tarasova said, smiling. "My role is to put these pieces together—please understand I am working on a jigsaw puzzle with missing pieces—and come to some conclusions about the likely future conduct of given individuals if they act consistently with their past conduct. I know that when we speak of political science, computer people smile. I daresay that there is less downtime in the practice of our science than in the running of computers."

She got her laugh again. *It's okay*, Thomassy thought. *They're liking her.*

"Is or was there anyone in your field, Professor Tarasova, who specialized in the same kind of work?"

"Oh many people have written about the KGB, sometimes unknowingly," she smiled, "but in my second field very few, most notably the late Professor Martin Fuller."

"Did you ever study with Professor Fuller?"

Eggshells.

"Yes. We worked together for many years."

"Were you surprised to learn that he died suddenly under unusual circumstances?"

"Objection!" Roberts was adamant.

Judge Drewson called Roberts and Thomassy for a brief conference at the bench. When they were back in place, Thomassy said, "I withdraw the question." He removed a sheaf of paper from the manila folder he picked up from the defense table. "Professor Tarasova, can you identify the contents of these pages?"

Roberts was on his feet again. "May I see those before they are shown to the witness?"

"Of course," Thomassy said. "As soon as they are identified, I expect to have them entered into evidence as Defense Exhibit H."

Roberts glanced at the top page, flipped through the rest. "In that case," he said, handing them back.

Thomassy handed the papers to Tarasova. "Can you identify these?"

"Oh yes," she said, "they are illegal photocopies of pages from one of my books."

"If it please Your Honor," Thomassy said, "I could enter a copy of the book. I thought entering just the relevant pages would make life easier for the duplication of exhibits if it becomes necessary. I don't mean to get into matters of copyright law."

Judge Drewson addressed the witness. "Professor Tarasova, I understand your feelings about having pages from your book copied without permission."

"It's all right," she said.

"Then," Thomassy said, "will you summarize what is on those pages?"

Roberts objected again. "Your Honor, the jury is perfectly capable of examining those pages and reaching its own summary conclusions as to their contents."

The judge tapped his impatience. "I see nothing wrong with the author characterizing her own pages, if that will speed the process of this court. Overruled. Will the court reporter repeat the question for the witness."

Tarasova didn't need the repetition. She said, "This is a list of known executions within the continental United States from 1931 to the present."

"Executions by whom?"

"By the KGB, of course, and its predecessor organizations."

"Executions of?"

"Americans. And other nationals living here."

In the press section, pens wrote rapidly. Judge Drewson asked to examine the pages.

In Thomassy's peripheral vision he could see Roberts standing. *The son-of-a-bitch is ready to rip.*

Judge Drewson handed the pages down to the clerk. "Admit Defendant's Exhibit H for marking."

"Your Honor," Roberts said, his Adam's apple bobbing, "I don't see the relevance of the line of questioning unless defense counsel is implying that the defendant's name will appear on that list in the next edition of Professor Tarasova's book."

You jerk, Thomassy thought. He didn't have to object. Judge Drewson, trying to restrain his reaction to Roberts's outburst, summoned them both to the bench.

Before the judge could speak, Thomassy said, "I move for a mistrial, Your Honor."

"I tried to head that off. Motion denied." The judge turned his wrath toward Roberts. "I would appreciate it greatly, Mr. Roberts, if you would remember that I am here to judge relevance, and the implication in your remark was—"

206

He stopped in mid-sentence to see what the commotion was about. Thomassy and Roberts turned.

A stocky, blond-haired man of forty with tortoise-shell eyeglasses had entered the rear of the courtroom after it had been closed to further spectators because of the absence of seats. The court officer at the door attempted to stop the man, who brushed the guard's hand away and moved across the rear of the room and down the right-hand aisle, the court officer hurrying after him. Everyone in the news section had by now also turned around to watch the source of the interruption.

The intruder attempted to move into the one row that had an empty seat.

"Your Honor," the court officer said at the top of his voice, "I have reason to believe this gentleman has a concealed weapon on his person."

The judge used his gavel to quiet the courtroom. He nodded to the court officer who'd administered the oaths, a signal to aid the other officer.

Quickly Thomassy strode back to the defense table, stood between Ed and the spectators.

Even at a distance Thomassy could see what had attracted the alert guard's attention. The man seemed to have some bulk under his jacket in the vicinity of his left armpit. Suddenly Thomassy's gaze caught an anomaly. Everyone in the courtroom was now watching the stocky man, who had managed to squeeze by other spectators and seat himself, the people next to him visibly pulling away from him. Yet Perry, unperturbed, was staring not at the man but at Thomassy. Just for an instant. And then, turning his attention in the same direction as everyone else's.

The first officer had removed his weapon from his holster with his right hand, and with his left was gesturing vigorously to the interloper to come back out to the aisle. Thomassy thought *Some innocent people are going to get hurt.* Then he felt the tug on his jacket and looked down. Ed Porter, still seated, was trying to attract his attention, make him bend down. When he did, Ed, terrified, whispered, "Who is that man?"

"I don't know," Thomassy said.

And then the three people between the stocky man and the aisle scampered into the aisle out of the way and the guard moved in, pointing his gun at the man's head. The second guard had now drawn his weapon also.

The stocky man stood up and raised both hands above his head. "My name is Ivan Christov," he said at the top of his voice. "I am

207

employee Soviet delegation to United Nations. I not have gun." He continued talking loudly in Russian. It sounded like a speech he had prepared.

Carefully, the court officer came close enough to reach the Russian's jacket. He unbuttoned it, and reached under the man's left arm. Surprise registered on the guard's face. He withdrew a handful of balled paper. He motioned to the other guard to cover for him, and with care he motioned the Russian to lower his arms and remove his jacket. The man was wearing a shoulder holster, the leather straps clearly visible. Sticking out of the holster was the rest of the paper wadding.

Judge Drewson turned to Tarasova. "What is he saying? Please translate what he is saying."

Tarasova, her face impassive, said, "He wishes to seek political asylum in the United States. He says he has much information of vital importance to the United States that he is willing to reveal to the proper authorities if his defection is greeted with political asylum."

The judge gaveled for silence. "The jurors will return to the jury room. They are not to draw any inferences from this event to this case and are not to discuss this incident among themselves or with others." As soon as the jurors were out, the judge instructed the guards to bring the Russian forward. There was no stopping the activity in the press section.

"Ask him why he chose this courtroom as a place to defect," the judge said to Tarasova.

Tarasova asked the question in Russian. The stocky man replied.

"He says it is safest for him to do so in a public place with many witnesses, particularly newspaper people from this country and many other countries present. He apologizes for the intrusion and wishes to be turned over to the proper authorities."

The judge saw that the reporters couldn't be contained a moment longer. "The court is in recess until tomorrow morning," he said, as the reporters headed for the phones.

The judge indicated to Tarasova that she could leave the witness box. He beckoned her closer. He also asked Thomassy and Roberts to approach the bench. Thomassy turned to the ashen-faced Ed. "Take it easy, kid," he said, "you'll pop a blood vessel."

One man who had not been bidden approached the bench. Perry said, "Your Honor," and laid a plastic ID card in front of the judge. "This event was not entirely unexpected. I took the precaution of arranging for a warrant for Mr. Christov's arrest from a judge in the Southern District. I am prepared to take him into custody. I have two federal marshals outside."

Judge Drewson jerked the lapels of his robe. "You mean to say you knew ahead of time this might happen?"

"Mr. Christov sought the advice of others as to the safest way to defect. He didn't want to be stopped. He didn't want to chance being drugged and taken to an Aeroflot plane at Kennedy on a stretcher. The people he talked to apparently advised him to make his declaration in a public place with the press present."

"You had the nerve to suggest this courtroom for your purposes?"

"I don't know who made that specific suggestion, Your Honor."

"Are you usually a casual visitor at county trials? What are you doing here, Mr. Perry?"

"I have been delegated as an observer on this case."

"By whom?" Judge Drewson's anger had not abated.

Perry glanced down at his ID card.

"Your presence here, Mr. Perry, could be prejudicial to the outcome of this trial. And your seeming foreknowledge of this interruption—I don't believe you didn't know more than you are saying—is an intolerable interference. I will reserve judgment as to whether you are in contempt of this court. I am going to require a lot more information from appropriate authorities before I will consider condoning what appears to me to be a staged public arrest in the midst of an important trial that may have been severely compromised by this action."

"Your Honor," Perry said. "I am sure everything can be explained to your satisfaction."

"Miss Tarasova," the judge asked, "would you be good enough to ask Mr. Christov where he got the idea of making a public defection in this courtroom?"

Before replying, Christov glanced at Perry, then mumbled something in Russian, which Tarasova had to ask him to repeat before she understood.

"He says, Your Honor, that he cannot say more. He is afraid for his life."

◻ CHAPTER THIRTY ◻

The trial had begun to disassemble Thomassy's view of the functional world. If you went to see a musical comedy, he thought, and a pretty girl came out on one side of the stage and a handsome fellow on the other, you knew the plot. They'd be kept apart by some villain, and get together at the end. That's the way people like things, good guys and bad guys. Perry Mason in the courtroom. You always knew how it would come out.

In actual courtrooms Thomassy was used to surprises engineered by him. Who had arranged that defection right in the middle of Tarasova's testimony? Was Perry still pulling the strings?

Whatever Tarasova thought, he was not naive. When he came up against an assistant DA like Scotty, as he had several times, a decent man bewildered by ambiguity, you could see the man's eyes pleading with the priest on the bench to relieve the strain on the altar boys. If you comforted Scotty, if you attacked everybody but him, he became grateful, a bit careless, and you won your case.

Or if you tried a case in front of a judge like Humberto Maldonado, anxious to be accepted by the gringos and to maintain his composure, looking like he'd died up there with his eyes propped open, all you had to do was goad the prosecution's chief witness to explode like a spic, and the judge would come to life on your side, coming down on whoever was behaving just the way the judge's mother and father had probably behaved, riding every emotion like a killer wave.

And then you'd run into a young lawyer playing Henry at Agincourt with such verbal resonance he missed seeing the naked belly in front of him when he had a skewer in his hands. Thomassy saw courtroom moves like a chess player, building questions two, three, four, and springing the zinger, check. Though the boy in him sometimes longed to revert to the days when you always knew which side everyone was on, he'd remember the fat boy he had protected and who had betrayed him. In life, if Perry Mason didn't cover his ass, plan, prepare, dissimulate, purposefully obfuscate, then clarify on his terms, Perry Mason would lose. Haig Thomassian had fled the Turks for the safety of Oswego, New

210

York, where they didn't massacre Armenians, just beat their sons up, and gave them an incentive for moving on. Would Francine some day think him a fool for not wanting to be a DA or a judge or running for some political office because ambiguities unsettled the other guys, and he didn't want to get caught in the same trap? Would she damn him for cloistering himself? For living in Dickens's world of the easily tagged? Or was he himself, because of this damned trial, suddenly vulnerable to the icebergs that were rising all of the way out of the sea to confront him, with all the world's television eyes watching.

That had been his dream on waking that morning: George Thomassy with a harpoon trying to spear ice.

Walking down the hospital corridor looking for Francine's room number, Thomassy thought *To hell with the trial. Everything is gravitating toward her. Charles Darwin, you son-of-a-bitch, is this how the species survives?*

Thomassy opened the door of the room, but did not cross the threshold. For a second he'd expected to see her propped up on pillows reading, as she'd been on some weekend mornings when he'd gotten out of the shower.

She was lying flat, staring at the ceiling. The light was streaming in the window on her face. He remembered how dark it had seemed in the intensive-care unit.

She'd heard the door open, turned her head slightly.

"It's me," he said. She looked shrunken under the sheet, a thin mummy in a large bed.

She said almost inaudibly, "Come in." Her voice reached him as if from across water.

Her broken left arm was no longer suspended from the ceiling. Without realizing it, he had stopped halfway to her bed. She cleared her throat. "It's not contagious."

He came the rest of the way quickly and took her right hand. It was like someone else's hand, without warmth, damp.

"I look terrible," she said.

"No, you don't."

"The nurse let me have a mirror."

"You look fine. It's a miracle you weren't smashed worse. What do the doctors say?"

"The damage wasn't divided equally between Tilly and myself."

"The doctors didn't say that."

"I said it."

211

"Your father has a thing he quotes about the serenity to accept things you can't change."

"I can't accept. Burt called me."

"Who's Burt?"

"Tilly's husband. He said I was a reckless driver. He's never been in a car with me. You know how carefully I usually drive. It was those men."

"Sure it was. I saw the police report."

"Burt screamed at me. He said he didn't know how to take care of two little girls. He said did I want to take Harriet and Frieda since I'd murdered their mother."

Francine was sobbing as the nurse came in, looked at them both, jumped to the wrong conclusion. "You'll have to leave, sir. The patient can't be upset." The nurse was younger than Francine, a kid with a starched white cap.

"He's not upsetting me," Francine said between sniffles, holding tight onto Thomassy's hand.

"I have to take her temperature," the nurse said to Thomassy.

"There's no point to taking her temperature right now," Thomassy said. "You can see she's upset. It's likely to be elevated."

"I have to put it down on the chart with the time."

Thomassy put down Francine's hand and walked toward the nurse. "Take yourself and that thermometer out of the room," Thomassy said. "Now."

"I'll get my supervisor."

Thomassy tried to lock the door behind her. There was no lock. He took one of the chairs and propped its back under the handle, doubting it would hold.

When he returned to her bedside, Francine said, "I love the way you are." She let a suspicion of a smile show. "You don't take shit from the world the way the rest of us mostly do."

Francine took a tissue from the box and touched the edges of her eyes. "How's the trial coming?"

"It's getting interesting."

"Oh George, you're like my father. You're not telling me anything. They won't let me read newspapers because the print comes off on the bedsheets. Hospitals are terrible. What's going to happen to the men who caused the accident?"

Thomassy let go of her hand long enough to pull his chair closer to her bedside. "Don't strain yourself," he said. "Whisper."

"Who's doing something about it? You said you'd look into it. If you love me, don't lie to me, George. Were they charged? What'll happen?"

"Nothing."

Francine's face flushed. "You can make them do something. Those men caused the accident on purpose. You believe me, don't you?"

"You're getting yourself worked up."

"You're getting me worked up. I counted on you."

She dropped his hand. She turned her head away.

He had to tell her. "I got the names of the three men in the Cadillac from the police report. I can't ask favors of Roberts with the trial on."

"Favors!"

"That's what they call it when you poke your nose into a case that doesn't concern you."

"*I* concern you."

"As far as they're concerned, I'm not your next-of-kin or anything. Just a lawyer looking to make trouble for them. I talked to an assistant prick in Roberts's office. The line is that the three men in the car all say that you smashed into them."

"They were drunks girl-chasing. They were reckless on purpose. They drove into our lane at an angle—"

"I know, I know. But the assistant DA said there's the three of them, and they'll find family and friends to swear they were with them just before and they hadn't had too much to drink and don't chase girls in cars. They have regular jobs. There'll be ten, twelve witnesses on their side. They don't like to prosecute against odds like that."

"What about the people in the car behind me?"

Thomassy lifted his shoulders as if to say *I'm not to blame.* "They're from Kansas. They gave a statement to the police. They said they were sticking around just for the two days it took to get their car repaired. The DA's not going to pay for them to be brought back here."

"But they saw what happened! *I* saw what happened!"

"Take it easy, Francine. Your best corroborative witness is dead."

He couldn't stop her sobbing. Someone was rattling the door from outside. A strong female voice was saying, "Open this door at once."

Francine tried to retrieve enough control to speak. "What about the toll booth attendant?"

"You said he wouldn't even put in a call to have their car stopped. He wouldn't want that to come out. He's not a witness you can count on."

"You mean they're not going to do *anything?*"

"The three of them were banged up. By the time someone took a blood sample in the hospital, their alcohol count was below the legal limit. The one with the cleanest count claimed he was driving."

"What about the insurance company?"

There was loud knocking on the door.

"Your company will pay for your car, minus the deductible. They'll go after their insurance company—if they've got insurance. Tilly's husband could file a civil suit."

"He's glad she's dead. He won't have to pay her alimony."

Thomassy had to take the chair away from the door. There were three of them out there, the young nurse, the supervising nurse, and a male hospital attendant.

"We're trying to have a private conversation," Thomassy said. He went back over to Francine.

"That's some justice system you work in," she said, pulling her hand back.

"I never called it a justice system." He meant the world. "They think of this as difficult-to-prosecute vehicular homicide. I'm glad you didn't get hurt worse."

"What hurts worst is Tilly. We were friends for life."

"You'll have to leave now," the supervisory nurse said.

"I'll be back," Thomassy said to Francine.

"Where are you going?"

"I'm going to pay a visit to Ramirez."

"Who is Ramirez?"

"The car was registered in his name. I'll bet he was the one driving.

The hospital attendant, a six-foot-two ham-handed neuter, had obviously been told to see him all the way out the front door. Thomassy went straight to his car, watched the attendant in the rearview mirror. The son-of-a-bitch stayed there till Thomassy drove off.

He drove four or five blocks till he saw a gas station with a phone booth. He pulled up, took out his wallet, checked the card on which he'd written the names. He dialed the hospital's number. "Information," he asked. When they came on, he said, "Room for Emilio Ramirez, please." "Hold on," the crisp voice said. The voice

214

came back on. "Four-six-nine, I'll connect you," but Thomassy hung up.

He drove back to the hospital, found a space in another part of the parking lot in a section that said DOCTORS PARKING ONLY. In front of it was a door marked "Staff Entrance." He walked in as if he owned the place and went straight for the stairs up to the fourth floor.

He found 469. It was a ward with six beds, three on each side. He looked for a Peurto Rican face. There were two, next to each other. The chart of the first one indicated admission two weeks earlier. The other one was admitted the same day as Francine. And the name was Ramirez, Emilio.

"You from the insurance company?" Ramirez asked.

Why not? Thomassy thought. He nodded, pulled over a chair.

"Mr. Ramirez," he said. "You're in trouble. The home office report says you were the driver."

"So? So what?"

"One of the women died."

"I told the cops. Her car hit us. I tell you the same thing I told the other insurance man."

Thomassy would have liked to yank the pillow from under Ramirez's head and put it over his face. The son-of-a-bitch could have killed Francine, too.

"The story's come out," Thomassy said.

"What story?"

"About you fellows drinking."

"Who said?"

"Witnesses. And another saw you nearly sideswiping the girls' car before you came to the Hutch toll booth. They had three calls on the police special number saying your white Cadillac was parked in the right-hand lane. The car behind the girls' had two people in it and they both swear you swerved your car in front of the girls' on purpose to scare them."

"That's lies. All lies."

"Keep your voice down, Mr. Ramirez. Remember, the company is on your side. I think you'd better get yourself a lawyer. You could get fifteen years."

"You crazy?"

"Your lawyer ought to cop a plea and get you inside as soon as possible."

"Inside? You nuts."

"You know the girl that survived? Her father is the mob's lawyer. You know what they'll do to you if you're walking around

215

loose? They might even try to get you while you're still here. They might even be able to get at you in jail. Mr. Ramirez, you'll be lucky if all they do is cut your balls off. Take my advice."

Thomassy got up and started toward the door of the room.

"Hey," Ramirez called. "Insurance man, wait a minute!"

Thomassy didn't stop.

From his office, he called Francine. Her room phone didn't answer. Maybe she was getting X-rayed or something. He called back in ten minutes and she answered.

He told her what he'd done.

"Oh George, you'll get into trouble."

"You found trouble without looking for it. Maybe I should learn from you."

He heard her breathing on the line. Then she said, "George, I have to get well fast. I don't want another woman running after you unless I'm around to trip her."

"I'm safe," he said. "I've got my cruise control on."

He was glad he'd made her laugh. She sounded alive. She'd sounded half-alive before.

She said, "Are there others like you?"

"Sure. I just hope you never find one."

They hung on, listening to the electricity on the line.

Finally she said, "What do you think that Ramirez person will do after your visit?"

"He'll hire a lawyer. He'll check around. He'll get some gray hairs. Maybe I'll follow up with a phone call. If someone figures out it's a hoax, who would they look for?"

"You're on TV a lot these days. He'll recognize you."

"So what. Like you said, the justice system stinks. You could search the statute books for a year and you won't find anything I did in them."

She laughed a second time. "You know what daddy always used to say. Some day I'd find a really nice man."

"That's somebody else, not me. Really nice men lose. All the time. Everywhere."

"Don't lose me, George."

CHAPTER THIRTY-ONE

Thomassy, finally home, the rest of humanity shut out, sat in his living room, his legs up on the ottoman, a drink at his side, the evening paper spread before him. DEFECTION BY RUSSIAN OFFICIAL DISRUPTS TRIAL. Thomassy, a tight steel spring all day, read the story twice before his mind strayed.

He had never counted himself among the lonely of the world. He would rather listen to Mozart at home than in a crowded concert hall surrounded by strangers. If, at the beginning of some particular evening, he had a sudden appetite for companionship, there were several women he could call who, if home and alone, would be likely to say something like *Come on over, George, if you don't mind sharing a casserole.* What any one of them would also share was a friendly kiss at the door, a bottle of good wine that Thomassy could be counted on to bring, and after dinner, the woman, energized by hope, was quick to touch, the kisses not casual now, honey stirring in the pot, the erogenous brain longing for the gentleness to become less gentle, and the welcome final nerve-end spasms that after rest brought peace.

This evening he did not reach into his jacket pocket for his phone book. His loneliness, he realized, was for a specific other person.

Was this continual longing for Francine a weakness? Once, when he was fifteen, his father, whose true love was killed by the Turks, had said to him *George boy, you think tough as nail? Nails bend. Armenian needs be tough as hammer.* Hadn't he gone out into the fucking world as a hammer? If you were a good enough hammer, they wanted to use you. Clients, women. Why was he bending now? When he was roaring, any woman could stroke the lion's head, but now the lion trusted a particular woman to hold his head in her arms. In the hospital, amid the instruments of intensive care, he'd found fright, a courtroom spinning out of his control, and suddenly it didn't matter whether you were forty-five or twenty-eight, he saw it could happen any time, a brick from a building, an aneurysm, a crazy driver on the road. You just couldn't live forever.

217

He loved her. It wasn't capitulation. It was two people hang-gliding in the same direction over the rest of the world.

The telephone clanged into his thoughts. He strode to answer it. Her voice said, "Find any cute nurses to keep you company while I'm laid up?"

He laughed. Like a balloon filling. And she laughed too. And he laughed louder, celebrating their life.

□ CHAPTER THIRTY-TWO □

Judge Drewson had asked both Roberts and Thomassy to a meeting in chambers, a return to the war.

Nobody shook hands. Civility could contaminate.

"I have four things I want to say to you both," the judge began. "You two don't like each other. I accept that. But this trial is an adversary proceeding, not a spitting contest. Which brings me to the second point. The purpose of this trial is for a jury to determine, on the facts, whether a particular defendant is guilty of a particular crime with which he is charged. The third thing is that we have had an unholy interruption in our trial that must not permit these proceedings to be tarnished. Of course it is inevitable that the brouhaha yesterday is going to affect some of the jurors in some way none of us is wise enough to determine."

The judge looked at each of them in turn.

"I feel obliged," he said, "to advise you that I had a phone call from Washington. Mr. Christov's defection was genuine. The reasons he gave for doing so in a public place were also genuine. But . . ." He knew he was on dangerous ground and chose his words carefully. "I must ask that this next point be in confidence. Do I have your agreement?"

Roberts nodded too quickly, Thomassy thought. *Was he in on it?*

The judge was waiting for Thomassy's agreement. He couldn't seem to be uncooperative while Roberts was kissing ass. Thomassy nodded.

"The government suggested this courtroom as the locale for the defection because they wanted to send a signal to the Russians. One of the things yet to be written in the late Professor Fuller's manuscript was an assessment of the younger members of the Politburo based on whose protégés they were. That information is desperately needed now. Mr. Christov is in a position to supply some of the facts needed by the people who will be making that assessment now that Fuller is dead. The Soviets are apparently much stronger than we are with agents in place in Britain, France, West Germany, and here that have not yet been identified. We apparently have an advantage in that it's largely a one-way street with defections from East to West. Christov's defection couldn't have been more timely. It could focus the Politburo on their internal power struggles and away from the Middle East, Africa, and Latin America, where their clients have been gaining ground."

Thomassy thought he saw uncertainty flicker in the judge's face. "Gentlemen," the judge said, "I'm no expert in foreign affairs. My expertise lies here. I know that each of you might have grounds for a mistrial. If granted, that would be a great and in my judgment unnecessary expense for the people and for the defense. I hope my sharing a confidence with you will abort any such thoughts you have had overnight. I want to say that in my instructions to the jurors I will tell them to disregard the scene we witnessed yesterday. I will focus them on the issues in this case. I have a lot of faith in what happens once jurors are closeted for discussion. My advice to you would be to do whatever you feel you must do for the record, but to consider the consequences. Moreover, I want you to know ahead of time that I find it inadvisable for either of you to interrupt summations. Remember that if either of you will have reason to appeal—and I don't like to have my cases appealed any more than anyone else on the bench—the grounds will have to come from the trial itself and not the summations. If either of you waxes eloquent, I'll rub that wax off. Understood?"

They both nodded. Thomassy didn't like judges talking kindergarten to him. Maybe it was meant for Roberts.

"My last point, Mr. Thomassy, is this. Professor Tarasova's testimony was interrupted in a way that required me to ask her to translate some things that have nothing to do with this trial. If you feel you must continue with her testimony—and if you, Mr. Roberts, feel you must cross-examine—we'll just pick up where we left off. May I have your thoughts?"

Thomassy, as always, did his homework at home. But last night's thoughts, the phone call from Francine, and his thoughts about the defection left him unprepared. "May I have a minute, Your Honor?" Thomassy asked.

"Take your time," the judge said, and left them in his chambers.

□   □   □

"I'm sorry about your girl friend," Roberts said when they were alone.

"Thank you. I'm sorrier about her friend."

"I gather the driver of one of the other vehicles had a strange visitor in the hospital," Roberts said.

"Oh?"

"It wasn't you by any chance?"

Thomassy looked at the key chain across Roberts's vest. Roberts looked down as if his fly were open. "Anything wrong?"

"Why don't we stick to this case right now."

"I was just being civil about your girl friend. I understand how you feel. I think you need to be careful."

"Thank you." No point in getting Roberts angry.

"Tarasova's testimony sent a lot of red herrings swimming in front of the jury," Roberts said.

"We had to look at all the possibilities."

"You going to continue with her testimony?"

"If I don't, will you cross?"

"You'd like to redirect, I imagine. Take them through all that KGB garbage again. If you let it go, I'll let it go."

When Judge Drewson reentered, Roberts said, "We've had a chance to discuss the matter."

"I assumed you would. Gentlemen?"

"Your honor, I am obliged to move for a mistrial," Thomassy said.

"I know of your obligations, Mr. Thomassy. Your motion is denied."

"In that case, Your Honor," Thomassy said, "I won't resume Professor Tarasova's testimony."

"Good," the judge said. "Let's get the show back on the road."

When Tarasova was dismissed as a witness, she wanted to take a seat in back of the courtroom, but her throat was dry as if from fever and so she went out to take a long drink at the water fountain before returning. As she raised her head from the fountain and touched her handkerchief to the corner of her mouth, she saw Leona Fuller coming out of the courtroom toward the same water fountain. Before Tarasova could turn away Leona saw her and stopped. They were ten feet apart, twenty years of memory spinning between them.

Tarasova nodded her head. Leona's bright eyes blazed. Footsteps clattered on the marble floor all about them, but they sensed only each other, isolated in remembrance.

Leona nodded.

So much time had passed, they might have shaken hands, but they did not. Tarasova stepped aside so that Leona might have a clear path to the water fountain. Leona did not move. And so Tarasova, instead of going back into the courtroom, which belonged to Leona now, headed for the exit, the air, and the world outside.

Tarasova, walking around the courthouse, let the memories come: Martin Fuller, the lion lover, so enormously physical. Her fantasy had been to eat his brain. What a tempest they had been! What fun they had had!

Enough. The breeze cooled her face. The walk did her good. The all-clear sounded in her head. Leona had had him back for twenty years. His insurance was *hers*. *Hers* the proper widowhood. But his mantle was Tarasova's. She, once Martin's other wife, must return to the trial. It was his brain that they had stopped.

□ CHAPTER THIRTY-THREE □

During his Mellon Lectures, Thomassy had told the law students, "Over a period of time you can tell as much about a man by his choice of clothes as his choice of a wife. Clothes are easier to change. What's more, the defendant's wife, if he's got one, doesn't sit at his side in court. But his clothes are there, and they talk to the jury all the time."

The usual courtroom costume for someone Ed's age was a dark suit, white shirt, and a conservative tie designed to make jurors feel they weren't watching a "young person" but someone who was on the way toward being an accepted part of the community once these flimsy accusations against him could be got out of the way.

"I don't want you looking like you'd got yourself ready for a wedding," Thomassy had said to Ed before the trial. And so Ed wore slacks, a sweater over a solid-colored sports shirt, and a corduroy jacket. For his appearance on the witness stand, however, Thomassy had Ed substitute a cream-colored button-down shirt and a knit tie. The sweater under the sports jacket remained. "I'm going for a young professorial look," Thomassy said. "An almost authority."

"Do I keep my fly open or closed?" Ed said.

"We're not trying to cop insanity," Thomassy snapped. "We want serious attention paid to your answers. I don't want to have to appeal this case. Think you've got the answers straight, or do you want to rehearse again?"

"I'll be okay."

"Remember, the DA is going to be bobbing up and down with objections, sometimes just to rattle you."

"Don't worry."

"The judge might pull Roberts and me over to confer at the bench. That leaves you hanging in the witness chair with the jury watching you twitch."

"I won't twitch."

"The whole idea of having a living witness instead of an affidavit is that you form as much of an impression from how someone says something, and how he looks when he says it, as from what he says."

"I got it, I got it. You have any idea what kind of Spanish Inquisition Ph.D. orals are like? With two, three years work on the line?"

"You've got thirty years on the line here. When I'm through with you, you'll have to face a new script I didn't write. In his cross-examination, Roberts'll try to show inconsistencies in your testimony. He'll make you look shifty, he'll get you nervous, he'll throw you off balance. He's a prick, I've seen him work. He doesn't care if you're guilty or innocent, he only gets a passing grade if the jury finds you guilty, understand?

"Do you care?"

"Care what?"

"If I'm innocent or guilty?"

One of the notations in Thomassy's devil book said *Never let a client know your verdict. If you opt for innocence and lose the case, it'll be your fault. If you opt for guilty and win the case, he'll think he can get away with anything the next time as long as you're his lawyer.*

"I'll tell you," Thomassy said, "it doesn't matter what you are anymore. Just be grateful your lawyer isn't innocent."

Before court convened, Ed said to him, "You know I don't believe in taking the oath."

"You could have told me earlier," Thomassy said.

"Is it important?" Ed asked.

"Its omission would sure as hell come across as important. Most normal people take the oath without even thinking about it. I want

222

you to come across as a normal person. If you can't put your hand on the Bible and affirm the oath in a way that sounds like you mean it, I'm not putting you on the stand."

"You're blackmailing me," Ed said.

"That's right."

"I'm a free person," Ed said.

"Temporarily. If you want to cut your own throat, you can do it under somebody else's auspices."

"State your full name," Thomassy began.

"Edward Porter Sturbridge, sir."

Attaboy.

He asked Ed where and when he was born, where he went to school and graduate school, what his majors and minors were, and how he came to select Soviet Affairs as his field of special interest.

"Because of its incontestable relevance to our future," Ed said.

"Who do you mean by 'our'?"

"The United States, of course. If I were making a choice of major today, I might opt for China."

"Would your choice of such countries as subject areas be because you thought of studying the potential or actual enemies of the United States or was your interest derived from a desire to see us emulate their governments?"

Roberts was on his feet. "Your Honor, I have to object. This is a murder trial, not a classroom."

Judge Drewson slowly turned the ring on his fourth finger in a full circle, as if invoking time in the hope of invoking thought. "I will let the question stand. All of the charges involve intent. The jury is entitled to know all it can about the defendant's intentions, including those that relate to the work that brought him and Professor Fuller together."

"Thank you," Thomassy said, then turned back to Ed with a nod.

"I believe," Ed said, "that if political science is to be of value in practical affairs, foreign governments should be viewed objectively rather than as friends and enemies. The U.S.S.R. was our ally in World War II. Now the very Chinese government that excoriated the U.S. for thirty years because of its backing for Taiwan, is considered an ally of sorts. Times change. Conditions change. If political science is to be even partially scientific, it must involve the accumulation of fact and perception, not the buttressing of a prior theory or view. Otherwise, we will never be able to adapt to changes in our subject matter. I believe that's what Professor Fuller taught and the principle that I hope I learned from him."

Well, he pulled it off, Thomassy thought. The perfectly reasonable young specialist. He bet Roberts was thinking something like *That son-of-a-bitch is going to try to make his client sound like a saint.*

Thomassy asked, "When did you first meet the deceased, Professor Martin Fuller?"

With care, Ed described the first of Fuller's lectures he had ever attended. He had, of course, read Fuller's masterpiece and some of his other books, but hearing the incisive mind at work was, Ed said, "an electrifying experience that changed my life." In response to further questions, he went on to describe how he had qualified to attend a post-Ph.D. seminar given for Soviet Affairs specialists who were planning to make a career in the foreign service.

"Did you intend to pursue such a career?" Thomassy asked.

"No, sir," Ed said.

"Did Professor Fuller know that when he admitted you to the seminar?"

"Yes, sir. He said that since American policy toward the Soviet Union was so unstable, it was always useful to have knowledgeable experts work outside the government as he always had. In fact, he welcomed my taking the course because by that time we had established a kind of mentor-student relationship outside the classroom."

"Can you explain to the court what that entailed?"

"Well, that's when I first started being invited to his home along with others, getting a chance for long one-on-one discussions, too. I had a feeling that in Professor Fuller's head was the most valuable method for understanding another political system and how it functioned that existed anywhere in the country and I was determined to learn whatever I could from him directly, or by inference and osmosis."

Good boy, we wanted words like that.

"Now then, Mr. Sturbridge—" He'd prepared Ed for the fact that he would use the name. "With His Honor's permission I'd like to ask you a question not normally asked in the courtroom. Have you ever belonged to any political party?"

Judge Drewson looked over in Roberts's direction. Roberts did not seem inclined to object. "You may answer," the judge said.

"No, sir," Ed said.

"Let's narrow that a bit," Thomassy said. "Have you ever belonged to the Communist party?"

"No, sir."

Thomassy didn't hear the answer, as if a sudden deafness had descended on him in which he could only hear the voices of two women, Tarasova proclaiming him naive and Francine, trying to help him, explaining that Christopher Boyce hadn't belonged to a party or a movement—he'd just hated enough to focus on the biggest enemy in sight, his father's country, and had given the Soviets a present of all three guardian satellites. Had Ed given them another gift he thought they'd want, the stopping of Fuller's brain?

Thomassy glared at Ed on the witness stand. "Answer my question," he said, and suddenly realized he was attacking his own client and that every lawyer in the country would consider that improper. My client right or wrong! *Wrong* he wanted to shout because it was within these walls, within his head, that he was beginning to grasp the intolerable complexity of the human condition and that Martin Fuller, his greatness unchallenged because he had understood everything about the enemy, in the end, by accepting Ed Porter, may have been, like Trotsky, naive unto death.

Judge Drewson was beckoning him over. "Are you all right, counselor?"

"Yes, Your Honor."

"The witness had answered the question."

The courtroom was painfully silent.

"I'm sorry, Your Honor."

"Continue."

Thomassy went over to the witness box. Ed seemed frightened of him. *It must be my expression.*

Gently Thomassy asked, "Mr. Sturbridge, have you ever belonged to any group or organization affiliated with the Communist movement in any way whatsoever?"

"No, sir."

"If you had, would such affiliation have gone undetected by Professor Fuller during the course of your many discussions?"

"Objection," demanded Roberts.

"Sustained."

"I withdraw the question." Thomassy picked up a book from the defense table, and brought it to the witness box. "Do you recognize this volume, Mr. Sturbridge?"

"Yes," Ed said, smiling for the first time.

"Will you tell the court what it is."

Roberts was on his feet, coming over to see what the book was. He regretted his move, just as Thomassy was saying, "Your Honor, I intend to enter this volume into evidence as Defense Exhibit J."

"Continue," the judge said.

"Will you describe this book, please?"

"It's a copy of *Lenin's Grandchildren* written by me and published last year by the Oxford University Press."

"You were twenty-three at the time of its publication?"

"Just about going on twenty-four."

"And who wrote the foreword to this book."

"Professor Fuller."

"Do you know if Professor Fuller was paid to write the introduction to this book?"

"No, sir. It would have been impolitic for me to offer an honorarium. The publisher may have. I don't know."

"Would you characterize this book as procommunist, anticommunist, or any other way?"

Roberts objected. "Your Honor, I question the relevance."

"I can see a possible relevance," the judge said. "Please rephrase, Mr. Thomassy."

"Would you characterize your book, briefly of course."

"I hope it's objective. That brief enough?"

Ed got a tinkle of laughter from the press.

"And what is the book about?"

"It deals with the Latin American and African revolutionaries of the last thirty years, and the influence of the Soviet Union on their countries."

"Would Professor Fuller have written an introduction to the book if it were markedly procommunist?"

"Of course not!" Ed said before Roberts objected and was sustained by the judge.

"I think," Judge Drewson said, "that a question like that might have been more appropriately asked of Professor Tarasova or some other expert witness. The jurors will note that the question and the answer are both being stricken from the record and they should not consider either in their deliberations."

"Now then," Thomassy said, "would you please describe the events of the evening of April fifth in the home of the Fullers to the best of your recollection."

Ed described the conversation at dinner and Barry Heskowitz leaving.

"Did Mr. Heskowitz offer you a ride into the city?"

"He did."

"Did you accept?"

"No, sir."

"Why not?"

"Well, it was only eleven-fifteen—"

"How do you know that?"

"I looked at my watch."

"Do you wear your watch all the time?"

"I sure do. Except when I take a shower."

There was a titter in the audience. Okay, okay, Thomassy thought.

"Do you wear your watch when you sleep?"

"If there's no alarm clock in the room, so if I wake up I can tell what time it is without fumbling around."

"At what time did you all go upstairs to bed?"

"Mrs. Fuller broke up the discussion just about midnight."

"Did you all go up at the same time?"

"Yes, we did."

"Each into your own bedrooms?"

"Yes."

"Did you hear any unusual sounds during the night?"

"Just the usual athletic activities."

"What do you mean by that?"

"Doors opening, closing, springs going up and down, nothing serious, except I had to use the bathroom once and the damn door was locked, so I had to use the downstairs bathroom. I hated to do that because I didn't want to wake the Fullers up."

"Wasn't there a nearer bathroom?"

"As I said, yes, but the door was locked from the inside. I rattled the knob. Then I went downstairs."

"Fair enough. Did you slip on any garment when you went downstairs, such as a bathrobe?"

"I have a superlong T-shirt. It's like a nightshirt on someone my size."

"But you didn't put it on when you ran down in the morning?"

"That was an emergency. I heard the screaming."

"During the night when you went down to use Professor Fuller's bathroom, did you raise the toilet seat?"

"I always do."

"Did you notice whether or not you were wearing your watch when you left the bathroom?"

"No, I didn't."

"So it might have fallen off as you raised the seat?"

"Objection!" Roberts said.

"Sustained."

"I withdraw the question," Thomassy said. "Did you during the course of the night go out to the garage?"

"No, sir."

"Now, apart from that night and the previous evening, did you at any other time shortly before that use Professor Fuller's bathroom?"

"About two weeks earlier, Professor Fuller had asked me to fill up his kerosene heater from the can kept in the garage."

"Which you did?"

"Which I did."

"Did you ever mow the Fuller's lawn?"

"Many times."

"Did you fill the lawn mower with fuel from the same or a different can?"

Ed smiled. "I've never tried running a lawn mower on kerosene. I doubt it'd work."

"Are the two cans clearly labeled?"

"Oh yes, in Professor Fuller's own handwriting. On wide duct tape pasted on each can. He was very careful about things like that."

"Now, let's be clear. Between the time two weeks before the accident and the date of the accident, did you at any time refill the kerosene heater in Professor Fuller's bathroom."

"No, sir."

"We have heard testimony that Mr. Fuller used the heater every morning. Would it hold a two-week kerosene supply?"

"I doubt it. Frankly, I don't know."

Jesus, he's forgotten, Thomassy thought.

Ed caught himself, continued. "Actually, I did fill it three weeks earlier, too, so it must hold only about a week's supply."

"Thank you. That would seem to indicate that someone else filled the heater at least twice since you did, once a week earlier, and once between the morning of April fourth and the morning of April fifth because if gas had been mixed with the kerosene in the heater accidentally or otherwise, it would have blown up earlier than the morning of April fifth."

The judge held up a hand. "Mr. Thomassy, I'm certain you can touch on these matters in your summation."

"I'm sorry, Your Honor." He turned back to his witness. "All right," Thomassy said. "Did you have any reason to want to see Professor Fuller die?"

Ed's face looked as if all expression had suddenly drained away. His eyes moved within their sockets as if taking in everyone in the courtroom from left to right without seeing an actual person.

228

Thomassy couldn't tell if Ed was thinking, daydreaming, or lost. *His soul has fled.*

"Did you hear the question?" Thomassy asked, keeping his distance from the apparition.

The ghost-head on Ed's shoulder made a barely perceptible nod.

"Please answer," Thomassy said.

"I have never wanted anyone to die."

Thomassy saw the character he had helped create for the jury's eyes turning into vapor. "Please speak up," he said, coming closer to Ed. "Did you have any reason to want to see Professor Fuller die?"

Ed's face snapped back from wherever it had been as he said louder than anything he had said before in that courtroom so that it sounded like a wail. "I loved him!"

That wasn't what they had rehearsed. He hadn't answered the question.

Thomassy glanced at the judge, caught in a freeze-frame. Thomassy turned to Roberts, expecting an objection that never came. And so, his voice as normal as he could make it, Thomassy said, "Mr. Sturbridge, did you at any time ever mix gas and kerosene in Professor Fuller's heater or any other heater?"

"No, sir."

"Did you kill Professor Fuller?"

Thomassy could feel the acute silence in the vast room. He'd told Ed not to answer instantly or to wait too long.

After two seconds, Ed said, "No, sir," and he was actually sobbing, crying and sobbing, reaching frantically for the handkerchief in his pocket, and none of that was in the script.

"Thank you," Thomassy said. "Your witness, Mr. Roberts."

As Thomassy returned to the defense table, he noticed Tarasova sitting halfway back. She hadn't been able to keep away. The dead man belonged to her, too.

Roberts's two young assistants were busily skimming Exhibit J, *Lenin's Grandchildren*. The sandy-haired one was glancing down the left-hand pages, while the other skimmed the right-hand pages. "So far nothing," the sandy-haired one said.

Roberts told them to hurry as he pulled his vest sharply down and proceeded to his post in front of the witness.

Preparation is ninety percent of the battle, Thomassy thought, yet winging it without preparation for a particular turn of events gave him an adrenalin high. When he saw Koppelman and another

229

young assistant DA busily skimming the places they had marked in Exhibit J, Thomassy wished he'd spent time with that book of Ed's, trying to figure out what they might use, or at least—he looked at Ed sitting in the witness box, his chin cupped in his hands—he should have questioned Ed as to what in the book might be used against him. But Ed wouldn't necessarily have pointed to the right things. He's playing a double game, what he tells the world, what he tells me. How different are they?

The large flat envelope on the prosecution table bothered Thomassy. Did they contain the photographs? Roberts would have used them during his witness's testimony, when Francine was on the stand, if he had them. If he had them *then*. What if he'd just gotten his hands on them? What if Roberts was smarter than he thought and had saved them to demolish the defendant's testimony? Could he have prepared Ed to deal with the photos? Were these oversights in his planning because of the rush of things, or was he doing less than a hundred percent? The ache of doubt was not something you wanted nibbling at your gut while the defendant was being cross-examined. You can't push the clock back. This is it, go with it.

Roberts pulled his vest sharply down and proceeded to his post in front of the witness. He looked like his family had owned the world for a long time.

"Mr. Sturbridge," Roberts said, "when did you first adopt an alias?"

"What alias?"

"You testified here that your name was Edward Porter Sturbridge. Prosecution Exhibit A was an identification card found in your possession on which you used the name Porter as a last name. My question was when did you first start using that alias?"

"Your Honor," said Thomassy, objecting, "the word *alias* has a perjorative connotation that might be misinterpreted by the jury."

"Sustained," the judge spoke directly to Ed. "Would the witness clarify his use of two last names."

Ed's mother and father sat frozen like Grant Wood figures in the back row.

"Your Honor," he said, "Porter is my mother's name. Sturbridge is my father's name. I used my father's name, as is customary, until I left home for college. My father, as Your Honor may know, is a well-known pharmaceutical industrialist and I didn't want to be stigmatized by my peers for any views they might have about my father's wealth or reputation. The simplest solution seemed to be to use my mother's name, which is much more common and not associated with anyone in particular as far as I know."

Good boy, Thomassy thought. *Keep it up.*

Roberts, his gambit blown, decided to pursue another avenue. "Mr. Sturbridge, you testified that you never were a member of the Communist party. Had you been, what would have been your answer to the question, 'Are you or have you ever been a member of the Communist party?'"

Thomassy objected. "Your Honor, that is secondhand speculation."

"I'll let it stand," the judge said. He nodded to Ed. "You may answer."

"I want to repeat that I am not a member of the Communist party. Had I been, however, I would have denied that I was."

"Does that mean you would have lied under oath."

"On that issue, of course."

Thomassy wasn't happy with the outcome of that interchange. He could ask for a conference at the bench. He could appeal to the judge's desire to avoid reversible error. The question was hypothetical, though Roberts hadn't flagged it as such. It was speculative about a large group of people. The hell with it, he thought, let it ride.

Koppelman caught Roberts's eye and motioned to him. He handed him the copy of Ed's book opened midway and was pointing an excited finger at a passage, which Roberts quickly read. Koppelman whispered in Roberts's ear. Roberts nodded.

"Mr. Sturbridge," Roberts said, a touch of relish in his voice, "on page one ninety-two of Exhibit J—your book—it says, and I quote, 'Murder may be both an end and a means.' Would you explain that statement?"

This time Thomassy was in a mood to fight. "Objection! Your Honor, the book speaks for itself. Any elaboration that the district attorney wants may involve the writing of additional text or a pony, but I don't think the witness should be required to elaborate."

The judge said, "Counsels please approach the bench."

As soon as they were both close, Roberts opened up. "Your Honor, murder is the central issue of the indictment. Intent is central to the concept of murder. Here we have a most unusual opportunity for the jury to understand exactly what the defendant thinks about that subject."

The judge nodded to Thomassy, who replied, "Your Honor, I have no objection to letting the jury read anything that's in that book in context, but it is in violation of the defendant's rights for him to be forced to elaborate on a text that the defense itself committed to the record. If Mr. Roberts wants each member of the jury to read that book, I'll be happy to supply eleven other copies, but the context of that statement is the paragraph it's in, and the context of that paragraph is its chapter, and the context of the chapter is the book as a whole. As Your Honor knows, the Supreme Court has taken the position on the issue of obscenity that a work must be taken as a whole because nothing can be judged objectively and accurately out of its context."

Judge Drewson reflected on his isolation. He could not show the anger he felt. He couldn't leave the bench on some pretext, as he sometimes did; his daughter would see through him as easily here as she sometimes did over the dinner table. *Thomassy, you Armenian bastard, I'll throttle you some other time.* In his most controlled voice, the judge said, "Mr. Roberts, why don't you—without referring to the exhibit—just ask the witness any question you want to about murder."

"Your Honor," Thomassy said, "I have to object to that. I can't let my client be jeopardized by an abstract discussion of his views on any subject, much less murder."

"Look, Mr. Thomassy," the judge said, "I've been patient with you both. You put the defendant on the stand. I don't think you can deny the prosecution legitimate questions on the grounds of the defendant's possible self-incrimination. And please don't give me a dissertation on context. The context of anything the defendant testifies to is everything else he testifies to in front of the jury. Let us proceed. We're wasting time."

"Your Honor," Thomassy said, "may I quickly read page one ninety-two?"

"You did not read Exhibit J?"

"No, Your Honor. In preparing for trial I only had a chance to skim it briefly."

"Very well."

What Thomassy read on that page did not assuage his alarm. "May I confer with my client, Your Honor?" he asked.

"Not during his testimony. You ought to know better than that, Mr. Thomassy. Come on, gentlemen, let's get the record going again or we'll be here till Christmas."

As Roberts walked up to the witness stand, Thomassy hoped that Ed, entirely unrehearsed in this area, wouldn't fall into the pit.

"Mr. Sturbridge," Roberts said, "is your book a correct and accurate statement of your true beliefs?"

"Of course."

"Will you tell the court then what your beliefs are with regard to murder as a means to an end and as an end in itself?"

As Ed reflected for a moment, Judge Drewson wondered if he hadn't indeed opened the trapdoor of reversible error. He could still strike it from the record, though whatever happened now could not be stricken from the jury's memory.

Finally, Ed spoke. "Murder is generally regarded as the second-worst crime, after treason. The taking of a human life is, of course, abhorred in all societies we call civilized, though subsections of such societies have different views of murder. When it is a means to an end, the end may be the elimination of a potential enemy, or as an ostensible lesson to others—as when society commits capital punishment. However, murder is often committed in the heat of anger, jealousy, or some similar emotion and becomes like any emotion an expression or an end in itself."

"And why does a reference to murder as both a means and an end in itself," Roberts asked, "appear in a book that is about revolutions in Latin America?"

Ed was soaring. He didn't know if they were wholly understanding him, but all of them were focusing their attention on his every word. "One frequently hears it said about communist and fascist societies that they consider every means—including murder—not only permissible but perhaps even desirable if it accomplishes a just end as defined by that society. In capitalist society, profit is considered an end so desirable as to involve such activities as repossessing homes where mortgages are in default. Many people, perhaps most people, view war as permissible murder, permissible in that it is justified as self-defense or warranted attack."

Thomassy stood to attract the judge's attention. Ed looked at him as if to say what did I do wrong? "Your Honor," Thomassy said, "with respect, I cannot see how we are doing anything else here than confounding the jury, which is here to judge fact and only fact. I move that the entire discussion relating to Exhibit J be stricken from the record."

With great relief, Judge Drewson said, "Motion granted. Strike it out. The jury will disregard."

"Exception!" Roberts said, putting it on the record, and glancing at Koppelman.

They were setting up for an appeal, just in case, Thomassy thought.

Roberts looked relieved. The defendant wasn't being judged by his peers. Most of those jurors probably hadn't read a book of political theory since school, if then. If that last garbage had stayed in the record, they'd camp in the jury room forever. Roberts looked confident as he went back to the real world.

"Mr. Sturbridge, before the events of April fifth, what was your personal experience with kerosene?"

"My parents used to heat the greenhouse with kerosene heaters. I used to help the gardener when I was a kid."

"Can you tell the difference between kerosene and gasoline?"

"Sure. They smell different. They also look different. And in the Fuller garage, they're labeled differently."

Okay, okay, Thomassy thought.

"Then," said Roberts, "if you were to mistake gasoline for kerosene it wouldn't be a mistake?"

"Objection!"

"Sustained."

"Do you read detective stories, Mr. Sturbridge?"

Judge Drewson preempted Thomassy's objection. "Let's see where it goes."

"I've read a few."

"Good. Then perhaps you can tell us what you believe is meant by the perfect crime."

"In detective stories?"

"In detective stories or anywhere else."

"I guess it would mean a crime that would go undetected."

"And why might such a crime go undetected?"

"Because of the means used."

"Such as?"

"A poison that doesn't show up in laboratory analysis of the victim's blood or body tissues, something like that."

"Would you consider a bit of gasoline mixed in secretly with kerosene to be a means like a poison that doesn't show up in laboratory analysis?"

"I never read about any such thing in any detective story."

"Did you invent that means yourself then?"

"Objection!"

"Sustained."

Thomassy thought, Roberts ought to take lessons in cross-examination.

"All right," Roberts said to Ed, "did you ever visit the buildings that house the United Nations?"

234

"Of course," Ed said. "Several times in connection with my research."

"And was it research you couldn't do at the university or elsewhere?"

"Absolutely."

"And when was the last time you visited there?"

"I can't remember."

"This year, last year?"

Careful, Thomassy was thinking, *this is the trip-wire.*

"When I was doing my dissertation."

"And not since Professor Fuller's death?" Roberts asked.

"No, sir."

Roberts headed for the prosecution table, where Koppelman, all smiles, had the large envelope ready to hand to him. "Your Honor," Roberts said, "I would like to have these four photographs marked as People's Exhibit R."

Four? Thomassy had seen three in Widmer's house. *What the hell was going on?*

Judge Drewson looked at the photographs. The first three drew no special reaction from him. The fourth did.

"May I inspect the exhibit, Your Honor," Thomassy said.

The judge nodded, at the same time that Roberts said, "Of course," handing them from the judge to Thomassy, who glanced at the first three so as not to betray his anxiety to see the fourth.

The fourth was an extreme close-up of Ed and Trushenko. Their expressions were of men in heated argument. *Why hadn't Perry shown him all the pictures?*

Judge Drewson motioned both lawyers to the bench out of earshot of the jury. "Mr. Roberts, can you clarify the purpose of introducing these exhibits?"

"Certainly, Your Honor. We don't have a smoking-gun case, but one of circumstantial evidence. This evidence, Your Honor, may be objectively verifiable proof that the defendant committed perjury when he said he hadn't been to the UN building since Professor Fuller's death when in fact he was there when these photographs were taken within a few days afterward. More importantly, it establishes a link between the defendant and Soviet officials, which speaks to the point of intent if he was in fact operating under instructions from them."

Thomassy didn't know whom he was most angry at. "Your Honor, that is a tenuous chain. Photographs can be dangerously misleading because a jury of laymen has been brought up to be-

235

lieve that what the eye sees is proof, but the proof being offered by the government does not speak to the point of the events preceding the death of Martin Fuller."

The Judge asked Roberts, "Who took those photographs?"

"Your Honor," Roberts said, "each is stamped on the back. They were taken by an agent of the Federal Bureau of Investigation, which has certified on the back of each the date and approximate time taken."

Drewson turned to Thomassy. "Will you stipulate as to the source?"

There was no point to fighting what he knew to be fact. "The defense stipulates that the government is the source of those photographs. But Your Honor, I still believe . . ."

Thomassy wanted to go on, but the judge said, "Let's get on with it," and that was that.

At the witness box, Roberts was ready to break Ed. "I show you photograph one. Can you please examine the photo closely and see if you can identify any of the people you see?"

Ed looked at the photo. His lips were tight. "There are a lot of people there."

"Please focus on the people who are not walking. Can you identify any of these three?" Roberts asked, pointing to Semyonov, Trushenko, and the young man with his back turned.

"The picture isn't very clear. From what I can see, I can't identify any of those persons."

"Well then," Roberts said, "can you identify that short man I am pointing to right now who is wearing a jacket exactly the same as the one you are wearing now?"

"Objection!" Thomassy shouted.

"Sustained," the judge responded.

"Can you identify the short man," Roberts said, keeping the pressure on.

"No, sir. His back is turned."

"Well, then," Roberts said, taking the photo back and handing Ed another, "here is a side view. Does that help you identify the man?"

Ed looked at Thomassy. He was hoping for an objection. There was nothing for Thomassy to object to.

"I can't identify any of them," Ed said, swallowing.

Don't let the jury see you swallow like that.

Ed responded to photo number three the same way. But when he was shown the fourth photo, he asked, "Is this a different photo?"

"It is a blow-up of a section of photo three," Roberts said, "to help you identify those persons."

Ed pretended to study the photo, using the time to think. Finally he said, "I'm not sure."

"You're not sure," Roberts said triumphantly, "that that person I'm pointing to right now is you?"

Thomassy was on his feet. "The witness answered that question already, Your Honor."

Roberts asked to approach the bench. Both lawyers came forward. "Your Honor," Roberts said, "I beg the court's leave to ask for an adjournment to ascertain if the government will permit the agent who took the photographs to testify and as an expert witness, to bring up from Washington the Bureau's chief expert in identification procedures involving photographs."

"I object, Your Honor," Thomassy said. "The prosecution has had its chance with witnesses."

He saw the flicker in Judge Drewson's face. He wasn't dumb. He wouldn't take an obvious chance with reversible error.

"Sustained," he said.

Thomassy tried to keep his smile in check. Roberts started to burble his objections, but the judge cut him short. "Sustained," he repeated.

Roberts tried to compose himself. "Your Honor," he said, "while the testimony of the defendant is fresh in the jury's mind, I request the court's permission to publish all four photographs to the jury."

"Granted."

They all watched the faces of the jurors examining the photos. Some of the jurors took extra time over photo number four, looking up at Ed on the stand, then back at the photo. One of them looked over at Thomassy. The last thing in the world Thomassy wanted to communicate was worry. He smiled. *Those photos don't mean a damned thing.*

When the jurors were through, Judge Drewson ordered them sequestered for the night. Then he asked to see Roberts and Thomassy in chambers.

"Gentlemen," he said, "let's do a little horse trading. Mr. Thomassy, are you planning to redirect on those photos?"

"I'll reserve my answer," Thomassy said, "until I hear the other half of the horse trade." He didn't want to redirect. The less focus on those pictures the better.

"Mr. Roberts," the judge said, "if you get your FBI people on the stand, they'll bore us all to death, and you know Mr. Thomassy is going to feel obliged to tear their testimony to the point where the jury'll doubt they could recognize their own mothers in a photograph. If you'll withdraw your request for additional prosecution witnesses, perhaps Mr. Thomassy can be persuaded to skip his redirect. We'll save a day and you can get to your summations. Perhaps your own comments on those photos, Mr. Roberts, may be more impressive than what the FBI people might have to say. And you get the last word without Mr. Thomassy's objections. What do you say, gentlemen, shall we call it a day?"

Smart, Thomassy thought. Roberts can't resist that. And Drewson's avoided error.

"Well?" Judge Drewson prompted Roberts.

"Deal," said Roberts.

Thomassy nodded his assent, and in two seconds they were on their way back into the courtroom. As he gathered up his papers, Thomassy told Ed, "I have to visit a friend in the hospital. Stay in your place. I want to talk to you tonight."

"Did I do all right?" Ed asked.

"The first half was brilliant," Thomassy said. "The second half depends on whether the jury thinks you're lying about the photographs."

His throat tightening, Ed whispered urgently, "What do they prove?"

"In their minds? That you're a liar. If you lie about those photos, you could be lying about everything."

"But I'm not."

Thomassy was already on his way. Through his mind flitted the thought that one of the virtues of not being married was you didn't have children like Ed. He passed the Sturbridges on the way out of the courtroom. Mr. Sturbridge had the face of a long-dead Pharoah. Only Mrs. Sturbridge, a mother used to pain, turned to nod at him.

□ C H A P T E R   T H I R T Y - F O U R □

The logistics made sense to Thomassy. After a full day in that hardwood chair in the courtroom, the ache in his lower back needed fifteen minutes of stretching out. He'd go home, sack out for that quarter of an hour, freshen up, drive down to Ed Porter's, then shoot over to the hospital to see Francine without a time limit hanging over his head. Hell, I'll sleep with her in the hospital, he thought, and laughed at the ideas that sometimes came into his head.

One thing he didn't like about late October was the switch from daylight saving time to what he thought of as daylight losing time. When he pulled up in his driveway and got out of the car, he did something he hadn't done for quite a while. He looked up at the night sky. It was spangled with stars. One of them had to be Haig Thomassian. Another his mother. That's what he wanted to believe, the dead who continued to live in his brain spoke from the stars. That was a suitable compromise for the idea of heaven. He'd share that with Francine on whatever day Episcopalians started to believe in miracles.

First he heard the car door slam. Then a second slam, and footsteps coming up the gravel. Give them your wallet, he thought.

"Hello," said Perry. "Hope we didn't startle you."

Randall was with him.

"We left a message with your service," Perry said.

"I didn't call my service."

"You're seeing Ed Sturbridge tonight."

How did they know?

"We wanted a couple of minutes before you did. We hoped you'd stop home first."

He had no choice. "Come on in," Thomassy said.

They didn't want a drink even when he poured himself one.

"You look tired, Mr. Perry. What's on your mind."

"Christov's been talking a blue streak."

"Who the hell's Christov?"

"Sorry. Remember the man who defected in the courtroom?"

"Nearly got me a mistrial. You don't think anyone in his right mind wants to try this case twice."

"Christov says Trushenko was Ed Sturbridge's control."

"What does that mean?"

"You know damn well what that means. Semyonov's left for Moscow. We need to know whatever Sturbridge will give us before Trushenko's gone, too. He could be out of our hands tomorrow."

"Does Roberts know any of this?"

"Of course not."

"Then how the hell did he get the pictures if you're not cooperating with him?"

"The pictures were to put pressure on Sturbridge."

"And get him convicted?"

"Not in your capable hands. What would Sturbridge get if he were convicted?"

"Of what? Accidental homicide? He's not getting convicted."

Perry took a single sheet of folded paper out of his breast pocket. "If Sturbridge will give us an affidavit on Trushenko, we'll pick Trushenko up. We won't let the affidavit out until after the trial. We want Trushenko. There's at least one other American in his control."

"Who?"

"If we knew we wouldn't need anything from Sturbridge."

"You fellows play a dirty game," Thomassy said.

"I'd expect to hear that from a nurse, not a criminal lawyer. The affidavit doesn't need to be in exactly that form. Just the substance."

Thomassy tore the paper in half. "Get out of here," he said.

□ CHAPTER THIRTY-FIVE □

There was a time when Ed thought he could count on Trushenko. He had a kind of Slavic charm, a friendly gruffness, a laugh that came from an up-and-down movement of his whole chest. Ed asked him if he had once worn a beard, and he remembered how that question startled Truskenko. "How did you know such a thing?" he demanded.

Ed said he stroked his face with his left hand as if he had once had a beard there. Trushenko thought that was a very clever observation. "A painter, an artist sees such things." Later Ed learned that he didn't mean artist. To Trushenko, the highest art was espionage. Trushenko was a soldier during the Great War in defense of the motherland. "A soldier," he said, "gives his life to protect against the enemy. In espionage, a man sometimes gives his life to the enemy in order to bring back something more valuable than his life."

"Nothing," Ed argued, "is more valuable than a man's life."

"That," said Trushenko, "is the fallacy of individualism." He stood in admonishment, ready to leave. "Society matters. What kind of socialist are you?"

"One clever enough to fool you, even anger you at will," Ed said, laughing. "Do you think I am a believer in rampant individualism as in the earliest days of the capitalist era? A Neanderthal?"

Trushenko sat back down, shaking his head, his left hand stroking his chin. "Why are you willing to help us? You could get into trouble."

"If I answered money, you would accept that?"

"Of course," said Trushenko.

"Then read my book, *Lenin's Grandchildren*. You respond to capitalist assumptions as they appear in books and not in life. What kind of Neanderthal socialist are you, Comrade Trushenko?"

"For a young man you are easily insubordinate."

"If I work for you, I will take your orders, not before." Ed hoped his ballsiness wasn't putting Trushenko off. In Fuller's company Ed was always the student. In Trushenko's he could be the teacher. In the next two hours Ed convinced Trushenko that Ed knew more about Marxism and Soviet history than Trushenko did. Trushenko probably considered himself an educated man compared to the police-mentality bureaucrats he often had to put up with. Ed could tell he was winning the older man's admiration. Trushenko had a weakness. He could be seduced by intelligence.

"Here," Ed was saying, "we learn Marxism in three dimensions. From its progenitors, its followers, and its antagonists. You learn the second dimension only." He leaned forward on his elbows. "I can be valuable to you."

"Oh you can shine like a star among the intelligentsia, I'm sure," Trushenko said, "but when it comes to my kind of work you are a baby."

"We shall see, won't we?"

How could he not try Ed? To test him, the first thing Trushenko asked him to do was to bring him a page of Fuller's famous doodling. No harm in that.

When Ed brought it to him, Trushenko said, "Did Fuller see you take it?"

Ed assured him not.

"Did his wife or anyone else see?"

"No."

"Fuller will know it's missing."

"No."

"How can you say that with such assurance?"

241

"I took it out of the wastebasket."

"Why didn't you say so?"

"You didn't ask. Why should I reveal my methods if you are not yet ready to accept me," Ed said, enjoying himself, knowing he had already moved himself closer to acceptance.

"I don't know how useful you can be to us. Of course you are there so often. And he obviously respects and likes you. You are a likable sort, I suppose."

Ed didn't hear from him for more than a month. When he did, Trushenko said, "I have read *Lenin's Grandchildren*. It is a very clever, very offensive book. It derides Ché Guevara, it holds the Arab Marxists up to ridicule."

"I deride those who have failed, not those who have succeeded."

"Some would say your book is anticommunist."

"Would you expect me to be useful to you in Professor Fuller's household if I had written a procommunist book? I would be useful to nobody."

Trushenko stroked his no-longer-existing beard. He said, "My colleagues who have not met you have expressed a certain concern over your attachment to Professor Fuller." When he saw the ice in Ed's eyes, Trushenko quickly changed the rhythm of his speech. "Of course, of course, no one is saying anything bad, nothing like that, just worshipful, a very strong bond."

"Do you have a wife, Comrade Trushenko?"

Trushenko was startled. In all his years of service, no one had asked that question. Those who knew him well, knew, those who didn't, didn't ask. He did not want to lose this arrogant young pigeon, and so he answered. "I have a wife."

"You are attached to her?"

"Even when she is in Moscow and I am here."

"What if you were to find out, Comrade Trushenko, that your wife was working with someone else?"

"What do you mean 'working?'"

"Working."

"Why would she be doing that?"

"You see how you feel right now, Comrade Trushenko? You are full of emotions that redden your face. How do you think I feel after giving my total devotion to Professor Fuller, studying at his feet, and I find he is setting down the most profound elements of his system, the core of his knowledge particularly of the next generation of the Politburo, in a manuscript that he will not let me, his closest young friend, read or even get near, yet when it is finished he will hand it over to some stranger in the government?"

"I see," Trushenko said.

"He is disinheriting me!"

Trushenko remembered his wife was ironing when he asked her point-blank whether she made love to anyone else while he was in America. She'd left the iron on the collar of his shirt till they both smelled the burning. Then she lifted the iron and held it so that its bottom faced him, as if it were suddenly not something with which to smooth clothes but a fierce weapon that could split a skull. Was that an admission of some sort? Was his own reaction so strong because he himself had been unfaithful to her with a secretary of the embassy? Or was she merely reacting to an unfair accusation? He had never learned the truth. All he took away was the image of the raised iron and the smell of burning.

To Ed he said, "I need to consult with my colleagues."

"Why does everything have to be cleared with Semyonov?" Ed said impatiently.

"How do you know that name?"

Ed arranged a slight smile on his face.

"Is he in Fuller's manuscript?" Trushenko demanded.

"I have not read Professor Fuller's manuscript. Semyonov's name comes up around the dinner table. All the Columbia people know he's the KGB's top dog at the UN."

"Why do you use a word like dog?"

"It's an expression. Top dog. Chief honcho."

Trushenko had to restrain himself from telling the impudent youngster that all of the American experts were wrong, that Semyonov was number two. "We will meet again in a few days," he said.

"A few days is acceptable," said Ed, who felt time racing. Fuller had made a mistake in cutting him off from the manuscript in which he was imbedding things Ed didn't yet know. If he'd given it to Ed as his rightful heir, Ed could bring to the international barter tables the new generation's spirit of rapprochement, to replace the system of congenital warfare with the triumph of a socialist peace for all time. Of course he had loved Fuller until he'd seen that Fuller's method of political analysis was not a process for understanding but a monstrous mechanism for dividing East and West forever. In his head Ed heard the billowing of words to fill the immensity of his feeling: *I hate Fuller.*

□   □   □

To Semyonov, Trushenko reported, "The boy is an intellectual, the most dangerous species in the world. He believes ideas are real."

Semyonov, a stocky man, laughed with the full expanse of his chest. "You sound like Lenin."

Trushenko said, "Thank you, comrade. I was born the year that Lenin died. Perhaps there is some connection."

Semyonov laughed harder. "Not enough or you would be party secretary today. What is your assessment of this intellectual in terms of our immediate need?"

Trushenko had thought carefully. This report could be a turning point for his career. Slowly, he said, "The boy came to sit at Fuller's feet. To suck his brain. To become his heir. Fuller will not let him read the manuscript. The boy feels betrayed."

"Could he kill?" There was no longer a trace of laughter on Semyonov's face.

"A man in profound love is untrustworthy."

"But you reported Fuller trusts the young man as a son."

"That makes it worse. The son expects more. When he gets less, he is a danger to everyone. That is my opinion, comrade."

"We must get him to copy the manuscript right away."

"It isn't finished."

"I know, I know, but we can then send Porter Sturbridge, whatever you call him, to Europe for a time on some invented errand and let him return when the manuscript is nearly done."

"How will we know that?"

"Clearly you have not inherited Lenin's brain. As Fuller nears completion, he will have Washington people on his doorstep every day, waiting to snatch his knowledge away to a safe place."

"We could have it copied once it reaches Washington."

"And risk someone who has been in place so long? Don't be a complete fool. Better by far to risk the young man."

And so at their next meeting, Trushenko pumped Ed's hand and announced, "Congratulations, comrade. I have your first assignment for you." He wished the young man's eyes didn't dance so. He gave Ed the address of a copying service ten minutes from the Fuller home. "They have a 9200. It can copy a large manuscript in few minutes. Take the front page off or anything else that identifies it. Those people don't look at what they're copying. Pay them extra to do it at once if you have to. Make certain it's the original you put back. If you can manage this, we have even more important work for you to do."

□　　□　　□

244

Ed believed that almost everyone at one time has a fantasy of fame—an Olympic champion, a film star, a computer king, a political David who slays Goliath. His was to attend a meeting in Geneva or The Hague, a huge room with a horseshoe table for the principal participants, all hushed as Ed opened his briefcase and produced the Two-Part Plan that would cause the stubborn Warsaw Pact delegates and the equally stubborn NATO functionaries to forfeit their obstinate downward plunge to mutual destruction and instead seize the Plan, kiss his cheeks, shake his hand in long lines of grateful delegates. His visionary plan's two parts consisted of the East's guide to understanding the naive West, attribution Edward Porter Sturbridge, and the West's guide to understanding the practical East, attribution to Martin Fuller courtesy of his greatest pupil. The Nobel Peace Prize had sometimes gone to the wrong people, terrorists like Menachim Begin and dictators like Anwar Sadat, but it could now go to the youngest worthy man in history to receive it.

"Are you well?" Fuller had asked him immediately after Ed returned from his last meeting with Trushenko.

"Of course," Ed said.

"Your eyes look like you have a fever."

It wasn't fever, it was bounding excitement. "I am very grateful to you," Ed said. "I want to help with your work."

"Ah, but you are. Have I neglected to say that our evening discussions, you and Leona and I, and all of us with the others when they visit, stimulate the way I develop my thoughts each day? If I haven't thanked you, it is an oversight."

"No, no, no," Ed protested, "I mean I want to help directly, perhaps to read behind you, pointing out the small things everyone misses in his own work, let you have memoranda on these points, speed up the process of completion so that when you get to the end little or no revision will be necessary."

Ed saw Fuller regarding him without speech. Had he said the wrong thing? Quickly he added, "We could work out a schedule that would not interfere with your hours. When you finish in the late morning, I could work in your study, read behind your work of the day—I could catch up quickly on what you've already done—and when I finish you could lock up for the day so that I would never have to have the key and the work would never leave your study. Wouldn't that be safe and expedient and benefit the time needed for completion so that you and Leona would be free to go off on that long holiday abroad? What do you think?"

□   □   □

245

Fuller had sloughed off the offer to help as something to think about and discuss later. But when he was alone with Leona in the kitchen and Ed was in his room upstairs, he said, "What do we know about Ed?"

Leona seemed surprised by the question. "Too much. The auto-biographies of the young are so similar."

"Do you think Ed is what he has represented himself to be?"

"What do you mean?"

"I think he wants to read my manuscript very badly."

"Of course. So do I."

"Not for the same reasons."

"I'm sure that in his secret heart he yearns to drain every ounce of your expertise."

"Why do you say *drain?*"

"A young scholar's thirst is for the ocean."

"I wonder."

"Don't get paranoid."

"Something is very wrong. I think we should not invite him frequently. Perhaps not anymore."

Since the weather had improved, they went out into the garden for a walk and whatever they then said was not recorded on the voice-activated tape recorder Ed had left behind in the breadbox.

When Ed retrieved the recorder and listened to the tape upstairs, his euphoria turned into panic. The Russians had at last given him the go-ahead and he was to be cut off from access. And that is when the thought came to him: *He will not thwart me. I will stop his work.*

Ed thought Trushenko's gratitude would be unbounded when he did *more* than he was asked.

Never use the phone booth closest to your home, Trushenko had instructed Ed. So he went to a farther one, put in a dime, and called the number. Ed was not to give his name, just say hello. Trushenko would recognize his voice. "Fuller is dead," Ed said.

"Of course," Trushenko bellowed. "We see the newspapers, we hear the radio. Was it an accident? We must meet at the designated place, say four o'clock—"

"I did it," Ed said, wanting acknowledgment for the most important act of his life.

"You fool," he said, and hung up on Ed.

Ed never felt more alone in the world.

Two hours later, the walls of his apartment screaming at him, he went back to the same phone booth. There was a black man vomiting in it. He ran to the next one and dialed the number again from memory.

The number you have called is not a working number.

It was working just two hours ago! He dialed carefully, making sure he got every numeral right.

The number you have called is not a working number.

He was frantic. *They can't cut me off like that.* He hailed a taxi. He had the cab drop him off a block away, then walked to the door of the Soviet UN Mission.

"Can I help you?" the stout woman said. Ed told her he would like to see Gaspodin Semyonov. He thought the "Gaspodin" would help establish something. What did it matter if he was going over Trushenko's head. The woman, a wax smile on her tight lips, said, "There is no one with that name at the mission." Ed thought if this stupid woman knew what he had accomplished she would be smiling as if to a Lenin prize recipient instead of giving him the run-around. "Perhaps Comrade Trushenko can help me locate him?"

She telephoned someone and spoke in Russian. Did the fool think Ed didn't understand the language? He didn't need to be thrown out of there by one of their hoodlums. He left on his own.

He expected them to get in touch with him. They are loyal to their people. They even get them out of jail if they can't exchange them for one of theirs. If they weren't in touch with him, perhaps they had good reason. Maybe Trushenko was under surveillance and didn't want to compromise Ed. Something like that surely. But Ed couldn't stand the isolation.

He knew both Trushenko and Semyonov went to the UN building frequently. That's when he got the idea he would simply be a tourist, a visitor, and pass them a note in the lobby, arranging for a meeting to receive further instructions. The UN lobby was crowded most of the time. The chances of meeting at least one of them were good. So they didn't want him seen in the mission. On reflection, he could understand. He had been indicted for a crime they wouldn't want to be connected with. Surely they were pleased that Fuller is dead and can't do any more harm? Ed needed to know why they had cut him off. Could they get him out of the country? All his note said was for Semyonov or Trushenko to meet him at the Forty-second Street station of the Eighth Avenue subway at 5:00 P.M. or as soon thereafter as possible that day. Surely that was an inconspicuous place to meet? That station was always crowded with strange types.

It rained like a waterfall that afternoon. He is late, Ed thought. He even got solicited while waiting, this man no more than thirty with long blond hair and leather pants. Ed pitied the blond man, but shook his head till he went away. And then the subway cop, who'd been watching Ed, came over and told him, "No loitering." Ed had never taken any shit from cops. He said to him, "It's a free country," and the cop said, "Not down here. Move on or take the next train." Ed left by the nearest entrance and ran two blocks getting soaked in the rain, and down another entrance, hoping he hadn't in the elapsed minutes missed Trushenko.

When eight o'clock came, he felt as if he were coming down with a terrible cold. Why had he waited for three hours? Trushenko would never come. They would not throw him a life preserver.

All I have left now, he thought, is Thomassy. Then the doorbell rang. *They have sent someone to kill me.*

"Who is it?" Ed asked through the door.

"Open up," replied Thomassy's voice.

Ed took the chain lock off the door to let him in. Oh how beautiful his Armenian face suddenly seemed to him! He put out his hand. Thomassy looked at it, shook it perfunctorily. *Doesn't he shake hands with clients?* Ed remembered Thomassy had never shaken hands with him.

Thomassy sat in the chair Ed usually sat in. Ed sat down opposite.

"Coffee?" Ed asked him.

Thomassy shook his head.

"Anything?"

Thomassy shook his head again, then said, "What are we going to do with this case?"

What did he mean by that, he was the lawyer? He knows I have no one else. Of course, he wants more money. That's how they do it, just before the summations they ask for more money, is that it?

Finally Ed said, "You want more money."

Thomassy laughed. Ed didn't want to be laughed at. "Leave it to me in your will," he said. He must have seen the expression on Ed's face. "They don't have capital punishment in this state," he said.

"How does it look?" Ed asked.

"If you were the lawyer," Thomassy said, "how would it look to you?"

Ed couldn't answer that, knowing what was in his head.

Thomassy saw Ed as a rabbit chased up against a fence, turning, eyes frantic for another escape route. "What happened to the key to Fuller's study?"

Ed said nothing.

"Don't tell me *How should I know?* His wife didn't take it out of his burning bathrobe pocket. She was trying to save his life."

"So was I!"

"Listen, kid, nobody hears what you say to me. It's privileged client-lawyer talk. What did you do with the fucking key?"

The rabbit, unable to run, whispered, "I threw it in the toilet."

"Which toilet, upstairs or downstairs?"

"Upstairs."

"Suppose they'd taken apart the soil pipe, top to bottom?"

"I wrapped it in toilet tissue. I flushed the toilet fifteen times. That's nearly a hundred gallons of water. Even if they'd found it, they could never prove I'd thrown it in. I'm not stupid."

Thomassy felt heady, like the time he'd taken Francine to climb the two hundred rickety steps to the fire tower in Pound Ridge. The fire tower shook in the wind. It was like looking down from the top of a swaying toothpick. *The people versus whomever he was defending. Look what he was defending.* "If you were a juror," he said, "what would you be thinking?"

"About the key?"

"They don't know about the key! About the case!"

"I would want to be fair." *Thomassy, you are my Clarence Darrow, my brilliant advocate, my hope.*

"Were you fair to Fuller?"

Ed could hear screaming inside his skull.

He could hear Thomassy saying, "Don't tell me you were only following orders."

"What are you talking about?"

"Was Trushenko your control?"

Ed couldn't believe what he was hearing.

"I said was Trushenko your control, yes or no?"

"No, of course not!" Ed said, summoning strength.

"Will you sign an affidavit saying that he was not your control?"

"I won't sign any affidavits for anyone. Who put you up to this? Are you my lawyer or are you working for someone else?"

"You've lied on the stand. You've lied to me."

"What lies?" Ed stood up.

"Sit down!" Thomassy yelled. "Tomorrow I'm supposed to sum-marize this fucking case to the jury. If you were a child molester, I'd let them have you because I wouldn't want to see you on the streets again until your cock withered. Putting you away isn't

249

going to bring Fuller back. The kind of rehabilitation you need you won't get in prison. You know what I hate most about this case?"

He didn't want an answer from Ed.

"I'm supposed to go in front of the jury and conjure those people, lie to them the way you lied to me. Like hell I will."

"You can't abandon me!"

"Like hell I can't!" Thomassy said. "My father loved this country because it took him in. I take it for granted. But you'd give it to the barbarians. I came here to tell you face to face. You stink."

Ed's eyes blurred. He put his arm up in front of his face, thinking Thomassy was about to strike him. Then he heard the terrible thud of the wood door slammed.

□ CHAPTER THIRTY-SIX □

Thomassy's anger was like a black ball of acid corroding his gut. He walked in belligerent rage through the streets of New York, unnoticed.

I will not appear in court tomorrow. They won't find me.

He glanced up at the night sky, expecting stars, stumbled badly over a crack in the sidewalk. An old bagwoman noticed, squealed through a harpie's missing teeth, "You could have broken your head, mister."

Insane. As if there aren't enough murders, we kill ourselves.

He stopped to lean against a parked car, breathless, dared look up again. His view, blocked by buildings ablaze with rectangles of artificial light, showed in the narrow patch of permitted sky, not one star, nothing. Haig Thomassian had drummed into the young boy's head that his Armenian forebears were the first Christians. Was he now making waste of his life among the last?

Faced with an impossible choice, he put tomorrow off till tomorrow and rushed to find the aphrodisiac of life today.

When Thomassy got to the hospital, the round-faced lady at the desk said it was after visiting hours. When he was younger he would have raised his battering voice, telling her who he was, threatening wrath from above. . . . He glanced to his left. In front of the elevators a uniformed guard was at his post.

250

He left without a word, went once more around the periphery of the building to the door marked "Staff Entrance." Inside, a starched white-garbed woman said, "Doctor?" with a question at the end of her voice.

"Yes?"

"I didn't recognize you."

"Sorry," he said, "I didn't recognize you either," and went straight for the staff elevator.

"One minute, please," she said too late for the doors of the elevator closed on her prey before she could reach it.

At Francine's floor, Thomassy stepped out of the elevator, saw in a second that he'd never get by the nurses' station. Quickly, he stepped back into the elevator, went down one floor. Francine's room would be all the way down the corridor, just before the stairway at the end. If he went to the end of this floor and took the stairway up . . .

The floor was like a holding pen for old people, milling around, chattering. They looked gregarious, not sick. He moved through them as a doctor might, smiling here and there, and they smiled back, watching the friendly newcomer's back as he bounded for the far stairway, and unlike the other doctors, who always took the elevator, went up the stairs with the kind of energy some of them remembered once having.

On Francine's floor, Thomassy opened the stairway door slowly. He was not ten feet from Francine's room. All the way down the hall at the nurses' station the white, starched birds fluttered over what, a joke? He walked the ten steps, opened the door. Safely inside, he went quickly to her bed. He watched her face. She seemed a child, too young for him. The gap of seventeen years would never narrow. When she grew older, he'd be old. He lifted a chair silently, silently set it down next to her bed, and without a sound, he sat down.

She couldn't have heard him, yet her eyes opened, first small slits, then large and alive. "How long have you been in here?" she breathed, quickly darting her good hand to him.

"Missed visiting hours. Had to sneak in like jail." He stood up, bent over her, kissed her forehead.

"That's what my father did."

"What?"

"Kissed my forehead."

And so he kissed her the way he had been used to kissing her.

"You're looking better," he said.

She touched the front of his pants with her fingers.

251

"It's still there," he said.

"Can you hang a sign on it, like the real-estate people do, saying sold or something like that."

"How about rented?"

"Always the lawyer. George?" She clenched his warm hand.

"What?"

"Last night, in the middle of the night, I woke up and thought I was dead for a minute. They'd given me some stupid sleeping pills. George, just because you're older, that doesn't mean you have to die first."

"What kind of dope have they been giving you?"

"I never really believed I could die before the accident. And if I can die, you can, too. You run so fast I bet you never think about it."

"I think about it."

"I'm getting out in two days."

"Why didn't you say so?"

"I'll have to take it easy for a couple or three weeks. My mother says I should stay with them so she can watch me daytimes. You can't stay there at night." She sighed. "This is getting impossible. Half the time it's death on my mind and the other half sex."

"That's the standard battle."

"Can you make love to me now? Gently? The nurses don't come by at this hour. You could put a chair under the door handle. George, make love to me so the dying will go away."

Thomassy glanced at his wristwatch. Francine was peacefully asleep, her face just barely visible from the blue-gray light filtering through the window blinds.

He got dressed quickly. He wanted to leave her a message. Nothing to write on. He started to scribble something on the back of a calling card, scratched it out. Words were no longer good enough. Gently, he removed the chair from the door, looked back once at the undulations under the sheet, the face now turned away from him. It could have gone the other way, Tilly husbandless in the hospital, Francine husbandless in the morgue. Who watches us when we are not watching over ourselves?

Out the door, without thinking he turned left, realizing the direction he'd taken only as he passed the nurses' station, and the solitary night guardian looked up.

"What are you doing here?"

Thomassy leaned over her desk, his hands flat within inches of

her hands. "I was ministering to the lady in six-oh-eight. She's one
of this country's great women. Please care for her."

He removed his hands, stood straight, turned to go.

"Are you a doctor?" the nurse said.

"Tonight," Thomassy said, "I think I was."

□ CHAPTER THIRTY-SEVEN □

Ladies and gentlemen of the jury, Thomassy began, *before you stands a
lawyer who last night, after visiting hours, sneaked illegitimately into the
hospital room of a female of the species, and in acts that some of you would
condemn, held hands, kissed multiple times with great intensity, and finally achieved the most gentle, wonderful illicit sexual union. This holy
act—and I say this because only a god could have invented nerve endings
suited to such a grand binge of heartburst and semenspurt—this holy act
not only did the recumbent, injured lady in question no harm, but she was
restored, renewed, and overjoyed to be fully orgasmic and alive after beginning to recover from a brutal car crash deliberately arranged by three Spanish-speaking males who confused courtship with a cock fight. I am here to
tell you that in the not-so-long-ago, I was myself a mere man like them,
brought up on locker-room language and only belatedly learned that all
those man-to-man descriptions of humping, thumping, pumping, and so
on, are fraudulently inaccurate renderings of what can and does take place
when a man and a woman are ready for each other. Gentlemen of the jury,
if any of you have not experienced the feeling of frenzied butterflies around
the corona of your penis caused by the purposeful circling of a skilled,
loving, grasping vagina, you are missing something Napoleon would have
given Europe for. And what an anticlimax it is for me to be with you this
morning to speak ostensibly in defense of mere murder.*

"Mr. Thomassy," Judge Drewson said, "are you ready for your
summation?"

I am ready to walk out of this courtroom.

"I said are you ready for your summation!"

I have been giving my summation! "No, Your Honor," he said
aloud. And not aloud, *Francine, I love you.* Then Thomassy turned
to the courtroom in which every seat was filled, his gaze on the

253

doors at the back, trying not to see the more than a hundred pairs of eyes looking at him.

Through his paralysis he could hear the murmur of the spectators and then the judge's gavel.

"The court will stand in recess," the judge said. "Mr. Thomassy, can you hear me?"

"Yes, Your Honor."

"Will you step into chambers, please."

Why was the gray-uniformed guard holding the door to the judge's chambers open for him, did the man think he couldn't open it himself? The back of his scalp felt wet. Thomassy touched his forehead with the back of his left hand; it came away damp. How clearly he remembered losing his patience with the students, snapping *There's nothing that says you have to take on a client, but once you take him on, it's like giving birth, the case is yours until the client doesn't need you anymore.* And the young, tall, shy boy way back in the lecture hall had held up his hand and said, "Sir, how do you know ahead of time it's a case you want?" And Thomassy had replied, "Because you have the perception of a god!" which got a laugh, but was a lie, so he added, "Sometimes you get stuck!"

Where did he get that crap about children? He had been a child. If he felt helpless now, where was *his* Thomassy to rescue him?

Judge Drewson, sitting opposite him at the end of the long walnut conference table, hadn't said a word.

Thomassy took out his handkerchief and carefully wiped his forehead and then the palms of his hands. But he couldn't meet the judge's eyes for fear he would betray the banging terror in his chest.

At last the judge said, "Mr. Thomassy, I've had counsel unprepared for summations before this but I've never heard one admit it."

Thomassy said nothing.

"Are you ill?"

A loud, distracting knock on the door was followed by Roberts entering. "Your Honor, I was wondering —"

"Come in, come in and sit down, Mr. Roberts. I was not discussing anything relevant to the case with defense counsel. I was inquiring about his health."

Thomassy shook his head as if to clear it. "I'm okay, Your Honor. I apologize."

Why the hell was Roberts staring at him like that?

254

"Nothing like this has happened to me before," Thomassy said to the judge. "I'm sorry. I've been under a strain."

"I understand your fiancée was in a bad auto accident."

"It's not Miss Widmer, Your Honor. I had a very difficult conversation with my client yesterday . . ." How could he talk with Roberts present?

There was another brief knock on the door. When it swung open, Thomassy could see the court attendant trying to block Jackson Perry from entering the room.

"Your Honor," Perry was saying, trying to get the guard to lower his arm, "I was concerned that—"

Judge Drewson interrupted him. "Mr. Perry, do you understand plain English?"

The guard lowered his arm.

Perry nodded.

"Then stay the hell out of here!" snapped the judge. Then he turned to Roberts and said, "I think you'd better leave too. You have my word that nothing affecting the evidence will be discussed between us."

Roberts, his face flushed, rose. "Your Honor, I must protest—"

"All you like, to whomever you like, but I want to have a few words with Mr. Thomassy in private. Understood?"

When Roberts left, the judge, his voice calmed, said, "I'm not a doctor, but you looked a bit out of it in the courtroom as if you had suddenly been taken ill . . ." He spoke slowly, choosing words carefully. "Or were having a garden-variety anxiety attack. In how many murder cases have you acted for the defendant?"

"Sixty-one, Your Honor. This would be the sixty-second."

"Let me hazard something. I believe you accepted this case not in your normal routine but at the instigation of others, that you expected to be defending, as you have in the past, a defendant accused of murder. I could make an educated guess and suggest that in the course of this trial you have yourself formed an indictment different from the one handed down by the Grand Jury. Please don't acknowledge by word or even headshake whether I am correct. There are some attorneys who shirk no case that produces income for them. You are in the unusual position of having elected to defend a man whom you have turned against on knowledge of the nature of his actual crime. Mr. Thomassy, to desert that defendant now, for any cause, would be an act of treason."

The word reverberated in the room like a curse. *I know,* Thomassy wanted to say, *I know.*

Judge Drewson was saying, "When I was a young man I was in love with a woman who was aspiring to be an actress. We went to the theater a lot, upstairs in the cheaper seats. I remember how one night we managed to get to the theater in a snowstorm because we didn't want the tickets to go unused. I really couldn't afford to buy them again. We got there ten minutes late, wet and cold, but the curtain wasn't up because the star had canceled, ostensibly over illness. The audience was thinned out, but of those that had gotten to the theater, not one person believed the star was ill. We thought she had chickened out. There are certain roles in life that require our appearance no matter the weather outside. Or inside."

Judge Drewson suddenly seemed embarrassed by his turn of phrase. "It wouldn't be like you to quit," he said.

Thomassy looked at Drewson and saw the man behind the courtesy. *Even if he made up that story about the theater, it was an act of kindness.* Thomassy had always thought of judges as the people up there, politicians, hacks willing to be bored in exchange for the mantle of authority. *Not this man. He is civilizing me, like Francine.*

"I'm sorry," Thomassy said, his voice a shroud.

"I will not find you in contempt if you walk out of this courtroom," the judge said, "but I believe that you will find yourself in contempt of yourself for the rest of your career as a lawyer if you don't get out there and do the kind of job you have a reputation for. The only tolerable decision is that of the jury. And you and I and the defendant will have to live with their determination. Now, if you want some time, I'll recess till this afternoon."

Thomassy felt shame for the wetness in his eyes.

"You can use my bathroom to wash up," the judge said, pointing.

The white ceramic glare of the immaculate bathroom blinded Thomassy for a moment as he tried to focus on his face in the mirror, the red deltas of his eyes, the streaked cheeks of boyhood tears. Despite the sweet bullshit of the judge, he heard himself thinking *I can't do it,* and then, plucked from memory were the same words.

He'd been eleven. His father, before heading for the stables, had said to his mother and himself, *When a man breaks leg, they fix cast. When horse breaks leg, finish. What kind of God sins against horses?* He'd slammed the door so hard the dishes on the table rattled.

"Go to him," Thomassy's mother said.

Thomassy didn't want to be with his father when he was railing.

256

"Go," his mother ordered.

In the farthest stable, away from the whinnying of the other horses, he found his father sitting on the ground with his arms around the mare's neck. The mare's huge right eye betrayed its fear.

Thomassy saw the pistol lying near his father's knee. He wanted to run back to the house. *Can you do it?* his father had asked. *You put the gun against the side of the head behind the ear and pull the trigger just once.*

Thomassy ran from the barn, and his father had run after him, the gun in his hand. When Haig Thomassian caught up to his son, he held the gun pointing heavenward for safety, and said to the quivering boy, *When I am dead and you are the man, you will have to do what is necessary. God is a coward. Do you understand?*

Thomassy had stood rooted in the field, watching his father walk back to the barn in the moonlight, and then, after an endless time, he'd heard the shot.

He'd gone closer to the barn, and when his father finally came out, he remembered his father put his arm around his shoulders and Thomassy had instinctively put his arm around his father's waist, and the two had walked in mourning together back to the house where Marya waited.

When Thomassy emerged from the bathroom, his hands and face and eyes were dry. He said, "You are a very understanding man, Your Honor."

The judge said, "We've all been touched by the same thing."

Not quite the same.

"I will do what is necessary," Thomassy said, grateful that in the carnival of the law, he did not have to pull a trigger.

□ CHAPTER THIRTY-EIGHT □

Thomassy, facing the twelve rapt jurors behind their wooden barrier, felt like a man who had come out of a terrible fever. He was back in his world.

He began his summation with the words he always started off with. "I wonder if you and I couldn't talk this thing out."

The jurors strained to hear him. That meant the judge and the spectators would be straining even more. Straining helps the attention.

With his eyes he was saying to the jurors: *This is between you and me.*

"When I got out of law school," he said, "I did a lot of civil liberties work because I was interested in justice and I saw a lot of injustice around to older people, black people, Spanish-speaking people, people people. I learned that there are a few individuals with a lot of power, most of them working—when they're working—for the government. Since 1776 we don't have a king, we have a lot of little kings who get their kicks out of coming after the people who don't have power. Looking at you I'd guess your parents came from a lot of different backgrounds. My parents were Armenians. They came to this country because here you can fight back. The law here doesn't let the little guy get beat up in some back room and thrown into the jug to rot the way they do today in a lot of places. The law gives us this big room so what we do is in public view. And we pick twelve citizens who are as clean of prejudging other people as we can find and let them know that they are the sole judges of the facts in this case."

Before this trial he had always enjoyed what he thought of as *jury bullshit*, building their egos, palsying, flirting, pretending, talking down, telling them what to think, and they loved it. But as he walked along the front of the box, looking at each one of them, making sure they knew each one was under the tent he had erected to seal them and him off from the others, he knew he no longer loved it.

Even lawyers can grow up, George.

Go away, Francine. I've got a job to do.

258

"There is much about this case that is confusing, even how it got here in the first place. We all know the biggest growth industry in this country is violent crime. We all know that billions of dollars of hard drugs come into this country, that kids the defendant's age and younger get hooked on hard drugs to the point where they have to steal and rob and commit violence to support their expensive habits. The government admits they get only about ten percent of the drugs coming in, and you'd think with our concern about the violence that results from just this one habit that the government would go after the ninety percent like gangbusters. But they don't. The government is going after an accomplished young man, a scholar with two graduate degrees at the age of twenty-four, and a respected book to his credit. And what do they go after him with? Circumstantial evidence. Not real hard eyewitness evidence—I saw him do this or I saw him do that—but what I call 'maybe' evidence."

Thomassy turned his back on the jurors and looked directly at Roberts. "The prosecution," Thomassy said, "has the burden of proof of every issue that's been raised in this trial. In New York— and that's what we're operating under here, New York law—Section three eighty-nine of the Code of Criminal Procedure says that if anyone is accused of a crime, the presumption is in favor of his innocence. No ifs and no buts. The defendant is entitled to rest upon the presumption of innocence in his favor unless the prosecutor offers evidence that so far outweighs the presumption of innocence that each and every one of you without exception is convinced of his guilt beyond a reasonable doubt.

"The easiest way to understand reasonable doubt is that if you are a hundred percent sure of someone's guilt, okay, but if you're only ninety-nine percent sure, the other one percent is reasonable doubt."

The judge may hang me for that definition but the jurors will remember it.

"You've probably been in a lot of situations in your life where you felt your opinion didn't count for all that much. But here it's different. If eleven other people are one hundred percent sure and you're not so sure, that's enough reasonable doubt for an acquittal. This is one election in which your personal vote can be as important as everyone else's put together."

Francine, this is the first time in an exemplary legal career that I am delivering a summation with half my mind. I have to work. Take your hands off my thighs. Stop kissing my arms. Stop making me need you so much!

Thank God the jury still had its attention fixed on him. He took a deep, ghost-chasing breath. "Now that that's settled," he said, "let's take a look at the so-called evidence that the prosecution has offered here for your inspection. There's the button that the detective detected in the garage. It could have come off the accused's jacket, or the detective's raincoat or any of thousands of other MacGregor jackets or raincoats that we don't know about. Does that prove that the bathroom fire wasn't an accident? That anybody did it on purpose? And that Edward Porter Sturbridge in particular committed assault with intent to murder with a deadly weapon? Or are we talking about a button found in a garage?"

Thomassy looked down at his jacket. "Just checking the buttons," he said. "You never know what someone will make out of a dropped button. If they don't have a case.

"What are some of the other things that have been said here? Edward Porter Sturbridge slept over at the Fullers' lots of times. Do you invite someone to sleep over if you have any reason not to trust them? You heard Mrs. Fuller in her grief say she trusted the defendant. The night before the accident the defendant was one of three people who slept over at the Fullers. If sleeping over ever becomes a crime, you'd have to lock up a significant portion of the teenage population. And maybe some of the adult population as well. Actually, the only crime that's been admitted in this courtroom was the adultery committed by the other two people who slept over. Were the goings-on in Miss Troob's bedroom a cover-up for some more insidious activity? There's been no more proof of that than there's been proof that the defendant did anything that night except what he said he did, use the downstairs bathroom because the hall door to the upstairs one was left locked by Mr. Melling.

"We heard some testimony about some strange detective work. Detective Cooper found some folded curtains stashed on a high shelf in a closet. I don't know how normal it is for guests to go prying into their host's closets, but Detective Cooper is a detective and I guess that gives him a chance to do what we folks abstain from doing. He pushed the curtains aside and found some old magazines of a kind that I assume didn't belong to the Fullers, but he didn't inquire as to who they might have belonged to in order to ascertain how long those magazines had been there. But behind the magazines, lo and behold he finds a flask of the kind he used to take to football games. There has been no link between that flask, used for carrying liquor, and the accused, who testified he does not drink liquor. No initials. No identification. You heard ab-

260

solutely zero proof that the stashed curtains, the magazines, or the flask belonged to the defendant, and ladies and gentlemen, you are here to examine proof and not to get romanced into a lot of speculation of a kind that could be said about anybody who stayed overnight anywhere. We have heard that the accused ran downstairs naked. If you run downstairs naked because you hear someone screaming for help and you don't want to take the time to even slip something on—is that a crime or the act of a samaritan? Or a friend? Pushing a six-foot torch under the shower to try to get the fire out, does that sound like someone trying to hurt or to help? Common sense tells you it was to help, and any other interpretation requires you to turn logic upside down.

"Being someone's disciple is not a crime. Helping out around the house, doing chores older people sometimes find difficult, like mowing the lawn, is not a crime. When you get into the jury room, you take a good long hard look at the counts of the indictment because, ladies and gentlemen, those are the crimes. If the evidence you've seen doesn't support those counts beyond a reasonable doubt, you're going to find the defendant innocent.

"Suppose what happened was not an accident? Nobody has proved it wasn't, but let's do what the prosecution has done, rely on some conjecture. Who would want to kill Martin Fuller. He was doing important work for the United States. Who would want to put an end to that? Obviously, the enemies of the United States, and I'm afraid we've got quite a few. My question to you is were the disciples of Martin Fuller, the young people who were his friends and junior colleagues, threats to him? Please remember that all of those people got some kind of security check from the federal government. Wouldn't those experienced people have sniffed out someone who was potentially dangerous to Professor Fuller? If so, where must we then look? You heard testimony here from Professor Ludmilla Tarasova, second, perhaps, only to the late Professor Fuller in the field of Soviet experts, how the U.S.S.R. has had people killed in this country for decades. Have those killers been caught? And if they haven't, is that what's so embarrassing to the government, that we can't stop hired dedicated foreign assassins from operating on our turf? We don't yet know if President Kennedy was killed by a loner or as part of a well-worked-out conspiracy. If there was a conspiracy to kill Martin Fuller—if his death wasn't an accident—where are those conspirators? Why isn't the law chasing them down? The point I'm making is that all of the potential or probable killers of Martin Fuller have not been put on trial here. The government took the easy way. They picked one young man, devoted to Professor Fuller, who was his mentor, and who—you heard the testimony—whom he loved.

Thomassy looked around the courtroom. *All you angels filling those seats,* he wanted to say, *do you know the statistics? That you kill someone you love much more often than you kill an intruder, an enemy, someone you don't know? In Europe, according to Francine the Intelligent, pleading a crime of passion is practically a guaranteed way of getting a client off. Was this a crime of passion?*

Some of the faces seemed to be wondering why he was not speaking.

I am not obligated to tell you the whole truth, only what I choose to tell you. I do not have the responsibilities of a witness. I am an advocate, and that word, advocate, ladies and gentlemen, sticks in my fucking craw. Is this what every ambassador for every country in the world feels like when he feels revulsion at the message he's been ordered to deliver?

Judge Drewson said, "Mr. Thomassy?"

"Sorry, Your Honor. Just getting my second wind."

He adjusted the knot of his tie. No one ever faulted you for adjusting the knot of your tie.

Then he said, "Which brings me to the subject of intent. Ladies and gentlemen, without proof of intent the government has no case. The judge will support me on that when he instructs you on the law.

"I'm afraid this case is flimsier than the paper the charges were typed on. It was irresponsible to bring those charges into this or any other courtroom. Governments, where the power lies, should act with greater responsibility. But we say that all the time, don't we?

"Under the New York law, it is a well-settled rule that where the prosecution relies wholly upon circumstantial evidence to try to establish the guilt of the defendant, the circumstances must be—I repeat *must* be—of such a character as, if true, to exclude to a moral certainty every other hypothesis except that of the accused's guilt. And I say to you that each of us has lots of other hypotheses rattling around in our brains as a result of what we have seen and heard here. The law says all those other hypotheses have to be ruled out before you can begin to think about the defendant losing his presumptive innocence.

"Which brings me to my final point, a point that I want you to take into the jury room if you take no other. It doesn't matter whether you memorize it word for word or remember the idea behind it. The most important words of this trial are: The defendant is entitled to rest upon the presumption of his innocence unless it

262

is so far outweighed—so far outweighed, remember those words—by the evidence offered by the prosecution that you are convinced of his guilt and nobody else's possible guilt beyond a reasonable doubt. If there are only four words you should remember exactly they are: beyond a reasonable doubt."

Thomassy spotted the woman in the front row of the juror box move her hands as if to applaud and catch herself just in time, blushing embarrassedly. He looked at her and nodded as if to say it's all right. He hoped she'd feel the same way after the prosecution got its last licks in. Just once, just once he'd like the last words to be his.

□ CHAPTER THIRTY-NINE □

Thank heaven there wasn't a lineup at the phone booths. Thomassy closed the door, plunked in his dime, heard the mechanical voice ask for thirty cents, and his right hand fished in his change pocket for two more dimes, plunk and plunk, and when he was connected, asked for Francine's room.

"One moment, please," the woman at the hospital switchboard said, then got back on the line. "Not putting through calls to that room right now. Doctor's orders."

"Let me have the nurses' desk on that floor." He hadn't meant to bark an order.

"Okay, okay," the woman said.

He waited. The goddamn way they make you wait, hanging. Finally, a voice.

Thomassy said, "I'm calling about Miss Widmer in six-oh-eight. They're not putting calls through. What's up?"

"Who is this calling, please?"

"Mr. Widmer," Thomassy said, almost without thinking. He had a prerogative, a right to know.

"Oh," the voice said, "there's another Mr. Widmer right here. I'll let you speak to him."

Christ. Ned Widmer said, "Yes?"

"Ned, this is George. I have no credentials so I said I was you. Or her husband. What's the damn matter?"

263

"I just got here, George. Priscilla says her temperature went up."

"How up?"

"Hundred one. The doctor ordered some tests after he'd made his rounds. Her white count's up. Possible she has an infection somewhere. They're doing a lung scan just to be sure they didn't miss anything on the X-rays. He said with auto trauma they go after the obvious things first, like the broken arm, sometimes miss some minor internal injury. It could be something totally unrelated to the accident like an infection of some kind. They're checking that, too."

"Do you think it's serious?"

"No, I'm sure nothing serious."

It's very serious. I love her crazily. "Ned, they're beginning the prosecution's summation in just a few minutes. I'm tied down here."

"There's no reason to be concerned."

I made her worse.

Widmer continued, "I'm coming back over to the courthouse, George. I'll see you there."

Thomassy crossed one leg over the other. Then reversed. *A good fuck always made you feel better not worse. Francine said she felt wonderful.* It's your fault, he said to the place where his crossed legs joined.

Ed Porter touched Thomassy's arm. "That man," he said.

Thomassy, from his distraction said, "Which man?"

Ed pointed to Roberts.

"Oh, he's just working himself up for his summation," Thomassy said. "What you're seeing is a cold fish trying to warm his blood a bit. I wouldn't worry about it."

"When was the last time you lost a case?" Ed's eyes seemed to be shimmering.

"Look, Ed," Thomassy said, "consult your horoscope. What counts is how we make out in *this* trial *this* time. If you don't like Roberts staring at you, stare back."

Ed, pinching the edge of the wooden table in front of him, turned just enough to face Roberts directly. Instantly, Roberts looked away.

"See," Thomassy said, busying himself with his marginal notations, "rabbits run."

"Why does he get the last word?" Ed said, worrying the cuticle of his middle finger.

"I wouldn't do that within sight of the jury," Thomassy said. "They'll think you've got something to be worried about. Relax."

"Why does the DA get the last word?"

"Because it's the custom."

"Your Honor, ladies and gentlemen of the jury," Roberts began. He repeated the specific charges, emphasizing the words *assault, deadly weapon, intent, death*. They had been written into the law. Now use them. See if they fit. He positioned himself perhaps eight feet in front of the jury box. "You are here to determine the facts. Not the judge. Not me. Not the defense counsel. You've been exposed to rhetoric, of course, but to reach your conclusion, all you are required to examine is the evidence and the testimony. The testimony you have heard can be summed up this way. Professor Martin Fuller, a much honored scholar engaged in important and, alas, unfinished work, is no longer among the living because in the early morning of April fifth, as was his custom, he went in for his morning shower and ignited the kerosene heater in his bathroom, as he had done every morning for years. He was incinerated, a human torch dying a horrible and undeserved death because some person—I hesitate to say a human being—mixed a quantity of gasoline in with the kerosene in the heater."

Roberts turned away from the jurors and as if looking past the first few rows for someone, walked to the press section. *Just a reminder, boys and girls, of who's playing the lead.*

Come on, Thomassy thought, get on with it!

Roberts, as if tuned in to Thomassy's signal, glanced at his opponent and got himself back to the jury box. "Evidence," he said, "was introduced to show that the separate containers of gasoline and kerosene kept in the Fuller garage were uncontaminated by each other, meaning someone brought some gas—it could have been a relatively small quantity—and poured it into the fuel opening of the heater that already contained kerosene. Who *would* do such a thing?

"You heard Detective Cooper testify that he found a flask hidden in the closet of the room occupied by the defendant in the Fuller home, a flask that had recently been washed out. What was washed out? There were traces of inflammable fluid near the defendant's bed. He told Detective Cooper he spilled some lighter fluid. Yet he couldn't find his lighter—surprise!—and he had no cigarettes—surprise!—and then you heard evidence that he doesn't smoke. You'd have to be deaf and dumb and blind not to see the connection between the flask and the spilled inflammable fluid and the middle-of-the-night visit to the downstairs bathroom—where he slipped up and left his watch—and the explosion the following morning.

"Why would he do such a thing? Why would he commit such a monstrous act?

"The defendant's counsel has made it clear, through the testimony of Professor Tarasova and otherwise, that Martin Fuller was engaged in work that was important to the national security of the United States and that stopping that contribution dead in its tracks was of greater import perhaps than knocking one of our early-warning satellites out of the sky. Every day people kill for gain or revenge or out of jealousy, but there's been no evidence here that any of these common motives apply in this case. Common sense would tell us that Professor Fuller was killed for one reason and one reason only: to stop the work he was doing. Therefore, I ask you, who would benefit from his death? Not his wife, not his friends, not anyone who would call himself a friend of the United States. However . . ."

Thomassy didn't think Roberts would have the guts to do it, but he did. Roberts came straight over to the defense table and staring straight down at Ed he said, "This defendant has sworn that he was a friend and disciple of the deceased." Roberts looked up, and strode over to the jury. "I hope none of you counts as a friend someone who would insinuate himself into your life, pretending to be—"

"I object!" Thomassy roared. "Your Honor, this jury is innocent of experience. In the impaneling room we learned that none of them has ever served on a jury before. When the district attorney used works like 'insinuate himself into your life' he is not talking about the defendant or this case or the evidence in it or the testimony that was taken. Your Honor, the learned district attorney is here to sum up and not invent."

Judge Drewson often said at home over dinner that you preserved your vanity on the bench and got cases done with by knowing what missteps to overlook. But George Thomassy was not letting this get by, and now, with the world's press observing, he could not. He summoned counsel to the bench.

Thomassy knew that the lecture that was given both of them in order to preserve the judge's stance of impartiality was not a matter of great consequence. What he had accomplished was to break Roberts's stride. *Lingua interrupta.* He'd have to grab the jury's ears all over again. First, he'd have to yank his vest down. And as Roberts positioned himself in front of the jury box, yank he did.

Roberts said to the jurors, "I apologize for the interruption."

That son-of-a-bitch, Thomassy thought.

"I suggest," Roberts continued quietly, "that we look dispassionately at the first question I asked. *Who* would perpetrate the kind of murder that has been described here? The defendant's counsel has attempted to obfuscate the facts by dragging a carload of red herrings across the courtroom, by attempting to indicate how many, many people might have been motivated to commit a barbaric act of this sort.

"But ladies and gentlemen, the *only* question—I repeat, the *only* question—for you to consider is do the facts point to a particular individual doing this deed? This wasn't a vague act committed against an anonymous person by an equally anonymous killer. This was an act of deliberate murder committed against a particular person, the distinguished professor, by a particular killer, ironically someone he had learned to trust and love. And by trusting the defendant, Edward Porter Sturbridge, by counseling him, giving him friendship, offering him the hospitality of his house time and again, Professor Fuller, a man of considerable sophistication, made a mistake as great as the mistake Eve made in the Garden of Eden, because this defendant, this young man of a rich father who had the best of everything, was the snake who, in the middle of the night, would sneak down to the Professor's bathroom with a flask full of gasoline and pour it into the kerosene heater with intent to kill."

Thomassy stood. He said nothing. He just stood there till the judge noticed him and Roberts noticed him and stopped talking.

Judge Drewson said, "Mr. Roberts, I think the people ought to get out of the Garden of Eden and away from the snakes. We are considering an event that happened this year."

"I'm sorry, Your Honor," Roberts said. "It was a simile that sprang to mind."

Thomassy said, "Your Honor, may we approach the bench?" Once there, he said, "I must move for a mistrial, Your Honor."

The judge looked at him. "You make that motion and I'll grant it and then where would you be? I think everyone would benefit if Mr. Roberts were able to conclude his remarks without further objections and interruptions."

"I did not object, Your Honor," Thomassy said.

"You stood up."

"I stood because I felt sure Your Honor would object to the prosecution's improprieties, as Your Honor has."

The judge sighed. "Well, Mr. Roberts, let's resume."

Roberts strode over to the prosecution table to gather up some papers. Thomassy thought *He's buying time.* Thomassy glanced up. The judge was looking at him instead of Roberts. Was it a silent warning not to rattle Roberts's bones anymore? Thomassy nodded. Message received. He settled back to watch what he knew would be Roberts's climax. *I hope he comes all over that vest of his.* Was something sexual larded into courtroom combat? The anticipation. The jockeying for position. The combat governed by rules. The amount of ego invested in the outcome. He'd always thought the process of winning was the process of winning. Francine had said *It's a dance with both partners trying to lead.*

Roberts was ready. "Ladies and gentlemen," he began, "common sense is a very good guide. Common sense, in this case, tells us that if gasoline had been introduced into the kerosene heater sometime before the previous morning, the heater would have exploded the previous morning. Therefore, the gasoline had to be introduced between the time Professor Fuller took his shower on the morning of April fourth and the explosive morning of April fifth. During that period there were five people other than the deceased in that house. Did Mrs. Fuller do it? There is not a shred of evidence to indicate that she would have the motive to do it. One of the people, a student by the name of Barry Heskowitz, the one who didn't stay overnight, arrived before dinner, stayed through dinner, and left immediately after dinner, in full sight of the others present the entire time except for one trip to the bathroom. You heard testimony that visitors commonly used the professor's bathroom because it was nearest to the living room and dining room, but none of them left their watches in that bathroom except the defendant. Are we to believe that Barry Heskowitz had a container—say a half-pint container at least—in his pocket and secretly slipped into Professor Fuller's bathroom in order to pour the gasoline into the heater and then take off so that he wouldn't be around when the explosion happened the next morning? It was brought out in testimony that Barry Heskowitz, though he visited the Fuller home from time to time, never stayed over. What purpose could he have had? Nothing was introduced that would prove intent. Barry Heskowitz is just one defense red herring for the garbage pail.

"Three of the guests did stay over. We heard Melissa Troob testify—with visible embarrassment—as to her reason for staying over. Her motive was clear. It was not murder.

"Scott Melling also testified as to his movements that night. Do you believe he put the gas into the kerosene and then locked the upstairs bathroom door to force the defendant to use the down-stairs bathroom in order to implicate him in this crime? Hardly. Mr. Melling told the truth here at the peril of his marriage. As with Melissa Troob it is up to you and you alone to judge the truth of his testimony and whether he had any reason for doing harm to his host.

"Finally, we come to the defendant. We heard testimony to the effect that not only did he stay over at the Fuller house frequently, but he cut the Fuller's grass, he was in and out of their garage where the lawn mower was kept, he had plenty of occasions to see the two cans, one of gasoline and one of kerosene, and time to formulate a plan that would make Professor Fuller's death look like a terrible accident. No guns that could be traced. No obvious other weapons that might or might not have worked. But a weapon that was a common household object that required only a bit of tamper-ing once and his mission was accomplished."

Thomassy watched Roberts's face carefully. *He's putting the black cap on. Here it comes.*

"Ladies and gentlemen," Roberts said, "nobody knows what went on in the minds of the members of the Grand Jury when they indicted Edward Porter Sturbridge and made him the defendant in this trial. What matters is what you think based on the evidence you saw and heard. You saw four photographs taken by the FBI who had certain Soviet diplomats suspected of being KGB mem-bers under surveillance. They weren't taking those pictures for the heck of it, they were trying to photograph their contacts, Amer-icans cheating on America."

Thomassy had to restrain himself. The son-of-a-bitch was going far beyond the testimony. But Thomassy knew that if he inter-rupted the summation a third time, it might be the last straw for Drewson. And the jurors didn't like summations interrupted ei-ther. Well, he'd taken license, now Roberts was taking it. Tit for tat.

"A photograph is worth a thousand words," Roberts said, "If that's true those photographs are worth four thousand words all saying the same thing: This defendant was trying to make contact with the Soviets. Why? You don't have to be an expert in Soviet affairs, all you need is your common sense. He'd done his work. If they didn't know who he was, if he was a stranger, would the senior man have gone trotting off in the opposite direction? Would the other man have rushed away? Common sense tells us they reacted as if the defendant had leprosy because they recognized him and knew what he did. Was the defendant claiming his due?

We may never know the answer to that one, but I ask you, can you think of an innocent reason why Edward Porter Sturbridge was trying to make contact with two Soviet diplomats who were under suspicion by the FBI?

"To corroborate the message of the photographs, we heard evidence from an eyewitness. Not a witness to the murder, no one saw that, but to that attempt by the defendant to make contact with the enemy in the lobby of the UN building soon after Professor Fuller's death. What nerve he had to have! Yes, but what nerve it takes to snuff the life of another human being!

"You heard the testimony of Francine Widmer, walking in that same corridor in the UN, where she works. I asked her, 'Miss Widmer, did there come a time that you witnessed anything unusual on your way to work through the UN lobby and if so, would you describe it.' And she did, in meticulous detail. She saw with her own eyes the young man thrusting something that looked like a folded piece of paper at the Soviet diplomats. You heard her testimony. The young man finally caught up with the second Soviet diplomat and he took it. I ask you, would he have taken it if the young man was a stranger to him? Common sense will tell you otherwise. And then you saw the witness point a finger at the young man right in this courtroom because she recognized him as the same young man she had seen in Mr. Thomassy's office. Just as if she were pointing him out in a police lineup, she directed her finger—as I am now directing my finger—at the defendant in this case. Did you believe her?"

Roberts turned to look straight at Thomassy when he said, "As the daughter of one attorney and the close friend of another, she would surely know the perils of perjury. What motive would she have for lying? None. You saw her. You heard her."

I saw her, Thomassy thought, but the image was not of Francine on the stand but in that hospital bed, a wounded eaglet, her wounded wing still in a sling, her body still black and blue in spots from contusions, her spirit subdued, her soul soaring to his touches, her announced anguish at not being able to throw her hands and body into motion as before, and yet, with it all, it had been a lovely lovemaking, full of the feeling of coming back to life. Afterward, she'd touched the sticky spot on the sheet and said, "You ought to give some of this to the sperm bank, George. The world needs more lovers like you." In all the years before Francine he'd met some interesting women, but none capable of saying something like that by way of *I love you*.

I love you, too, Francine, he discovered himself thinking as he looked up, wondering what he had missed as Roberts rested his hands on the top of the wooden barrier that protected the bottom halves of the men and women in the jury box from the gaze of others, as he talked to the twelve upper torsos supporting faces, not one of them as radiant as Francine's, each trying to attend with intelligence every word that Roberts put before them.

"Yet," Roberts was saying, "the defendant under oath, in front of you, said he had been there to do research before Professor Fuller died and not after. Did you believe him? Or was he lying? Edward Porter Sturbridge and Francine Widmer can't both be right. In that garbage pail full of red herrings the defense has sloshed in front of you during this trial, the biggest was the suggestion that the Soviets would have benefited most from Martin Fuller's death and that they could have sent any one of dozens of agents to kill Professor Fuller. They could have killed him on the street, or at the university, or in any one of dozens of places, but the fact is that none of these things happened, that Professor Fuller died in his own home, and only five other people were in the Fuller house during the period in which the means of his death was conveyed into the kerosene heater. Do you believe that Mrs. Fuller did it? Or that Mr. Heskowitz or Mr. Melling or Miss Troob did it? Or does the testimony and evidence convince you that the likely perpetrator was Edward Porter Sturbridge acting on his own?

"If he did it on instructions from anyone else, that would not affect the charges against *him*, understand that.

"Counsel for the defendant has attempted to denigrate the evidence on the grounds that it is largely circumstantial. Those of us who spend our working lives bringing criminals to justice know that one rarely finds the killer standing next to the body, surrounded by eyewitnesses, a smoking gun in his hand.

"Consider this. You're out looking for a new house, and the real-estate agent takes you down to the basement, it's right after a heavy rain, and one wall of the basement is wet. It looks wet, it feels wet to the touch. Do you think the owner threw a pail of water up against the basement wall because he really doesn't want to sell the house? You decide to look at other houses because we live in a world where most of our actions are governed by circumstantial evidence, and it is on such evidence that we make daily decisions in our lives.

"What we are here for, you are here for, is to determine, as I trust you will, that Edward Porter Sturbridge intended to and did in fact kill Professor Martin Fuller by the use of a weapon he made deadly by mixing gasoline into a kerosene heater, and that you will therefore find him guilty as charged on all counts."

Ed whispered to Thomassy, "Son-of-a-bitch."

"He's doing his job," Thomassy said.

The judge's instructions to the jury were concise and clear. He defined everything carefully. He left nothing out, including the fact that they were to disregard the district attorney's reference in his summation to Francine Widmer's testimony, which did not meet the criteria he had set down. The jury was then sequestered and the reporters were permitted to head for their telephones.

"What do we do now?" Ed asked.

"We wait," Thomassy said.

Ned Widmer made a phone call, then took Thomassy down to the cafeteria for tea. Thomassy ordered two cups of coffee delivered together with Widmer's tea.

"Doesn't that jangle your nerves?" Widmer asked.

Thomassy said, "You can't shake a milk shake that's already shook." He noticed that Widmer sipped tea with pursed lips like Francine. "I believe your Washington friends, despite their denials . . ."

Widmer put the teacup down carefully.

". . . got the photos of Francine to the DA," Thomassy said. "If you didn't."

"I didn't."

"They wanted the link to the Russians ballyhooed by the press."

"I don't know," Widmer said.

Widmer unwrapped the paper from around a lump of sugar. Then he tried wrapping it up again. He lifted his head and looked Thomassy directly in the eyes and said, "I am an amateur, George. Like your client."

Thomassy finished his second cup of coffee in silence before Widmer added, "I'm sorry if I was the conduit. I should have understood more."

"No need," said Thomassy. "I understood even less. Francine can testify to my ignorance. What's the news from the hospital?"

"Priscilla says all she's getting right now is the usual double-talk."

"I feel like I ought to be there."

"You can't leave here now. And you can't do any good there." Widmer's voice cracked slightly. "I envy you, George."

Thomassy looked at Widmer. When someone like him said something like that you paid attention.

"I think Priscilla and I were once briefly insane about each other the way you and Francine are now. I hope your insanity lasts longer."

272

"I'll see what I can do," Thomassy said, feeling for the first time that the ice floes he and Ned always stood on when talking to each other had drifted together.

When Widmer and Thomassy went back up, the jury was calling to have a portion of Tarasova's testimony read to them.

"I'm going to run over to the hospital," Thomassy said. "If it looks like they're close to bringing in a verdict, phone me quick, will you?"

"They won't let you see her now."

I got in last night.

"Let her rest."

I'm not going to let her rest for the next thirty years.

"Priscilla's there. She'll call me if we're needed."

I'm needed.

"Your client wants you, George."

Reluctantly, Thomassy went over to Ed.

"What does their calling for Tarasova's testimony mean?" Ed asked.

"How should I know," Thomassy said irritably.

A while later the jury asked to hear Detective Cooper's testimony read to them.

"Is that good or bad?" Ed asked.

Thomassy looked at Ed's face. The kid, who'd flam-boozled everyone with his professional double-talk, looked like a frightened twelve-year-old. Unfamiliar turf makes jelly out of rock.

"Don't pee in your pants," Thomassy said. "If a jury's asking for things, it means they're not agreeing. Disagreement works in your favor."

"Why Cooper's testimony?"

"Maybe they're interested in the cigarette lighter. Or the flask. Or the button. Probably the button. Was it yours?"

"How should I know?" Ed said.

The way young people shrug their shoulders is ugly, Thomassy thought. For the first time in his life he was prepared to take a verdict of guilty.

Thomassy felt the tap on his shoulder. When he glanced around, he saw Ned Widmer's smile.

"Priscilla says Francine's temperature is down to normal. Blood count, too."

"What was it?"

"We may never know, but it's gone."

"What the hell good are doctors for? Half of what they do is guesswork."

"Some lawyers I know still use leeches."

Thomassy laughed because it suddenly hit him that Francine would be okay and that Ned Widmer had the makings of a friend.

At four-fifteen the jury sent out word that it had a verdict. Everyone was reassembled in the courtroom. "All rise," the court officer said as the judge came through the door from his chambers and ascended the bench.

Ed watched the face of the foreman, but she wasn't giving anything away. The judge asked her if the jury had reached a verdict.

"We have, Your Honor," she said.

It occurred to Ed that the judge didn't know the answer either. Over his left shoulder he saw the family contingent, mother, father, and Franklin Harlow. Only the father was looking at him. The others were watching the foreman.

Thomassy poked Ed. When it came time for sentencing, judges sometimes added a few years for defendants who hadn't paid attention.

The foreman cleared her throat. She was looking at the judge. The judge nodded to her. And so she said, "The jury finds the defendant not guilty on all counts."

Ed looked like he wanted to hug somebody. Thomassy, who was thinking of Francine, didn't offer his hand. Ed glanced over at his family, but they were already leaving the courtroom.

Out in the hallway, Ed saw Scott and Melissa. Had they heard the verdict? He started over to share the good news but they turned away.

"There are TV cameras outside," Thomassy reminded him.

"What do I say?"

"Don't say anything."

On the steps of the courthouse, Franklin Harlow came over to them, keeping his back to the TV cameras. "Your father would like to see you," he said. "Over this way."

And so, the cameras grinding away, they separated, Ed stepping along with Franklin Harlow to where the Sturbridges waited for them, and Thomassy hurrying down to the other cluster, the smiling string-pullers Jackson Perry and Randall, and Ned Widmer with his arm through Tarasova's. The men all wanted to shake his hand.

"Hey," one of the TV reporters yelled. "You guys get closer together so we can get you in one shot!"

Something made Thomassy glance over at the other group. Mrs. Sturbridge was embracing her brilliant son, scholar, author, hugging to her a devious lying conniving ultimately thoughtless human being who, against the occasional courtesies and decencies and kindnesses that enabled people to survive in God's huge tent, had struck at his friend and mentor, burned his brain, and by doing so had lashed out against every class and kind, unleashing his personal warhead against the whole society. Thomassy could hear Mrs. Sturbridge chanting, "I'm so glad, I'm so glad," but he saw Ed twisting his face toward Mr. Sturbridge, wanting reassurance of his vindication from the man. Ed put out his hand to his father, thinking his father had his hand out to shake his, too, and what Thomassy saw and heard was the irrevocable thunderball slap of Mr. Sturbridge's hand striking Ed's face.

Franklin Harlow, a peaceable man, stepped forward, thinking Ed might strike at his father. But Ed merely took two steps back out of harm's way.

Mrs. Sturbridge, who had been thanking her God for her son's court-proven innocence, cried as if it had been her face that received the resounding slap.

Ed, who, after all, was an extremely intelligent young man, understood. He rushed past his mother for the taxi at the curb.

Thomassy saw the taxi pull away. As it did, a car he hadn't noticed before left the curb, following the cab. He didn't get the whole license number, just the FC that stood for foreign consulate.

"Jesus," said Perry, who'd also noticed.

"They are not wasting any time," said Tarasova, who unlike the lawyers present, understood justice very well.